THE
VIRUS
CHRONICLES

MICHAEL D. ACOSTA
ERIC DONALDSON, PH.D.

THE
VIRUS
CHRONICLES
THE CULLING

TATE PUBLISHING
AND ENTERPRISES, LLC

Published by Tate Publishing & Enterprises, LLC
127 E. Trade Center Terrace | Mustang, Oklahoma 73064 USA
1.888.361.9473 | www.tatepublishing.com

Tate Publishing is committed to excellence in the publishing industry. The company reflects the philosophy established by the founders, based on Psalm 68:11,
"The Lord gave the word and great was the company of those who published it."

Book design copyright © 2015 by Tate Publishing, LLC. All rights reserved.
Cover design by Bill Francis Peralta
Interior design by Shieldon Alcasid

Published in the United States of America
ISBN: 978-1-68164-367-0
Fiction / Science Fiction / Action & Adventure
15.09.17

Dedication

For my family who has patiently allowed me to take many trips into exotic, violent, and fantastic places where they cannot follow: Brecker, Miles, Michela, Elijah, and the linch pin who holds the world together, Beth. You provide me with more than you require, and I love you. To my mother, who never held me back and taught me to fight for every inch. To the teachers and mentors who provided inspiration, encouragement, and believed no box existed that I should have to think outside of. And to Him who has allowed me to fall far short but still loves and accepts me as I am.

A special thanks to my coauthor Eric, who is in a real and constant battle to save humanity from viruses. His expertise is invaluable.

—Mike

For Shawna, Callie, and Tristan who make it all worth while; for Ralph Baric who taught me that science can be fun; for Marcie McClure who showed me that science is much better in the lab than in the classroom; and for Tim Harmon whose storytelling skills inspired my creativity.

—Eric

August 5, 2018

Perhaps it would be for the best if human beings were all but extinct, culled from the planet. I agree with Dr. Jonas Salk, the Earth would certainly be better off. We've been on this path of destruction for a very long time, and no matter how you analyze it, our species is screwed. All the signs have been there, the warnings, but we just unconsciously continued consuming as if only we mattered, and as if all of the resources on the planet would last forever. We have been mindless consumers, driven to buy things to fill the gaps in our souls. We've consumed everything available. Starvation, greed, and stupidity rule the land now. Instead of rising to the occasion, we have withered into desperation.

This will likely be my last journal entry. Truth be told, I don't believe anyone will survive to read it. I should be spending my last days and hours trying to work it out; after all, that was what I was trained to do. It doesn't really matter at this point, because even a cure wouldn't ameliorate what we've become. It's ironic that we're more like it than we can comprehend. You can't blame it for wanting to survive, for acting on the most fundamental instinct to live. I guess I admire its resilience, its earnest desire to live for nothing other than life itself. No other motivation, both simple and profound. We're both fighting for our very existence, and yet it seems to know the stakes far better than we do. It's battle-tested and fully aware of the consequences. We're like spoiled children demanding our way because of a false sense of superiority. Perhaps Jeremiah is right. Is this God's vengeance? Is this how life ends on Earth?

Tony Van Lee, PhD

Chapter 1

May 3, 2018

I T WAS A lazy day on the Gulf of Mexico. The hot midday sun warmed the sands along the coast, as the early afternoon breeze delivered the smell of fresh sea salt to the Louisiana shore. The beach itself was not romantic and beautiful like most Southern shorelines because a thick sludge of oily black foam tarnished its once golden sands. The pollution looked bad and smelled worse, which contrasted drastically with the gulf's natural beauty.

The landscape invoked a state of melancholy and a sense of fading hope that rested heavily upon the local scene. The coastal parish had built and placed barricades along the beach accesses in an attempt to prevent oblivious "accidental" tourists from wandering onto the contaminated sands and into the foul and potentially harmful ocean waters. The coastal and offshore drilling companies, which produce a sizable fraction of the US petroleum supply each year, dotted the local shores and seascape, and these companies were skilled at taking the necessary precautions to avoid potential liability claims.

Dr. Carrisa Harrison, MD, once a youthful beauty now in a graceful middle-aged decline, waded hip deep into the ocean water, toting a large floating environmental sampling box. Her skin was in the process of being baked to a painful red by the sun, her dark hair showed signs of being bleached on the ends, and the view of the upper half of her body standing in the dark and black polluted ocean water gave the illusion of her torso being cut at the midline.

While many of her MD colleagues eventually settled to one place, developing a practice where they cared for the same patients year after year, Carrisa was not even remotely interested in such a lifestyle. She was always much more comfortable studying microorganisms that strived and adapted for every opportunity to survive, than tending to humans who frequently squandered their lives. So she dedicated her life to the work of collecting, analyzing, identifying, and characterizing microbes and the diseases that they caused.

Working at the American College of Medical Microbiology and Toxicology (ACMMT) afforded her an opportunity to serve as an epidemiologist and medical doctor without the confines of the examination room. It was her passion to identify the underlying causes of disease, and she quickly dispatched her duties on this beach collecting water samples from the polluted ocean water. She collected marine water samples, sealed them in carefully labeled tubes, and placed each sample into her collection box in the proper order.

The state of the local environment literally made her feel sick to her stomach, and she knew that if she was feeling sick, the locals were feeling it too. However, she was only too aware that these locals were mostly illegal aliens, and it was not lost on her that the language barrier meant that they had no voice with which to complain. It troubled her that the giant oil companies intentionally manipulated the middle class, knowing that they were the financial engine that drove the capitalist American economy that filled their coffers, while mercilessly exploiting the illegal workers that were the tires upon which their armored vehicles cruised to the bank.

"Carrisa? It's time," a young dark-skinned man yelled from the shore.

"Got it, Charlie. I'm coming."

Carrisa folded up her sample collection box and was slowly maneuvering her way toward the shore when a fish popped up to the surface, floating on its side.

"Hmm," she said aloud to herself as she looked closely at the fish. After a few moments of deliberation, she bagged the fish and placed it into the box.

Life at the La Playa Hotel felt like a scene from a Hemingway novel. There were more outsiders than locals and even fewer tourists, which meant that everyone that happened to be there belonged to an eclectic group of people either hiding, running, relaxing, or studying. Identity didn't mean much at a place like this, because people were either reserved and quiet or shallow and polite, and everyone paid their bills; no questions asked. The ambiance of the place seemed too perfect, the atmosphere too real. Illusion is not always a bad thing.

The large-leafed ceiling fans twirling overhead stirred up just enough of a breeze to keep the heat to a minimum, which made the guests feel more comfortable. Charlie and Carrisa sat at a small table in the dimly lit bar, where they had already enjoyed just enough drinks to feel relaxed.

Charlie was a recent college graduate who wore an immature optimism that made him come across as slightly arrogant. He had been awarded a prestigious ACMMT internship and had requested Carrisa as his mentor. He was assigned to work with her for the summer before continuing on to medical school in the fall. Even though she didn't think he was particularly gifted intellectually or incredibly creative, Carrisa liked him. He was not afraid to discuss his ideas, even when he was wrong.

What she really liked, however, was that he did what he was told and was always on time. He was trustworthy, and Carrisa felt reassured that she could count on him in a pinch. They argued as they did each night, playful and combative. Carrisa with wisdom and the young man with hope and naïveté.

"What are we supposed to do, stop using gas? How the hell do you think you flew down here?" Charlie quipped, being only half serious but knowing he'd get a rise out of her.

"That's not what I'm saying. How about, be responsible and accountable, it's an endearing quality, sweetie," Carrisa retorted, taking a hard pull off her Corona.

"Good luck with that. If there's a way to make money outta it, then they'll do it."

"So cynical and so young," she offered.

"Just realistic. How were the sample reports that you got back today?"

She shrugged."The samples I took last week had one one-thousandth of a microgram of naphthalene in the ocean water. There's still plenty of tar and asphalt run off. I mean, it's measurable. The refineries aren't doing enough, but these reports will get buried with the rest I'm sure."

"What happened to the eternal optimist? So cynical, so…"

Carrisa smiled and playfully kicked him under the table as she took another healthy pull from her beer. Her smile was in recognition of the truth of his assessment of her. Her optimism, although still present, had begun to wear thin over the years. Her belief that people were generally good had been beaten down time and time again. She had given up lucrative contracts and offers at brick and mortar practices to run off and save the world as an epidemiologist, but it was an exhausting job that didn't pay well. And most of the so-called epidemics ended up being the direct result of irresponsible human behavior, like pollution, contamination, and encroachment into new habitats.

She didn't really have a choice, of course, but she knew that she had to be out in the field as much as possible, in the lab a limited amount of time, and with patients only on rare occasions. She had spent eight years at the Center for Disease Control and Prevention (CDC), during which she served about half that time in a lab. While she was there, she had almost lost her mind. She needed to be outside under the sky, and her job at ACMMT allowed her to work the perfect balance. But even so, she missed her more stable friends and colleagues from the CDC who she had worked with and who had trained her, at least the few that were not too full of themselves.

Carrisa shook an empty beer bottle at the bartender, who acknowledged that she was ready for another drink, and then returned her focus to the conversation with Charlie. The two passed the next hour or so in casual conversation, listening to the sounds of the local musical fare, and being bathed by the din of the crowd. After his fourth beer, Charlie's eyes began to linger a little longer on her legs.

"Okay, that's enough, Charlie," Carrisa said playfully.

"What?"

"You know what."

"Wait a minute now…"

"It's never going to happen again. I'm old enough to be your mother, and I definitely know better!"

Charlie laughed, obviously having a blast poking fun at her. She was feisty and not gullible at all, but it was easy to get her goat, and Charlie loved teasing her.

One night three months earlier, she had had one too many drinks, and Charlie walked into the bar at precisely the right moment. "Against All Odds" by Phil Collins was playing on the jukebox, and Charlie remembered that she was in a good mood from the start. Luck, being what it was, the night went extremely well for him, although the next morning was a little awkward. Charlie never let her forget it.

"Fine, at least show me your tits," he guffawed as she tried to give him the evil eye but quickly gave way to laughter instead.

The two toasted by clicking their bottles together.

"To saving the world," she said sarcastically, "one contaminated seashore at a time."

"To saving the world." At that moment, a young fisherman stepped into the lobby out of breath and approached the bar.

"*Quienes*, uh, *el* Dr. Harrison?" the young man asked the bartender with a thick Mexican accent.

"I think you have a visitor?" Charlie pointed toward the man.

Carrisa turned in her seat to see the man whose voice she could barely hear from across the room. She glanced over just in time to see the bartender point toward her.

"Esta, Dr. Harrison?" the man asked as he approached her table.

"Yes."

"*Nosotros necesita en la playa.*"

"I'm sorry, what can I help you with?" she asked, as she recognized the look of terror on the man's tired face. An overwhelming sense of alarm arose from the pit of her stomach, overriding her buzz.

"We need ju at water. Sick. Very sick! Come now, *por favor, ahora,*" the young man said urgently, struggling hard to speak in English.

The small village of San Tomas was just south of Pecan Island and didn't exist on most maps. It was a Mexican-style shantytown comprised mostly of fishermen and oil riggers who worked as laborers on the oil platforms and at the refineries along the coast. The young fisherman ran ahead, stopping frequently to allow Carrisa and Charlie to catch up. He waved his hand feverishly, in a vain attempt to hurry them along, but no matter how hard they labored, they were unable to meet his expectation.

When they arrived at the edge of the beach where the man led them, the scene resembled that of a nightmare. Several bodies were scattered across the tarnished beach. Loved ones knelt over many of the victims, weeping madly as the sick struggled and doing whatever they thought they could to help them survive or to will them back to life.

"Jesus Christ!" Charlie said, his eyes opening wide in shock.

"Stay back, Charlie. We have no idea what caused this," Carrisa said, assuming command as she contemplated their next move. "We've got to contain this thing, whatever it is, right now."

Charlie stared at the gruesome scene, horrified by the sudden change that had come over what hours ago was a quiet, deserted place.

"Charlie, stay right here and do not go near any of the sick. I'm going to go get my medical kit and call the CDC."

Carrisa got the attention of the young fisherman who had come for her and told him that she would return shortly. She couldn't decide if the expression on his face was one of doubt that she would return or fear that no one would be alive by then.

When she returned with her medical kit, she donned a disposable N95 respirator mask over her face. She threw a N95 mask to Charlie as she approached and ordered him to put it on. Then, she immediately opened the medical kit, put on a pair of goggles, and then a pair of latex gloves, followed by a second pair of gloves. Charlie followed her lead, and then the two went from patient to patient, confirming that each victim had already succumbed to the unknown sickness that ravished their bodies. She had Charlie put a red ticket with a number on each dead body they examined.

After examining several bodies, Carrisa walked over to the Mexican fisherman and grabbed him by both arms.

"What happened here? You have to tell me everything that you can," she exclaimed in an urgent voice that was muffled by her respirator.

"*Como?*" he responded, not understanding.

"What happened to these people…uh, uh, *que paso el gente?*"

"*No se.* People get sick now. In the day, okay, now very sick. *Mi padre' es aqui, por favor,*" the boy said, looking even more alarmed than before. He motioned for her to follow him.

Carrisa followed him to one of the small shanties just a few hundred yards from the beach. An older man lay awkwardly on a small bed, bleeding from his nose and mouth. His skin was chalky white and his forehead was covered with beads of cold sweat. His face bore a vague similarity to the young Mexican boy's face.

Carrisa examined the older man, studying his eyes, nose, mouth, and then pushed gently on his stomach to assess potential abdominal distention. The old man groaned each time she touched him, and it was obvious to her that he was experiencing an immense amount of pain. She placed an IV in his arm to help with fluid replacement and electrolyte imbalances, but she knew that this procedure would only buy her a little more time.

Inside the man's mouth, she noticed several blisters. She removed a sterile hypodermic needle from her medical kit, lanced one of the pustules, and drew a murky yellow fluid into the chamber of the syringe. She placed the sample into a sample tube filled with a buffer that would preserve it. She then labeled it and handed it to Charlie.

"As soon as we are finished here, take this sample back to your room and put it on ice. I'll swing by later and package it for transport back to the lab."

She then discarded the empty hypodermic needle into a sharps container in her medical kit and proceeded with her examination of the old man. As she monitored his vital signs, she noticed that his eyes slowly grew large, and his breathing became more and more labored. She witnessed the life leaving his body a little at a time as he grew weaker and weaker. She was fully aware that there was nothing that she could do to save him. He was overwhelmed. His body was fighting and losing, and it would soon be over.

At his bedside, the man's wife moaned sorrowfully. In that moan, Carrisa could hear the desperation of this woman, and in that moment, she knew that his death was not as bad as the pain of his loss would be to her. As the man went into cardiac arrest, Carrisa thought carefully about what her next move would be and finally decided that she hadn't tried everything at her disposal.

"Hand me that syringe," she said to Charlie as the boy looked at her with hope in his eyes, but with no comprehension of what was said.

"This one? Epinephrine?" Charlie asked.

"Yes."

Carrisa had seen many things in her career. Ebola virus fatalities and terminal AIDS patients in Africa were among the worst. Those viruses were known killers, but whatever agent caused this outbreak hit faster than anything she was familiar with. It caused irreversible morbidity that led to rapid mortality.

She reasoned that it had to be a chemical contaminant that had spilled into the ocean water. The most logical assumption was that it was probably a pollutant generated by the large oil refineries that operated largely above the law and insulated by convoluted and absurdly complex government regulations. They made money by exploiting these workers and then killed them with the refuse. These thoughts fueled her inner rage.

Charlie handed her the syringe.

"Cross your fingers," she said as she carefully inserted the needle into the man's neck and injected the medication. There was no immediate reaction.

"This might take a few minutes..."

The man's eyes opened wide as he drew in a deep breath, filling his lungs with desperately needed oxygen. Carrisa exhaled a sigh of relief, but she knew his recovery would only be temporary unless his immune system could gain an advantage against the unknown agent that was having its way with his life. Given the rapid rate at which victims were dying, she doubted that he would live much longer. She was hopeful that he might be able to provide a clue as to what was causing this outbreak, but attempts to communicate with him went unanswered.

Carrisa and Charlie continued to work through the night, with more and more sick people being brought to them by distraught family members seeking help. In some cases, those seeking help later became the lifeless victims overwhelmed by this strange disease.

At some time in the night, additional emergency response personnel arrived, but Carrisa barely noticed them unless one asked her a question. She was in the zone, focused and ready to do whatever she could. It was really the only way that she could cope with the situation.

Charlie was surprisingly composed as he attended to the victims and followed Carrisa's lead. But the warm and friendly face of optimism had long since been replaced with a look of exhausted bewilderment. He felt as if he would cry if he stopped working, and he wasn't sure if he would be able to stop the tears once they started.

The sun rose across the ocean water that morning, sending a dazzling array of colorful light dancing across the waves. Carrisa contemplated it only long enough to note the contrast between it and the dead bodies that were strewn across the beach, covered by blankets and marked with red tickets tallying their deaths. Flashing lights atop ambulances circled rhythmically above her head as emergency response personnel scurried to and fro, looking disoriented, gathering up bodies, and asking questions of anyone who would sit long enough to provide an answer.

"How many did you count?" she asked Charlie.

"We looked at thirty-seven, all dead. I don't know how many others the paramedics already hauled out of here. Was there only one survivor?" he asked as he removed his latex gloves.

"Only one, the boy's father. But he won't make it very long without massive intervention, probably from above," she said halfheartedly, knowing that even divine intervention could not help him.

"My God. What the hell could've happened here?" Charlie asked as he wiped his forehead in exhaustion with his bare hand.

It was a question that rang in her mind, and one that she simply could not answer. The presentation of multiple symptoms occurred so rapidly that the only way she could think to describe it was as a generic global assault on several organ systems simultaneously. It was as if these patients were dying of sudden and rapid multiple organ failure. She could not think of a single toxin, not even weapons grade anthrax that acted this quickly.

"Ricin!" she exclaimed suddenly.

"What?" Charlie asked in a hushed voice as he looked around suspiciously. "You think this is bioterrorism?"

"I'm just talking out loud, Charlie. I saw no evidence of necrosis, no injection sites, but cyanosis, adnominal distention, multiple organ failure—and the blisters? Ricin would progress fast, but not this fast. There would have to be a common source to impact so many. Whatever this thing is, it has the potency of a super toxin and the infectivity characteristics of a microorganism. It doesn't make any sense."

She racked her brain, trying to identify a clue that would help her solve the riddle, but nothing seemed obvious. In her exhausted state, she pretended that the agent responsible for these deaths was the fatal poison, ricin. Beyond that, she was stumped.

And she knew that the cost of identifying and characterizing an unknown agent that worked this efficiently and killed this effectively would likely be hundreds, maybe even thousands of lives. Containing an agent that worked this quickly was like trying to extinguish a forest fire with a garden hose.

"The locals say there was an omen in the sky. Like fire from heaven or something. I couldn't quite make out the full details of what they were saying, my Spanish has always sucked, even in college," Charlie broke in.

Carrisa laughed sadly.

"The meteor shower. It happened a few days ago."

As Charlie and Carrisa turned away from the scene of bodies and walked back toward the hotel, a white Suburban with Center for Disease Control and Prevention written on the side pulled up next to one of the ambulances. A team of scientists got out and quickly organized to establish a mobile containment facility. A man in field gear approached them, extending an official-looking plastic badge, identifying him as an officer in the Epidemic Intelligence Service.

"Are you Dr. Harrison?"

"Yes," she replied, barely having the strength to be polite. They're really taking this one seriously, she thought to herself. An EIS officer in charge?

"I'm Dr. Moreno, thanks for calling this in. What do we got?"

"I don't know for sure," she started. "Whatever it is, it hits hard and fast. Most of these people were alive and well a few hours ago. Whatever they came in contact with killed them so fast that I couldn't even characterize the clinical presentation of symptoms. One had a highgrade fever over 105, signs of systematic organ failure, and extreme abdominal distention. I treated him for emergency cardiac arrest, but unless his immune system rapidly overcomes whatever this is…" She didn't have the strength to finish the sentence.

"No detectable preliminary symptoms? Were there any signs of illness prior to onset of death?" Moreno asked.

"Nothing. According to the locals, everyone was in good health. Onset was sudden and progressed to a fatal outcome within a matter of hours. Some of the family members that were attending to sick loved ones later developed the same clinical presentation and died within two or three hours."

"Two or three…Jesus! How many fatalities?"

"We counted thirty-seven, but there are more. The only survivor is in that shanty over there." She pointed to the house where the young fisherman took her earlier.

"Not much of a house, huh?" Moreno tried to add some levity, but it didn't work.

"She thinks it might be a ricin attack," Charlie piped in shyly. Moreno looked at him and then at Carrisa.

"Ricin?" Moreno questioned.

"I was only thinking out loud. It's a long shot at best."

Moreno cleared his throat as he deduced that ricin wasn't the likely culprit.

"You collect any samples?" he asked.

"I got blood and mucus samples from a couple of victims. You want to take them back to the CDC?"

"We'll get ours, thanks, it's—"

"Protocol. I know. I'll log it."

"That's right, you used to work with us. Didn't you and—"

"Dr. Moreno, if that's all, I'm sure you and your crew have this covered. I'd like to go get some sleep," she said, fatigue firmly taking hold.

"Sure, sure. Hey, we'll let you know what we find"—he handed her a card—"and let's get a sample of your blood before you go. Just in case."

Charlie and Carrisa removed their masks as they cleared the disease zone and went back to their rooms. After sterilizing every square inch of her body, Carrisa climbed into her bed and closed her eyes, but she could not sleep because her mind raced. She tossed and turned for a couple of hours, finally falling asleep just a few moments before there was a loud knock on the door.

"Who's there?" she hollered. "And what the hell do you want?"

"Carrisa, it's Charlie. You've got to come see this."

Carrisa quickly got out of bed, threw on some clothes, and followed Charlie to the beach where they had been working hours earlier. Hundreds of fish, squid, jellyfish, and other marine life littered the beach. The stench was overwhelming, as the dead forms baked in the afternoon sun. Dr. Moreno and his colleagues worked furiously, gathering samples from a wide array of dead marine animals. The CDC had set up its mobile lab and several members of the team worked anonymously behind the scenes.

The deceased victims had been bagged and removed, but a few of the red tickets still littered the sand. Several emergency workers navigated around the area in biosafety suits. Carrisa placed a fresh N95 mask over her nose and mouth and looked back to make sure that Charlie had done the same. As they approached the site, Moreno noticed their arrival and trudged over to meet them. He was exhausted, and it showed.

"They started washing up this morning a couple of hours after you left," he said, the lightness in his voice no longer present.

"Do you think it's related?" she asked.

"Best guess?"

"Best guess."

"I think it's the water. The foam layer shows traces of contamination with a variety of chemicals. I think it's poisoned the fish. The main staple of the villagers around here is fish."

"You think it's infectious?" Carrisa asked, a little concerned.

"We've ruled out norovirus, cholera, and a whole panel of waterborne pathogens, but really, any agent that could do this type of damage would have had to cross the species barrier and I think that's improbable. It's most likely a toxic chemical, it's gotta be. Lot of rigs out there, who knows what they're draining off," Moreno said.

"But some of the victims appeared to get sick only after contact with sick loved ones. You'll test for rare infectious agents too, right?"

"Of course, we're not idiots." His eyes bunched with a smile, which took the edge off.

"I'm sorry, I didn't sleep well," she apologized.

"No problem. We've got lots of samples that we will test for everything known and do some metagenomics to see if there is anything unknown. We'll keep you informed, and I'll send a tech down to ask you some questions before we pull out. I'd like to know what you find out with your follow-up analysis of the ocean water."

"Sounds fine," Carrisa sighed, a little embarrassed.

She and Charlie started back toward the hotel to go get some well-deserved coffee.

"Oh, by the way," Moreno yelled, stopping the pair in their tracks. "The good news is it doesn't appear to have spread to other humans. If it's infectious, it killed so fast that it didn't transmit to others. If it's a chemical contaminant, we're confident that keeping people from eating seafood will stop this disease. We did contact tracing to identify anyone who was in contact with the victims, and none of villagers we have quarantined have had any symptoms whatsoever," Moreno smiled.

"How's the old man?" she asked.

Moreno's face faded from joy to sorrow.

"He didn't make it. Sorry. You did what you could."

Moreno turned from them and walked back toward the work area.

Charlie and Carrisa were hungry, but neither felt like eating. Instead, they sat at the same table where they shared drinks the night before, looking at the food that they ordered. It was a miserable way to end the expedition.

Charlie seemed out of it. "I've never seen anything like this. I just wanted to help the environment, you know? Do something instead of just bitchin' on the couch," he said, feeling unsure of the situation.

"You're doing good work, Charlie. Eat your breakfast."

"But it's three thirty. Way past lunchtime," he said dryly, still in shock.

Carrisa forced a laugh, trying to calm him down. They both needed to let off some steam.

"What are we going to do?" he asked.

"The CDC will be here for at least a week, so we'll be wasting our time if we stay. I don't play well with others. Go home to the West coast, see your family, and we'll regroup in Atlanta, see what the ACMMT lab wants to do there. I'll get the samples I have in for analysis. And I have to see my mother, or I'll never hear the end of it."

Later that afternoon, Carrisa met Charlie in the hotel lobby and kissed him on the cheek as he carted his suitcase out of the hotel. She then checked out and went back up to her room to collect her bags. On the bed was a large rolling suitcase with her sample box and medical kit strapped to it, as well as her trusty backpack that had seen better days. With one last dummy check, Carrisa opened the hotel room door and nearly walked right into a thickly built man in an army colonel's uniform who was standing directly in front of her door.

His pants were tucked into his boots, he wore a beret on his head, and he had several rows of medals prominently pinned across his crisply ironed uniform jacket. He wore an intense expression on his face, which was highlighted even more by his tightly groomed mustache. Behind him stood a smaller, younger clone of himself without the mustache.

"Ms. Harrison?"

She stopped abruptly, attempting to catch her breath as it dawned on her that this was not an accidental meeting.

"It's Dr. Harrison."

"You were at the kill zone last night, correct?"

"I'm impressed! The army boys have arrived, and they are calling it a kill zone! What, is this one of your experimental biological weapons gone awry?" she chided.

He smiled curtly with no friendliness in his eyes.

"Listen, ma'am, I understand you were first on the scene," the colonel said.

"Yes, I was."

"Did you collect any samples?"

"Water samples."

"I'll need them. All of them."

"Why do you need my water samples? You are welcome to get your own. The ocean's right out there," Carrisa pointed through the wall in the direction of the beach, noting that she didn't like his attitude one bit.

"This is a national security issue, ma'am. We are counting on your full cooperation…"

"How about a name and some credentials? I'm not in the habit of turning over my research samples to just any clown in a sergeant's uniform. Don't you have a procedure to follow?"

This time, his smile had more appreciation in it. He realized that this wasn't your typical scientist or typical woman. No, he could tell that this lady was tough and smart, and it occurred to him that if it had been under different circumstances, he might have allowed himself the luxury of a dinner with her. He might have even gone about this in another way if time had allowed, but his orders were clear and time was sensitive.

The colonel had come from a long line of men, all of who had served in the United States military dating back to the Revolutionary War. His father served in Vietnam, his grandfather in World War II, and his grandfather's father in World War I. His family's military history was well documented, and the military life was so ingrained in his blood, it might as well have been encoded in his DNA. He was, however, the first member of his family to make the jump from a combat officer to a medical officer. After receiving his MD, he joined the army and went into special forces, serving in the field in several campaigns. He quickly rose through the ranks to become the director of the bioweapons division under the auspice of the army's medical research division.

"I'm sorry, Doctor, perhaps I have not made myself clear. Give me the samples," the colonel exclaimed, nodding calmly to his smaller colleague, who detached and opened her sample box.

"I am going to need an itemized inventory of everything you take, and an address where I can inquire about your findings. This research is funded by a grant from the National Institutes of Health to the American College of Microbiology and Toxicology. They own these samples, and it's my ass on the line if they disappear."

The colonel smiled sardonically.

"I don't think that a list is necessary, and your ass will be just fine, Dr. Harrison. Thank you for your cooperation!"

"As if I had a choice. They were a lot of work you know."

The protégé nodded to the colonel, who looked in the box full of organized sample tubes.

"Is this it?"

"Yeah, that's it," she snapped.

The colonel stared at her for a moment then rummaged through the sample box. At the bottom under a cold pack, he found the fish that had floated to the surface of the ocean water. He removed her medical kit from the suitcase, opened it, and examined its contents. He removed the samples that Carrisa had taken from a few of the victims and the sharps container before handing the kit back to her. She snatched it abruptly from his hands.

The colonel looked at Carrisa, but he couldn't tell if she responded with an expression of appreciation, contempt, or disappointment. Whatever her expression, this woman intrigued him. She was definitely tough, and he liked that—he respected it. It had taken him most of his adult life and many bungled relationships to understand what he wanted in a woman, and he sensed that this woman had it all.

Secretly, he dreamed that someday he could focus his attention on his own needs instead of on duty. Time was catching up with him, and things weren't as black and white as they used to be. But those dreams would have to wait.

"Take the sample box and put these medical samples and the sharps container in it too," he ordered.

Carrisa reacted immediately to stop them. "Wait one damn minute," she yelled, moving toward them. But she stopped in her tracks when she noticed the colonel's protégé moving his hand toward his sidearm.

"Lieutenant!" the colonel commanded.

"Sorry, sir," he said as he pulled his hand away from his gun, closed Carrisa's sample box, and placed it under his arm.

The colonel looked at her apologetically but quickly regained his stoicism.

"On behalf of a grateful nation, ma'am," he said with the same sardonic smile.

She couldn't tell if he was a prick or if this was his way of flirting, but regardless, she concluded that the man was charismatic. He was interesting, and he certainly looked capable of using brute force, but she was surprised by the intelligence in his eyes. He was that intelligent bad-boy type that she had already figured out would not work for her.

"Up yours," she muttered as she watched them disappear into the elevator.

Unzipping a pocket on the side of her backpack, she reached in and pulled out two vials. One contained the sample taken from the old man, and the other a water sample taken that morning after the accumulation of dead marine animals littered the beach.

"Pricks. Let them waste their time rerunning my old water samples. I have everything I need right here."

Chapter 2

April 28, 2018

I<small>T WAS A</small> dark night in Delta, extremely dark. The small southwestern Louisiana town of White Lake might have been famous for its darkness, had anyone of importance been aware that the town even existed, but this fact was only known to the town's three hundred residents who welcomed the obscurity. For the most part, White Lake's residents were simple people who lived by the conservative, Southern Creole traditions with which they were raised. They embraced their quiet little town, and they thrived in the familiarity of knowing all of their neighbors. Most of these folks had never had a reason to travel much further than the thirty-mile trip to Abbeyville for supplies or on special occasions, the sixty miles to Lake Charles to get whatever Abbeyville didn't have, or to take in the occasional show and eat in style.

On this dark night, an overworked 1978 Ford F-150 Super Cab pickup bumped along down a narrow parish road outside of White Lake, with dim and dirty headlights barely producing enough light to guide the way. In the cab sat a young, golden-haired girl named Sara. She was a precocious, grade-school beauty destined to mature into a local convenience store cashier, a job that seemed to be reserved for all the pretty young women of Delta who were unable to escape.

The fate of these young women seemed to be the same. Perhaps it would be a high school football star or a banker's son, it didn't really matter; someone in town or nearby would marry her right out of high school, and she would live there, have children, and pretend to be happy. Having nothing to compare her existence to, she might actually believe that she was happy, but by most modern standards, no woman in this conservative backwoods parish could truly attain happiness.

Sara's father, Don Boussard, drove the bouncing truck down that narrow road toward home. He was a professional jack-of-all-trades, who prided himself on being able to work at many different trades, but he excelled at none. He was a slave to mediocrity, but mediocrity paid the bills, and since Mrs. Don had left two years earlier, he was the sole source of financial and emotional support for his daughter. He quickly decided that there would be no more commuting to Lake Charles for his work. He decided that he would rather do odd jobs around town so that he would always be close by to raise his daughter.

Don and Sara spent a lot of time together. He took her with him on his evening jobs in case they ran longer than expected, which was often the case. Don was a good father, and Sara was a good daughter, and they both deserved more than their present circumstances provided.

"Daddy, when I'm eleven, can I stay up to nine thirty?"

"You just turned ten last week, sher'. Should enjoy being ten, no?" he asked with a definite Cajun drawl.

"Yeah, I like ten, but I want to be eleven."

Don smiled while he wiggled the dial to tune the radio. The knob on the old truck's radio was worn, a bit of white paint outlined a barely visible musical note pictured on the front. The radio signal wavered in and out as he moved the dial, broadcasting equal amounts of static and broken voice.

"Talking with Professor Richard Bondurant, an astrophysicist and director of the International Space Institute at Cornell…"

"Damn thing. Can't get nothin' out here."

"All the good shows come on at nine, and I never get to see them," Sara continued.

"Shhh. I wanna try hearin' this, you."

"Size of some of the bodies, and it is on a trajectory that will probably…Earth's gravitational field…paradigm suggests that ice

cannot make it through the atmosphere without being destroyed by the intense friction that would result. However, mathematically we cannot rule out the possibility that a giant body of ice entering the Earth's..."

The voice faded to complete static.

"Damn, damn!"

"Potty mouth," Sara smiled.

Don fiddled with the tuner some more, trying to find the station again.

"Why are bodies gonna get burned?" Sara asked.

"They mean heavenly bodies, it be another name for meteors."

"Why don't they just say meteors then?"

"Smart people use big words sometimes."

"You're smart, and you don't use big words."

Don laughed out loud at the supposed compliment.

"Well, thanks, sher'."

"Wouldn't it be neat if they weren't meteors at all, but little spaceships and aliens were on them?"

"I guess that would be pretty neat."

"Do you think there's people on other planets, Daddy?"

"Maybe so, but not in the way the movies say. Anywhere there be water, there be a chance for life, sher'."

He continued adjusting the dial in an attempt to find just the right setting for the broadcast, but with little success.

"Don't worry, Daddy, it'll come back on in a minute."

Don smiled past his frustration and looked over at his sweet little girl.

"I know, honey, I know."

"Why do you like the stars so much anyway?" Sara asked.

Don bent his neck down in a position that allowed him to look up through the dirty windshield and see some different heavenly bodies twinkling above.

"I always wanted to study them. Space, life on other planets, everything that was out there and not down here is what I wanted to know about when I was young. I even went to community college for a while, but…well, it didn't work out."

"Is that why you have so many books at home?" she asked with genuine interest.

Don didn't talk that much about the past; as a matter of fact, he didn't talk that much at all, so anytime he did, Sara was sure to listen. He smiled at her, feeling proud of the perceptiveness and curiosity of his daughter.

"I guess so, sher'."

As the truck continued down the tree-lined country road, they came to a large clearing. The static on the radio faded, and voices could be heard faintly at first, and then louder as the signal became strong.

"Let's listen, okay?"

"Okay, Daddy," she said quietly and hunkered down, lying her head underneath his arm.

"Sky this Thursday night. Dr. Bondurant, please tell our listeners… minor meteor shower…be spectacular…"

Don deftly tuned the radio once again, moving the dial very slowly as if one wrong movement might knock out the reception all together. The voice came in crystal clear.

"Disintegrate in the atmosphere before they can even make impact with the surface of Earth. It is possible that some of the larger bodies of ice could still be intact by the time they reach the surface, but we expect these to be extremely small by the time friction from our atmosphere melts them, probably to the size of a marble or a golf ball at the most. In fact, most of these will probably land in the ocean, where they will pose no threat to our environment."

"Dr. Bondurant, one more question before I let you return to your busy schedule. With the recent discovery of ice on Mars as determined by the Phoenix Mars Rover spacecraft, is it possible that these large bodies of ice originated from a different planet?"

"That is an interesting question, and one that we do not know the answer to at this time. I would speculate that this is possible.

MICHAEL D. ACOSTA & ERIC F. DONALDSON, PH.D

However, it seems highly unlikely given that bodies this large would seem to indicate a traumatic planetary event. I would suspect that we would have seen evidence of an event like that while it was occurring. However, we cannot rule it out."

"And what about life, Dr. Bondurant? Water is the magic elixir for life, does the fact that ice exists on Mars suggest to you that there could be life elsewhere in the universe?"

"Well, it's an intriguing possibility. Mars has similar mineral and rock formations as Earth, and now we are learning that there is ice and even silica and sulfurous salt residues just below the dusty surface of the planet. The chemical elements necessary for life to evolve may have been present on Mars, we simply do not know enough at this time to make any definitive claims."

Once again the static drowned out the voices, and Don turned off the radio in frustration, while trying not to wake the sleeping beauty under his arm.

"Sher' can't wait to be up later but already be asleep before her usual bedtime," he said softly to himself.

Chapter 3

May 6, 2018

THE BEACH GARDEN was among the finest in the region by most normal standards, and it looked particularly amazing as the gentle North Carolina breeze bent the tall plants and cooled the air. The garden belonged to Darrin and Minnie, who cultivated it carefully and took great pride in the vegetables it produced each year. However, their garden did not even come close to measuring up to the garden next door, which drove them crazy.

"Sorry, Darrin, the secret's all mine."

"Come on, just a hint," Darrin pleaded as he juggled a pair of cantaloupe-sized tomatoes that his neighbor brought to him.

Darrin was a retired dot-com yuppie, one of the few who had enough sense to get out of the business before the World Wide Web market crashed. He was in his late fifties, lived with the only goal being to enjoy life, and made it a point to not flaunt his wealth to anyone, especially to his "mad professor" neighbor, Tony Van Lee. Darrin was one of those guys that wanted desperately to be funny, but just didn't have the knack or the timing. He never met a punch line that he didn't bungle somehow.

Darrin and his wife, Minnie, were great neighbors. They were always good guests when they were invited over, rarely showed up uninvited or unannounced, and were gracious hosts when they threw their monthly dinner parties for most of the local neighbors in this small, eclectic North Carolina beach town. Tony enjoyed his friendship with Darrin, mostly because he was so much fun to mess with.

"Sorry, Darrin, no can do," Tony said.

"What if we're attacked by giant space creatures in spaceships, and I need to grow your super vegetables just to survive?" Darrin asked, trying to make a joke but failing miserably.

"Let me know when that happens and we'll talk," Tony replied.

At that moment, two extremely well-groomed young men wearing crisply ironed white shirts and black ties with neat backpacks walked up, pushing their bikes ahead of themselves.

"Good afternoon," said the taller boy to Darrin and Tony.

"Good afternoon to you," Darrin replied.

"Have either of you accepted the Lord Jesus Christ as your personal savior?" the young man asked in an endearing voice and offering a sincere smile.

"Sorry, guys, I'm not into mythology," Tony said, climbing onto his custom-made, over-engineered, high-tech solar scooter, which was obviously an evolving prototype.

"But, sir…," the other young man started.

"Save it," Tony said dismissively, "unless you're prepared for an open-minded debate. I'm not interested in hearing the embedded theology your church has spoon-fed you."

The young men glanced at each other uncomfortably but did an admirable job of keeping up their smiles as they focused their attention on Darrin.

Darrin tried to disguise his discomfort by introducing himself quickly to the missionaries and then turning to catch Tony's attention before he rode off and abandoned him all together.

"Please?" Darrin said.

Tony smiled an uncomfortable smile and waved as he situated himself on the driver's seat.

"Fine, but I'm telling Minnie that you grow cannabis in your garden!" Darrin shouted with a familiar smile and waved back at Tony.

"You do that." Tony shook his head, and called out a fading "see you later," as he drove off on the noiseless scooter, reaching a speed that was greater than would have been possible with the original factory model.

Darrin turned his attention back to the missionaries.

"Gentleman, would you care for some iced tea? My wife makes the best lemon tea in the South," Darrin said, now feeling a sense of obligation toward the two young men with whom Tony had abandoned him.

It was another pleasant spring day on the North Carolina coast. The ocean waves rhythmically washed across the white sands, as seagulls circled overhead, waiting for the right moment to claim whatever food they might find. A strong breeze blew the late spring heat and humidity away as Tony cruised along the narrow beach roads on his scooter. While the scooter was an engineering marvel, it was not a pretty thing to look at. The back half of the scooter was basically a large basket, and a makeshift roof that doubled as a solar panel covered the seat area. Smaller solar panels were mounted near the front headlight and mirror, which gave the vehicle the appearance of a large mechanical insect. It was an ugly thing.

Tony was soothed by the lovely ocean breeze that blew gently across his face, forcing his hair back, and the methodical sounds of the wind and the sea were almost enough to wash away the bitterness that motivated his self-imposed exile. While Anthony Van Lee was not a bitter man by nature, he couldn't quite let go of the past, and over time, it devoured him.

After years of struggling to live in the high-stress world of scientific innovation, wearing his bitterness as a badge of honor, he had finally given up on that life and moved to the beach. It helped that he had been fired from his former position because of "philosophical differences" with the US Government, and it was apparent that he had been blacklisted when no one responded to any of his job queries, even though he had been highly recruited by a number of institutions prior to his dismissal.

Tony was a hotshot, and he knew it. He was always the smartest person in the room, and no one was able to grasp things quite as quickly or as detailed as he could. Unfortunately, being extremely intelligent, and knowing it, often made him cocky, which in turn made him reckless. And as intelligent as he was, his blind spot was that he could not perceive how others would react to his arrogance and recklessness or see how his actions impacted the people around him. It was this arrogance and recklessness that cost him his career, and his relationship with Carrisa. As was often the case, he didn't believe he had anything to do with either.

Tony's beach house was a charming 1950s cottage that had been fully modernized with a few of Tony's innovations. It was built in a quiet area of town only a short walk from the sands of the beach. The roof of his cottage was covered in solar collector panels that were lined internally with intricate networks of gold threads. The gold fibers were assembled inside the panels by a replicating virus, the M13 bacteriophage, using a nanotechnology and material sciences approach that he modified for the sake of efficiently wiring the nanowire network of the cell to improve its capacity for collecting and storing solar energy for his home.

The gold nanowires efficiently transferred the energy of the sun to electricity that was stored in solar batteries designed to provide several days worth of power, and this process allowed Tony to completely power his home, free of charge, from the rays of the sun. Tony had conceived the idea for this nanotechnology a couple of decades earlier and had run it by his colleagues who rejected the concept as too extravagant and too expensive to produce.

Tony and his silent scooter rolled to a stop in front of the modernized cottage, where Tony maneuvered the scooter to be in the direct sunlight so it could charge. He then dismounted the machine, made a quick check of the solar batteries to ensure they were set to charge, and entered his yard through the back gate that opened onto a path that led through his garden to the back door of his house.

The entire backyard was laid out as a beautiful and efficiently designed vertical container garden that displayed beautiful and fragrant flowers, aromatic herbs and spices of many varieties, and enormous colorful fruits and vegetables that hung from stout branches and vines.

Tomatoes, cucumbers, lettuce, beans, apples, pears, cilantro, basil—the bounty was endless. The tomatoes were the size of softballs, and many of the cucumbers were over a foot long. Tony carefully inspected each plant individually and used a spray pump to administer a dose of his biologically designed organic liquid fertilizer to each of the plants that didn't look quite right to him. When he was satisfied that every plant had what it needed to thrive, he retired to the house. The inside of the cottage was in stark contrast to the outside. It was disorganized, and even a little cluttered feeling, but homey with a "lived in" feel. As Tony entered, he pressed the button that was blinking red on an answering machine that sat on a table just below his old-school-style, wall-mounted telephone.

"Tony? Call me back! Asshole," said an anonymous female voice.

Beep.

"Mr. Van Lee, this is the Beaufort Vegetable Competition Committee. Your application has been received, and we look forward to seeing you next week."

Beep.

"Tony, its Ben. Call me."

Beep.

Tony opened the fridge and pulled out a generic brown bottle that was filled with one of his own healthy concoctions and took a drink. He stopped when he heard Ben's voice on the answering machine a second time.

"Ben again, when are you going to get a cell phone? We have something, well…I could use your…help"—a moment of silence then—"you're an asshole. Call me."

Beep.

Tony laughed; it seemed everyone thought he was an asshole. Ben and Tony had a long history together, starting in graduate school, but to say they were friends would be stretching the definition of friendship, but stretch it they did. Ben hated the fact that Tony was smarter than him. In fact, it really irked him. All the way through school, it was the same old story, everyone noticed Tony and ignored Ben.

Tony suspected that Ben secretly felt vindicated when Tony was blackballed from the CDC, but Tony knew that Ben was too polite to ever say it. While Tony was reckless, a bit arrogant, and not very diplomatic, he wasn't completely out of touch. A part of him knew that he deserved to be fired from the CDC nearly a decade ago. He had grown accustomed to living life on his own terms, and he enjoyed an occasional phone call from Ben, who always reminded him that getting out of the rat race was the right thing to do. Tony had no regrets.

Tony climbed the narrow set of rickety stairs that led from the main floor of his cottage to an undersized door that opened into an attic. The top story of his house was fairly typical with dust-covered, nonessential items stacked incongruously around the open space. He walked straight over to an old weather-beaten dresser and slid it to the side along the wall, which opened a door that lead to a secret compartment.

The compartment was larger than the visible portion of the attic, and red light illuminated the entire hidden area. On the left side of the hidden room, several plants stood about six feet tall and spread out like bushes. These plants were unmistakably marijuana, however, the leaves on these plants were almost twice the size of normal cannabis leaves. On the opposite side of the room, there were rows of tables, and on the tables were much smaller plants at various stages of growth. The red lights hung directly over them.

"Good afternoon, my babies," Tony said in the most genuine voice he had used all day.

He inspected the smaller plants, spraying them as necessary and putting his finger in the soil to check moisture. A digital thermometer on the wall read 88°F, and just then, an electrical fan kicked on automatically. "Just right," Tony said with a smile of satisfaction on his face.

He carefully removed a few leaves from one of the larger plants, placed them in a pouch on his belt, and then exited and locked up the hidden room.

In the kitchen, Tony vacuum-packed a special cellophane bag containing several ounces of carefully harvested and dried buds and leaves using a reengineered Seal-a-Meal that removed all the air and sealed the contents. The bag flattened out to the size of a steak, and he stacked it on top of several similar packages. On the counter behind the kitchen table sat an extremely large antique telephone the size of a Teletype machine from the fifties. Next to it was a black plastic box with two round indentations on top, designed to cradle the receiver, and a digital number pad.

Tony picked up the receiver of this phone and dialed patiently using the round dial on the antique phone box. He listened for a ring and then placed the receiver onto the black box with the receiver in the special cradle. The analog sound of ringing was audible for a few rings and that sound was followed by the arcane sound of a 54k baud modem from 1993. Tony punched in a combination of numbers on the digital number pad.

A few miles away, an animated smiley face winked on the screen of a client's cell phone with the message, *Steaks are on the grill.*

The call was rendered completely untraceable by a novel signal encryption device contained in the black box. This device used an encryption algorithm to convert low-tech telephone signals into untraceable digital signals and was one of Tony's inventions that he kept to himself. While the sounds coming from the device beeped and screeched, Tony loaded the airtight packages of marijuana into a six-pack-sized cooler, covered it with ice, threw in a couple of packaged steaks and added a bottle of beer as the final piece.

When his package was complete, Tony cleaned up his small operation by putting everything in its proper place in plain sight. Tony knew that the only way to truly hide something was not to put it in some location out of sight where a seeker would eventually look, but instead, to hide it where the seeker's mind would never conceive to look in the first place. So every part of Tony's operation was hidden in plain sight in the main part of his home, the kitchen. And everything looked like it belonged in a kitchen, including the big phone, which doubled as a breadbox.

After his work was done, Tony put on a pot of coffee and settled into his favorite chair. He reached into an ashtray for a pair of worn silver hemostats that had a roach clenched between its teeth. Tony lifted the roach to his mouth, carefully lit it as he inhaled its therapeutic vapors, and settled into his chair as the calmness came over his body. He promptly fell asleep.

Tony was jarred awake by a knock on his front door that was way too loud for a serene beach afternoon. He moved slowly toward the door but was barely able to get his eyes open. The therapeutic effects of Tony's crop were powerful and profound. He finally opened the door at the exact moment that it occurred to him that he didn't have to open the door at all. By then, it was too late.

Behind the front door, a FedEx man greeted Tony with a charming smile and a package. Tony took the package, none too graciously, and signed the electronic box that sent the FedEx man and his smile back into oblivion. Tony took the package into the kitchen where the aroma of the brewing coffee mixed with the scent of the saw grass plant that grew on a kitchen counter in a small pot.

Tony filled his cup before the coffee was done brewing and sat at the table. He took a swig of strong coffee and then opened the package. Carefully wrapped in small bubble wrap inside the package was a DVD that was attached to a folder full of papers by a large rubber band. The letter was from Ben.

> Tony, I got a call from Carrisa, please don't stop reading! She saw something pretty rough down in the gulf area. The data are a little tough to wrap your head around. Thought you might be able to determine what the hell this is using your Walmart chemistry set. The video is no joke and she needs your help.
>
> Ben

As Tony was about to put down the letter, he heard another knock at his door, but this knock was not nearly as obnoxious. Tony knew that this knocker would be his paperboy, who absolutely loved his job even though it was rapidly becoming obsolete. The "boy" on the other side of the door was far beyond paper "boy" age. At about twenty-five, he was shaggy and thin with a pleasant smile, and he exuded all of the characteristics of a typical "beach bum" stoner. He even insisted that everyone call him Dude after watching the movie *The Big Lebowski*.

Tony greeted the paperboy who was holding his red beach bike that had a basket attached to the front handlebars. In the basket was a six-pack cooler identical to the one Tony packed earlier. The bike also had saddlebags attached to each side of the rear wheel, and these were laden with rolled-up newspapers. He handed a paper to Tony with a big smile.

"Hey, Dude," Tony yawned.

"Totally righteous afternoon, bruh."

Tony smiled. These two knew the drill. Dude removed the empty cooler from his bike and handed it to Tony who exchanged coolers with him.

"The Dude could use more steak, Doc. Another sixteen ounces perhaps?"

The marijuana that Tony grew was genetically engineered in a manner that made it a much higher grade without some of the typical side effects, like paranoia. It had become quite the rage in the area and beyond, but Tony was disciplined about his little business and knew it had to stay small and under the radar. Dude, on the other hand, knew that he had a product that could make them both rich.

"Sorry, Dude. You know the rules."

Dude nodded and tapped his chest with his fist.

"I dig where you're comin' from, bruh, much respect."

He stopped before pulling his bike around.

"Ya know, bruh, the Dude has raised his prices three times. He would understand if the limited supply and increased demand demanded an increase in wholesale price."

He left it out there. The Dude liked Tony, and his three semesters in business school, before dropping out to "find himself," served the small sales operation well.

"I charge what I need, Dude. Greed is the root of all evil."

The Dude smiled widely with his eyes open only a slit. He tapped his chest again.

"Much respect, bruh."

Dude secured the cooler in the front basket, pushed his bike to the road, and pedaled away.

Tony returned to his cottage, placed the empty cooler on the counter, and popped the DVD into his laptop while he took another gulp of his coffee. He stopped abruptly mid sip when Carrisa appeared on the screen, with the kill zone directly behind her.

"Damn it, Charlie, are you ready? We don't have a lot of time!"

The camera bobbled in and out of focus.

"Okay, Ben. This is pretty weird. I have no lead in clinical symptoms prior to almost complete systemic failure, concentrated fever over 105, signs of systematic organ failure, and extreme abdominal distention…it's fast, really fast. I've never seen anything kill so efficiently."

She dropped her head and pointed. The camera zoomed in on bodies lying on the beach. Tony moved to the edge of his seat, squinting at the screen. The bodies were swollen, and many had become chalky in color, some had dried blood near the nose and mouth.

"My God," Tony exclaimed, stunned at the sight.

Carrisa returned to her position in front of the camera while attempting to stay out of sight of the CDC workers that hovered to and fro in the background.

"I'm sending you the data that I have. I'm thinking this may be ricin…I hope. Maybe you know something I don't.

"It's not ricin," Tony said aloud to himself.

"Let me know, ASAP. I saw the army pull in early this morning. Something's not right. Oh, and, Ben"—she moved closer to the camera—"whatever you do, don't call him!"

The camera went black.

Tony rustled through the remaining papers in the FedEx package, quickly analyzing the limited amount of data. It didn't make any sense to him; the information simply didn't add up. He grabbed the phone, not at all happy with the information he had received so far, and his lack of understanding it.

The challenge of this event sparked a long dormant excitement in him, and his mind quickly started developing a scientific strategy that could be used to attack this problem.

"Ben, it's Tony," he spoke urgently into the phone.

The voice on the other end was tinny and cynical.

"Really, because I happen to know that Tony doesn't call back. Who is this really?"

"I saw the footage, what the hell is it?" Tony asked, too preoccupied to join in Ben's games.

"We don't know, but whatever it was, it's gone. We checked everywhere, even had a crew canvas air, soil, water, local wild life—its gone. If it was biological, it killed itself out. If it was a toxin or chemical, it has disappeared. Sorry I bothered you, but it was pretty serious for a while," Ben said nonchalantly.

"For a while...wait a minute, you guys are burying it? You don't know what it is, and you're burying it."

"You know how it goes, Tony, we fight what we can, lots of scary stuff out there. We don't have the budget to—"

"No symptoms, complete biological shut down, death within hours, and you don't have the budget? It's not ricin, Ben, you know that, right?" Tony asked sarcastically.

"We know it's not ricin," Ben answered, his voice breaking slightly.

Ben loved Tony for his brilliance, respected him for his work, but at a more personal level, he was terrified of the man who dominated him and unknowingly belittled him. The line remained silent for a few moments as Ben took a deep breath. He returned to the call in a calm and professional voice devoid of friendship.

"Look, Tony, there's a reason you're not here anymore. You never could understand the political part of the job."

"You asked for my help!" Tony felt emotionally charged. He had waited ten years for them to call him, and when they finally did, it was to screw him out of an investigation again.

"I thought we were in a bind because Carrisa was really shook up. It's hard to say no to her," Ben defended himself.

"What about the army? Why were they there? Is this one of their synthetic biological weapons that got out?"

"Tony, you're so paranoid. The army didn't even file a report, probably National Guard guys were dispatched to help with traffic."

Tony shook his head. *Same old thing, same old frustrations, same old Ben, a company man for life*, he thought.

"Same story, huh, Ben? CYA! Cover your ass."

"Tony, I'm sorry I got you involved. It's just that Carrisa was so shook up, and I wanted to...well, put her at ease. You know we should get together. It's been a while. I could get a flight down, and we could hang out, like the old days."

Tony never lifted his head and felt the pain of past years flutter by as he nodded unconsciously.

"Sure, Ben. Just give me a call," Tony said, already knowing that it would never happen.

Tony hung up the phone and stared at the frozen avatar of Carrisa on the computer screen, her eyes burning into his. The feelings that welled up inside him were mixed with anger, betrayal, and longing. He had loved her, still did, but his pride didn't allow him to admit this to himself, let alone to her. Sadly, the courage that he used to build a new life for himself was not up to the task of reaching out to her. He reminded himself that it was time to move on and yet, he had been telling himself that for ten years now.

He clicked off the TV and reached for the hemostats with the roach clipped in, but stopped short of lighting it. Something wasn't right. Something Ben said…the National Guard. Why the hell would he say the National Guard? Carrisa knew the difference between the National Guard and the army. They had all worked with both during their years at the CDC. Something was wrong, and he didn't have all of the proper elements to solve this particular equation. Same shit, different decade, he thought.

Chapter 4

JEREMIAH MARCONI WAS the son of Bullet Bob Marconi, a local Texas war hero from the Vietnam War. Bullet Bob had been shot several times while saving comrades-at-arms in that war. He received the Purple Heart four times, the Distinguished Service Cross for extraordinary heroism, and the Silver Star for gallantry. His status as a local celebrity helped him purchase a bar in the small town of Newton, Texas. Unfortunately, he lost that bar in less than a year due to a myriad of problems, including drug addiction, ever worsening alcoholism, and disastrous relationships with too many women.

It was not uncommon for there to be reports of Bullet Bob crawling naked through neighbor's yards, an M16 cradled within his arms, shouting to push ahead or to fall back. It was this life of basking within the shadow of a hero's greatness and the embarrassment of sifting through the posttraumatic delusions that drove Jeremiah to make poor choices and ultimately to turn to a life of crime.

By the time Jeremiah was eighteen, he had already served time in juvenile hall and served a coming-of-age six-month sentence in the county jail for breaking and entering. By twenty-five, he was serving a ten-year stint in prison for strong-armed robbery and assault, of which he served the first two years in a secured rehab clinic.

The crime itself wasn't nearly as damaging as his attempted getaway. While normally a smash and grab of under fifty bucks would have gotten him a thirty-day sentence in the county clink, Jeremiah rarely had that type of luck. After punching the cashier and grabbing a total of forty-two dollars and eighty-eight cents in change, Jeremiah left the convenience store, and also punched an off-duty female police officer in the process.

He then fled from the police on his motorcycle, leading them on a fifty-mile high-speed chase. Not only did he add to his sentence by leading the police on the chase, he also crossed county lines. In addition, the police officer that he punched was two months pregnant. That might not have had any bearing on the charge under normal circumstances; however, it happened to be an election year. So it didn't take long for a misdemeanor to evolve into a felony over the course of a few minutes.

The chase ended in a horrible accident, from which most folks believed Jeremiah would never recover. Whether he did recover or not was a topic of great debate within the community, because Jeremiah lost his spleen, a kidney, most of the cartilage in his left knee, and sustained irreparable damage to his spine to the point that he could no longer stand fully erect.

As hard as the accident was on his body, it was the damage to his brain that concerned the doctors. Jeremiah lay motionless in a coma for nearly two months, and when he awoke, he was simply not the same man. His temperament mellowed, as did his mental acuity, and his new demeanor allowed him to earn some privileges for good behavior.

Traumatic brain injuries were hard to study, and no one showed any real interest in helping a convicted felon. The turning point for Jeremiah came when he found God in prison and dedicated his remaining years to understanding and interpreting the Bible, mostly the Old Testament and the Book of Revelation.

With newfound belief, his demeanor mellowed even more, his loud and expletive-laden language became quiet and concise, and if he spoke at all it was about God, heaven, hell, or the apocalypse. He became harmless and everyone liked him much better that way.

When he got out of prison, Jeremiah spent two years living on the streets of Newton, preaching to anyone who would stop and listen to his fragmented and delirious sermons. He often garnered support from the goodness of those that remembered the sacrifice and celebrity of his father, who had died a tragic alcoholic death while Jeremiah was in prison.

Jeremiah didn't mind living on the streets; his focus was on God now, and he vaguely remembered that God had a son who lived on the streets as well. On Sunday afternoons, Jeremiah waited outside of the cafeteria for handouts, smiling dumbly, as his coffers filled with copper and silver coins from benevolent dinner guests. He occasionally mumbled "thank you," but no longer had the ability to form anything beyond sentence fragments.

On Thursdays, he got a free dinner and a box of food from the local shelter, and on Friday he could always expect a couple loaves of bread or muffins from the bakery that threw out products that hadn't sold by the expiration date.

He was always provided for, the people of Newton saw to that, but Jeremiah was waiting for a sign that would break through the cobwebs of his mind. A sign he believed God would provide directly to him, and one that would dictate the true purpose of his new life.

May 9, 2018

Jeremiah received his sign in the form of a sunny day and a large white cargo van with Centers for Disease Control and Prevention emblazoned on its side. After a few days in Louisiana, Dr. Moreno's crew had been dispatched to Texas to investigate a report of marine animal die offs occurring in a gulf coastal area of Texas. They were sent to determine if there were any additional human illnesses, and having found none, they were headed back to headquarters in Atlanta.

Dr. Moreno parked the van in a space in front of Jeremiah and stepped out with several colleagues to grab a quick bite to eat at a local diner. Normally, such a mundane occurrence would not have even registered on the damaged psyche of Jeremiah, but something very subtle occurred that day. The diner had a power pole behind it, which stood nearly fifteen feet higher than the roof. On the front of the building was a sign that read "Joe Mallot's Get It Hot." The sign was thin and directly in front of the sun, which created a shadow that was cast across the hood of the CDC van in the shape of a cross, a gigantic cross. Jeremiah stared at the effigy that was displayed in stark contrast to the white hood of the van. Unconsciously, he walked toward it and placed his hands on the hood. He walked slowly around the vehicle, never taking his hands off it. Eventually, he dropped to his knees next to one of the rear tires, hands folded in prayer, head resting on the tire.

"Father, I hear you," he cried. "Help me understand what you want of me, your humble servant."

Most people in town had become accustomed to the strange behavior of this man, so they ignored him as he prayed. And because he was ignored, no one understood the importance of this event in Jeremiah's life. After several moments, he rose, his face staring upward toward the heavens, and a smile spreading across his lips. A smudge of dirt and dried rubber were imprinted on his forehead, but he didn't notice, for he was filled with the assurance that he had been called by God.

As Jeremiah walked down the sidewalk, he was filled with a new sense of purpose, as an unknown agent began the process of overtaking the cells of his body. It entered through his nostrils and his hands, and immediately disseminated into his tissues and various cells where it began to multiply. The agent was much more efficient this time, because, through trial and error, it had adjusted to the human body. Instead of dominating completely and destroying the host, like it had at the gulf, it toned down its virulence and set itself on a course of symbiosis. By keeping the host alive, it could live to transmit its progeny to another host. In order for it to survive, at least some of its hosts had to survive, and the proper adjustments had been made.

More than a thousand miles away, two-time gold medalist, David Grace, rode a stationary bike, sweating profusely. The gym that he worked out in was a typical Southern California setup, with big windows, beautiful people, and superficial smiles that gleamed and permeated the air with unkindness. Huffing and puffing, David finished his workout and entered a door that took him to an indoor volleyball court. He was obviously the top dog of the pack.

After an hour of volleyball workouts, David sat down next to a huge muscular man in the locker room who had just finished showering. The large man looked at David and then injected a syringe full of clear liquid into his own leg.

"I'm tellin' you, man, this stuff puts you back on top," said the large man.

"Drug testing's too stiff now," David said. "You get caught, you serve two years with no competition. I'm forty, I don't have two years left."

"Suit yourself," the large man answered as he removed the needle from his leg.

From around the corner of the locker room, Charlie emerged. David noticed him right away and completely ignored the steroid activity that had been going on next to him.

"You need something?" David asked curtly.

Charlie came all the way around the lockers, smiling shyly.

"Uh, Mr. Grace, my name's Charlie, and I saw you play in the last Olympics."

Charlie's comment was met with silence.

"In China," he continued.

"Yeah, I know where it was. I won a gold medal."

Charlie felt very uncomfortable.

"Anyway, I just wanted to say I saw you win. You're great, and I'm a fan." He started to turn away.

"Wait a minute, man. Sorry, I thought you were one of those media geeks," David said with a warm smile as he extended his hand.

Charlie shook his hand and smiled, relieved to break the uncomfortable silence.

"Guess asking for an autograph would be kinda goofy?" Charlie said, hopefully, as he fidgeted with the pad and pen in his hand.

"Not at all, man, give it here." David took the pad and pen and signed his name, keeping the superficial smile plastered on his face.

Charlie nodded, thanked him, and returned to the next row where his locker was located.

"What a dweeb, man," remarked the large man.

"The price of fame, my friend," he said as he glanced from side to side. "You got any more?"

The big man smiled and pulled out another syringe and handed it to David. However, unbeknownst to David, the unknown agent was already working its way through his bloodstream, infecting cells, and beginning the process of generating millions of copies of itself. The transfer was seamless, from Charlie's hand to David's in one quick, fluid movement.

Charlie and David were unwitting accomplices that helped deliver the agent to the West Coast. Moreno and members of his team carried the unknown agent to the South and East, passing it on to all of those with whom they had contact. In just a few days, hundreds of people had contracted the agent, and these numbers would increase exponentially over the next few weeks, as those who were infected, but had no symptoms, traveled to large metropolitan areas. It would not be long before the effects of this agent were known across the globe.

Chapter 5

CARRISA HATED SCRANTON. While the town folks described it as a quaint little town with nice people, for her it brought back too many memories of the ugly duckling stage of her life, and the town made her think of her father who died as a result of working in the coal mines there. Her mother never left, and now at eighty years old, was more stubborn than ever.

Her mother was extremely mobile for a woman of her age. She still mowed her own lawn, got her own mail, and even pulled a little metal cart to and from the grocery store once a week. She wasn't unique in Scranton, though, as the town was filled with many stubborn old people who refused to sit down and waste away. They were the last of the Greatest Generation, but they were slowly giving way to the aging baby boomers. Nonetheless, her work ethic was still quite impressive.

Carrisa's mother, Dottie, knew everyone in town, which wasn't so unusual, because everyone in town knew everybody else. While most folks claimed this was part of Scranton's charm, it was among the many reasons that Carrisa would never return.

Dottie's house was one of the typical small homes built in this area in the thirties, with a rough cement cellar and a stone foundation. The house had small rooms but a nice screened-in porch that faced the sidewalk, which was perfect for gossiping in the evening.

Carrisa didn't like the way Scranton made her feel, but she loved the way that she could relax in her mother's house. The house she grew up in. It would soon be her house; her mother reminded her of this almost daily. Carrisa thought she should be more comfortable with the inevitable ending of her mother's life, particularly since her mother was in her golden years, but she had only grown closer to her mother over the years, and it seemed to her that it would be impossible to live without her.

She smiled to herself as she thought of what Tony would say if this topic came up, that it was a statistical certainty that one-out-of-every-one person will die. Her thoughts of earlier times with Tony were interrupted by her mother's voice that called to her from the porch.

"Come sit with me, girly," Dottie said in an abrupt but loving voice, so famous for her generation.

Carrisa finished stirring the teas and put the two cups on a serving tray.

"Coming, Mom," she said, walking carefully so as not to spill the hot drinks.

The porch was freshly painted white; it always seemed to be freshly painted and smelled of roses from the bushes that had been growing along the front of the house since she was a child. She handed her mother a cup.

"Here you go, Mom."

"Thank you, dear." Dottie sipped slowly, testing its temperature. "You should come see me more. This will be your house soon, and I'll be gone."

"I'm here now, Mom."

"So you are," she said with a subtle tone to her voice.

It was a familiar tone to Carrisa, a subtle way for her mother to remind her that she should have become a mother. Carrisa could not resist the temptation to make her repeat it.

"What did you say, Mom?"

"Oh, nothing, thank you for the tea," Dottie said, guilt now completely evident.

Carrisa sighed, putting her head in her hands. She knew what was coming, and there would be no peace until they talked about it.

"It's just that I wanted to be a grandmother."

"Mom..."

"Now, wait a minute. I'm eighty years old, and you're no spring chicken. Most women don't even think about kids at your age, but you still could do it. What happened to that funny young man you—"

"You promised, Mom." Carrisa's face tightened. "We weren't meant for each other. Working with him was too hard. He always had to be right."

"Right, wrong, who cares? Let him think he is right. Your father was the same way. All men are, you just have to know when to smile and nod, then do what you have to do," she said, waving a dismissive hand at Carrisa.

"You didn't have to work with Dad."

"Work is easy, try living with a man."

"Work's hard when someone always thinks they are right."

"Someone always thinks they are right, dear, even you. This work, it's too much. Go find a man, have babies, have a family. Make me a grandbaby. Now drink your tea before it gets cold."

Carrisa smiled. The inevitable soapbox conversation wasn't as bad as she thought it would be, but at least it was out of the way. Thoughts of a baby floated around in her head from time to time, but she knew that if she had a baby, her life's work would be over. She couldn't take a baby into an Ebola-infected zone or leave it at home with a babysitter halfway across the world for extended periods of time. No, a baby would change everything.

Besides that, she wasn't so sure that she would want to bring a new life into this world, with all the dangers and temptations it presented. She had questions of her own to answer before she could think about a baby. At least that's what she told her self over and over.

Her mother was right, though; time had nearly run out on her biological clock, and she had been worked obliviously on while it ticked away. Even if things had been different and she had settled down with a husband who wanted to bring a child into this world, she wasn't sure she had what it would take to be a good mother. She wasn't sure she could love unconditionally, and she doubted that she had the patience for it.

Honestly, she had decided against having kids long ago but didn't have the heart to tell her mother.

Chapter 6

TONY WAS ATTENDING to the garden in his backyard when he heard the rattling of the gate and a voice asking if anyone was home.

"I'll be right there," he said, stripping off his gloves.

On the other side of the gate stood Ben Epstein, wearing the ugliest brown suit imaginable. Ben shrugged and rolled his eyes as Tony walked up and opened the gate.

"Not a word about my suit," Ben said wryly, breaking into a smile.

They embraced each other like old friends, forgetting any bad feelings between them for the moment.

"Come in." Tony motioned toward the cottage. "We have a lot of catching up to do!"

Tony led the way through the large garden toward the backdoor of his cottage.

"Holy shit, you said you planted a garden, but what the hell did you do to those tomatoes? Are they real?"

"No, they're fakes, I thought it would be fun to put plastic vegetables in my yard...of course they're real," Tony said, partly annoyed, partly amused that Ben always resorted to a joke instead of a compliment.

"I guess I didn't realize that you had a green thumb to go along with all the rest of your bullshit," Ben joked.

Tony ignored him. It was the same old Ben that Tony knew and loved. Too insecure to compliment a friend, for it might mean that he actually had to stop comparing himself to others.

The two men walked into the cottage, and Ben sat down on a bench in the open sitting room where Tony motioned. The windows in the room were open, allowing the ocean breeze to flow gently through the room.

Tony prepared Ben a glass of his special concoction of fruits, vegetables, and vitamins. It didn't look very appetizing.

"Try this, it tastes better than it looks," Tony said, handing the glass to Ben.

"So what's going on?" he asked. "Why did you come to the beach in a suit?"

Ben inspected the drink and sniffed it before shrugging and taking a healthy swig.

"Wow, that's actually good. What is it?" Ben asked.

"I puree tomatoes, broccoli, and cucumbers, then dry them. Then I freeze them and blend them with pears or apples, whatever I have a taste for. And then I add a little organic pig poo, and wah-la."

Ben choked and spit the liquid back into the glass.

"Are you serious?"

"Everything except the pig poo part," Tony said, smiling wickedly.

"You'll never change, always playing around, never serious."

"I didn't have the privilege of a serious Jewish upbringing."

"Nobody's perfect, keep your head up," Ben said as he drank more of the smoothie.

"Still pissed you missed the boat on the whole *hey-sus* thing, huh?" asked Tony sardonically.

"Shalom," Ben said with a smile that equaled Tony's.

"I appreciate you coming down, but tell me what's going on, Ben, why are you here?"

"I'm not sure, and I'm sorry for the call the other day. I ran some more tests on some of the samples that came back from the gulf, preliminary stuff after we talked. Everything I tried came

MICHAEL D. ACOSTA & ERIC F. DONALDSON, PH.D

back negative. Whatever made those people sick is a new agent. I couldn't detect any known infectious agent in the tissues of the victims, in the dead marine animals, or in the water. And there were no unexpected chemical contaminants found, either. We had no choice, so we sent everything that we had up to USAMRIID," Ben said, shrugging.

"You sent everything to USAMRIID? Let me guess, you were just following protocol."

"That's right, protocol, something you know nothing about," he said, obviously harboring a bit of bad blood. "But I printed an extra report and sent it to you anyway because Carrisa was so shook up. I figured you could identify what this thing was, and I could calm her down. Then when the data came in later…anyway, no sooner than I had it out the door to you, then USAMRIID came in and shut it all down. They took the whole thing over, said it was out of our league."

"USAMRIID couldn't decode the alphabet, much less submicroscopic organisms," Tony said arrogantly.

"Almost twenty years on the job, and I've never seen anything like this. Samples, mock-ups, hard drives, anything we had on this thing was gone, and we were told it was contained. Well, some of the guys asked some questions yada yada, they were told it might be an isolated ricin episode."

"It wasn't ricin," Tony interrupted.

"I know that, we tested for it. Negative. Some of those same guys who asked questions have been reassigned, effective immediately. Security cleaned their desks out."

Tony shook his head, his anger was growing.

"Those bastards. They're covering something up, or they think they've found a gold mine."

Ben shrugged in response.

"Did you rule out bacteria?" asked Tony.

Ben took a moment to think and then shook his head.

"No, I don't think it's bacterial."

"Is it viral?" Tony asked. "If any pathogen could wreak this kind of havoc it would be a virus."

"I don't know, and I can't speculate. I didn't get a second look. Army's got the whole thing now."

Ben took another gulp of his drink.

"Are you sure it was contained? I mean really sure."

"I don't know. I think so."

"Ben, from what I've seen, this thing is possibly the most effective killer on the planet. You've got to be sure."

"What do you want me to say? I wasn't there," he said nervously. "If there was anything, the army would have grabbed it."

"What about Carrisa? Is she okay? Have you heard from her recently?"

"Not since she sent me the samples she had, but they asked lots of questions. Her name was all over this," he said, not happy with the insinuation.

"Damn government, it's the same old shit. We've got to get in touch with her."

"She's not going to like that," Ben warned.

"Hope you're wrong, 'cause you're the one calling her."

"No way, Tony, no way." He shook his head.

Tony's smile showed an expression that spoke more of his sinister nature than of his happiness, and Tony got his way by convincing Ben that the only way to make sure that she was free of danger was to get her to North Carolina. The only way to get more answers on this enigmatic agent was to put their collective heads together. And the only way to get all this done was to lie to her.

Soon after the phone call, Ben opened the front door of Tony's cottage and smiled when he saw Carrisa's face. It had been a while, and they were genuinely happy to see one another. After a heartfelt embrace, he invited her in.

"Nice place, Ben. Really doesn't seem like you though…" Her voice trailed off as Tony sauntered into the room.

Her face showed surprise at first then softened for only a moment before giving way to anger.

"You son of a bitch." She turned toward Ben who looked abashed.

"You shouldn't judge Ben's mother too harshly, Carrie," Tony defended him with a smile and laugh.

"Just…just…don't call me that!" Carrisa exclaimed as her anger overwhelmed her.

"Listen to me. If Ben thought enough to call me on this thing and you thought enough to call him, I'm thinking it's worth taking a look at all the facts together. Agreed?" Tony negotiated.

Ben nodded, still looking abashed and nervous. Carrisa glared at both of them and shook her head rigidly, seeing the logic, but not appreciating the circumstances or the subterfuge it took to get her here. It did not take long for her to relent, though, because she had a strong desire to solve this mystery, which meant that her anger would have to wait.

For the next few hours, they poured over the evidence, dissected the data, and studied the video. Hypothesizing, debating, constructing, and deconstructing. None of the biological or chemical agents that the three had worked with were capable of doing this much damage across so many distinct species.

The sun began to set, and the breeze drifting into the cottage became cool. Tony got up, closed the windows, and made them shakes that he spiked with a shot or two of his own blueberry vodka. Soon after, the conversation veered away from the unknown agent, and they began rehashing old times, laughing and accusing each other of instigating events none remembered very clearly, because most had occurred at least eighteen years prior.

They had a great time distorting and exaggerating the facts at each other's expense and catching up on the personal events that had transpired since the last time they shared a few drinks together. By midnight, Tony had brought out the big guns, and the three took to shooting straight tequila, reminiscing about an onsite *E. coli* outbreak investigation in Mexico and fighting over the worm. It did not take much of the tequila to knock Ben out, and he was soon curled up on the couch, snoring obnoxiously.

Carrisa giggled at Ben's loud snorting.

"Sounds like he's dying," she said, laughing more than was necessary for the comment.

"You're still the most beautiful woman I have ever seen," Tony replied, somehow aware that his comments did not fit in with the conversation.

"You're drunk," she said, her face flushing.

"Doesn't mean I'm not right."

"You always think you're right. That's your biggest weakness," she slurred and laughed despite herself.

Tony reached across and gently touched her face.

"Care to present evidence to the contrary, Doctor?" he asked with his eyes stuck on her.

"You bastard." She giggled and threw her head back. "I knew I shouldn't have had anything to drink. I've been trying to get you outta my head for years."

"I'm like a bad habit, I never go away." Tony smiled.

"Mmmm, more like a case of herpes, you lay dormant until I'm in a weak state," she quipped.

"I love it when you talk dirty."

The two embraced gently, as their long dormant passion boiled up to the surface once again. Tony caressed her hair with his hand as his lips pressed against hers. Hot tears poured down Carrisa's cheek as she surrendered to the passion that she had carefully suppressed for over a decade.

Tony came to the next morning hangover-free, because his concoctions were designed to prevent dehydration and loss of electrolytes. He remembered the details of the previous night, and he knew who was beside him in bed, but he took a deep breath before he looked just in case his mind was playing tricks on him.

He had dreamed about this moment for ten years and could only hope that when she awoke it wouldn't return to how it was. He moved the sheet just a little to allow for a better view of her face, which struck him as glowingly beautiful. He grabbed a worn, leather-bound diary off his bedside table and began to write, looking at her face often for inspiration.

After a few minutes, her eyes fluttered and opened, falling upon him immediately. She had no expression on her face and seemed to be caught between thoughts. For a single moment, she looked longingly into his eyes and then suddenly broke the gaze and slapped him across the jaw. Tony recoiled as Carrisa ripped the top sheet off the bed, wrapped it around herself, and stormed off to the bathroom.

Tony smiled while moving his jaw around to make sure it still worked.

"Was it good for you?" he called behind her.

"Up yours," she shouted from behind the slammed door.

Tony put on a pair of loose-fitting pants and a light sweater and made his way into the living room where Ben was just beginning to stir.

"Morning, sunshine." Tony smiled.

The smile had just enough mystery to it that Ben wondered aloud.

"Where's Carrisa?"

Tony pulled a trio of cups from the cabinet and filled them with coffee from a pot that had brewed automatically. He nodded his head toward the bedroom. Ben looked shocked and then smiled in the way that frat boys smile when a brother gets lucky.

"Get the hell outta here," Ben whispered incredulously.

Tony smiled and brought him a cup of Joe, while flipping to a local morning news show on the television. Ben took the mug robotically, glanced at the TV and then at Tony. At that moment, Tony's face registered concerned as he processed the news that the broadcaster reported.

"Etymologists from North Carolina State University are baffled by this finding and are further investigating this situation in cooperation with the Environmental Protection Agency. It appears that hundreds of thousands of bees have been found dead in North Carolina, lying on the ground, apparently having fallen right out of the sky were they had been flying. We will have more information on this story on the News at Noon. This is Gerald Strum, reporting for North Carolina Coastal News."

"Where did you say Carrie was working when she encountered the agent?" Tony asked.

"The gulf."

Carrisa walked out at that moment, preparing for battle, but she saw the expressions on the faces of the two men and knew something was wrong.

Tony flipped through all the news channels in an attempt to gather as much information as he could. Carrisa, Ben, and Tony discussed the new information and rehashed the data that Ben had brought with him. For a second time, the trio went back and forth debating the possible origin and identity of the agent and attempting to determine if one agent could be responsible for killing humans, fish, and now bees.

Every possibility they discussed brought them back to the beginning. Every time one of them had a new idea, the other two would discount it. It was good scientific debate. Frustrating and annoying, but the process allowed them to arrive at a well-vetted list of possibilities.

Ben looked exhausted.

"Everything points to a chemical contaminant, probably a heavy metal like lead or mercury poisoning. Look at the fish. A waterborne contaminant makes sense, and it probably came from the refineries," he said, having assumed this from the beginning.

"With out prolonged symptoms? I'm not buying it. A thousand fish don't die at the same time. There would have been signs of this for weeks, maybe months. And humans don't die with such a rapid onset of symptoms, it just doesn't happen. But I suppose a contaminant makes the most sense at this point," Carrisa answered.

"What about the army? If it were a chemical pollutant, why would they be so interested? You said yourself that you've never seen anything like it, Ben," Tony said. "And how can we be sure that this isn't some engineered virus accidentally released by the army?"

"Come on, Tony," Ben started, "stop with the conspiracy theories. When are you going to grow up and realize that our understanding of science isn't advanced enough to create an engineered supervirus."

"You are infuriating and naïve. Just a few years ago, a research group at UNC engineered a Bat SARS virus that could cross the species barrier. They didn't even have a real virus to work with, just the sequence. If they could do that, just imagine what the army is capable of."

"The military is not in the business of making viruses. Hell, the navy can't even control the norovirus that costs them millions of dollars every year," Ben said defensively.

"What about Nixon?" Tony asked.

"Tony, let's not do this again," Carrisa said, feeling they were getting way off track.

"Let him go, Carrie. What about him?"

"He initiated the whole biological warfare and biological weapons research program in the 1960s through the National Cancer Institute and the CDC."

"So now the CDC is complicit with biological weapons research and—"

"Even after he signed the Geneva Accord and claimed that all biological weapons research and development ceased, it still continued. This is documented stuff, Ben, stop pretending! They were designing viruses that would wipe out the immune system, specifically for the purpose of infecting thousands of soldiers in the field."

"I know where you're going with this," Ben interrupted. "You think HIV is a man-made virus, custom-made by our military to wipe out the immune system. I've heard it all before, I read your research, and I was there when they booted you out for it. Time to learn a new song!" Ben said, feeling bad because he was afraid that he might have gone too far.

Tony exhaled deeply and loudly, feeling as if he were just kicked in the stomach. An uncomfortable silence fell over the room.

"I've seen the documentation," Carrisa interjected, trying to smooth the rough edges. "Nixon and Kissinger started the bioweapons research program. They ran it through USAMRIID at Fort Detrick and funded it under the National Cancer Institute. Taxpayers assumed they were paying for some lab to investigate cancer causing viruses, but they were really funding research designed to create viral weapons of mass destruction."

"What does all of that have to do with the current situation?" Ben asked. "Do you honestly believe that this is a man-made virus?"

"Think about it, Ben. We have witnessed something that kills more efficiently than anything we know of. It leaves no evidence behind, and there appears to be no limitation to what it can infect. This whole thing smacks of a biological weapon to me," Tony stated.

The phone rang, and Tony answered but spent most of the time listening, thanked the caller, and returned to the conversation harried.

"What is it?" Carrisa asked, still trying hard to forget the events of last night.

"The bees," he answered.

"What do you mean the bees?" she asked.

MICHAEL D. ACOSTA & ERIC F. DONALDSON, PH.D

"This morning, we saw a report on TV. Hundreds of thousands of bees were found dead, as if they fell right out of the sky. It was reported on the local news, but now it's happened in six other states between here and the Gulf of Mexico. If the same agent that killed everything around the gulf is killing bees, then it is moving up the coast, and it is moving quickly!"

Ben looked frustrated and couldn't quite wrap his head around it.

"I'm lost," he said.

"Two days ago, bees started dying by the hundreds of thousands, falling out of the sky with no warning and no known symptoms," Tony restated.

"And?" Ben asked, frustrated.

"Could it be an airborne contaminant?" Carrisa asked to no one specific.

"It's got to be an engineered virus." Tony shook his head. "Nothing else could spread this fast, and what contaminant would be present in all six states? It has to be an engineered pathogen."

"Oh, come on, Tony," Ben said. "The army wouldn't engineer a virus capable of infecting multiple kingdoms. That would be a game changer. And if they did, they wouldn't release it on their own citizens!"

"I don't know what's going on, Ben, but this thing scares the hell out of me. Everything we have come up with points to a virus, one that kills efficiently and moves quickly in a multitude of different directions, crossing many of the barriers that stop other viruses. If this is not a creation of the army, then maybe it came from some terrorist group," Tony said softly.

Ben was worried.

"Look, I know you two are more familiar with viruses than me, but a virus simply cannot cross all those barriers. Viruses can only infect cells that have specific receptors that allow it to gain entry. If this virus infects humans, and insects, and fish, then something has gone terribly awry."

"That's not completely true, Ben. There are several viruses that have life cycles that include different species. Look at West Nile Virus, it infects humans and horses, birds, and mosquitoes. What if this is a virus that uses some unknown generic receptor found on a variety of different cell types?" Carrisa asked, trying to be open to the improbable.

Tony nodded.

"Okay, let's say for the sake of argument that it is an engineered virus that uses a common receptor found on cells from several species and kingdoms," Ben began, "that doesn't explain how it is spreading so quickly. Whatever this agent is, it is traveling across state lines in a matter of hours. Come on, nothing infectious can move that fast. It's got to have an incubation period."

"For a virus to spread that quickly, it would have to infect rapidly, replicate in record time, and shed to a new host within hours," Tony said. "And if it were adapting to infect other species from different kingdoms, then it would have to have a mutation rate greater than anything known."

"We don't have enough evidence that this is a virus, engineered or not, and we don't even know if what is killing the bees is the same agent that killed those people on the gulf. You guys are grasping," Ben said.

The moment of silence was filled with tension, and Tony locked eyes with Ben. "Ben, listen to me just for a moment and set aside everything you have ever learned about absolutes. Once upon a time, we knew that the world was flat. Once upon a time, we knew that there were nine planets. Less than 150 years ago, we were completely unaware of germs. If anything is capable of breaking or reinventing all the rules, it is a virus. They are the fastest-evolving life forms on the planet, and if they find a niche to exploit, they will find a way to exploit it."

"Then where did it come from and why did it stop killing?" Ben asked sarcastically. "A virus can exploit a niche, but this is more than one niche, there are several barriers here."

Ben looked to Carrisa, who seemed worried. She smiled kindly at him.

"Let's just look deeper. If we don't, who will?" she asked in a kind manner. "We can't just let the army bury it and be done with it. Remember when we just started, it was about saving the world from deadly diseases and toxins, and curing cancer and—"

"Maybe, it hasn't stopped killing, maybe it's just attenuated so that it's not killing humans anymore," Tony said.

Ben looked at the two of them as if they were crazy and then checked his watch.

"I need to go. I'll do some checking, but I gotta be honest. I don't buy this, I need evidence to support it, and I'm definitely not comfortable calling it a virus yet. I'll check around anyway, for the sake of the old days and saving the world." Ben smiled sardonically and kissed Carrisa on the cheek.

They said their good-byes and watched as Ben left, leaving them alone to deal with their past and the present and the thick tension of excitement, frustration, and confusion that was brewing between them.

Chapter 7

May 11, 2018

J EREMIAH MARCONI FELT the changes occurring in his body within a few hours, and he knew that it was the life force of the Father that had been bestowed upon him during the revelry of his vision. He soon began to comprehend that God's hand had changed him forever, and he knew that it was time for him to make people understand the awesome power that was the Alpha and Omega. Slowly, but surely, God's plan became clear inside him.

God revealed to him that the Apocalypse was coming, and it was time for all of God's children to repent for their sins and accept the punishments due each of them. Through the pain of fire, there would be absolution and life eternal.

Jeremiah smiled in a way he hadn't smiled in years, and he began to run as his broken body no longer felt quite so rigid. Inside his body, the agent worked to restore depleted muscles and scarred bones. There was much to remake, especially in the central nervous system and the brain, but the agent made due, repairing this broken human.

As Jeremiah ran, his mind focused upon a distant sound that cleared into music and voices, many voices. The voices were singing hymns, and they sounded glorious. He ran toward the music, feeling called by the Almighty. With every step, the sound of the music became more and more clear and seemed much closer than it actually was. He felt the urge to reach out and touch it, but somewhere in his mind, he realized that the music could not be touched. With each passing moment, Jeremiah's brain cleared, and he began to understand a great many things that had not made sense for many years, if ever. He felt sad that he had wasted so much of his life being driven by a crowded mind filled with distracting notions and discombobulating thoughts.

After running for nearly a mile, Jeremiah was surprised that he still had not reached the source of the music. He realized that it was remarkable to hear something so clearly at that distance, but he felt reassured because he knew that nothing was impossible for God. When he finally arrived at his destination, he saw that it was a large First Assembly of God Church, and he knew what God wanted from him. He knew this would be the place where he began his ministry to teach, preach, and prepare the world for the coming Apocalypse.

It was clear to him that nothing could stop it, and it would be his job to lead as many sinners to God as he could. He had been bestowed with the glory and authority of the King, and he would demonstrate his obedience by using any force necessary to honor this truth.

He opened the door and looked at the backs of nearly five hundred finely dressed congregants singing songs of praise. Jeremiah closed his eyes, turned his face upward toward God, and allowed his tattered coat to fall off his shoulders and onto the floor.

For a moment, he felt self-conscious as he could feel his disheveled hair shooting out from his head in all directions, and his beard was long and ungroomed, but he recognized that God never sent prophets that regular people would expect. No, God sent prophets that false Christians would fear and righteous Christians could identify. He would make them all bow, every last one; it was God's will. And with that, he spoke the first lucid words that he had uttered in many years.

"Behold the glory of our God, Jehovah," he said in a voice that boomed over the singing.

The music died down, and everyone turned to see who had disrupted the service. Jeremiah loomed over the congregation. He was a big man, like his father, standing well over six feet tall.

He was also blessed with a naturally muscular physique, which he had managed to not lose despite inadequate nutrition over the last few years. He hadn't stood straight in years, due to the accident, but he did so now and his presence was imposing and intimidating. No one moved as he strode down the aisle, peering into the eyes of anyone who dared make eye contact.

An elderly pastor meekly stepped forward.

"Jeremiah? What can we help you with, my son? We're right in the middle of—"

Jeremiah pointed and stopped him in mid-sentence.

"God has chosen me to prophesize and gather His children. He has chosen this place to be the genesis. The beginning of the end starts here and now."

The pastor smiled kindly and went toward him, still under the impression that he was mentally confused. He laid his hand on his shoulder and tried to guide him to the side. Jeremiah gathered together the front of the old pastor's robes, kissed his forehead, and lifted him above his head with one arm.

"Those who are unwilling to listen to me are unwilling to listen to the very voice of God. Those who do not listen to God will travel the path of perdition and burn in the febrile fires of Gehenna," Jeremiah preached and slowly brought the pastor down and released him.

The congregation was stunned and sat quietly, while a sense of collective expectation and curiosity traveled from person to person.

"Hear me, children, hear my testimony, hear the words the Almighty has given unto me. Fallen is Babylon the Great! She has become a home for demons and a haunt for every evil spirit, a haunt for every unclean and detestable creature. For all the nations have drunk the maddening wine of her adulteries. The kings of the earth committed adultery with her, and the merchants of the earth grew rich from her excessive luxuries."

Jeremiah looked from eye to eye, demonstrating a clarity that he had never known. The pastor stepped back, stunned by the sudden speech from a man who could barely put a proper sentence together only a few days earlier. Some congregants left the church immediately, fleeing to their cars. Jeremiah continued, unfazed.

"Brothers, sisters, a storm is coming. In God's mighty wisdom, He will set upon those of us who do not accept his offer of forgiveness and eternal life. With such violence, the great city of Babylon will be thrown down never to be found again. The music of harpists and musicians, flute players and trumpeters, will never be heard in you again. No workman of any trade will ever be found in you again. Accept this offer. Accept my prophecy and join me, for a plague is coming to this land."

Jeremiah grew increasingly charismatic with each word. Intense and frightening, something had changed drastically. More than half the congregation still sat riveted by his testimony, believing that a miracle had taken place in him right before their eyes. The pastor stepped forward once again, his old bones showing how frail and afraid he was, but his anger and fear were just as obvious.

"You are a false prophet. Do not believe these lies," the pastor said, his voice shaking with emotion.

Jeremiah smiled contently, showing another expression that hadn't been seen on his face for many years. He looked calmly and kindly at the old man.

"You will be one of the first. Your blood will boil and burn within your body. You will not live past tomorrow because of your transgression against God."

The old pastor did not back down.

"These are wicked words, Jeremiah. I beg of you to repent them now, please do not condemn yourself this way. You are not well, and this is blasphemy."

"You are the blasphemer, old man. And you shall be paid the wages of sin," Jeremiah said softly.

The congregation began to mumble, swaying with the odd and tense meeting on the dais. The old pastor spoke in a feverish pitch, holding his Bible aloft.

"When I say to a wicked man, you will surely die, and you do not warn him or speak out to dissuade him from his evil ways in order to save his life, that wicked man will die for his sin, and I will hold you accountable for his blood."

Jeremiah discounted his words with a smile and made contact with the congregation, spreading his arms out wide, inviting them into his prophecy.

"And I saw the dead, great and small, standing before the throne. And the book was opened, which is the book of life. The dead were judged according to what they had done. The sea gave up the dead that were in it, and death and Hades gave up the dead that were in them, and each person was judged according to what he had done. Then death and Hades were thrown into the lake of fire. The lake of fire is the second death. If anyone's name was not found written in the book of life, he was thrown into the lake of fire. I ask you now, is your name in the book?" Jeremiah asked, looking at the congregants who remained.

Many members of the congregation were unsure of how to answer.

"Is your name in the book?" he asked again, forcefully. "Will you accept God's invitation? Will you accept?"

The congregation answered softly with "amens" at first, and then began to gain confidence and fervency. Their eyes were large and intoxicated with Jeremiah's message. The old pastor could only stand by the wayside and watch what he believed was the devil at work.

"Come to me, and we shall write your name in blood in the book of life," Jeremiah smiled widely, gleefully, fully in what he felt was the Spirit. One by one, the remaining members of the congregation rose from their seats and went to him kneeling before him.

"No! Stand, I am not the Lord, I am his messenger, stand and from this day forth kneel only to Him!" he said, his voice trembling with emotion.

The men and women all stood, and none of them could take their eyes off him. Jeremiah looked down at the first, a woman in her early twenties, fragile and pale, wearing a knit sweater. Her face was peeked and hair flaxen, a thin girl not in the greatest of health. He took her face gently in his hands.

"Do you accept God's word?" he asked.

"I do," the sickly girl answered.

"What is your name?"

"Jessica."

"Jessica, do you accept the invitation to spread His message and do battle for Him? Are you ready for your name to be written in His book?" he asked, his voice getting louder and louder as he spoke.

"I do," the girl said almost inaudibly, shaking like a leaf.

"Let it be written in blood!"

Jeremiah reared back his huge fist and slammed it into her face. Blood exploded from her fragile nose and the blackness of bruising began to swell beneath her eyes, as a collective gasp rose from the parishioners. The young girl fell unconscious on the people behind her. Jeremiah picked her up and wiped the blood from her ruined face. He smiled and treated her as a child.

"You are the first child. The first to accept His name, you shall have a place high in the Army of God."

The girl smiled briefly through her broken face and then slipped back into unconsciousness. Jeremiah laid her down and looked at the others.

"Who's next?"

When Jeremiah left the church that day, he had gained nearly two hundred followers dedicated to helping him build God's Army. They came from all levels of society, but what was most significant was the fact that they were all devoted to his vision and believed that he was God's chosen prophet. In fact, for those who knew him from before this change, he was the miracle made manifest.

Chapter 8

B EN WAS ANNOYED by his visit to North Carolina. It wasn't that he disliked Tony and Carrisa, or that they hadn't bought his assessment, it was that he believed their hypothesis, and he didn't like it. The thought of this agent being a virus engineered by humans bothered him. He knew that it was dangerous, but it was the fact that it had all but disappeared at the gulf that bothered him most. Viruses just didn't do that, at least not so quickly.

He knew that it was improbable for a virus to survive and evolve if it adapted so quickly that it couldn't sustain itself in a population. He also knew that most viruses didn't adapt to become less virulent, at least not quickly. They established a symbiotic relationship with their host, adapting to become virulent enough to outfox the immune system, but not so virulent as to completely destroy the host. Give and take. If this thing was a virus, it was not playing by the known rules. It appeared to be either all give or all take. It made no sense.

Ben knew that he had to be careful. The fact that the army boys were on this case meant that containing this thing was their top priority, and most probably, as Tony said, it was destined for weaponization or was some government weapon already gone awry. Either way, Ben knew that he had to find something, anything that would help them determine if the army had halted the unusual outbreak. If not, the consequences would be dire, probably for the whole world, and certainly for Carrisa.

Ben was a company man, he knew that—hell, everyone did— but at the core, he was a scientist, and Carrisa was right. It was all about bettering mankind, saving the world. Those things meant something to him once, and he felt that this was his chance to do something worthwhile.

Back at his office, he went to the directory that contained all the information for the event at the gulf to search through the data one more time, but just to be safe, he used a computer terminal that was in a common area and used by many users. To his surprise, there was nothing left on the hard drive. It was wiped completely clean.

The lack of any information whatsoever indicated to Ben that there was indeed a cover-up. After all, this was government work. Every incident required a pile of paperwork, followed by an after-action report, and then a written conclusion. It was protocol, and Ben knew protocol.

For the first time in nearly twenty years, Ben was forced to do something that he knew how to do but had only done once before. It meant breaking the rules. Several years earlier, Ben had stolen a password from his supervisor, Ken, in order to have porn advertisements sent to his .gov e-mail address as a joke. Against all regulations, Ken had never changed the password, and now it was Ben's key to more information.

Over the next couple of days, Ben waited until the time was right and then used the same terminal to access Ken's secure files while everyone in the immediate office was out for lunch. Working quickly, he scoured through the classified directories and documents for nearly twenty minutes.

At first, he was unable to find anything that looked like it pertained to the case, but then he stumbled upon a directory labeled "Pecan LA." It contained no information about the agent, but he found written orders by Army Colonel Adrian Bragg whose office was located within USAMRIID.

Ben's mind raced as he searched the entire database using the colonel's name. After a brief delay, a directory page opened with a biography of the officer. Col. Bragg was an infectious disease specialist in the bioweapons division.

Ben clicked on a link to "Ongoing Investigations," which revealed that the Army Bioweapons Division was investigating an unknown outbreak that occurred on the Gulf of Mexico under the direction of Colonel Bragg. In addition, it listed the agent as "an undetermined agent with high weaponization potential."

At the bottom of the report in the section marked "Additional Considerations" was a single sentenced that made Ben gasp. The sentence read, "Investigation initiated to determine identity of the agent, and to refute allegations of an internal domestic terrorist attack."

Although there was not much information on the agent, his search shed a lot of light on the situation, and Ben felt disheartened. The army didn't know for sure what it was, but someone was alleging that it was an internal agent that was released by someone at USAMRIID. He sent the information to Tony and resolved to take more invasive measures to get more answers.

May 21, 2018

Tony and Carrisa spent several days, mostly in silence, cohabitating together at Tony's cottage at the beach. They had agreed that this would be the safest place for Carrisa to stay until Ben learned more about what the army was up to, and whether or not they might try to come after Carrisa. While this living situation was awkward for them both, it was obvious that each enjoyed having the other as a companion. Tony enjoyed knowing that Carrisa was one wall away, and Carrisa enjoyed the secure feeling that she felt, knowing that Tony would do everything he could to protect her.

But they also had their shortcomings, some of which came with a long history of annoying the other. Carrisa hated sitting still or lying low, because she always felt the urge to be on the move and outdoors. Tony was perfectly content staying at home and looking after his plants and his inventions. In many ways, they were as different as two people could be, but that they still cared for one another was obvious. That she didn't like him smoking marijuana was proof, but she didn't say anything, only gave him a look that said so. He didn't like that she still bit her nails, so he left the room when she did.

He also had to keep his illicit distribution operation on the down low, but Tony prided himself on how well he covered every step, and for the most part, Carrisa had no idea that he was moving a pound of marijuana every week. However, Dude was not an easy person to forget, and Tony had to dodge the occasional question about him from Carrisa.

One afternoon, Tony's reengineered Teletype machine beeped to life and quietly printed out a long ticker tape receipt. Tony tore the paper from the machine as soon as it stopped printing and began to read it.

"Carrie," he hollered.

She came in and watched him closely as he decoded the message.

"Okay, he found the guy who is in charge, US Army Colonel Adrian Bragg. Infectious disease specialist…"

"Is there more?" she asked. "That is the smug prick who took my samples."

"He's in the Bioweapons Division at USAMRIID. We were right. I knew it," he said, feeling sad that he lived in a world that created biological weapons.

"They're investigating whether or not this is an internal domestic terrorist attack? What the hell does that mean? Do they think this is their own agent that was released?"

"Sounds to me like they don't know what it is or where it came from," Carrisa said.

"Or they recognize the destruction, but don't know who released it," Tony added. "We've gotta go."

"Where?"

"To the source. We need to collect fresh samples, and I need to get a look at the site. Regardless of the origin of this agent, the army is stuck. They don't know if it is theirs or not, and they are going to bury this until they figure it out. If we don't do something, it's going to be too late. Particularly, if they sit on this because they think it is theirs and it ends up being something totally novel. That would cripple any public health measures that would try to stop it."

"Are you sure you want to jump into the middle of this? The kill zone will probably be under guard. How do you plan to get in?" she asked, knowing that any plan he had would be irresponsible.

Tony smiled wickedly.

"Just pack," he said.

The flight to New Orleans went smoothly, and the two quickly deplaned and rented a car for the 150-mile trip to the beach town south of Pecan. The main highway provided easy access to Vermillion Parish, but from there, they got onto Highway 82 and headed southwest, taking the only road that went in or out of Pecan.

The landscape in the area was mostly marshy, which was typical for the Delta, but it had a certain charm. On many of the sunny, humid days, the locals would pass the day by gathering along the marshy banks to catch and boil crawfish and drink beer.

However, the landscape changed drastically as they got closer to Pecan. Many of the vibrant greens of the marshy grasses became tinted with brown, and the brown plants became more prevalent as they progressed southward. The color change was subtle at first, but Tony was looking for anything unusual in this area. Carrisa noticed the differences too. And while normally she would have written it off as signs of a drought, she knew that these grasses were green just a couple of weeks before.

"This isn't right," Tony said, noting the distinct difference in foliage as they travelled.

They stopped for lunch in the small seaside village of Pecan Island, which the sign proudly proclaimed as unincorporated. And while that wasn't completely true, their selection of services was limited to one small, overpriced grocery store that doubled as a diner of sorts and a bait shop. A few locals sat at tables scattered around the interior of the dining area. A hostess in her late fifties rang up a customer. Something about her seemed odd to Tony. She looked…vibrant, almost defiant of her years. *It must be the spice,* he told himself.

Carrisa and Tony sat down in a comfortable booth and ate a fantastic lunch of traditional Creole shrimp and eggs. Afterward, the same hostess delivered the bill to their table, but the amount was about twice as much as the prices listed on the menu. Carrisa discovered the difference and called the woman back over to the table.

"Ma'am, I think there's been a mistake, why is our bill so much?"

The woman spun around quickly, ready to do battle.

"Prices went up. Animals no doin' so good. Sorry, mon ami," she said as she pointed toward a piece of paper on the wall that announced the new prices. She tried to leave again, but Tony got her attention this time.

"What do you mean?" he asked.

She huffed, now outwardly annoyed at the break in her routine.

"Cattle's been dyin', all sick. Hay has begun to fail, so we can't feed the cattle. Chickens are laying less eggs, even the shrimp is hard to get now. *Nous avons un problème you?*" she asked, sensing a potential refusal to pay.

"No problem." Tony pulled out a fifty and handed it to her. "Please keep it. Can you point us to any of the farms that are losing animals?"

Once back in the car, they followed the hostess' directions to a nearby farm, which led them down a pothole-laden gravel drive. They bumped their way along the road until they saw a shabby farmhouse and then parked. Inside the fences, hundreds of cows roamed and grazed on wilted and browning grass. Most of the cows looked haggard and thin, too thin for beef cattle.

A man in overalls was watering the cows when he saw them pull up, and he immediately dropped what he was doing and headed their way. Surprisingly, he jumped over the fence in a single bound, as if he were a hurdle runner. Tony and Carrisa were impressed with his spryness, especially when they saw up close that the smiling man was probably in his late fifties.

"*Bonjour. Peux j'aide?* Can I help you?" the farmer asked in a French Cajun accent.

"Hello, I'm Tony and this is Carrie. We heard that you were having some problems with your cows and we wanted to take a look."

The farmer immediately became suspicious.

"You real estate people?" he asked.

"Oh no." Tony laughed. "We're scientists and just wanted to ask some questions. Is that okay?"

Upon hearing that the two were scientists, the man brightened.

"Sure you. You thinking you can help them?" asked the farmer.

"Can you tell us exactly what you've seen and when?"

The farmer told them that his cows began getting thinner a week ago at about the same time the hay crop began to go bad. He described it as an "early fall," and he indicated that everything was changing too early, even the grass was dying and the leaves on the trees were dropping off. Some of his cows died with a fever, but most seemed to die of starvation, wasting away and falling were they stood. The veterinarians took blood and stool samples, but so far had found nothing. They had administered all varieties of antibiotics and antivirals to combat the sickness, but nothing had any effect.

The damage at the farm was devastating and getting worse by the minute. Tony knew that this man's farm would be completely depleted in two days time, and the man seemed to sense this too.

MICHAEL D. ACOSTA & ERIC F. DONALDSON, PH.D

"It's a funny thing," he said. "I have never felt better in my life. Now I am ready to work hard all day long, and the crops are drying up and my cows are dead."

The farmer's words haunted Tony and Carrisa. Everything around that farmer was dying, and yet he was thriving. Something about that scared the hell out of Tony. *Could this all be linked to the same outbreak? Is it some new virus?* he wondered.

Tony and Carrisa continued their journey to the site on the gulf where the original outbreak occurred. As they approached the ground zero area, Tony carefully parked the car far enough away to avoid notice. From a distance, they observed that the army was managing the site. Humvees were parked about with armed soldiers guarding the area. There were no signs of people anywhere, which indicated that either the entire area had been evacuated, or that this town was now operating under martial law.

Tony and Carrisa removed their gear from the trunk of the car and began trekking through the marsh. They narrowly avoided notice more than a few times, as the army had deployed armed guards even in the marshes. They moved slowly and deliberately as there wasn't much cover, and the greenery in the area was completely gone—long past the browning stage and now rotting away. Once they reached the edge of the sand, they saw that several tents had been set up on the beach. Soldiers wearing biological grade gas masks guarded the entrances, and men in fully self-contained biosafety suits walked in and out of the tents often, many of them carrying trays of sample vials.

"There's no way to get in from here, let's go down a little farther," Tony said.

"I think we're in over our heads, and I thought you had a plan?" she said sarcastically, but not without a little fear.

"This is my plan."

"Great."

"What happened to the optimist?"

Carrisa rolled her eyes and muttered something under her breath.

"I have a plan B too, Carrie, I just don't know what it is yet. Let's go."

They moved just in time to avoid being detected by a roving guard. After sloshing in the mud and sand for an additional thousand yards, they reached the outer edge of the perimeter. The first thing Tony noticed was two dead cats and a dead dog.

"I think this will do. Why don't you collect some samples, and I'll have a look around," he said.

Carrisa quietly unpacked her case and went about the business of doing what she did as well as anyone in the world. She collected several samples from a broad range of flora and fauna. She swabbed mucous membranes, took blood samples, and isolated several animal tissues in formaldehyde. She even collected more ocean water, took large aliquots of the black foam and sludge, and harvested several plant leaves. The plants seemed to be dying in waves, as if they were caught in a concentric circle of death that was more potent at the circle's center, but decreased in potency as it extended away from the kill zone. She carefully contained each sample in a small, portable dry ice container that she brought with her. Tony looked closely at several plants before focusing on the dead animals, which appeared to have been emaciated prior to death.

When they completed their mission, the two darted back into the marsh under the cover of the dying plants and trees and hiked back to their rental car. As they approached the site where the car was parked, Tony grabbed Carrisa's pack and tossed both his and hers behind a tree. He then grabbed her and threw her roughly onto the ground, pulling at her shirt and yanking at his own pants. Carrisa fought back, nearly in shock.

"What the hell are you doing?" she gasped as he attempted to kiss her.

"Just go with it," he whispered back at her as he proceeded to passionately attack her.

Tony successfully unlatched her pants and climbed on top of her.

"Hold it right there, folks!" said a deep voice from behind them. Both Tony and Carrisa froze.

"Let's see some hands."

Tony slowly rolled off her and raised his hands, leaving him in a precarious and embarrassing position. His pants were partially down and hers were unbuttoned, unzipped, and pulled down just past her hips. They both raised their arms from the prone position.

When they looked up, they saw a large, angry-looking soldier who stood in full military stance, pointing an M16 assault rifle directly at them. He carefully looked them over, and when he was satisfied that they posed no threat, he pulled his rifle back.

"What do we have here?" the soldier asked.

Tony smiled and shrugged his shoulders in the dirt then laughed nervously.

"I feel like I just got caught by my mom. Did we do something wrong?"

Carrisa looked confused and said nothing.

"I'm gonna need to see some ID. Go ahead and get up and… zip up."

Tony and Carrisa got up from the ground, fixed their clothing, and handed the guard their identification cards. The soldier looked at them and handed them back.

"You're not local."

"We're on vacation. Trying to put the fire back into our relationship, if you know what I mean." Tony lifted his eyebrows in successive motions.

The soldier hesitated a moment and then laughed. A voice called over his radio.

"Alpha six actual. Alpha six-one. Are you clear?"

"Alpha six-one, copy. All clear," the soldier responded into the radio.

"Look, you can't be around here. I'm gonna do my round, but I'll be back in ten minutes. I know that's not a lot of time, but do what you got to do and get lost. Copy?"

Tony nodded, adding an appropriately embarrassed smile.

"Oh, we copy," he said.

They waited until he was at least fifty yards away before Tony pulled her down slowly to their knees. He eyed the soldier warily until he was out of sight.

"Sorry about that—"

Carrisa slapped him several times on the shoulder.

"You son of a bitch, I was scared to death. Why didn't you warn me?"

"How the hell was I going to do that? Look, we gotta go," he said as he retrieved their packs from behind the large tree and moved to the car as fast as possible.

The ride back to New Orleans seemed twice as long, and the brown and dead plant life was even more pronounced. They were both exhausted and bothered by the data they were presented with: dead and dying animals, withering plant life, and a large army presence at the site. None of it was a recipe for anything good.

Chapter 9

B EN HAD BEEN sweating bullets since he illegally used his supervisor's computer terminal. He had successfully found what he was looking for, though, so he was not about to let his own fear stop him now. Not this time. He knew that he needed more security access, but he was at a loss as to how to get it. Then a solution presented itself.

He had been assigned the task of determining the identity of an unknown agent that had originated in Indonesia. He had acquired a small but unique snippet of the pathogen's genetic DNA code, and he had run a search using that DNA sequence to query the non-redundant nucleotide database at the National Center for Biotechnology Information. A match of the unknown DNA sequence to a known viral or bacterial sequence would help identify the unknown pathogen. However, this sequence did not match any DNA in the public database. And then it hit him.

Ben went to Ken's office and entered without knocking.

"Ken, I need access to..." His voice trailed off, as he realized that he was talking not to Ken but to a woman he had never seen before.

"Oh—excuse me, didn't mean to intrude. Is Ken around?"

The woman appeared to be dressed according to some sort of regulation, every crease was perfect, and every gig line straight. Her red hair struck him, as it contrasted strongly with her dark-green pantsuit.

"No, I'm afraid he's not," she said with little or no emotion.

Ben noticed that she was unpacking a box and putting her things on Ken's desk. She removed a nameplate that read "Diane," a coffee mug that had "Soldier of the Quarter" embossed on it, and a picture of her graduating from West Point.

"Why are you in his office?" Ben asked, completely confused.

Finn smiled and walked around to shake his hand. The superficial facial expression sickened Ben, who was the master of superficial.

"I'm Diane Finn. I'll be replacing Ken as division director."

"Replacing? Why, where is he?"

Diane's expression became cold at first, as she lowered her hand that had not been taken by Ben. Her expression saddened.

"Were you a friend of Ken's?" she asked.

"What do you mean *were?*"

"He died in a car accident last night. I'm sorry to be the one to tell you. I assumed they made an announcement."

Ben froze, conspiracy theories running amuck in his brain. His first instinct was to run, but he couldn't; he knew that would be a sure way to get caught. But he realized that it was time to close things down and hope that Tony could solve this thing on his own. Ben couldn't take any more risks.

"No, they didn't," Ben said and turned to leave.

"What is it that you wanted access to?" she asked.

Ben froze for the second time that morning.

"Nothing, I'll figure it out."

"Listen, I know this is awkward, but I am your boss. So if you need something or have something to tell me, just let it go. I'm here to help," she said with the very same superficial expression as before.

"I, uh…I have been working to identify an unknown pathogen that came in from an outbreak in Indonesia. I isolated a DNA band and sequenced it, but the sequence didn't retrieve any hits from the non-redundant nucleotide database. So I thought it might be in another database, perhaps in our classified infectious disease database or the rare pathogens database or perhaps even in the Top Secret database," he said as he raised his eyebrows and indicated something mysterious.

"So before I put it up on the unknowns list, maybe I could look a little deeper...perhaps I could find something similar, instead of just letting it go."

"I'm afraid I don't know what you mean," she answered sharply.

Ben whispered, "It looks synthetic to me. The codons appear to have been optimized for human tRNAs, but it isn't a human sequence. It might be one of our military bugs, and I don't want to raise a red flag where it doesn't need to be raised."

She stared at him for an uncomfortable moment.

"Your file said that you were a good employee, and that you understood the important aspects of this job. That's good, having a man like you working for us. Before I give you access, did you BLAST it against the non-redundant nucleotide databases in Europe and Japan? What about SwissProt?"

"Yeah, nothing. There were no matches," he answered.

"Okay."

She wrote a ten-digit code on an index card.

"This will expire in forty minutes, so get on it. This will provide clearance for level-four access only. If it's not in those databases, then I'll have to check the restricted Top Secret sequences myself."

Ben left shaking like a leaf and feeling like he no longer wanted to play this game. But he knew that this was never a game, and that he should have kept his head down, like always. He had never been a very brave man, but he was a tireless researcher, and he had a sharp mind. That's how he stayed where he was for so long. He had always viewed his life as a success, because he got paid to do what he loved to do, but now he found himself in a place that he had avoided at all costs for his entire career.

Ben went to his terminal and navigated onto the secure server, and then entered his temporary pass code when prompted. He pulled up the identifiers of the Indonesian agent and looked through the search options, but he was really looking for something else entirely. He glanced nonchalantly over his shoulder at the young redheaded woman often, trying not to look nervous.

And then suddenly, there it was! He had found the pathogenic profile for the agent that killed people in Pecan. The page contained a complete listing of the unknown agent's code name, the symptoms that were observed, the route of transmission, the epidemiology, and the demographics of the victims. Interestingly enough, there was additional information on the agent, indicating that it did indeed infect other species from different kingdoms. And most terrifying of all was that the army didn't know what the agent was. The report speculated that it was a virus that utilized some universal receptor found on a variety of eukaryotic cells, but there was no conclusive evidence. The current research focus was to determine if the unknown agent was a prion.

"Tony was right," Ben said as he memorized as much information as he could. "*Ich kann es nicht glauben,*" he said in German.

"I can't believe what?" Finn asked from directly behind him.

Ben jumped halfway out of his shoes.

"You startled me. You speak German?" Ben asked as he scrolled through the code, trying to act naturally.

"I picked some up here and there," she said. "So what can't you believe?"

"Oh, that I've gone through this for almost forty minutes now and found nothing."

"Do you need more time?"

"Oh no," Ben answered a bit too quickly. "I'll go back and make sure that I transcribed this sequence correctly. Maybe I missed something."

"I certainly hope that's not the case. You're a Jew, right?"

"Um, yes?" Ben answered, caught off guard by the direct question.

"Did you know that several Jewish scientists fled Germany in the thirties and helped develop weapons against Hitler's regime?"

"I did," Ben said, the hackles on the back of his neck beginning to rise.

"In Germany, they were considered to have committed treason. *Treason*, what a terrible word."

Ben was incredulous. "What are you talking about?"

"I was only making conversation. Obviously you're sensitive to the issue. I apologize," she said with no expression at all.

"I'm not sensitive—" He was interrupted again.

"Anyway, keep up the good work. *Ich werde aufpassen*," she said and left without looking back.

Ben was very upset by her last remark. He learned German as a young man. His grandparents were German-speaking Jews who fled Germany in 1935 after the Nuremburg Laws went into affect. He had studied German in college and became fluent. The words "*Ich werde aufpassen*" translated to "I'll be watching." Ben just sat for a moment, but for the first time in his life, he felt more anger than fear.

"Up yours, lady. *Herauf ihr*," he said, smiling sardonically at her as she entered Ken's old office.

In that moment, Ben felt empowered. Perhaps it was the disdain he felt for his new supervisor or the fear that overcame him as he realized that the army was going to keep this thing quiet so that they could exploit it. Whatever it was, Ben reacted as he had never reacted before in his life. He quickly copied the classified document and sent an electronic fax to Tony's encrypted line. *This time, the Jew wins*, he thought.

The New Orleans airport was busy. Carrisa and Tony had to stow their samples carefully, as they knew that transporting unknown infectious material across state lines, and particularly by air, would be sufficient cause for imprisonment. The security line was long and annoying, and every passenger was required to take off their shoes and belts, throw away perfectly good bottles of water, and submit themselves to what seemed an endless array of stupid questions asked by uncaring faces. And to make matters worse, their flight was delayed an hour and a half, in ten-minute increments. They were both relieved when their flight was finally called to board. Just as Carrisa was reaching to turn her phone off for the flight, it rang. She answered and expressed her displeasure as she handed it to Tony.

"It's Ben, he sounds worried," she said.

Tony took the phone. "Ben, what's up?"

"Listen, they are on to me."

"Who's on to you?"

"Just shut up and listen. They have it."

"Have what, Ben?"

"Will you listen? The virus, the army, they have it. You were right about the bees. Somehow, it also infects plants and animals the same way. I didn't have time to look. I'm sending you all I have, Tony. I can't do anymore. I think they killed my boss."

Tony laughed nervously. "Why would they do that, Ben?"

"I'm not kidding around here. I used his password to get myself into some secure files yesterday, and today he's dead. I'm scared shitless here, and I'm not doing anymore. I wish you the best of luck, but I'm not putting my ass on the line anymore. Stupid little German bitch!"

"German who? Okay, okay. It's fine. Everything is fine." Tony shook his head in confusion at a worried Carrisa as he tried to sooth Ben.

Ben continued talking, but they lost him as they walked down the ramp to board the plane.

"Ben, I'm losing you, I'll call when we get back in town," he said and then hung up. "I lost him."

"What the hell was that all about?" she asked.

"He found something. Apparently, the army has confirmed that the agent crosses kingdoms and the species barrier," he said as he began to understand the calamitous events that could unfold.

Carrisa looked shocked. "Oh my…"

"Yeah, we gotta get cracking here or this is going to be a devastating event."

Ben left the office in a hurry, constantly looking over his shoulder as he recklessly drove home. Everywhere he turned, he imagined someone was watching him, and he nearly caused several accidents. Once home, he rushed inside, locked the doors, closed all the blinds, and poured himself a large glass of scotch.

As soon as he had settled himself down a little, there was a loud knock at his front door that made him jump. He knew whom it would be but snuck to the door and peered through the peephole to confirm. Two casually dressed men who looked suspicious stood on either side of Diane Finn. She knocked again as Ben scurried around his home, looking for a way out. He thought about calling 911 but knew that no one was going to arrive on the scene in time to save him.

"Dr. Epstein?" she called.

As the truth of his predicament settled upon him, Ben relaxed and walked over to a wall full of pictures. Most of the framed photos were family members, but there were a few of him with Tony, and even a few more were candid shots of Carrisa. He removed his favorite picture of her from the wall and held it in his hands and stood there and stared, as the knocks on the door turned into the sound of someone attempting to kick it in.

"Oh, Carrie, I should have said something years ago," he said aloud.

Thump.

"I've been a coward my whole life."

Thump.

"Now time's run out."

Tears streamed from his eyes and rolled down his cheeks. His love for her had remained hidden for years because he was afraid that if he confessed his love and she didn't feel the same way, he would lose her forever. And now it didn't matter. He held the picture up to his face, leaned in, and kissed it gently with his eyes closed. This was the one tragic mistake of his life, of having loved and never letting it be known. It was his only true regret.

"I love you with all my heart, Carrie. I am sorry I failed you. Good-bye, my love," he said aloud to the photo as the door shattered in the background.

Finn was the first to walk in through the busted door, and she moved slowly as she looked around the home before focusing her glare directly at Ben. Ben didn't react at all. His eyes were glued to the picture of Carrisa. The two men held their side arms in their hands, but stayed back, as Ben didn't seem to be a threat.

"*Kann ich hereinkomme?*" she asked.

"Please do." He motioned robotically for her to enter. A useless gesture, since she was already inside his house.

The men motioned for Ben to sit down and he obeyed. His face was white and bloodless, but his demeanor was composed. *They may be here to take my life*, he thought, *but my dignity is not theirs for the taking.*

"We've got a problem, Dr. Epstein. You see, we know that you've sent some privileged information to someone, information that is classified and of the utmost importance to National Security. Some people might see this as a treasonous act. Do you know that we can still execute civilians for treason, Dr. Epstein?" she asked, her eyes settling upon the photograph Ben was looking at.

"You don't scare me," he said.

"No?"

"No!"

One of the men behind Ben hit him in the head with the butt of his pistol, sending him straight to the floor. Ben grabbed his head in pain and felt blood on his fingers.

"Dr. Epstein, we need to know exactly what you sent and to whom," she said calmly.

"You can't control it. It adapts too quickly, there are no parameters. This will annihilate everything!"

"Everything can be controlled, Dr. Epstein."

The other man lifted Ben off the floor, slamming him back into the chair and then punched him in the jaw. The blows put Ben in a state of quasi-consciousness. The man slapped him lightly back to the present.

"Who and what, Dr. Epstein? You don't seem to understand how bad we can make this."

Ben gathered his thoughts into a coherent response.

"I cure diseases, and all you know how to do is destroy life. You are the disease, why should I tell you anything?"

Finn pretended that his comments hurt her. She picked up the photo of Carrisa that Ben had dropped when he was hit from behind. Finn knew that he was in love with this girl, that much was obvious, but as she looked closely at the photograph, she couldn't understand what Ben thought was so special about this woman. The thought began to infuriate her the more she thought about it. By Finn's assessment, the woman wasn't as pretty as she was, wasn't as young, and certainly did not have her well-defined body. Why did he look at her like that?

It occurred to her at that moment, she must find this woman and dispose of her. She was a menace, a loose end, and the one most likely with the information that Ben leaked. Finn refused to acknowledge any thoughts of jealousy or of obsession, for this was for the sake of National Security.

"I guess since I can't seem to get you to tell me anything, I'll have to try Dr. Carrisa Harrison. Maybe, she'll be more pliable."

Ben tried not to blink, although just the mention of her name made his stomach tighten. He knew this was the end of his life no matter what he did or said. The thought made him want to cry, but not because he was so scared. He was sad for the things he would miss. A good scotch, Tony's overly intellectual jokes, hopes of saving the world, and Carrisa's smile. He looked down and saw his glass of scotch on the coffee table.

"May I?" he asked.

"Please," she answered thinking that maybe he was ready to talk.

"*Ein für die Straße,*" he said in his mind, one for the road indeed.

Ben took a large gulp and savored the taste in his mouth, then let it slide down slowly, burning in that good way that only good scotch can. *Maybe I'm saving the world after all,* he thought.

"So, Dr. Epstein, who did you send the information to?"

"You know, I can't seem to remember," he said with a smile that said much more than his ordinary smile.

"I am through playing with you."

One of the men hit him with the flat of his gun and followed that blow with another.

"Who and what?" her voice got louder as her patience fled.

Ben recovered, blood flowing freely on his face.

"Do you know who you are playing with, Dr. Epstein?" she asked, her face becoming as cold and rigid as ice.

"I do. You're an Aryan twit with no self-esteem and bad shoes," he said with the corners of his mouth turned up.

It was ironic that the single bravest act of his life would also be his last. Before he could take another breath, a silent bullet pierced his skull, and his lifeless body crumpled to the floor.

Chapter 10

JEREMIAH CRUISED DOWN the two-lane highway on a black flathead Harley. Wearing only a pair of dark sunglasses for protection, he was followed by a dozen or so other bikers. The group pulled into a roadside bar just outside of town as the sun began to set.

Jeremiah had accumulated a following of close to five hundred disciples since his first gathering at the Assembly of God Church just a few days earlier. At the end of that ceremony, Jeremiah had prophesied that the old minister would die before the end of the next day, and when his prophecy proved to be true, more than a hundred other members of that church joined his group.

Most of Jeremiah's followers were ordered by Jeremiah, who had been ordered by God, to build a series of structures on the outskirts of Newton that would serve as their headquarters. The group began calling itself the Sons of the Apocalypse. Although Jeremiah did not come up with the name, he let them use it. It gave them an identity, and he knew they needed to feel a sense of ownership and connection.

Over the past few days, Jeremiah's thoughts had become very clear. For the first time in his life, he knew what he wanted to accomplish for God, and he knew that he did not have all of the skills necessary to complete the job himself. So he recruited people who had the skills that he needed to do God's work, and he converted as many of them as he could to his cause. Architects, bankers, accountants, organizers, and ex-military vets. He called upon them all, and once they converted, he gave them authority over specific aspects of his growing ministry.

The sheriff of Newton did not like this large group that had been forming, and he still had reservations about Jeremiah's intentions. The whole thing made him nervous, and his nervousness was only slightly tempered by the fact that Jeremiah struck a deal with him.

The agreement was that Jeremiah would focus on converting criminals to the service of the Sons of the Apocalypse, and in exchange, the sheriff agreed to go easy on enforcing laws that would interfere with the growth of Jeremiah's army. The sheriff didn't have much to lose, as he couldn't do much about the Sons of the Apocalypse anyway. They hadn't broken any specific laws, but a large group of fanatics was always a danger. So the sheriff was happy to have an agreement in place with the leadership.

Jeremiah began living up to his part of the agreement right away. His first stop was at the spot where most of the crime started in the county, the Broken Spoke Roadside Bar & Grill. Jeremiah climbed off his Harley and waited for the other bikes to settle in behind him. When all the bikes were quiet, he ordered his men to wait outside while he did a first sweep.

A day or so earlier, one of the Sons, an ex-Marine, demanded that he accompany Jeremiah into a church to provide protection. Jeremiah slammed the man to the ground by his chest, a feat that illustrated his strength was becoming superhuman, and then reminded his followers that they had agreed to complete obedience. The ex-Marine sustained a broken sternum and a collapsed lung, but later thanked Jeremiah for instructing him.

Jeremiah entered the Broken Spoke and found a fairly average gathering of bikers: old, young, bearded, and the longhaired— every stereotype that could be imagined. Most of them were men and all of the men wore leather cuts and jackets, some with colors, some without, and all had bandannas.

Jeremiah walked straight over to the jukebox and pulled out the power plug. A small crowd that was dancing abruptly stopped, and everyone in the bar looked over to see what happened to the music. When the crowd realized that someone intentionally pulled the plug, looks turned into glares as they studied the man that they were about to beat.

"I am Jeremiah, and I come with a mandate from God and with an invitation to you all."

"Get the hell outa here, freak!" someone yelled from the crowd, which laughed in response.

In this place, Jeremiah was not the largest man, and he did not intimidate this crowd as he had others. However, Jeremiah remembered from his own experience how these people thought. He knew what he was walking into, and he knew what had to be done to convince the crowd. Only a show of supreme force would get their attention. Jeremiah had come to believe that most people were slow learners, but he knew these criminal types would be even slower. For the sake of God, he would do anything.

A large man was the first to attack. He charged Jeremiah but didn't make it very far. Jeremiah knocked him out with a single blow before he was close enough to do any damage.

"Your name may only be added to the book by blood," Jeremiah said.

"Kill the freak!" shouted another voice as the crowd rushed him from all directions with blades and broken bottles ready for battle.

Jeremiah charged right into the middle of the brawl, an exuberant expression on his face. The group tried to take him down, but Jeremiah was too powerful, with each blow he destroyed faces and broke bones. He continued to preach while he fought without once losing his breath.

"Fear the Lord your God, serve Him only and take your oaths in His name. Do not follow the gods of the people around you, for the Lord your God is a jealous God and His anger will burn against you, and He will smote you from the face of the earth. Do not test God and His strength," he said as he picked up two large men and slammed their heads into one another.

The fight was extremely violent, and Jeremiah took many blows, cuts, and stabs, but he didn't even notice his wounds. He continued to fight until he had taken down over twenty bikers in the bar. Some of his followers peered in through windows to watch the fight, while others watched through the crack in the door. All of them observed in amazement at Jeremiah's display of power.

One of the bikers stood up with blood running down his face, pulled out a large knife, opened it with a flick of his wrist, and waved it toward Jeremiah with obvious skill.

"Who the hell do you think you are, man?" he asked.

"Who is this that darkens His counsel with words without knowledge? Brace yourself like a man. I will question you, and you shall answer Him," Jeremiah said.

"This is our place, man."

"Where were you when He laid the earth's foundation?" Jeremiah asked.

"I said this is our place, and we don't answer to no one!" he said as he rushed Jeremiah.

Jeremiah grabbed him around his neck with one hand, as the man's knife blade plunged deep into his abdomen.

"Every man answers to the name of God," Jeremiah said and squeezed until the man's body went limp.

Many of the other bikers watched him kill their friend so easily, but they were not cowards and wanted revenge. They continued to get up and fight on, and several attacked Jeremiah as the blood seeped through his shirt, turning it beet red. Jeremiah was oblivious to the pain; he felt nothing but the power flooding into him, as the unknown agent acted quickly to clot and heal his injuries. He deflected the simultaneous blows of his attackers with such speed and agility that he appeared to be superhuman.

"Your stubbornness and unrepentant hearts will face the day of God's wrath when His righteous judgment will be revealed. He will give to each person according to what he has done,"

Jeremiah said as another man dropped to the floor, dead, his throat destroyed by a massive and crushing blow.

"There will be trouble and distress for every human being who does evil," he said as the remaining men backed away, most of them physically unable to continue.

Jeremiah stood solid on his feet; the stab wound no longer bled, and his nose and mouth only showed smears of blood. Compared to the men he had fought, he was in great shape.

Jeremiah smiled a warm and inviting smile.

"But there is glory, honor, and peace for everyone who does good. God does not show favoritism, my brothers, only truth and love. Let us stop this, I am filled with His power and shall not perish. Repent of your old ways and accept my invitation of salvation through blood. For all who sin apart from the law will also perish apart from the law."

"What do we do?" asked a female voice from the back.

"Your name must be added to the book of life. It must be written in blood. I can show you the way."

"Some people say you're a miracle. Are you?" asked one of the men who had battled fiercely.

"We are all miracles in God's eye, brother. Join me. Take your place by His side and join me!"

The man began to cry and fell to his knees, weeping.

"I'm a bad person. How can God love me?"

Jeremiah gently helped him get up.

"You kneel only to Him, brother, and it is not those who hear the law who are righteous in God's sight, but it is those who obey the law who will be declared righteous. God's law is above man's law."

The biker smiled through bloodied teeth and nodded his head. In an instant, Jeremiah smashed his face, dropping him to the floor like a large sack of potatoes.

"Brothers!" Jeremiah yelled and a dozen men came in the front door.

"Help this man who has accepted glory. Clean him and clothe him and give him gifts of gold."

The Sons helped the man up off the floor, and Jeremiah embraced him warmly.

"Welcome home."

At that moment, several other beaten-up bikers stepped forward and received the same treatment, but at least ten men looked on, shaking their heads, wanting no part of what Jeremiah was offering. Three men lay dead on the floor.

Jeremiah had his followers escort those who had accepted his invitation out of the bar and then focused his attention on the men who had pushed back to the far wall.

"I ask one last time, brothers. Join me. I beg of you," he said humbly.

"Screw off, freak," said one of the brave men.

Jeremiah's face changed from humility to anger.

"You arrogant, overfed, and unconcerned pagans. You who will not obey Him are profligates and drunkards."

Jeremiah ordered his men to dump gasoline throughout the bar.

"Then, all the men of this town shall stone them to death. We must purge the evil from among you and cleanse you by fire."

With that, Jeremiah left the bar without looking back as the Broken Spoke went up in flames, burning the remaining inhabitants to death.

The fire department arrived in time to put out a few sparse fires, but the building was nearly gone by the time they got there. The sheriff pulled up and met the fire marshal who explained to the sheriff that this fire appeared to be arson. The sheriff explained to the marshal that outlaws and bikers frequented the place, and they both agreed that it served the county better if it was explained as a grease fire. As the sheriff got in his car, he took one last look at the coroners putting body bags into a van. A shiver ran up his spine as he wondered if he had made a deal with the devil.

Chapter 11

COLONEL ADRIAN BRAGG sat in his base office at Fort Detrick, Maryland, with an especially sour expression on his face. The woman, Lieutenant Dianne Finn, had come highly recommended but was far too motivated, and way too ambitious. She was smart and got things done, but too often in the six months she had worked for him, she decided to do things her own way. The colonel was confronted with yet another one of those times.

The phone rang.

"Yes?" he said.

"Lieutenant Finn, sir." "I gave you a direct order that he was not to be hurt—"

"Sorry, sir, there was no other—"

"I said listen!" he yelled, losing his cool for the first time in many years.

Those who knew the colonel best called him the cryogenic man because he never lost his cool. Losing his temper at Lt. Finn was just another piece of evidence that proved to him that he was getting too old for this job, or it was changing too fast. He had been a practicing doctor at one time and had desires of finding cures and healing people, but instead ended up working with viruses and engineering them into weapons. It wasn't the same world anymore, nor was it the same army.

Politics within the army itself was far different than when he joined. He was able to stay above it for the most part because most people feared him, but that, too, was getting old. Lt. Finn wanted his job, and he knew it. He rarely had someone on his staff that wasn't after his job these days. They were all smart, all ambitious, but this one was cold and detached, and he thought she was probably a sociopath. She had been able to get around the psychological entrance testing, but she was not fooling him.

"You disobeyed a direct order, and now there will have to be a cover-up."

"With all due respect, sir. Sometimes more aggressive measures are required."

"You just don't get it, do you? Report to my office immediately, close of business."

"Sir, I'm in Atlanta."

"That's your problem. Close of business or your resignation." He slammed the phone down and looked out his window.

Colonel Bragg's subordinates at the lab couldn't get a bead on this infectious agent. Outbreak investigations were sometimes a slow and grueling process, he knew, but something about this one bothered him. This agent killed at an incredible rate, and it was still doing so in the lab. He had a couple of primates infected with a sample of the agent, and they were dead within ten hours; however, a second sample didn't kill primates at all but instead seemed to increase metabolic rates and aggression. It was odd, and even more than that, it was something he had never seen before.

No matter how hard his lab tried, they simply could not isolate any RNA or DNA associated with the agent. In addition to the unusual symptoms, he was also bothered by the way this agent seemed to evolve. He knew that viruses couldn't adapt that fast, but this agent had, and there was nothing in the middle—an isolate that killed and an isolate that seemed to improve health.

It was fascinating, but he didn't like dealing with things that he didn't fully understand. He had spent his career following the four basic steps to scientific investigation: observe, explain, predict, and control. With this agent, he knew they were still very much at the observe stage. And not having all the facts readily accessible opened the door for too many mistakes, and he didn't like mistakes.

Lt. Finn stood in the middle of Ben Epstein's home. Men in coveralls worked all around her, wiping the house down. They were hard-looking men. One of them tended to the body, which was sprawled out on the floor in the same position as when it fell. All traces of Lt. Finn's presence and the presence of her men were being erased, but this was not what was bothering her. It was the old man. He disrespected her, treated her as a child. The old fool completely failed to see how valuable she could be if he would only let her do things more efficiently.

Ben's phone rang, and Lt. Finn moved to get it. One of the workers in coveralls stopped her from answering the phone by grabbing her wrist.

"That is not procedure," he warned her.

Lt. Finn glared at the man as she subtly reached into her uniform pocket, removed a small knife, and tapped his groin area with it. The man froze as he looked down and saw the knife.

"Won't you be the running joke in the locker room?"

Slowly the man let her wrist go as his faced tightened into a smile devoid of joy. Lt. Finn picked up the phone without taking her eyes off him.

"Hello?"

"Hello?" said an unsure voice. "Is this Dr. Epstein's house?"

"Yes, it is, but he's a little indisposed at the moment." She giggled with a hint of sexual implication. "Can I take a message?"

"This is Charlie Brooks. I work with Carrisa Harrison, a friend of Ben's, and I'm in town…"

"That's very interesting, Charlie, Ben was just asking about her. Would you like to meet him somewhere?" she asked, a vacant and hungry look entering her eye.

"Uh, sure."

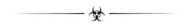

Lt. Finn sat in a black car in a parking lot and watched as a young man with slightly curly hair walked to the curb where the café was located and looked around. *Fish in a barrel*, she thought to herself, but she knew that she still had a part to play. She rolled down the window and waved Charlie over with a sweet smile.

"Charlie?"

He waved and walked in her direction.

"You beat me," she said. "Hop in."

Lt. Finn didn't wait for an answer; she reached across and opened the passenger door. Charlie climbed into the passenger seat feeling a bit apprehensive, but being reassured by her friendly smile and the fact that the car was not running.

"I'm Charlie, don't you want to go in and get a coffee...?"

Lt. Finn smiled sweetly. "That's okay, this won't take long, and I have a plane to catch."

"Where's Dr. Epstein?"

"He asked me to come meet you. He is also very interested in finding Dr. Harrison. Do you have any idea where she might be?"

"I'm guessing she's at her mother's house, that's where she said she was going the last time I talked to her."

"How nice, and where would that be?"

"Scranton, but Dr. Epstein knows all of this already. What did you say your name was?"

"Do you have an address?"

Charlie sensed that something was wrong. Suddenly, he realized that this woman was not as genuine as her smile. She made him feel cold inside and afraid. And he had a strong urge to get out of the car, but he didn't want to offend her if he was just being paranoid. He casually glanced around the interior of the car and noticed that the backseat driver's side window was broken out. Shards of glass were all over the back seat.

"Did you know your window is broken?"

"And what's her mother's name again?"

"Dottie Harrison," Charlie said, resolving to get out of the vehicle and away from her. "I forgot, I got somewhere I have to be."

"Certainly, sorry to keep you from your evening plans, thanks for meeting with me," she said and offered her gloved hand to shake.

This helped Charlie relax a little and he reached over to shake her hand.

"Good meeting you."

Lt. Finn pulled him toward her as soon as she had a grasp on his hand and thrust a Taser to his throat. Charlie seized and shook violently, but Lt. Finn did not loosen her grip until Charlie stopped resisting. His mouth drooled as his head slumped to one side, unconscious.

She then removed a knife from her pocket and cleanly sliced each of his wrists. Next, Lt. Finn wiped down the knife and placed it in his right hand and allowed it to drop to the seat. Finally, she locked all the doors except for the passenger side door and exited the scene, making sure nobody was watching. When she was satisfied that it was safe to leave the scene without notice, she got into her own car and drove as quickly as she could to the airport.

A knock at Col. Bragg's office door woke him up. It took him a moment to gather himself—a nap, he never took naps, especially at the office. His recent odd behaviors were helping him realize that he was getting old, which didn't leave him in a good mood.

"Enter," he commanded.

Lt. Diane Finn entered rigidly and stood at attention in front of his desk.

Col. Bragg looked at the clock.

"It's fifteen hundred hours, two minutes, which means you are late, Lieutenant."

Her bearing dropped for an instance, enough for Col. Bragg to enjoy the chink in her armor. In her defense, he thought, she didn't say a word edgewise.

"At ease. Sit down," he said, softer this time. "Tell me all about it."

Lt. Finn explained what she had uncovered at the CDC and Ben's unauthorized searches. She reported with little embellishment the meeting at his home and the subsequent murder, which she felt was necessary and justified. Col. Bragg was quiet through the entire explanation. He didn't ask any questions because he already knew what information she had to give. The men who were with Lt. Finn during Ben's murder were all loyal to him, and they had already given him a full report.

"It was the wrong move to kill him," Col. Bragg said.

"He would have drawn too much attention later, in my humble opinion, sir."

"And you think a homicide won't?"

"We made sure it seemed appropriate for a break-in."

"Really? You don't believe that two CDC agents working in the same department that die within a couple days of one another will be newsworthy? Conspiracy theorists will have a field day."

"I...," she stammered.

"It was my call to make, not yours. Moving on, we traced his information transfers to North Carolina, but that's where the trail runs dry. The traces just hit a dead end, so we have to assume that whoever received this information knows we are looking for them. Dr. Harrison took a flight to Wilmington, which will help narrow things down a bit. And we got a cell phone hit in New Orleans, but the phone was turned off afterward, so we don't know where she went. I want six teams working around the clock.

We need boots on the ground and ears on wheels. The wrong people get hold of this information and we've got a big problem," he said.

"I understand, sir, I'm on it."

"Now, Ms. Finn, if you make any decisions outside your pay grade again, you might find yourself somewhere very unpleasant."

Lt. Finn took a defensive posture. "Is that a threat, sir?"

Col. Bragg laughed just under his breath.

"Ms. Finn, I don't make threats, they're dramatic and a waste of time. But if I want you dead, you're dead. There will not be one thing you could do about it. You're dismissed," he said.

She left without a word, feeling thoroughly chastened, but Col. Bragg knew that her confidence would soon recover, and he would have to be ready. He saw it in her eyes—the desire for power. Col. Bragg was worried that he may be underestimating her psychosis, because he believed that she was a psychopath in the making, and he vowed to himself that she would not be allowed to stay in his service for long. After she finished this assignment, he decided that he would ship her off or possibly worse.

Lt. Finn left his office feeling the proper amount of self-pity, but it quickly turned to resolve. The old man was getting soft, and he stood in her way. She was convinced that she must find a way to get rid of him. The sexist old bastard was only holding her back. It was laughable that he thought she cared about his rank and authority.

Everyone warned her about him, but his reputation was much more sinister than he was. He was a coward who didn't even want to break a few eggs along the way. Sometimes bold action was necessary, and decisions needed to be made on the battlefield, not in the office.

She knew what must be done, and that's what she intended to do. The means justified by the end. His superiors would see, and besides, he wouldn't be around to add his opinion much longer in any case. The thought of taking him out made her feel warm inside. It was a feeling she didn't enjoy very often.

Chapter 12

Tony and Carrisa walked in through the front door of Tony's beach home. They both felt a little weary from their whirlwind trip to the gulf. Tony dropped their bags on the floor by the door, and Carrisa set her sample collection box on the table next to the Teletype machine. On the way over, she noticed a long ticker tape rolled up on the counter and falling onto to the floor.

"Look at this," Carrisa said, unraveling the tape for emphasis.

Tony grabbed the ticker tape and ripped it off, surprised at its the length.

"I guess Ben came through," he answered.

Tony went to his computer and began the process of decoding the message. Carrisa flipped on the TV and allowed herself a moment to relax. The news came on, and she tried to listen but quickly began to doze on and off.

"This is great, lots of data here. It looks like Ben got through the government firewall using a back door into the secure army server. He faxed me a classified document. Wow, he really came through on this one."

Carrisa didn't hear him because she head-bobbed herself awake, and a news story had caught her attention. A reporter was saying that emergency room visits were up 70 percent in the last two weeks and that many patients were being turned away from large hospitals and being sent to nearby small hospitals and urgent-care facilities.

The reporter stated that scientists feared this could be another influenza virus outbreak with possibly a new strain of that virus. The symptoms reportedly started out like the common cold, and then increased into flulike symptoms with a high fever. Public health officials were alarmed at the number of fatalities associated with this disease.

After realizing the significance of the information that Ben transmitted to him, Tony became concerned for Ben's safety. This wasn't the type of information that just anyone could access through normal channels, so he had to stay focused and hope that Ben would be safe on his own. Tony was impressed by the information Ben provided, and he studied it carefully.

"This is incredible. Listen to this, Carrie, they think it is a virus that uses a generic eukaryotic cellular receptor to infect cells, and they say it infects nearly every organism it comes into contact with. It must be some ancient eukaryotic pathway that is conserved at the most basic cellular level. So that's how this thing is crossing the kingdom and species barriers! It doesn't operate like anything we've ever seen before. It has to have a source, the Amazon, ocean trench maybe…" He looked up and noticed Carrisa staring at the television.

"What's wrong?"

"I think we found the bug."

Tony glanced at the TV as Carrisa turned it up, but by that time, most of the report was over and two analysts were discussing it.

"People are dying again, and the media is calling it a superflu. How original."

Tony returned his focus to the documents that Ben had sent.

"I'm calling Ben. They must have deployed on this already." She dialed Ben's number on her cell.

"Hang it up and turn it off," Tony said.

"What?"

"Turn it off!" he said, his voice expressing his sudden concern.

Carrisa did so, but she was not sure why. "Okay, now what?"

"Ben sent a warning, he said they were listening."

"So they're tracing our calls?"

"They can trace cell phones to a physical location if they are powered up. Take the battery out."

"What about calls you make from here?"

"My phone can't be bugged or traced."

"Oh really?" she said, not appreciating his arrogance.

"I'm not kidding. All these lines are encrypted, there's no way in, but we have to assume they know you're involved and maybe me too. It's only a matter of time until they track us here. We've got to find a safe place to hide out. Preferably, somewhere with a lab."

"Tony, I'm no conspiracy theorist, but how are they going to know I'm here on the beach in North Carolina?"

"How did you pay for the ticket to get here?"

"Credit card, of course…which is why you paid in cash for our ticket to Louisiana. Okay, I get it, you're paranoid."

A knock at the door interrupted their conversation and put Carrisa on edge. Tony answered it, only after looking through the peephole. It was Darrin.

"Hey, neighbor. I came by yesterday, but nobody was around," Darrin said, something obviously bothering him.

"Hi, Darrin, how are you?"

"Been better. Minnie's not feeling well, and you know how she gets sometimes."

"I'm sorry."

"It's fine. Listen, you think I could get some vegetables? I'm going to make her a special dinner, maybe cheer her up a bit."

"Help yourself, Darrin."

"You are a lifesaver. Hey, who's your lady friend?" Darrin asked, stepping further into Tony's house.

It was obvious that Tony was uncomfortable, but he couldn't stop Darrin from entering without making it apparent.

"Hello, I'm Darrin," he said, reaching to shake her hand.

"Carrisa."

"Oh my, the one that got away. Well, I'm so glad you two are back together," he said with a pleased look as he headed out the back door toward the garden. "I just love happy endings. Thanks again, Tony," he said as he disappeared into the garden.

Carrisa looked at Tony with a smug expression.

"The one that got away?" she asked with her head cocked to one side.

Tony couldn't respond, one of the rare times he had no words or thoughts that could get him out of an uncomfortable situation.

"Why didn't you ever call, Tony?"

"Why didn't you ever get married and have kids?" he responded a little too harshly.

Carrisa smiled and wrapped her arms around him. He was uncomfortable at first, but then settled into the embrace, allowing himself the luxury of succumbing to his emotions.

"It's a little too late for kids, I'm afraid, but maybe we can work on this for a while," she said softly.

"I've been waiting for you to apologize for ten years." He snuggled his chin into her neck.

Carrisa froze and detached herself from the embrace.

"Apologize for what?" she asked with a smile that was barely skin deep.

"You know."

"I'm afraid I don't. You'll have to explain it to me."

Tony took a moment to analyze a situation that was quickly beginning to spiral out of his control.

"What was done to me was unfair. No, more than that, it was wrong, intellectually dishonest, and you sided with them."

"I did no such thing, and I told you what would happen if you published without getting support from the community first, but no. The truth will speak for itself. Isn't that what you said, the truth is larger than any one of us or some such other bullshit?"

"You haven't changed a bit, have you?"

"Me? Are you kidding?"

"All I needed was your support, Carrie, that's all."

"And you had it, but you didn't listen to me, you never listen to anyone. You're so damn sure of yourself that you never even see it when it's coming straight for you," she said, her fists balled up and knuckles white.

"I was right!" Tony almost yelled.

"And look where that got you!" she replied just as loud.

Their argument was interrupted by another knock at the door. They stared at one another, tension thick, until Tony broke away to get the door. This time, Don Boussard appeared, holding the hand of his little girl.

Tony studied Don through the peephole. He was a tall, lanky man, in his mid-forties wearing worn blue jeans and a tattered work shirt. The fact that he had a little girl at the end of one of his hands was enough to convince Tony that he was probably not a government agent.

"Can I help you?" Tony asked as he opened the door slowly.

"Sure hope so. You do be Dr. Anthony Van Lee?"

"I am," Tony said, not sure he did the right thing in admitting who he was, as his paranoia came back to life.

"I'm Don Boussard, and this be my daughter, Sara. She the one that need your help," he said, pointing to Sara who looked a little piqued and not very energetic.

Tony motioned for them to come in and gave Carrisa a seething look. He showed his guests to the kitchen table were they sat down and talked. Sara looked nervous and stayed very close to her father.

"How can I help?" Tony asked.

"Sure you heard about the superflu. Well, in our parts, it killed twenty kids in two days," Don said gravely.

"I heard about it on the news, but you should have taken her to a hospital if…"

"She's not sick yet."

Tony looked at the girl, who looked exhausted, and then looked back at his guest with a puzzled expression on his face. Don leaned in close to whisper, where his daughter could not hear.

"So far, children over eleven years be just fine. Mon sher' here is just turned ten," he said and pulled back away, smiling at his daughter disarmingly. "You be the one everyone say to go to and find out how to be safe."

"Why me? How did you even find me?"

"I belong to a group. Just regular people who like to talk about things. Mostly amateur scientists."

Tony sighed. He had run into these types before. He was once invited to give a talk to an amateur scientist group that turned out to spend as much time chasing pseudoscience as they did employing the scientific method. Most members of that group spent their evenings hypothesizing about aliens and paranormal activities. Crackpots mostly.

"You didn't really answer my question, Mr. Boussard," Tony began to get slightly nervous.

"In this group, there be people who can do a good many things. Computers is only one."

"Nothing in my house is on a network, and there's no access to my systems."

"That be true and my friend say to compliment you on leaving no footprints, but not everyone orders the type of supplies you do. Certain things only get used by certain people and your suppliers use UPS. A little research, tracking keywords, and hacking the UPS database and there you go. It not so hard as you think. You just have to be creative and this group do be creative," Don finished with a smile.

"Right, look, Don, I'd love…"

"Its no crazy people here, this is not area 51 fanatics. It be a network called the Technology Underground. Stargazers, computer programmers, and inventors, but many very smart people."

"Anarchists."

"That's not entirely true, Dr. Van Lee."

"Nothing is ever entirely true, unless you have all the evidence without variance, Mr. Boussard."

"You are well known and highly regarded in this group."

"With my record, I'm sure I'm wacko royalty, but I've never heard of the Technology Underground in any event. Don, I'm pretty busy, we really have to get back to work."

Don laughed. "I read your article on HIV and Monkey Pox, it was very intuitive. To me it proved you were correct when you got the boot. Big medicine do not like the truth, but people thought you do be crazy anyway. Just because you speak crazy or look crazy, don't mean you be crazy."

Tony froze, as if this were a chess match that he was losing.

"You have a point," he said, surprised that someone who looked as plain as Don and spoke as unintelligibly had read his research.

"I need your help, Dr. Van Lee," Don said quite seriously. "My daughter needs your expertise. There be nobody else I trust with my baby's life."

Tony smiled and sighed then signaled for Carrisa to come into the kitchen. She did so while simultaneously shooting Tony a look of death, which made Don uncomfortable.

"Carrie, this is Don Boussard and his daughter Sara. They came all the way from…where did you come from, Don?"

"White Lake, Louisiana," he said.

Tony and Carrisa froze as they looked at each other. The anger was gone from their blank faces.

"Just north of Pecan Island?" Tony asked.

"Yes, indeed, 'bout an hour and a half north," Don answered.

"That's close to ground zero, Tony," Carrisa said.

Tony was delighted by this sudden turn of luck. A live subject possibly infected with the unknown agent, who lived within a hundred-mile radius of the original site of the outbreak. Along with their samples and a little luck, they might be able to learn something about this agent.

"Is there somewhere Sara can go?" Don asked.

"She can go look at my garden."

"Go head, sher', see if Dr. V got a green thumb or no."

He watched his daughter go outside and then turned back to Tony.

"You got a bit of a problem coming soon," he said.

"What do you mean?" Tony asked, alarmed.

"Army men stopped me thirty miles from here and searched my truck. They had a picture of you, miss," Don said.

Tony shook his head. "Sometimes paranoia pays off. We have to get out of here. How about your mom's place?" he asked a stone-faced Carrisa.

"If they have my picture, I'm guessing they know where my mom lives, *genius*," she said, barely able to contain her anger.

"We have to get the little girl to a lab," Tony said, looking at Don and trying to ignore Carrisa.

At the same time, he was feeling pissed off that Carrisa chose this time to get all worked up and stay mad. It was always like her to get angry at the most inopportune times. It exhibited the type of selfishness that had kept them apart all these years.

"Any ideas, Carrie?" he asked with a tinge of sarcasm.

She only stared at him coldly.

"I can help, but you have to promise something. My Sara, you have to keep safe," Don said.

Tony thought for a moment, allowing his mind to undertake as many preparations and calculations as necessary.

"The facility has to have an electron microscope," Tony bartered.

Don nodded with understanding.

"I'll do what I can," Tony said. "I can't promise anything. At this point, I haven't learned anything about this agent, the disease it causes, or even the source."

Don laughed robustly, catching Tony off guard.

"That's easy, *mon ami*. It came from up there." He pointed up toward the ceiling.

"It came from my attic?"

"It came from space. There was a meteor shower close to a month ago go by," Don said.

"You know this for a fact?" Carrisa asked, moments before she remembered hearing the locals at the gulf talking about an omen in the sky.

"You know, you're right. There was a meteor shower just before the outbreak. The locals thought it was some type of an omen in the sky."

"It the only thing that makes sense. I thought you people would know this? Look here, there was an ice meteor shower over the gulf on April 30, it was a Thursday night."

"That was the day before I got there," Carrisa said.

"Three days later, 128 people die on the beach south of Pecan," he continued.

Tony remained polite. He still thought he might have a crackpot on his hands, however, he realized the serendipitous meeting of his daughter was a gift horse.

"Don, with all due respect, the odds of a meteor successfully carrying a virus into our atmosphere is negligible," Tony said without giving it much thought.

"But it no impossible. I heard an astrophysicist say so," Don replied.

Tony ran the possibilities in his mind, *An infectious agent from outer space? It's a stretch, but if a virus was frozen in an ice meteor that landed in our ocean, who knows what type of cell it could infect, or how it might replicate. It could completely change the game, but for there to be a virus, there would have to be a host. Its just too improbable.*

"Where did you go to school, Don?"

"Lake Charles Community College, but I did no finish."

"Right…. Listen, the possibility that this is an extraterrestrial pathogen is just not realistic. If it had come from a meteor, whatever the agent is would have had to survive immense friction as it came through our atmosphere, and then it would have to survive impact with the ocean or land. Even if it survived all that, many pathogens would not survive the freeze thaw cycle without a proper buffer. Not to mention the fact that there has been no sign of life of any kind found in our universe. I don't want to come off as rude here, but it's just not a valid argument," Tony lectured.

"I heard once that the molecules necessary for life come from the stars," Don argued, beginning to enjoy the debate with Tony. "The universe has had 13.7 billion years to create one hundred billion galaxies with one hundred billion stars each. You think only one of those galaxies and only one of those stars supports life? Seem to me that sound silly, no?"

Tony was impressed with Don's knowledge and quickly realized that even though he came across as a bit of a redneck crackpot, Don was no average Joe.

"And our oceans contain fifty million viruses in every milliliter of water, most of them have not been characterized. What about the oceans of Jupiter's moon Europa? Maybe there be viruses in that ocean too," Don said.

"Don, that makes for a great campfire story, but I don't buy it." Carrisa joined the fray, looking for any reason to go against Tony at this point.

"You were the one that told Ben to forget everything he knew about absolutes." Carrisa hated when Tony thought he was right, and she didn't like the smug way in which Tony condescended to Don.

"Come on, Carrie, all the evidence we have so far indicates that this is man made. Germs and toxins don't stop killing. Viruses don't mutate this fast or become less virulent so quickly, so it has to be something synthesized for maximum damage and delivery. This has bioweapon written all over it. How else do you explain the army's interest? Why would the army be trying to stop information from spreading about the outbreak, unless they had caused it?"

Don sat amused, not bothered by Tony's pedantic attitude, but Carrie was livid.

"Just have to be right, don't you?" she said angrily. "Well, it still feels like a chemical to me. The wind carries the contaminated spray off the ocean to coastal flowers. Bees become contaminated by interacting with the flowers, and then die during migration. I'm sticking with my guns until we find something with teeth and not something you have just thrown together on a guess."

Tony took a moment to let the heat of the conversation subside.

"We have a couple days at best, let's get packed," he said and sent a questioning look toward Don.

"I'll do some research and find out where to go," Don said.

They commenced to prepare for their journey by gathering up and packing important items, while Don began searching for a lab in the Technology Underground on Tony's untraceable computer.

Carrisa took over the care of Sara and attempted to make her comfortable by feeding her soup and turning on cartoons. They sat on the couch, Sara laughing and Carrisa just staring at her, wondering what it might have been like to have a daughter.

"Is the soup too hot?" Carrisa asked.

"No. It's good, really good," she replied and slurped another spoonful. "Are you Dr. V's wife?"

"Dr. V, huh? No, I'm just a part-time friend," Carrisa laughed and sat back.

"My dad said we were going to see Dr. V, and he would keep me from getting sick like Tommy."

"Is Tommy your boyfriend?"

"Yuck." Sara scrunched up her face. "Boys are too immature."

"Amen to that, sister."

"Tommy was my best friend. Her real name was Thomasina. She'd been my best friend since first grade, but she died. Got sick. Daddy said it was the meteors, he knows all sorts of stuff," Sara said and got an excited look in her eyes. "Do you have a boyfriend?"

Carrisa hesitated and looked over at Tony who walked by gathering things.

"No."

"That's great, 'cause my dad could use one. My mom left and he was pretty sad, but you're pretty. Why don't you have a boyfriend already?"

"That's such a long story, Sara. First it was med school, then…"

"You're a doctor too!"

Carrisa stopped short. "Yes, I am."

Sara's eyes filled with wonder. "I didn't know you could be beautiful and smart. And I know you have to be smart to be a doctor."

Carrisa's eyes watered up, and she squeezed Sara in a hug and almost spilled her soup.

"That's the sweetest thing I've heard in years."

Tony decided he should let Don in on everything that they had learned about the unknown agent. As Tony explained the details, Don asked appropriate questions, and Tony was impressed with how fast he learned.

"Carrie be your wife?" asked Don.

Tony sat for a moment before answering, "No, just a friend."

"Well, it good to have friends," he said. "What we need for the trip?"

"We're going to need cash," Tony said, really talking more to himself.

Tony was lost in thought. His mind centered on his deepest regret. *I should have married her a long time ago*, he thought.

"I drove in on fumes," said Don.

Don had spent everything he had on the gamble that Dr. Van Lee would be where his contacts said he would be. He saw what the superflu did to some of the other kids, and he knew right away something was wrong. The plants and animals were all suffering, and he had to get his daughter as far away as possible, but he also knew she was probably already infected as she lost her best friend one day before they left. It was really the last straw for Don, and he drove over twenty hours straight to get to Tony's house.

"I've got a good amount squirreled away," Carrisa said. "We just have to stop at an ATM on the way out."

"Can't. They'll track it. Don't worry, I'll get us what we need. We need to pack as much food as possible from the garden to minimize us having to go into public," Tony said.

"Vegetables won't keep long," Don pointed out.

"Mine will. They're genetically modified and treated with my own biological elixir. They'll keep as long as the heat doesn't get too high."

Don and Carrisa went to the garden and picked the huge fruit and vegetables. They also packed clothes and other items that they would need. Tony loaded a computer with solar attachments into a hard-shell case along with several other pieces of equipment and testing supplies.

As the sun began to set, Carrisa laid Sara down in the bedroom and paused a moment to watch her fall off to sleep. The two had already developed a close bond.

Tony fired up a joint and took a good size gulp of red wine. He offered both to Don.

"I hope you don't mind," said Tony.

"I'm no capo, but I think I'll pass and stay with the wine, thanks." Carrisa grabbed the joint from his fingers.

"I'm not a big fan of this stuff, but I sure do need to relax," she said and took a healthy toke and then exhaled slowly. She coughed a little at first, and then suddenly looked sick and rushed off to the bathroom.

"She a bit of a tooloulou?" asked Don.

"I have no idea what the hell a tooloulou is, Don."

"I guess it no matter." They both laughed and enjoyed their wine.

Don curled up with his daughter Sara, and Tony curled up on the couch with Carrisa to rest for the upcoming journey. Due to the urgency of the situation, they put their anger at each other on hold for the time being.

Not twenty miles from Tony's home, the army made its rounds, searching car by car, house by house for Carrisa. Surveillance vans

Michael D. Acosta & Eric F. Donaldson, Ph.D

drove around, and all Internet sources and phone lines going into or out of this small town were tapped; all in an effort to track them down.

The next morning brought a gentle breeze, cawing birds, and the fresh aroma of coffee mixed with the scent of salt from the ocean. Tony looked out his window listening to the sounds of the waves. His diary was on his lap. He had grown accustomed to a morning ritual of taking in the sounds and sensations of the ocean while recording his thoughts in his diary. He felt certain that the ritual would end today.

He sensed that a change was coming, the magnitude of which had never come before. Something about the way things were going really bothered him. The way the army was pushing so hard, the unknown aspects of the agent, the bizarre deaths and infection of plant life. No, this wasn't something that was going to go away easily. He wondered if he would ever see this place again, and it gnawed at him.

"It do be beautiful," said a sleepy-looking Don from behind him.

"Morning, coffee's on," Tony replied.

A knock at the door interrupted the quiet of the moment, but Tony jumped up as if he were expecting it. After a quick check of the peephole, he opened the door to find Dude with two backpacks slung across his shoulder.

"Peace and love, bruh. Dude has arrived."

"Mornin', Dude. Did you bring it all?" Tony asked.

"Dude has brought it all. Look, amigo, is everything copasetic? This does not compute with the way the man has done business before," Dude said, hiding his brilliance in the guise of a beach bum.

"I need cash, Dude, that's it, and you get a bargain in the meantime. We still have a deal?" Tony said, not wanting to waste time.

"Dude said he would do the deal and the deal will be done," he said and snapped his fingers.

Four beach bum look-alikes strolled up to the door. At Tony's feet were four two-feet-by-two-feet cardboard boxes. They picked them up and left. Dude unslung the backpacks and gave them to Tony.

"You should count it, bruh."

"I trust you, Dude."

"And the Dude is trustworthy, but the man should not be so trusting."

Tony smiled; he genuinely liked Dude and knew that most of this was an act, that this was really a brilliant kid.

"I won't be around for a while, Dude. Keep an eye on things for me?"

Dude hesitated for a moment and pulled his sunglasses down to reveal his crystal blue eyes.

"As the movie says, bruh, the Dude always abides. This have anything to do with the army, bruh?"

"Why do you ask?"

"They've been scoping the area since before daybreak. Still down by the south side of town, but looks like they're moving fairly quick."

Tony's face got a little tighter. He didn't want to leave for a couple more days, but it was becoming obvious that they should leave immediately. He shook hands with Dude.

"It's been good knowing you, Dude. Best of luck."

"You too, Doc," he said, forgetting his beach bum accent.

The rest of the morning was a blur as the group prepared everything in a hurry. Tony loaded several sealed containers and two solar-powered scooters into the back of Don's truck. They roped everything down as well as they could.

Tony looked over his kitchen, trying to think about everything they would need and hoping he wouldn't forget anything that would be of value to them.

"What about Ben?" Carrisa asked, still looking queasy. Her stomach had been churning all morning.

"We're going to have to call him from the road. I left three messages, and he hasn't called back," Tony said.

"We need to let him know where we're going. He could be in danger as well," she said.

"I am aware of that, Carrie. I just said I tried to call him."

Don called from the living room. "What was the name of that guy you be calling?"

"Ben," Carrisa said ahead of Tony.

"Ben what?"

"Epstein," she said again and started into the living room.

Tony grabbed her arm, but she yanked herself away. Tony had put two and two together, and he dropped his head. Ben would have called; he had to be either dead or captured. It was hard to fathom that this whole thing was really happening. He knew he had to protect Carrie, no matter how much she disliked him.

"Did he work at the CDC—" he stopped short. Carrisa's face went blank as she looked at a report on the TV. A reporter standing outside Ben's home reported his death as a murder during a house robbery. Carrisa nearly fell apart, and Don took her in his arms.

"I am sorry for your friend, Carrie. I really do be," he consoled her.

Sara slid her hand into Carrisa's and squeezed.

Tony continued to stand in the kitchen, his fears confirmed by Carrie's outburst and whimpering. He knew they had no time to grieve, but Ben deserved a moment. They argued as much as anything else, but they were best friends, and Ben had lost his life getting the information Tony now had. He couldn't waste that effort, he knew that much.

The group was all loaded, but a silence had descended on them, and it affected everyone, even Sara. Tony stood at his doorway looking inside, running one more mental check when the phone rang. He didn't answer it but allowed the machine to get it.

"Mr. Van Lee, this is the Beaufort Vegetable Competition Committee. It was unfortunate you couldn't make the competition this year, and we look forward to your continued support and entry next year."

The routine nature of the call brought home the seriousness of the situation even further, and he locked up his home.

They piled into Don's old truck, with Carrisa and Sara in the back seat of the super cab. Sara looked better today.

"Hope you got an idea about how to pay for gas, *mon ami*."

"I think this will do," Tony opened one of the backpacks and it was full of cash, more than they would need.

"I think it will. You ready, sher'?"

"Ready, Dad," said Sara.

"Where to?" asked Tony.

"I contacted a friend, and he recommended South Dakota. They have a fully equipped lab in Pierre, with an electron microscope. I got directions."

"South Dakota?" Carrisa questioned. "How long of a drive is that?"

"Bout' a week in my old truck," answered Don.

"Certainly is out of the way. You sure, Don?" Tony asked. "That's a long drive and a lot of wasted time to meet a bunch of…"

"Somebody got to keep an eye on things, these people do that Dr. Van Lee, good people," Don said with a smile, but became very serious. "Statistics show that the Dakotas have a 74 percent chance of being last two states infected with an airborne contagion due to low migratory travel patterns. Only Montana get much better, *mon ami*."

"Okay," Carrisa said, lacking the emotional energy to debate it any further. The loss of Ben was a great weight to bear.

Don patted Tony's shoulder. "You need to trust me, Doc, because I trusting you to keep my girl safe." He looked back at his daughter who looked the slightest bit pale.

"And Dr. Carrie can help too. She's a doctor just, like Dr. V, Daddy. Did you know that?" Sara added.

"I did, sher'. Now you be in two good hands."

Tony had the feeling that Don didn't trust easily, so he nodded in agreement and off they went minutes ahead of the army search team. Tony's mind raced from question to question. He also wondered if he could keep his promise to Don's daughter. It would be a long drive with plenty of time to ponder the different possibilities.

On the radio they listened to the first CDC broadcast warning of a superflu outbreak and the recommended precautions to take. Just the mention of the CDC turned his stomach into a knot and caused Carrie to groan.

A feeling of impending doom came over him as he turned in his seat to take a last glance at his home on the beach. Something was indeed coming; he could feel it. His house slowly disappeared behind tall beach grass as Don's old truck chugged along down the old beach road out of town.

Chapter 13

May 28, 2018

THE FIRST THREE days of the trip were uneventful, but Sara had begun to show symptoms of a cold. The symptoms were consistent with how they were described on the radio, and they had her wear a mask when in public and limited her contact with people.

The onset of symptoms put the group in a state of anxiety because they didn't know who would come down with it next. It was apparent that the disease was spreading quickly throughout the United States. Real information was limited to what they heard on the radio, but reports of cases had already reached the entire Southwest as far as California.

The East Coast was infected as far north as Pennsylvania. The northeast was still safe. The midwest was the safest so far, as several of those states that were least populated including Iowa, Wyoming, Montana, Nebraska, and luckily the Dakotas were free of reported infections, as Don had predicted.

As feared by public health officials, preliminary reports of outbreaks were also trickling in from other countries. Cancun, Mexico, and Havana, Cuba, had reportedly been hit hard by the emerging disease. Other countries had enacted emergency legislature and in some cases resorted to martial law.

The group made decent time driving through the eastern states of Tennessee, Kentucky, and Indiana but the king cab Ford wasn't the most comfortable ride. It wasn't until they reached Illinois, having just left Indiana, that public anxiety became noticeable. People were getting scared, and scared people were dangerous. Looting and petty theft were on the rise as rumors of food shortages began to spread.

Stories of crop failures were all over the news, which was also reporting that nearly one-third of the beef cattle industry had been lost to the strange illness. Talk shows rattled on about conspiracy theories and doomsday and preachers ranted about the apocalypse.

Some pundits blamed global warming, others blamed the Chinese pollution problem. Tea Party republicans blamed the blue dog democrats for being too moderate and liberals harped on the radical right. However, none of these speculations helped anyone feel settled, and in fact, only added to the fervor, creating an even less stable environment.

"We have to stop. I need to call my mother," Carrisa said, turning the radio off.

The CDC had been issuing warnings on the Emergency Broadcast Network about the unusual outbreak, announcing what symptoms to watch for and urging those with symptoms to stay home. They also requested that caregivers of those with symptoms keep contact with the public to a bare minimum.

The CDC recommended that every person who had to go out into the public wear N95 masks, which were being distributed at designated locations in all of the major cities. Ultimately, the public health warnings only served to worsen an already bad situation. In addition, the CDC and World Health Organization had established a name for the unknown syndrome. They called it the Multivariate Accelerated Death Syndrome or MADS for short.

Don pulled into a gas station mini-mart, and they all hopped out of the truck to stretch their legs. Tony was outraged by the inflated gas prices of nearly five dollars per gallon that reflected the looming uncertainty of a population crippled by the fear of the unknown agent.

"Carrie, no cell phone," Tony said, yawning.

He watched her as she stretched and completely ignore him. She was glowing. Something about her was different; she looked younger. Even the way she walked reminded him of how she was ten years ago. Even her temper, which she consistently directed toward him over the past three days, seemed sharper and even more hostile.

She spoke to him, but only through Don. She would ask Don a question that he could not answer, which made Tony speak up and provide the information, and then Don would relay the information back to Carrisa. It was an emotionally draining game for the men but provided Tony with the time to think about what he had said to deserve such treatment.

Carrisa went inside the convenience store, got a handful of quarters, and called her mother using the payphone outside.

"Hello?" said a young voice she had not heard before on the other end of her mother's telephone. She knew immediately that something wasn't right.

"Hello, is Dottie there?" Carrisa asked a little confused.

"Oh, I'm afraid she is. Is this Dr. Harrison?"

"Where's my mother? Is she okay?" Carrisa was worried now.

"She's napping, but I'm not so sure when or if she'll ever wake up," the voice said with little emotion.

Carrisa's eyes began to tear up. "What do you mean?"

"Dr. Harrison, I'd advise you tell me your whereabouts right now. You are in enough trouble as it is. I sure would hate to involve your mother anymore than I have to."

Carrisa's lower lip trembled as she grasped the seriousness of this situation.

"What have you done with her?"

"Why don't you come on over and find out?" Lt. Finn asked.

"I don't understand. What is it that you want from us?" Carrisa pushed through her tears.

"I don't really understand it fully myself, Dr. Harrison. Nature chooses, you see? We all have a role to play, a place in this world.

Mine is to do her bidding, and yours is to succumb. It's simple really, once you've accepted your place."

"You're insane."

"I think we've had enough getting to know each other," Lt. Finn said, her voice becoming even more direct, even violent. "Now where the hell are you?"

Carrisa hung the phone up without saying anything more but fell to her knees and sobbed.

At the little home in Scranton, Lt. Finn stood over Dottie's dead body, holding a phone with no one on the other end. Her face was as cold as usual, but the woman's refusal to cooperate with her was infuriating, and she would have to pay. Lt. Finn pulled out her cell phone and called in a trace on the call.

The unknown agent had made its way through Lt. Finn's body days earlier, and she was starting to reap the benefits. Her senses became extremely acute, as if she could feel the hairs on other peoples necks move as she questioned them. She felt stronger, faster, her confidence swelled. The hunger inside her grew as well, becoming an unrelenting compulsion to cause death.

She didn't know where this new-found acuity came from, but it proved to her that she belonged in the big chair. The old man was over, a waste of skin, a relic. It was her time, and she knew how to get rid of him no matter how dangerous they said he was. The two men that accompanied her on these forays left the room as she began what she believed would be the end of Col. Adrian Bragg.

Lt. Finn removed a small glass vile, which looked empty, from her pocket and carefully swabbed its contents underneath Dottie's fingernails. Satisfied, she replaced the bottle in her pocket and tucked a business card into the cushions of the coach. On the face of the card, it read Col. Adrian Bragg, US Army Research Institute of Infectious Diseases. It was done.

She hoped this tactic would be enough to at least get him out of her way for a while. It didn't matter if it stuck or not; she only needed a little bit of room to work her plan. She couldn't risk allowing him the opportunity to make the next stupid decision that might foil her efforts to take over this operation. Her cell phone rang and she looked at the caller ID.

"Speak of the devil," she muttered aloud and then answered, "Hello, this is Finn."

"Did you find the mother?" asked Col. Bragg.

"Yes, sir, she was just lying around," Lt. Finn answered.

"Drop it. I need you back at Fort Detrick. We're shutting it down."

"But, sir, I've just received a great lead as to the whereabouts of Dr. Harrison," she answered, angry at his decision.

"This agent is beyond any containment and useless to us now. We need to create some space and start thinking defensively here. Get back here on the double. Oh, and Finn? Leave the old lady alive."

Without further warning, the colonel hung up.

Lt. Finn was furious and ecstatic at the same time. She wanted to continue with her mission. *That little bitch keeps evading me,* she thought.

However, she couldn't wait to see the look on Col. Bragg's face when he went down. She stepped over Dottie's body and began her trip from Scranton back to Fort Detrick with a light heart. Soon, she would have her way and be rid of the old man, and then she would be free to hunt whomever and whatever she chose.

Tony and Don stared off into a field full of green corn stalks. This was the heartland of America, but it could change very soon if Tony couldn't figure out exactly what it was that was infecting people and plants, insects, and animals. He thumbed through a newspaper, not really paying attention to Don.

"Most of the gardens were dying by the time I left. Maybe an astrophysicist is starting to put the puzzle together. Meteor shower, crops dying, people gettin' sick, you think?" Don asked, waiting for a response.

"Violent attacks are up 20 percent in the last two weeks. That seems a little odd, doesn't it?"

"You should no be so quick to disregard my hypothesis, Dr. Van Lee," said Don.

Tony sighed and looked over his paper at Don.

"Your hypothesis is circumstantial and coincidental. No offense meant, but it is. I'm sure we'll find a 'Made in the USA' stamp on this thing somewhere and when I do, I'll be the first to broadcast it to the world. We have to figure out what this thing is, if we plan to slow it down."

"You don't even know what it do be."

"I will once I get a look at it."

Don began to laugh so hard that he had to clear his throat.

"What's so funny?"

"You really believe that mess you do be slingin'?" Don baited him. "What do you really believe?"

"Okay, fine, I'll give you what I got." Tony folded up the paper. "The US government has been conducting chemical and biological experiments for decades. Neither one of us would trust the government with a nickel, much less a deadly agent, so what do you get when you cross an above average virologist with unlimited government resources, and a deadly virus? Trouble. You read my paper on HIV and the monkey pox vaccine. I laid it all out there in the discussion."

"I read it, you make no friends with dat," Don said, intrigued.

"We are witnessing something along those very lines. I believe it is an engineered synthetic virus that is transmitted to others through an airborne delivery system, and it was meant to kill a small portion of the population very quickly, but it got out of hand. It was probably designed to kill rapidly to minimize spread to others, but somewhere in the process, the virus adapted to keep the host alive. No host, no virus. But the biggest mistake they made was that they used a strain that allowed the virus to cross between kingdoms completely by mistake or via a mechanism they did not understand."

"Why's that a big deal with the kingdom thing?"

"There are literally thousands of viruses that do not infect humans, whatsoever, but if they evolve or are engineered to infect humans, then our immune system has to fight off something it's never seen before. A recent example of this was the virus that causes SARS. This virus normally infects bats. But in the Chinese live animal markets where bats are sold as food along with several other small mammals and reptiles, the virus was able to spread to other animals, and eventually into humans. Given the right environment, the virus was able to adapt."

"Well, that do sound a little scary, don't you think?"

"Viruses are the fastest evolving life forms on the planet. They'll find a way to adapt and thrive, and yeah, that's pretty scary."

"Are you saying that the government has developed viruses as weapons? That do be dark, no?"

"I'll give you dark! The US government has a long history of biological weapons development and testing. In 1900, US government doctors infected twenty-nine Filipinos with plague and beriberi to test the dual mortality rate of the two diseases. In 1915, twelve prisoners in Mississippi were exposed to pellagra by government doctors. In the twenties, hundreds of war veterans were exposed to mustard gas to test its long-term effects, while the vets were told it was a treatment. In the forties, prisoners were unwittingly infected with malaria for testing. In the fifties, marcesiens was sprayed over San Francisco. It goes on and on, but this is where it gets really good. In 1969, the Deputy Director of Research and Technology of the Department of Defense asked for appropriations to develop a synthetic biological agent that resisted immunological and therapeutic processes. That was in

1969, fifty years ago, Don. What do you think we are capable of now?"

Don stared blankly, trying to reconcile all the information.

"We even dropped Thrips over Cuba to kill their crops in the nineties," Tony said, emotionally drained.

"You really think that what this is?"

"I think it fits the profile of an engineered synthetic virus, yes."

Tony stared back over the vast fields of continuous corn and then went back to the truck where he found Carrisa kneeling on the ground, crying.

He ran to her and propped her up in his arms. She was weeping, and her body was limp with grief, shoulders shaking.

"What's wrong, Carrie?"

She could not speak for several moments, and Tony just held her until she was finally able to talk. She explained the phone conversation she had with the unknown woman and shared her fear that her mother was dead. The cold voice of the young woman on the other line made the futility of the situation all too real, and the probable death of her mother was devastating.

"Why would they go after my mother? She was innocent in all of this."

Tony couldn't provide her with much comfort, as he knew too well what the government was capable of. They had systematically dismantled his reputation after unveiling his study of HIV and AIDS. He believed that big medicine was in bed with the government. It was all the same; he had the truth, but the truth wasn't always the best thing for profits, so truth lost out.

That they would resort to killing meant this was extremely valuable to them, and that scared him more than anything else. He knew that they would be working on a plan to contain this agent, but that the most important data would never get out. He hoped they had developed a vaccine already, but that was founded on the assumption that the virus was developed by them or at the very least something they were aware of.

If Don was right or this was just an unidentified virus, the world was in deep shit. He knew that vaccines and antiviral therapies against viruses didn't just happen overnight, and this thing was moving much faster than normal.

Tony picked Carrie up and carried her grief-stricken form to the truck. Losing her mother on the heels of losing Ben was an overwhelming emotional blow, and Carrisa was crippled with grief. Tony could not afford to deal with the grief at the moment, because there were too many pressing problems to address on a much-larger scale. And besides, Tony preferred to handle his emotions in private.

"Is she okay, Dr. V?" asked Sara, who had grown quite attached to her.

"She's fine, just a little sad."

"I know how she feels. My mom left, but it didn't feel like she left. It felt like she died and I was sad too," Sara said as she wiped the tears from Carrisa's face.

Don looked down at his feet for a few moments, confronted with the same bad memories himself, and then he cranked up the old truck to resume their journey.

Chapter 14

COLONEL BRAGG WORE a lab coat and worked without sleep alongside his scientific colleagues. Although the agent they were working on was nearly indefinable, it was exciting for him to be working directly in the lab again. His job had turned him into more of a hunter than a doctor, and he resented that more and more as he got older. Devising ways to kill without being detected wore on a person's soul, and Col. Bragg was unsure of how much of a soul he had left. Perhaps, he could find redemption, perhaps not, but he didn't deserve it, and he understood that. The unidentified agent had worked its way quickly to the North, and his division was sequestered in their high-containment lab.

Col. Bragg and a colleague watched through a glass window into the biosafety level 4 chamber where several scientists in fully contained metallic biosuits worked with the unknown agent. It was a slow and methodical process.

"Did we get anything on the fish?" Col. Bragg asked.

"No more than anything else. It's just too damn hard to pin down. None of us has ever dealt with anything like this."

"Did you get the report I asked for?"

"Yes, sir, its here," he said and handed Col. Bragg a stack of papers.

The report provided data describing crop failures and beef cattle deaths. It was a global problem at this point, which was yet to be reported in the international media. Animals slated for food production were all dying before they reached slaughter, and this had reeked havoc on the commodities markets, which turned around quickly.

The economy had changed drastically in the past few weeks. The Departments of Agriculture, Defense, and Commerce had conducted similar international studies and had determined that the entire world had an eight-month supply of food. Once the food supplies were drained, countries faced starvation on a massive scale.

As soon as this information was released or more likely leaked to the international media, chaos would ensue. It was only a matter of time before some high-level official, overwhelmed by the coming onslaught, would disregard the rules and warn the public.

With no food and a failed economy, social decay would be fast on its heels. The government would call in the armed forces, but that would have little effect in the end. Frightened bands of starving citizens would quickly overcome any emergency infrastructure established by the military. Starving people never seemed to care about pesky rules.

The unknown agent was an efficient killer, but it would be these disastrous side effects that would lead to global destruction driven by chaos and anarchy. Col. Bragg looked at his colleague to gauge his reaction.

"This accurate?" Col. Bragg asked.

"Yes, sir. Everything I've seen tells the same story, sir."

Col. Bragg noticed that the man was scared to death.

"Are you married?"

"Yes, sir, and have two girls."

"Go home, take care of them. Report back in five days," Col. Bragg said.

"Thank you, sir," the younger man said, almost running out of the room.

Col. Bragg wondered why he was so concerned for this soldier and his family. He had never cared about things like this before. Old Father Time was creeping up on him once again.

Through the glass window of the observation room, he watched as Lt. Finn entered. She was a day later than he would have liked. Through his command network, he learned that she had killed a few more civilians, including the female doctor's mother and the ousted doctor's neighbors.

Lt. Finn had outlived her usefulness, and he couldn't watch over his shoulder while trying to figure this thing out. He had made a few calls and was having her transferred in the morning to a station in Reykjavik, Iceland, where she would meet with an unfortunate accident. He didn't feel entirely happy about this decision, but it was necessary. Col. Bragg proceeded to the observation room where she was waiting.

"Col. Bragg, sir," she greeted him.

"Lieutenant," he replied.

"I have traced the phone call from Dr. Harrison, sir. She called from a pay phone in Illinois. I'd like to request..."

"Finn, this has escalated into a national situation. We are no longer searching for anyone. In any event, it no longer concerns you. You've been transferred and are expected to report in forty-eight hours. Transfer orders are in your box. Best of luck," he said and turned to go back to work.

"It's men like you who lack commitment that make the world a place where cowards and weaklings climb the ladder of success, leaving out those capable of great things. It's your fear of being bested and left wanting that forces your feeble hand. Your time is done, old man, and I wanted you to know it was me who ended it."

Col. Bragg looked amused at first, but his expression quickly changed when two MPs entered with weapons drawn.

"Col. Adrian Bragg, you are under arrest for the murder of Dottie Harrison, sir. Please put your hands behind your back," one MP said as the other began to secure the colonel's hands in handcuffs.

Col. Bragg didn't look too concerned after his initial surprise. Lt. Finn had set him up; he realized that he was definitely getting soft. He smiled at her as he was taken away.

"This won't stick, Lieutenant."

"I certainly hope not, sir, but I promise to keep your operation going until you get back, Colonel," she said without a trace of contempt.

Lt. Finn watched him being taken away in handcuffs and the world inside her exploded with joy. Her plans were coming together, the old man was gone, and the look on his face was everything she could have hoped for.

Now she could resume her search for the female doctor, who consumed her thoughts. Lt. Finn was convinced that the woman doctor had to be extricated from her mind, and there was only one way that she knew to do that.

Lt. Finn's passion for death started when she was young. The culling, her father had called it. It was knowledge inexplicably given to her that allowed her to know who should live and who should die. It upset her very much as a child, but once her father had recognized the signs, he was able to help explain to her the role that she was selected to play in the world.

"Nature has ways of culling the unnecessary parts of itself," her father told her, "and humans are part of that nature, and often very unnecessary."

He had told her that it was like trimming a plant, cutting off useless blooms to allow more beautiful ones to grow stronger. Her father convinced her that she was the one who would do the trimming, just as he had done since he was twelve. She would deliver the fatal blow to the ones that were determined weak or unnecessary, and she would be guided by her own intuition.

Whether the decision was delivered by fate or by circumstance, the victims were mere unfortunate products of this preordained version of natural selection, of which she was nature's willing instrument. Of course as a child, she lacked the knowledge to recognize that her father suffered from psychosis. And she had inherited the same psychopathic genes, so she embraced her father's words as facts of life and killed him on her seventeenth birthday, as nature dictated her to do.

The brig was all but empty and very quiet. The hours Col. Bragg had already spent there frustrated him, because he wanted to know what was going on on the outside. He knew this charge wouldn't stick; he was sure of it. He had too many people who would provide him with an alibi, but it was taking longer than he anticipated to get released.

A pair of footsteps drew his attention to the bars of the cell door. An army major stood at the bars wearing a red beret, looking sympathetic. An MP stood beside him stoically.

"How's it goin', Adrian?"

"Fantastic, good of you to come by, Tom. When am I getting the hell out of here?" he asked a little more sharply than he would have liked.

"I came down here to tell you myself. JAG is requesting that you stay in custody."

"What? How the hell is that flying? Tom, I haven't left Maryland in weeks."

Major Tom Smith had been a friend of the colonel's for a long time. They were butter bars at the same time and crossed paths at many of the same duty stations. They weren't terribly close; no one got close to Col. Bragg, but they were very friendly. Col. Bragg liked Tom, knew he was honest, which was rare for a lawyer, even one working for the judge advocate general. The major indicated for the guard to leave, and he did so.

"They found DNA under the woman's fingernails. It's yours, Adrian."

Col. Bragg stood blinking, his head whizzing. *How the hell did she do that?* he thought to himself.

Col. Bragg sat down on the metal bed and put his face in his hands. Major Smith didn't like seeing his friend of twenty years in this shape. He knew Col. Bragg kept things on a tight tuck, but the evidence here was close to undeniable.

"So this is going Court Marshal," Col. Bragg said, disheartened.

"I'm sorry, Adrian, I have no choice. I can't turn you lose on a homicide with DNA evidence. It would be the end of my career," he said, hoping for understanding.

"I know, Tom, I'm not asking you to. But explain to me how I could be logged in at the lab here and in Pennsylvania at the same time. It's a setup."

"I know you deal in some really shady things. I can't even access your whole file. If what you say is true, we'll find out. You just have to be patient. Give me a few weeks, and I'll get you out."

"I don't have a few of weeks," Col. Bragg exclaimed, for in a few weeks he knew that the unknown agent would have spread from coast to coast and from continent to continent.

Major Smith was disturbed by his statement.

"What do you mean, Adrian?"

"I guess it doesn't matter," he said as he lay back on the bed and put his hands behind his head. "I'm stuck here, so I might as well take up smoking again," he said.

Major Smith pulled out a couple packs of cigarettes and a book of matches and smiled at Col. Bragg, who returned the smile and laughed.

"Thanks, Tom, you're a lifesaver. Just throw them on the table. How's your wife, Kathy right?"

"She's doing great. My eldest graduates from Columbia this year. How about you, any kids?" he asked as he slid a card through an electronic reader, which opened the cell door.

"Never got married," Col. Bragg replied.

"That's a shame." Major Smith tossed the cigarettes on the table. "I thought you were getting serious with that little number in Germany. What was that, fifteen years ago?"

"Kristina? Yes, she was something," Col. Bragg said as he darted out of bed and swept the major's legs out from under him. As Major Smith hit the ground, Col. Bragg slapped a flat hand against his throat, cutting off his oxygen supply and a preventing him from being able to speak. Major Smith rolled around on the cell floor unable to get any breath. Col. Bragg mounted him and held down his arms.

"I'm really sorry about this, Tom. I genuinely like you and that's why you're not dead. I promise you I was set up. You need to investigate Lt. Diane Finn. Be careful, though, she's dangerous. Maybe one day I can make this up to you," he hesitated, "and if I were you, I would go straight home, get your family, and drive northwest. Montana, Iowa. Probably the last place the virus will hit. Good luck, Tom."

Tom sucked in a huge breath of air only a moment before Colonel Bragg's fist slammed into his face, knocking him unconscious.

With no time to spare, Col. Bragg ran to the main door of the jail. He slid Tom's card through the reader, and the door opened. The guard stepped around, expecting Major Smith, and the hesitation cost him. Col. Bragg grabbed the guard around the throat and slammed him to the ground. The guard's head hit the floor hard, knocking him out. Col. Bragg dragged his limp body into the jail cell and placed him underneath the rack, He then removed his gun, keys, and cell phone. He placed Major Smith on the rack, covered him up with a blanket, and then closed the cell door behind him.

Col. Bragg didn't have a lot of time, and he knew it. A roving guard would be by soon. He had to get off base and out of the city, and he had about ten minutes to do it. The problem was that he wasn't sure where he would go after that. Knowing that he would be leaving behind the only life he ever knew, he took a detour for a quick stop at his office. He wanted to take the information that he knew Lt. Finn would be looking for, and even though there was a chance that she had his office under guard, it was a chance he was going to have to take. Maybe the only chance he had for redemption after all.

No one paid much attention to the colonel as he walked authoritatively down the halls because most enlisted soldiers tried to ignore high-ranking officers. Therefore, getting in and out of the various buildings and corridors wasn't too difficult.

The colonel's office was still in the same condition that he had left it. Col. Bragg went quickly to his desk, grabbed a portable hard drive, a sample box and collection kit, and several files, and then went in search of an escape vehicle.

No alarms had sounded, which meant that so far his escape was not noticed, and therefore, he still had a chance. Once the news of his escape got out, there would be alarms and the base would go on lockdown. He was headed to find a car when he noticed Lt. Finn talking with two young soldiers on the other side of a large parking lot. His blood began to boil on the spot, and it crossed his mind to kill her right there.

"Finn," he whispered.

At the sound of her name, she spun in his direction. He dropped behind a car to avoid being seen. Lt. Finn scanned the area for a moment before returning to her conversation. Col. Bragg couldn't believe she heard him, he knew that was impossible, but he sensed that it was not an arbitrary look. She was responding to something. He put it out of his mind so he could focus on his escape from Fort Detrick.

The transportation depot was only a few buildings down the street so he decided that this was his only way out. He could go there and hopefully convince some young officer to authorize a vehicle for him.

The corporal at the main desk was new and easily intimidated by Col. Bragg, and he did not make it easy for the young man. The colonel stormed in there, demanding his vehicle and berating the corporal when the reservation was not found. He ordered the corporal to stay at his post, telling him that he would prepare the Humvee himself, since it wasn't ready as ordered.

Colonel Bragg looked at his watch. Eight minutes had passed. He grabbed a few extra gas canisters from other trucks on the lot, as well as a box of ordinance, he had no time to check what was in it, and dumped his pack in the back. The Humvee appeared to be new, with no faded paint or welded bullet holes. He hopped in, pushed the start button, and pulled off to the base exit gate.

The gate was performing routine searches so the line was as long as usual. He checked his watch again, eleven minutes. He pulled up to the gate and saluted to the guard.

"Thank you, sir," the guard said.

Before Col. Bragg could press the pedal, the alarm sounded. The guard readied his weapon and stared at the colonel. Col. Bragg stayed calm and nodded at him.

"Lock it down as soon as I'm through soldier," Col. Bragg said and pressed the gas leaving a confused but obedient soldier in his wake.

The gate closed behind him, and the base was in a flurry. It would take at least thirty minutes for them to realize that Col. Bragg was no longer on base and even longer to circulate a picture of him for the guard to ID. Col. Bragg would be invisible to them by then, even if they sent in choppers, for he knew their playbook.

The bad part about breaking out and being on the run was it made him look guilty, but in his mind, he knew that if they couldn't get hold of this thing, it might not matter. Deaths were up 25 percent, ERs were flooded. The CDC had no clue, the World Health Organization was starting to panic, it was a grim situation, and it was getting worse by the minute.

Col. Bragg flipped open the onboard laptop and pulled up a back road route heading west, first to Illinois where Lt. Finn said the woman doctor was last seen, and then to wherever her trail led him. There was something about the Harrison woman, something he wanted to find out for himself. The doctor, Van Lee, who was likely with her, represented the best hope of decoding MADS of almost any man in America according to his file and Col. Bragg had exactly what they needed to do that.

Chapter 15

June 2, 2018

WHILE THE UNKNOWN agent was killing thousands of humans around the world, others who had become infected appeared to be improving. The unknown agent seemed to have the ability to take the broken pieces of a human body and rebuild them better than before, and it was able to focus the human mind to exemplify the most prominent characteristics of the human being's personality.

When Jeremiah saved his first disciple, Jessica, he nearly destroyed her. However, in the process of writing her name in the book of life with blood, he unwittingly passed along the unknown agent to her, and it helped heal her wounds quickly but left her nose a little crooked; even it couldn't fix that.

It did not take long for the unknown agent to make its way through most of the large group of Jeremiah's followers, and its drastic improvement of Jeremiah himself made him the unquestioned leader of the group, setting the stage for all others to be subordinate to him.

It appeared that the unknown agent understood the importance of order, and by producing dominance in some humans, it was able to increase the likelihood of its own survival. It constantly evolved and adapted to efficiently replicate in humans, and in the process, it seemed to mold some of these humans into the precise forms that would ensure its long-term survival.

In a sense, the unknown agent found and rapidly modified the perfect host, and they were reaping the benefits of its usefulness. More than that, the humans that were improved by the infection celebrated the new circumstances the unknown agent supplied, and many of them called it God.

It had been nearly a month since Jessica had accepted His grace, and her looks didn't matter to her anymore because every day she felt less and less self-conscious. As a matter of fact, she felt strong and more alive than she ever had in her life. Jessica knew that she had been touched by the very hand of God.

Jeremiah believed it too and put her in charge of all of his affairs. Jessica kept track of everything. This put her in a position of high esteem; people needed her, wanted her, and no one could meet with Jeremiah without her approval. She had power for the first time in her life, and she felt as if she would explode with joy.

Jeremiah believed that he had been told by God to devise a plan for salvation, and he left it up to Jessica to devise such a plan that would support the one true mission of salvation. Jeremiah explained to Jessica that her plan would save souls and build a path for God to return to the earth, and so she promised to devise the plan in intricate detail.

However, the thought of taking on such an enormous project frightened her. Doing God's work and saving souls was not the type of thing she was used to thinking about. Prior to being saved by Jeremiah, she spent the majority of her time crocheting and doing macramé. She cooked for the church on Wednesday nights and grocery shopped every Thursday morning. Her old life was one of routine and solitude, but that was her old life. She had been reborn.

Jessica worked on her plan for a week and did not stop until she felt it was perfect. Her plan called for a grand tour of revivals and invitations that moved northward, targeting certain major cities with populations over twenty thousand citizens.

Jeremiah's army would travel from Newton to Bismarck, and Jeremiah would pick up thousands of converts in each city. In this way, he would build his followers while doing the important work of saving souls.

Jeremiah touched her shoulder as he approached her and startled her. She was so engulfed in working through the details of her plan that she didn't hear him come in.

"Is it ready, sister?" asked Jeremiah with his soft but commanding voice.

Jessica almost squeaked she was so excited.

"It is."

He smiled and offered her a chair then took her eyes in his, gaining her full attention.

"Sister, I need you to display poise. You are my right hand, the rock on which His plans rest. The whole of this land's salvation will depend on your attentiveness."

"Have I displeased you?" she asked, lip trembling with the thought.

Jeremiah combed her hair with his fingers and shook his head ever so slightly.

"You could do no such thing. Show me the plan."

Jessica rolled out a map with red marker annotations marking the major cities and providing a precise route complete with nightly stops and lists of available resources in each area.

"We leave on June 6 and travel to Fort Worth," she said and continued outlining the plan.

The route would take the group out of Texas to Oklahoma and then on to Kansas, Nebraska, South Dakota, and finally to North Dakota where a second headquarters compound would be built. The Sons would then have bases of operation in the extreme north and south, severing the country in half.

The 1,600-mile trek would take nearly a month, with plans to arrive in Bismarck on July 1. They would spend a month in Bismarck building and then would return south hitting Rapid City, Pierre, and several other cities along the way. Jessica believed that this plan would allow the group to gain at least fifty thousand converts.

"You've done well, Jessica. You will be rewarded for your hard work," Jeremiah told her when he was finished examining the plan.

She demurred shyly, but was alight with his praise and left the room after he made it apparent he wanted a moment alone.

As soon as she left, he poured over the plan's details, checking routes, timetables, and schedules. Jessica was a sweet and well-meaning girl, but no one could be totally trusted with his plan.

Twenty-seven hours, forty-two minutes on the road, 1,616 miles, 250 men and women, 18,750 fifty meals, which would increase by 200 percent in every city with the addition of conversions.

He crunched the numbers quickly in his head and smiled in spite of himself. Only a short time ago, he could not string together more than a couple coherent thoughts, and now he was blessed beyond measure. Fifty thousand converts was a good guess, but Jeremiah had much bigger plans. He wanted one hundred thousand new names written in the book with blood. One way or another, every person that Jeremiah encountered was going to meet God, with Jeremiah over time or much, much sooner.

The last part of the trip to Pierre was more solemn than the first several days. Carrisa spoke very little, and Tony was equally consumed by her grief. Although Sara continued to show increasing symptoms of the superflu, she cared for Carrisa in every way that was possible for her to do so. It would have been sweet had they not all been weighed down with knowledge of the inevitable.

The truck passed through downtown Pierre, and the hustle and bustle was laughable compared to that of a busy city. The town had a distinctive Western flare and came across as a big town that was homey with people waving and smiling at each other.

Don followed the directions that had been written on a scrap piece of paper, and the route took them to a rural area out of town where there were no signs of people. A dirt road turned off the highway but was blocked by a long barbed wire gate, which was not tended or groomed, leading to the growth of vines and weeds that covered the fence and gate. It looked as if no one had been through the gate in a long while.

Tony opened the gate while Don drove the truck through and then Tony closed the gate behind them. The group proceeded down the grassy cow trail trying to avoid the deep ruts that had been worn into the road over the years, while traveling for several minutes and leaving the highway out of sight behind them.

They finally stopped when they reached a rusty convex shelter, the kind that was popular in the fifties. There was a small glass window thick with dirt and grime and a rusted door with a pad lock.

"This is it," said Don, looking at his directions, unsure if they were correct.

"You sure? This doesn't look like it was ever a lab," replied Tony as he looked around the old building.

Don shrugged. "No clue."

"What is this guy's name?" Tony asked.

"Don't know. I was only given an address and these directions. They said he would be expecting us."

"You've never met this guy? Never talked with him?"

"Quit your arguing and let's have a look around," said Carrisa as she pushed past them. Both men were surprised because she hadn't said much of anything for several days.

Carrisa pulled at the rusty metal door with the padlock. It was shut tight, so she knocked on it with the flat part of her fist, which seemed ridiculous. The building was partially grown over and looked like it had been abandoned decades ago. After several moments and no answer to the knock, they decided to go back to the highway to see if they could find another road.

Suddenly, as they were getting back into Don's pickup truck, a metal-clinking sound coming from the building stopped them in their tracks. Several thumps followed, as if someone was hammering metal, and then the door creaked open. On the outside, the door looked like a cut piece of rusted tin, much like the rest of the building, but when it was opened up, it was clear that the door was made of three-inch thick reenforced steel.

A quizzical-looking little old man stood in the open door frame, squinting out to see who was there. He wore a pair of horned-rim glasses, which sat crooked upon his nose and were taped furiously at one ear. His flannel shirt had one side untucked, and his brown shoes looked as if they had long since given up. His hair flew in every direction, pieces of brown, white, and gray disregarding the laws of gravity. Underneath it all were his eyes, bright and laser focused.

"Which one of you is the Cajun?" he asked in a voice that squeaked of old age and under use.

Don raised his hand. "I do be him."

"The Network folks made contact with me. Said you needed help," he said while looking Tony up and down. "So you must be the genius? Should've known. You have the look of a know-it-all."

"I'll say," Carrisa said under her breath.

"You're the arrogant one, and you're the woman doctor. Good, everyone's here. Get the child and come in, we have little time and much to discuss. We can unload the truck and hide it later," he motioned for them to follow him.

The interior of the shelter looked the same as the outside; it was rusted, dusty, and uninhabitable. The old man closed the door behind them as the group looked at the space dubiously. The old man then lifted up the side of an old rusty metal table and instead of tipping over, it swung as if on a hinge. Below it, a trap door opened, which lead to a lift platform.

The old man hustled everyone on board the platform and then maneuvered the lift, which took the group down to a hidden underground corridor. It was very post-WWII style cloak-and-dagger. Above them, the table swung back into its original position, leaving the entry room to look as if no one had been there for years.

They descended twenty seconds later into a lab, which looked like it was modeled after a 1960 science fiction movie. It was arcane by current standards, but on closer inspection, alterations and updates had been made. Tony was intrigued as it showed a level of ingenuity that only men like him could appreciate.

"Welcome to my lab. You are the first guests in at least twenty years…I think or maybe thirty. I'm Ramsey, pleasure to meet you all," he said as if it were a memorized line.

"I'm Dr. Tony Van Lee, it's nice to meet you, Dr. Ramsey." Tony reached out to shake his hand.

"I'm not a doctor, doctors heal, find cures, do good things. I am a destroyer of life, everything opposite that a doctor should be. So we can dispense of titles. Here, there are only solutions to be sought and questions to be asked. Every box we open, there will be two more in its place. I am Ramsey, merely an old man hoping for the chance at redemption," he said with a tinge of anger and sorrow, delivered with extreme frankness.

Tony was caught off guard by Ramsey's candor, and the rest of the group looked at him as if they could not decide if empathy or contempt was the proper response. But Ramsey wasn't interested in how others perceived him or if they liked him. He was dedicated to wasting no time in making a contribution that would help mankind. He began flipping switches at a fast pace, which fired up lights on a bank of computers along the wall and turned on fluorescent lights overhead.

"The girl needs to go in the clean room. We need to run some tests immediately. The woman is an MD, correct?" Ramsey asked.

"Yes, the woman's name is Carrisa," she answered curtly.

"Good. Clean room is that way, you can't miss it. Cajun, you go with them, I need a blood test from you as well, everybody eventually. Come here, Genius, and tell me what you have."

Tony felt as though he had just ridden into town on a rollercoaster. The crazy old man, who refused his own title, and his secret underground lab were all a little too much like an old movie.

"I'm pretty sure it's an engineered recombinant virus synthesized by the army or some rogue state as a bioweapon. I think it got out and is now out of control," Tony reported as Ramsey continued flipping switches and looking at readouts.

"Really? Where would something like that be developed?" Ramsey asked.

"I'm not sure. The first outbreak was in southern Louisiana."

"No government bio labs down there. Why do you think it's one of ours?"

"Friend of mine at the CDC discovered a bioweapons expert in charge of the investigation. And the way the agent attacks, it crosses species and kingdom barriers, it has to be manmade. Viruses just don't act that way on their own. And besides, my friend is dead now, the army killed him. So I'm pretty sure they're behind it," he said.

Ramsey studied Tony's expression, thoughtfully, which made Tony uncomfortable.

"Here, look at this. This was the last thing he sent before he died." Tony handed him a translated copy of the classified page that Ben had faxed him, and Ramsey looked it over very carefully.

Pathogen name: Unknown; possibly a virus that uses a universal receptor found on many eukaryotic cells or a prion of unknown etiology.

Code name: Zebulon

Pathogen target: The agent infects many eukaryotic cell types, including plants, lower animals, and humans. It appears to be completely fatal to most plants and animals, whereas there are differential outcomes among humans. Humans with a primary exposure died within twenty-four hours; humans with secondary infections show mild symptoms, with no obvious morbidity. Mechanisms of morbidity/mortality are currently unknown.

Pathogen transmission: The unknown agent appears to spread via multiple routes. It may be waterborne and also appears to spread via the aerosol route. Cell target is unknown, however, since it infects different species from different kingdoms, it likely utilizes a common and possibly ancient molecular pathway to cause morbidity/mortality.

Pathogenesis: Mechanism unknown. In plants and lower animals, the agent obliterates the cells and tissues, quickly destroying the organism. In humans, the agent does not appear to target any specific cell, but rather multiple cells within the whole organism.

Mortality: Current mortalities among primary human infections that occurred in Pecan Island, Louisiana, include 128 persons aging from thirteen to sixty-eight, median age twenty-seven. Reports of secondary infections in humans are currently being investigated. Mortality rates among plants, animals, insects, and fish appears to be nearly 100 percent.

Current investigation: Current speculation is that the unknown agent is a virus that utilizes a universal receptor found on a variety of eukaryotic cells, however, there is currently no conclusive evidence. Preliminary experiments have failed to identify RNA or DNA. Further investigations are being conducted to determine if the unknown agent is a prion.

Principal investigator: Col. Adrian Bragg, MD, Bioweapons Division, USAMRIID.

This report silenced Ramsey for a moment. "Hmm," he mumbled with a faraway look. "According to this, they don't appear to know the source either. So it can't be one of ours… or it could be that the investigator wasn't aware of the research of some other branch. This is the US government we are talking about here. The right hand doth not always know what the left hand doeth," Ramsey said with a sarcastic smile.

Ramsey tapped a meter on the face of an ancient central processing unit that stood six feet tall. The level on the meter was in the green range. Tony wore a puzzled look.

"Power," Ramsey said. "I've got solar panels above ground. I run this whole thing that way. No one can track you by the power you use if you are off the grid. Got to keep an eye on power levels, because I'm not used to having people around."

"Wait a minute. What did you mean one of 'ours'?" Tony asked, alarms beginning to fire in his mind as he searched the area, retracing the steps necessary to get the group out of the shelter in the event that this was the enemy.

"Calm down, Genius. I'm not the bad guy, at least not this time." Ramsey sighed heavily and allowed his pieced-together glasses to fall into his lap as he sat in an old roller chair.

"In the sixties, the government put together small teams of molecular biologists to study the effects of certain chemicals on the nervous system."

"Like mustard gas," added Tony.

"Well, that was before my time, but yes. Slowly it evolved into finding ways to bypass the body's immune system, and it didn't take long before viral weaponry was born."

Tony stepped back, anger plastered on his face. Ramsey was the personification of everything he fought against as a professional. He was the type of scientist that had thrown him out for trying to reveal the truth. He was a killer.

"You sick son of a bitch."

Ramsey smiled sadly and nodded, his eyes fading into another time.

"We did many good things here for nearly ten years. In 1969, there were eight of us here. Our work was mostly autonomous and classified. Only three high-ranking officials even knew we existed. There were labs scattered all over the midwest. None of us knew the whereabouts or personnel of the other labs. Security reasons. My wife Shirley and I were among the eight that ran this facility. Most of our time was spent investigating the exposure of nerve agents on primates. We had a state-of-the-art monkey house, just through that corridor over there." Ramsey pointed to a door that had been blocked by a long table and now held an inverted microscope.

"And then one day," he continued, "out of nowhere, we were given the assignment of developing a two-part viral attack system. The first step was to develop a virus that would infect cells and reprogram them to express a specific protein receptor. A second virus was designed and engineered to utilize the new receptor and deliver a lethal gene to anyone that had that receptor. The idea was to use this system to assassinate those who had been exposed to both viruses. The first virus exposure was to be very specific, and it set the stage for the fatal blow. Whoever was infected with the first virus had the receptor necessary for the second virus. The second virus was simply a modified rhinovirus that normally causes the common cold. However, by utilizing the specific co-receptor that was engineered into it, the combination of the two viruses resulted in immediate death. And the most interesting part was that the person who died appeared to die of the common cold. No evidence left behind, no smoking gun."

"An assassination virus," Tony said, finding it hard to believe what he was hearing.

"Yes. Internally, we called it the Mad Man system, because we always assumed that whatever genius devised this system was mad."

"But you built it?" Tony said incredulously and with disgust.

Ramsey became quiet, but stoic.

"Yes, we did. We used reverse engineered superinfection exclusion. In many cases, when a virus infects a cell—"

"It blocks other viruses from infecting," Tony interrupted.

"That's right, so we took advantage of that by having the first virus express the receptor for the second virus, allowing the first one to open the door. It was so elegant, we lost track of what it would be used for. It was like a game, and it didn't seem real."

"A game? You are an assassin! Maybe you didn't pull the trigger, but all the same—"

Ramsey put his hands up to settle Tony, who was ready to burst. Using viruses as weapons went against everything for which he stood.

"It was very nearly perfected when the accident happened. We worked without sleep much of the time, which probably led to the accident. One of my colleagues inadvertently released the first virus into the lab, thinking it was the harmless second virus. The first virus was not permitted in that lab but was brought in by mistake. Within seconds, the scientists inside realized it was the first virus and panicked. In the scuffle that followed, a flask containing a culture of the second virus was knocked to the ground and broke open, sending the death sentence into the air. There were no safety protocols in those days. It was a different time. Five scientists were inside, including my wife. She sealed the door and stayed inside with them. They all died within four days, four excruciating days. The second virus was designed to kill immediately, but the whole process went out the window when both viruses were delivered at the same time. I couldn't move, just sat next to the door watching her for a week, hoping to die too. There was no cure, no stopping it, only pain and heartache and the guilt of knowing that I had killed my own wife. She smiled at me, you know, tried to tell me it was okay. Imagine that, she was the one dying, and she was still trying to take care of me."

Tony felt the guilt well up within him and saw the pain in Ramsey's eyes. He looked as if it happened only a day ago.

"I'm sorry," Tony said softly.

"When I went topside, I found my other two colleagues shot to death and the lab sealed up. They had witnessed the events too and went to the upper lab to hit the alarm. They were killed to keep it silent, and no one even checked to see if anyone survived, so no one knows I even exist. This was a classified project. I'm not so sure anyone alive still knows its whereabouts. At least nobody's paid a visit in fifty years."

Tony felt sorry for the old man but was entranced in the cloak-and-dagger–like story. He had heard other stories like this, but they were always just that, stories; and now to have one confirmed sent a shock through his soul. Tony looked at Ramsey and noticed that he had a funny look about him. Suddenly, his expression changed, and he took a defensive posture as he looked around at the walls.

"Did you hear that?" he asked.

"Hear what?" Tony replied alarmed.

"Screaming, they're screaming again. I'm coming!" he yelled and scurried off.

Tony recognized the signs that Ramsey displayed as those of senility or schizophrenia, which one he was not sure.

"What the hell was that all about?" Carrisa asked from behind him.

"I don't think our host has a full load of bricks."

Don walked in behind her holding gauze over his arm.

"Maybe I steer us in the wrong way?" he said, following Ramsey's path with his eyes.

Tony sat and thought about things, contemplating where else he could go and what else he could do. First, he had to deal with stabilizing Sara then isolate the source and identify exactly what they were dealing with, and then try to identify some part of the life cycle to attack to stop it. If he could even do any of this, then he would be on the right track to stopping the unknown agent.

"Crazy as it sounds, I think this guy can help us like no one else could."

Tony decided that the others had no need to know about Ramsey's past, as it wouldn't help the situation. Tony had enough difficulty dealing with it himself, and he didn't want to burden the rest of the group with the information.

"Feeling better, Carrie?"

"No, but if I'm going to be of any help its time to suck it up."

Tony nodded, for the lack of any other way to respond. Don looked at her with respect.

"When my wife left me and sher', I no felt like walking or breathing. My heart kept pumping, but I don't know how. From the living room I heard crackling, so I go in there to see sher' sittin' watching TV, eating saltine crackers. I say, 'Hey, why you making so much noise,' and she say that she just hungry. Then I remember that I did no make lunch or dinner, maybe no breakfast. I say the same thing, time to suck it up, take care of my sher', 'cause she still here and my wife is gone," said Don, who left the room without waiting for a reaction.

Carrisa let the tears flow for Don and his daughter, and for her mother, who always strived to take good care of her.

"I'm so sorry things are so—" Tony tried to apologize to Carrisa but couldn't finish the sentence before she interrupted.

"Me too, Tony. Let's get started."

The underground lab was fairly large and needed a thorough cleaning and lots of organizing. There were several rooms that might have been originally designed for quarters, a pantry, and a kitchen but these had been repurposed for storing junk.

There were packaged rations stored in the facility and running water. It had everything they would need to hunker down and study the disease that was killing all around them, but it would take a little while to get it up and running as an efficient facility.

Carrisa set up the clean room as a patient exam area and the observation chamber as a lab. Don helped Carrisa set up the rooms and was a very quick study concerning the medical procedures and tests she discussed. Tony took inventory of the hardware he had to work with and distributed his samples and other data on a table. Dusty chalkboards were wheeled out, and Tony began writing his hypotheses and results on them.

After a day went by, and Ramsey had not returned, Tony decided to look around for him. In the common spaces, he was nowhere to be found, so he ventured deeper into the lab. He passed the sealable room, where Ramsey's wife likely died. It was dark inside, and he could not see, but the metal door with its small window was foreboding, considering what had happened.

He walked to the back down a narrow corridor and into a room that looked to be a storage area. Steel racks and shelves held boxes of antiquated masks and lab coats, as well as labeled boxes that Tony couldn't read. The room was dark, but he could just make out a heavy-looking door at the back of the room. The door had to be dogged like a naval hatch, as it was airtight. Behind it was another narrow corridor.

He felt for a light switch and flipped it on. A string of tiny lights hanging by bare wires that attached to a thicker bare wire lit the hall, which stretched on for several hundred feet. Tony followed the hall and noticed that the walls were cut roughly here, not smooth and manicured as in the lab, much more a tunnel than a hallway.

Once Tony came to the very end of the tunnel, he discovered a door. It was unlocked and swung easily, indicating that it had been used often. Behind the door was a set of steps that ascended into darkness.

A rack of flashlights was mounted on the wall, so he grabbed one and started climbing up the stairs. After a few minutes and with fatigue starting to set in, he arrived at a dead end. The stairs ended at what appeared to be a section of the concave metal roof. He pushed on the roof and a hidden swing door easily swung open. Tony noticed that the door was built with hidden hydraulic arms. Light flooded into the narrow corridor, blinding him. Once his eyes adjusted to the light, he saw a garden planted in a quasi-greenhouse.

He climbed out all the way and allowed the hydraulic door to swing back closed and become part of the floor. The walls and floor of the greenhouse were made of translucent plastic that tinted brown to match the exterior landscape. Vegetables and plants lined the floors of fifty-yard long greenhouse.

Twenty feet behind him was a screen door that led outside. The roof was covered in camouflage netting, as well as much natural overgrowth. The vines and plants seemed wild and untended, but Tony saw that they were trimmed and groomed to look wild to conceal the greenhouse further. The structure was impressive and most probably invisible from the air, which was Tony's guess as to all the camouflage.

The produce and vegetable selection was also impressive. Tall sunlamps stood along the walls, presumably for quicker ripening. More than Ramsey would need to survive and stay healthy. He was definitely here for the long haul.

Off to the side was a small patch of purple violets and a rustic wooden bench. On the bench sat Ramsey, who stared at the flowers motionlessly as if in a trance.

"Ramsey?"

He didn't look up but motioned for Tony to join him on the bench. Tony did, while trying to gauge his condition.

"I have a garden myself at home," Tony said, trying to break the ice.

"She liked violets," Ramsey said quietly. "She would have liked this. The quiet, the solitude, growing old together."

Tony didn't know how to respond, so he just kept him company.

"I have spells sometimes. They've been getting longer, happens once, sometimes twice a month. How long have I been gone?"

"A day."

"Hmm, well, there's nothing to be done, I suppose, and I think you'll be here for a while considering that animal you've got to deal with. So if I end up missing, this is where I always end up."

"Why do you think that is?"

"Sins. They always come back to haunt you. It's a helluva thing."

"Why are you still here, Ramsey? Why didn't you ever go public or—"

"Or what? I was as good as dead if I went public and eventually dead here if the virus got me. You wanna know what's funny?

I never got sick. After I found my friends dead, I went back downstairs and pried open the seal. I sat with her for two days, watching her decay and nothing. Immune, can you believe that? What are the chances that I was resistant all along, and she died? The cure was in my blood."

"I can't imagine what that's like," Tony said sympathetically.

"No, you can't. This bug of yours is my chance for redemption, my ticket to heaven."

Tony smiled smugly. "Ramsey, you can't tell me that as a scientist you believe in the existence of an omniscient being?"

"Don't you dare lecture me about beliefs or being a scientist."

"Surely science casts doubts upon—"

Ramsey cut him off sharply.

"The only thing that science demonstrates is that with every question and answer comes more questions and more answers. Science can't address where it all began and where it all ends. A smart man like you ought to have figured that out by now."

With that, Ramsey stood up sharply, opened the trap door, and descended the stairs with Tony following, a little unsettled. It was hard for him to understand a scientist believing in a deity with no empirical proof. However, somehow Ramsey, even in his declined state, moved him to ponder the idea ever so slightly.

Chapter 16

June 6, 2018

L<small>T. FINN HAD</small> finally gotten the old man out of her way and was now requisitioning troops for her search. With the chaos going on surrounding the unprecedented number of deaths and rumors about the superflu, it was easy for her to get the signatures she needed to implement her agenda. It was like taking candy from a baby, and all in the official name of national defense.

Truthfully, she no longer cared about the army or national anything. All Lt. Finn cared about was finding and destroying the woman doctor and mastering her place of dominance in this world, just as she had when she was just a child. She had played the game by society's rules for too long. *So, the bitch went west*, she thought. *And so that's where I will look.*

Lt. Finn no longer cared about the pathogen either. She couldn't get the woman doctor's face out of her mind. She was haunted by the weak, pitiable face that was smiling in the picture at Ben's house and the way that pathetic creature Epstein looked at it just before he died. Disgusting. Lt. Finn could not rest until the woman doctor was removed from the face of the planet, and only a painful death would do, to serve as an example. Lt. Finn believed that she had been called to fulfill the job of culling humankind, and nature could not be let down. She had never let her down before.

Now, Lt. Finn had the flexibility and resources at her disposal to do anything that she deemed necessary. She was aware that the group she hunted would need a lab setup, so she identified every lab and university from Illinois to Montana that had possession of an electron microscope, as it seemed elementary to assume that this is what they would be looking for. With three teams dispatched and a timetable enacted, it would only be a matter of time before she found them.

Lt. Finn no longer cared how long it would take or how many men would be expended. None of that mattered, only that she found this Dr. Harrison and brutally killed her. It was the only thing that Lt. Finn felt could make her feel whole again. It was the only thing in the world that mattered to her.

Lt. Finn started her search by taking a team of soldiers to Chicago herself. Traveling was not easy on the East Coast, as widespread panic had erupted into complete chaos with the appearance of MADS. It took her group twice the usual amount of time to get to Illinois, and she quickly discovered that nearly half the population of Chicago was sick and dying.

That didn't bother her at all. She saw death as a natural part of life, and events like the plague pandemic or Pompeii, or any number of other natural phenomenon that killed large portions of the population were just natural remedies to the life process.

It was an example of natural law and inevitability that nature had to cull the weakness out of its own self every so often. And it had happened over and over again throughout natural history. Natural disasters and major extinctions always gave rise to beautiful new radiations and creations, where exceptional creatures could survive, evolve, and thrive. And that's what she intended to do. Help the exceptional by culling the weak.

Her other teams had reported to her about a large organized contingent of people moving north from the southern border of the US. They started in east Texas and were headed north, driving anything and everything from motor homes and cars, to trucks, and motorcycles; but it was not clear if they were traveling together.

The large crowd went from city to city, staying for a few days in each major city. When they left each new place, the crowd was larger. Best estimates had the crowd at approximately ten thousand people, and growing every day. Lt. Finn's men had no idea how many they had started with, although they determined that the crowd arrived in Wichita a day or so prior, by way of Oklahoma City, and from the looks of it, had gathered another thousand or so people.

Lt. Finn listened intently to the report from her scouts. She did not like unknowns because unknowns were dangerous. Know your enemy before they know themselves. That was the motto she had used to pounce on unsuspecting prey. She studied their habits, learned their schedules, knew their flaws, and it all added up to weaknesses that she could exploit. This large crowd was a new player; however, it was one that she had very little information about, and it bothered her.

Telecommunications in the continental US were becoming increasingly difficult because cell phone usage reached an all-time high, and line and tower maintenance issues went unattended, especially in the east. To circumvent these problems, Lt. Finn picked up her satellite phone and called her scouts.

"This is Lt. Finn. What's your position?" she asked into the phone.

"We're ten clicks to the north of Wichita, ma'am, keeping an eye on things as you ordered."

"Do you have any additional information?"

"Yes, ma'am. The group calls itself the Sons of the Apocalypse. Their leader is a man called Jeremiah. He's some sort of pseudo Christian cult leader. They're ripping things down pretty good, and people are following them in droves. Would you like us to make close contact?"

"Affirmative, I want direct contact and find out what they are doing and where they are going, Sergeant. Deadly force is authorized for anyone who resists. I repeat, deadly force is authorized. I have confirmation code, lima, mike, centaur, five."

"Yes, ma'am. I copy, deadly force is authorized, lima, mike, centaur, five. Over and out."

The deadly force code was a safety measure used on domestic soil to prevent accidental civilian deaths. The army was not a police force and was trained to kill, not protect, so domestic actions had dual protocols in place. However, she had requested the codes and authorized them herself, as no one was really paying attention in the heightened state of national anxiety. For all intents and purposes, she had her own private little army.

Lt. Finn didn't want to take the time out of her hunt to deal with a religious cult, but it occurred to her that the woman doctor could be hiding in the group for safety. She realized that she must account for this possibility, and so she designed a plan of attack to intercept the group. Looking at a map, she guessed that the Sons of the Apocalypse would land in Lincoln, Nebraska, in less than a week. So far, they had hit all the major cities, and Lincoln was right in their path. She decided that she would direct her men to cut across Missouri and hopefully beat them there by a couple of days, allowing her to gain a strategic advantage.

Lt. Finn called her soldiers together and ordered them to the coordinates she laid out, heading west on a collision course with the Sons of the Apocalypse.

Chapter 17

June 18, 2018

Tony sat in a corner, writing in his journal, as he watched Carrisa run to the bathroom to puke her guts out. He was worried that she had contracted whatever this infectious agent was from her close contact with Sara. Sara had gotten worse; she was now running a low-grade fever and was starting to exhibit more severe cold symptoms. Her health had declined rapidly once they got to the lab.

Tony monitored her situation with great concern, but he still had no idea what type of illness he was dealing with. And other than a few comfort measures, there was little he could do to help the little girl.

It had taken him longer than he would have liked to get the lab up and running with all the proper safety equipment in place, as well as separate rooms for different studies to prevent cross contamination. They were ready now, but Tony decided it was time to get some more information. They had been at the underground lab for a couple of days, and being cut off from the rest of the world during a major crisis left him feeling anxious.

He decided it was time to go to town and find out what was happening in the real world, as well as pick up some additional supplies. It was necessary to reinforce the solar collection units in order to fully supply the lab with the needed electricity demands, and he planned to make a few modifications to some of Ramsey's antiquated gear. He also wanted to get a radio and a television. Ramsey made a phone call to someone he knew in town who had gotten supplies for him in the past and scheduled a meeting for them to pick up the things they needed.

Don, Carrisa, and Tony piled into the truck and drove the twenty minutes back to Pierre. Once there, they split up to collect some necessities and personal items and planned to meet at a restaurant in the middle of town where they were to meet Ramsey's contact.

Don collected seeds and some farming tools for the greenhouse. Carrisa picked up some routine medical supplies and several personal items. Tony purchased the electrical items he needed, which included a radio and small TV.

They met at the restaurant at the agreed upon time but found the place to be way too empty for dinnertime. They were thankful for the privacy even though it didn't feel right. A television played in view of their table, showing a sitcom, as a waitress came to take their order. She was young and plump with what appeared to be a permanent smile on her face.

"Ready to order?"

Tony put his menu down. "Is it normally this empty around dinnertime?"

"Well, ever since the Mad Hatter, people are a bit skittish," she said, the smile ever present.

"The Mad Hatter?" Carrisa asked.

The waitress looked embarrassed. "You know, the super virus and how it makes all the kids and old people die."

"MADS, the Mad Hatter, you're very clever," said Tony, not really amused.

"Shoot, I didn't make it up. It's on the TV," said the waitress.

Tony and Carrisa glanced at each other, trying to maintain their composure. Don saved the moment.

"Anyone get sick 'round here, *mon sher*?"

The waitress giggled at his accent.

"Naw, not yet. Hope never," she responded.

The group made their orders and asked if she would change the channel to a news program, which she did right away. What they saw shocked them.

The news reported that the Mad Hatter, what the CDC called Multivariate Accelerated Death Syndrome or MADS, had made its way overseas and killed at least twenty million in Europe, forty million in India, and over sixty million in Africa. The numbers were staggering.

Emergency rooms were flooded with victims, and it seemed to zero in on a particular demographic. The elderly were particularly vulnerable. There were tens of millions of cases of people over the age of sixty-five succumbing to the superflu, and this age group was dying off the quickest.

The next most susceptible demographic was children under the age of ten. The information wasn't quantified yet, but preliminary reports from various locations corroborated the findings. Tony reeled and glimpsed at Don, whose instincts had been correct—something he would have to keep in mind.

What was happening seemed impossible to Tony, but he couldn't argue with the facts that were confronting him. His thoughts returned to what deadly agent might have gotten out of some bioweapons lab. This was a nightmare. A total of forty-eight million elderly and young people had already died in the United States.

The most frightening information of all was that the mortality rate appeared to be 100 percent for those under ten and over sixty-five. Not one single patient in those age groups had reported to a hospital with the illness and later recovered.

In addition to the high mortality, the violent crime rate in the US and worldwide was on the uptick, increased brazen and aggressive attacks were occurring in broad daylight. Homicides were up 20 percent, rapes, break-ins, all across the board.

The reporter interviewed a few people, most of whom seemed frightened, but others seemed apathetic to the situation and demonstrated a strange nervousness and aggression toward the reporter.

The group sat in silence staring at the television and then looking at their food.

"That be 8 percent of our population. How can this be?"

"I don't know," Tony said reluctantly and looked at Carrisa for support, but she was as numb as he was. The death toll was unfathomable, and Don was thinking of his daughter.

"One hundred seventy million people in a month. Tony, that's not possible," Carrisa said, her lips trembling and face pale.

"Oh, it's possible, mate," said a voice with a distinct Irish accent.

The group looked up and saw a tall, well-built man in his thirties with a smile that said he knew something and wasn't telling.

"Can I help you?" asked Tony.

"It's I that can help you, mate"—he offered his hand—"I'm Irish."

"Never would have guessed," Tony responded sarcastically.

"You're a quick one, that's for sure. Ramsey asked me to meet you with supplies."

Tony shook his hand as did the other two, and they all greeted him warmly.

"How did you know we were who you were supposed to meet?" Carrisa asked suspiciously.

"Well, lass, it's not like there are many to choose from, if ya get my meaning," Irish smiled and looked around the nearly empty restaurant.

"Things are getting a bit hairy back east. Not so different out west. The Mad Hatter will be here fairly soon."

"What makes you say that, Irish?" asked Don.

"Murphy's Law. If it can get worse, it most certainly will."

"Murphy's Law, you say?" Don asked, not buying his reasoning.

"Aye, Murphy was Irish, and the Irish are never wrong." He smiled. "Let's get you loaded up. My truck's out front."

Tony asked the waitress to wrap up their food because they had all lost their appetites while watching the news, and it was time to get back to work. If this epidemic were allowed to escalate out of control, it would put humanity in danger of total extinction. After all, with no kids surviving, mankind would be one generation away from extinction.

Irish had a decent-sized truck, much like a U-haul. A giant lock held the roller door closed tight. It took two keys inserted simultaneously to open the large padlock. Irish saw the others looking at him oddly. He looked down at the lock and shrugged.

"When you're a man that can get things, your livelihood depends on keeping the items secure until delivery. Never can be too safe," he said.

The back of his truck was full of boxes, but he seemed to know exactly where to go. He pulled a few down and shoved them to the edge.

"Are they all sterile?" Tony asked.

"Hermetically sealed. It'll do ya well, I guarantee it," Irish cut through Tony's uncertainty with practiced charm.

"I guess you do guarantee all products. Would that be from the manufacturer, or do we contact you?"

"I'm afraid you'll have to go through me, as I'm sure the manufacturer won't be so happy to hear you have a problem."

"I guess we can assume that these are stolen then," Carrisa added, beginning to feel a bit nauseous.

"Now, that's not polite. I don't ask you what you want with live specimen containers in the middle of nowhere now, do I? Of course not, that would be your business, my business would be getting things. And as for these products, you'll have no problem with them."

Tony reached up to grab a box, but Irish placed his foot on top and stopped him.

"Did Ramsey tell you about the price we agreed upon?"

Tony pulled out a large roll of cash and handed several bills to him. Irish eyed the money and watched where Tony put it with much interest.

"That'll do," he said and pulled down several more boxes from the back of the truck.

Don grabbed the boxes and began loading them in his truck.

"Have you heard any other news? I assume you know how to get information as well?" Tony asked as he subtly pulled a hundred-dollar bill out and folded it into his hand. Irish did not miss the movement.

"Aye, I've been known to hear things now and again."

"Anything else on the agent?"

Irish looked at him, slightly off-kilter.

"Do ya mean the Mad Hatter?"

"Yes," Tony answered, annoyed at the need for people to come up with coy and colloquial versions of such deadly agents.

"Well, the news reports on the old folks and the kids, but it never mentions the others."

"What others?" Tony became interested very quickly.

"Drug addicts."

"Are you putting me on?" Tony asked.

"I know a good sort about and around. Not so many around anymore. Seems the addicts get sick faster than the old folks. Die in a day. Die badly. The Mad Hatter is an unkind killer," Irish said. He was not so energetic while talking about this.

"Would you know what kind of drug users we are talking about?"

"Not really, but mostly hard stuff. Crack, the dragon, ice, meth. Drugs you would see in an alley. At least that's what I've seen. Nothing more I can say for certain."

"Marijuana?"

"Can't say."

Tony handed him the money, but Irish shook his head.

"I enjoy a profit, but not on this. The Mad Hatter is not goin' away, I think." Irish shrugged. "If you're doin' what I think you're doin', best you do it quick, or they'll be no one left to cure," he said and nodded to the others as he left.

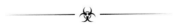

The trip back to the lab seemed as if it took forever with no one saying a word. The idea that MADS had infected such a large swath of the population was frightening and so unlikely that they had a hard time accepting it. Once they arrived, Don offered to park the truck and left Carrisa and Tony alone in the darkness under a thousand stars.

"He loved me, you know," she said.

Tony took the information in but didn't know what she meant. "Who?"

"Ben. He was in love with me."

"Get outa here," Tony said, reacting as if she might be joking, but then realizing that it looked like she was being serious. "Is that what he said?"

"No. He never said a word. You intimidated him."

"Are you sure?" Tony offered, not sure how to take this.

"You remember that study in Mexico? We went to a formal at the embassy."

"I remember you wore that burgundy dress," he said shyly.

"Yeah, I loved that dress. Ben and I had a dance while you were mingling, probably drumming up funding or something like that. It was the way he held me, like I might break. And you know Ben, he was never without something to say, but he didn't say a word the entire dance, just soaked up every minute."

Tony relived the memory and allowed himself a brief mourning of his friend.

"I didn't have a clue."

"You only see what you want, Tony. It's always been that way. You were the smartest, and Ben and I were only along for the ride."

"That's not what I wanted…"

Carrisa put her hand up and silenced him. Her face was very sober, and she locked onto his eyes with hers.

"Time to live up to your potential. Time to pay the piper. You have a gifted mind, and you have to stop this thing. You! We'll help anyway we can, but this is beyond me and beyond the rest of us. You have to do it. You are the hope for the next generation."

She paused for a moment, looking as if she had something more to say, and then reached out to caress his face, but suddenly stopped short and spun around, leaving him standing alone under the starry night. Don came around from hiding the truck and saw Tony alone.

"Everything okay?" Don asked.

Tony couldn't answer; Carrisa was right. For all of his posturing and self-righteous deliberating, it was time to deliver.

Chapter 18

THE NEXT MORNING, the team began to seriously study the MADS agent and hunkered down for a long day. Although it needed quite a bit of organization, Tony was surprised to find that the lab was so well equipped. While much of the equipment was leftover from the 1960s, it had been well maintained, and the lab was surprisingly well stocked with modern plastic ware, some of which they had just gotten from Irish. Overall, the lab had all the modern scientific conveniences of the day. Carrisa and Don were also in the lab, where Carrisa unpacked and thawed the samples that she had collected at the kill zone, and Don assisted her.

Tony made sure he was out of earshot of Don and Carrisa before talking with Ramsey. He didn't want to frighten them any more than necessary.

"Okay, so no one knows you're here, and you want to keep it that way, but you use a shady guy like Irish. I don't get it," Tony said to Ramsey.

"No one in the government knows I'm here. However, I have many colleagues in the network who subcontract with me to do routine lab work," he replied.

"I get some supplies from those labs, but because Irish is a 'shady guy' is exactly why I use him. He knows how to keep a secret. All men are loyal to one thing, Genius. For some it's power, some it's their women. In Irish's case, it's money and his ability to get that money depends on his ability to keep a secret. If you want to be an effective scientist, it's important to know what motivates people.

"Viruses are not so different," Ramsey stated, amused by Tony's puzzled reaction.

Tony took it in and was ready to respond, but he caught the funny look in Ramsey's eye, that faraway look that he had seen before.

"Let me give you the tour," Ramsey said and trailed off, walking toward a hallway.

It took Tony a moment to realize that Ramsey was having one of his episodes and that he obviously forgot that Tony had been here for nearly a week. Ramsey showed Tony around the lab, indicating where each important piece of equipment was located, and Tony nodded politely. Then, they went through a narrow doorway into a small room filled with a gigantic machine that took up most of the space in the room.

"There she is," Tony said, "the electron microscope."

"Yes, she's a real beauty," Ramsey said. "I don't use her that much, but I'm never unhappy with the results when I do."

They finished the tour and returned to the main room. Ramsey took a minute to reorient himself, because as he began returning to the present, he was unsure of where he was for a moment. Tony watched him, fully aware of the Alzheimer's and now very much sure of it as a diagnosis.

"Ramsey, were you going to get the lab coats?" Tony offered.

The comment seemed to reconnect Ramsey to the present, just as the others walked in to find him smiling as he opened the closet door. He reached in and produced a stack of what appeared to be freshly laundered lab coats and handed them out to everyone in the room.

"Listen up, everyone," Ramsey said, his voice clear and mind back in the now. "We must be very careful here. Everyone must don a mask. We have no idea what this is, and we certainly do not want to spread this thing around. I think in order to be on the safe side, we must assume that it is spread by both personal contact and through the air. Use your best judgment, and please, please be careful."

They all put on an N95 mask and began their work. Talking with the mask on made it a little difficult to hear what each person was saying, but they quickly learned to adjust their voices to accommodate the mask. Tony knew that Ramsey was having a borderline event and was unsure of his complete cognizance, so he tried to lead the conversation carefully.

"I was thinking that we should start by using some of our samples to infect immortalized cell lines. Maybe we can isolate a pathogen. Do you have access to any cell lines?"

"I do," Ramsey replied. "They're in the deep freezer. When I got the message that you were coming, I thawed and started cultures of several lines to save time."

"Do you have a wide range of species?" Carrisa chimed in.

"I have delayed brain tumor cells from mice, baby hamster kidney cells, Vero cells from primates," Ramsey started, looking at his list as he continued. "Oh, and LLC-MK2 cells from monkey kidneys, CaCo2 cells of the human colorectal tract, A549 cells from primate upper respiratory tract, and C636 cells of the mosquito."

"I do hate to break up a party, but what be immortalized cells lines?" Don asked, feeling completely out of place.

"Sorry, Don," Tony answered. "Cell lines are immortalized cells, which just means the cells grow continuously. They were first discovered in cancer tumors that seemed to grow without limitation. Later, as research progressed, it became understood that most cells stop dividing when their DNA becomes damaged. However, some cells found ways around this, and they are called immortalized because they keep dividing for extended periods of time. Immortalized cells can be passed from culture to culture, and when properly maintained, form a very nice monolayer of cells on the bottom of the flask," he finished.

Don nodded and allowed the concept to run through his mind, and then he blinked with another question.

"That all makes sense, but what is a monolayer?"

Tony continued, "A monolayer is like a blanket of cells, one cell thick, that coats the bottom of the flask, and these cells mimic cells in a tissue. They have receptors and in many cases excrete chemical messengers. They are perfect for growing some viruses."

"So we use those cell lines to find a way to keep sher' from getting sick? 'Cause it act like regular people cells," Don rehashed in English.

"You got it, Don. These cells will be good for screening the samples," Tony said and turned to Carrisa as an idea crossed his mind.

"What about media plates? We could try to isolate colonies from some of the samples, in case it's a bacterial pathogen."

"I made some Luria Bertani Agar plates with various additives, and we can test a number of these," Ramsey said, obviously already a step ahead of Tony.

And even before Don could ask, Ramsey continued with Tony's science lesson.

"LB plates are rich media plates that contain the nutrients that bacteria need to grow. Because different bacterial species use different nutrients, there are a wide variety of different plates that can be used to grow them, and determining which medium a bacterium grows upon will provide important clues as to its identity. Once we know what it likes to grow on, then we can conduct a whole variety of experiments to figure out what it is."

"You got to know a lot to do this work," Don said, adding, "but important work it do be, no?"

Tony and Carrisa began preparing the samples they had collected at the kill zone. First, they moved all the unthawed samples into a biological safety cabinet designed to provide a safe and sterile environment for working with the pathogens. The safety cabinet looked like a library table–sized cabinet with a large metal hood that covered everything above the surface.

An opening in the front was covered partially with glass, with just enough space beneath it to allow a person to insert their arms into the work area. Fans drew the air out of the workspace and up through HEPA filters that removed all potential pathogens before allowing the air to flow back into the room.

Once the tubes containing Carrisa's samples were inside the safety cabinet, they were prepared for use in infecting cells and plates. The plant leaf samples were crushed to a fine powder using a mortar and pestle, and resuspended in phosphate buffered saline (PBS) solution.

The tissue samples were also suspended in PBS and homogenized to break up the tissue and release any pathogens. The blood samples that were taken from everyone were prepared such that any pathogens present would be released by serum proteins that might be bound to them. The suspensions were then filtered with old Chamberland filter that Ramsey had saved from the 1950s.

"Jesus!" Tony stared at the old thing. "Sorry, but this thing is older than I am."

"Well, it still works like a charm," Ramsey answered. "Just 'cause something is old, doesn't mean it doesn't work."

"What does that thing do?" Don asked.

"It's really pretty simple," Tony began. "This filter has tiny holes that will only allow very small objects to pass through. That means that we can filter our samples and anything that is smaller than the holes will pass through. Most viruses are smaller, and all known bacteria are larger than the holes. Hopefully, we will be able to identify if the pathogen is a bacterium or a virus using this method."

"Those viruses must be really small," Don said. "How do you even know they be there?"

"That's the tricky part, most of the time we just have to use some experimental evidence like the destructive effect on cells, or isolation of viral DNA or RNA, or take a picture of them with an electron microscope," Tony said.

"I know that an electron microscope sees smaller particles than a regular one, but how does it do that?" Don asked, soaking up information.

"A normal microscope uses light and magnification to see things that are small, but viruses are too small to be seen using light waves. An electron microscope uses electrons instead of light waves, so it can visualize things that are much, much smaller. Once Ramsey runs the samples through, I'll let you take a look."

"I'll run one of the human tissue samples that you prepared and we can look for virus, right now," said Ramsey.

"What if it not be a virus?" Don asked.

Tony thought a moment before answering.

"Then we would have dodged one hell of a bullet but still have to figure out what is causing the MADS outbreak."

Carrisa looked on silently, knowing exactly what Tony meant. Finding a virus only began the long, tedious, and potentially unsuccessful process of finding a cure. If the MADS agent was a toxin or a bacterial pathogen, it would not change or adapt very quickly. The MADS agent, however, seemed to adapt rapidly and repeatedly; therefore, she would be surprised if it was not a virus.

Ramsey gathered the sample that he prepared for the electron microscope and exited the lab through the narrow door, while Tony and Carrisa prepared and filtered the remaining samples. Once filtered through the Chamberland filter, the solution for each sample was divided into equal quantities and applied to each of the cells lines.

"So if there is a bug in the sample it will move into the water and then from the water onto the cells?" Don asked.

"Exactly," Tony said, "except the filter will remove any bacteria and only allow something much smaller through, like a virus."

The cells were incubated with the MADS agent in nutrient-rich media that was added to the flask to feed the cells during the course of infection. All of the infected cell lines were incubated at body temperature for at least twenty-four hours.

For each sample, the Chamberland filter used to separate viruses from bacteria was rinsed with PBS solution to collect any left behind bacteria into a solution, and these washes were then streaked onto a variety of rich media plates in an attempt to grow any bacterial pathogens that might be present in the samples.

"We should harvest total RNA and DNA from the samples that we have left," Carrisa said to Tony. "Just to see if we can detect anything that looks remotely like a pathogen."

"Couldn't hurt," he replied. "Have you seen any TRIzol Reagent?"

"There was some in the refrigerator over by the hood. I'll get it."

"How long has Ramsey been in the EM room?" Tony asked.

"It's been a couple of hours. Those things take forever."

"Keep an eye on him, but be discreet," Tony said, trying not to oversell his concern.

"You know, Tony, I am a medical doctor," she said accusingly.

Not catching the hint, Tony went on, "Yeah, I know."

"Then why is it that you believe you're the only one who suspects he has Alzheimer's?"

Tony stopped and looked at her shyly.

"I didn't want to worry you. I think he's very useful, just—"

"I'm not breakable. Just try being honest," she said, not waiting for a retort.

Carrisa went to the refrigerator and returned with the TRIzol Reagent. She and Tony carefully added it to each of the remaining samples, mixed them well, and placed them in the deep freeze for the next day.

"We've been at this for nearly nine hours now," Carrisa said. "We should get some rest before the next phase."

"Sounds good," Tony said. "We probably won't see anything in the cells or on the plates for at least twenty-four hours."

Just then, Ramsey emerged from the EM room holding a handful of photographs.

"You got to see these," he said, pausing as he studied the images more carefully. "I have seen many viruses in my day, but nothing this complex, this beautiful."

Tony, Carrisa, and Don gathered around to look at the micrographs, which they studied for a moment in silence.

"Can this be?" Tony asked.

The micrographs showed similar pictures of very complex and very large viral structures in the shape of a perfect icosidodecahedron.

"Well, I think this is pretty strong evidence that we're dealing with a virus, and it's completely novel. I've never seen anything this unusual. I can't wait to see what genetic information is required to reproduce this giant," Ramsey said with a mixture of excitement and wonder.

Don didn't share his enthusiasm. Sara's condition had been gradually declining, and her fever spiked several times in the last couple of days. He was becoming increasingly anxious over the lack of speed in this process.

"I don't see how this is a good thing. If you no mind me saying."

Tony understood his tone and tried to get back on track.

"Which sample was this, Ramsey?" he asked soberly.

Ramsey stared nervously at the micrograph that he was studying. After a few moments of awkward silence, he looked up and then at his shoes.

"This came from the lady doctor's blood sample."

Tony's face dropped, as he slowly swung around to look at her. Carrisa stood stone-faced, not allowing any emotion through.

"I beat cancer once, I can beat this too," she said matter-of-factly.

"That's not all," Ramsey said even softer, "the routine panel of tests that I ran on her blood indicates that the lady doctor is pregnant."

The next morning, Tony and Ramsey checked the LB plates for bacterial colonies and found nothing. They placed them back into the incubator to continue the growth process for a couple of additional days. Then, Tony went to the incubator that housed the cell lines inoculated with the different samples. He took the flasks and placed them next to an inverted microscope to check for destruction to the cells.

"This be where you see if the cells were killed by the virus, no?" asked Don.

"Yeah, we might make a scientist out of you, yet." Tony smiled, glad to take Don's mind off things.

Tony turned on the microscope and placed the first flask under the lens. He spent a few moments focusing. Then he looked at the label on the flask before announcing his finding to the rest of the lab.

"Looks like blood collected from the dead dog at the kill zone contains a virus. It has completely destroyed the monolayer of Vero cells," Tony said.

He placed another flask on the microscope and focused the lens.

"And the dead plants collected at the site contain a virus, too, the monolayer of Caco2 cells is also shot."

Don sat back, unsure what everything meant as Tony placed the next flask on the microscope platform, focused, and then quickly grabbed another. He continued this process until he had looked at every single flask.

"Every one of these cell lines is susceptible to this virus, and everything that we sampled appears to have been infected with it," he said.

"Not only does this virus infect multiple cell lines, but it kills every one of them efficiently. These cells have only been in the incubator for ten hours, and they are already destroyed."

"What should we do next?" Don asked.

"We need to set up a series of controls to make sure that this is an infectious virus and not some chemical that is causing the cells to die. Second, we will need to dilute the samples to determine the titer, so that we can determine its lethal dose. And we need to start testing a variety of drugs to see if any of them prevent the virus from infecting the cells."

"Sounds easy enough," Don said with a shrug.

Tony looked at Don and carefully weighed his optimistic response. *I hope so*, he thought to himself, knowing the price if it took a long time to characterize this novel and deadly virus.

Chapter 19

COL. ADRIAN BRAGG had been driving for many days. He wore a military-grade chemical defense mask that gave him the appearance of a character from a science fiction film as he sped by other vehicles in his Humvee.

The traffic had deteriorated rapidly after the media leaked erroneous information concerning MADS, which most people now referred to as the Mad Hatter. He had left instructions for one of his aids to share the information his team collected with the CDC, but he assumed that somehow it all went wrong.

Some politician, most likely one trying to set himself up as the "MADS savior," had leaked the information to the public. Col. Bragg couldn't help but think that the stupid bastards had no idea what this thing was, and now people were doing exactly what they shouldn't be doing.

Col. Bragg spent much of the next few hours on the shoulder of the road, more so than he did on the asphalt. He knew he had to outrun the army, which would be after him, but he was also concerned with staying ahead of the effects of the virus.

The real trouble, however, was the lack of law and order as people began making runs on supermarkets and gas stations. Reports of failing crops and sick beef cattle had caused the commodities market to plummet and supply and demand forced stores to jack up their prices to ten times higher than normal.

At least one-third of the sitting US senators had already died of the virus and an equal number in the House of Representatives. The loss of such a large number of leaders had destabilized much of the government, as well as the people's trust in it.

The story was consistent globally, the colonel had learned, when he made some calls on the satellite phone to friends overseas. Governments had simply vanished when senior members died. Looting and violent crime was through the roof in Europe. The United States wasn't far behind; he had seen the evidence as he drove along. Total social breakdown and anarchy would engulf the country once everyone realized that the food supply would eventually run out.

It seemed to Col. Bragg that the big question was not how many would die from the virus, but how many would starve to death? How many would die during the fight to survive? The colonel knew that without a cure the country he served for his entire adult life would be reduced to a third-world nation in a matter of weeks or months.

Military protocols would kick in very soon, martial law would be enacted, but by that time, it would be too late. The chairman of the Joint Chiefs was dead, the secretary of Defense was dead, the Homeland Security chief was dead, the secretary of the Interior was dead, and the clock was ticking faster than the country could react.

With a third of Congress also dead, confirmations of new and younger cabinet secretaries were delayed as the federal government waited for the states to appoint replacements. And the states all faced the same dilemma. Widespread mortality had crippled the democratic process, and political pundits espoused fear that the president would draft an executive order essentially turning the US into a military dictatorship. Fear, which had already gripped an entire nation, would soon become the law of the land.

Once Col. Bragg crossed the Iowa state line, traffic stalled to nearly a complete standstill, and after a few hours sitting in his Humvee listening to doom and gloom on the radio, he took off the gas mask. The media reports were varied and often inaccurate, and one mistakenly reported that MADS couldn't survive in cold weather.

This set in motion a massive migration of people from the southern US toward the north, as everyone tried to escape the pandemic by heading north. All this misconception really accomplished was to put people in closer proximity to one another, which allowed the virus to spread faster.

Col. Bragg tired of the slow driving and the mundane scenery. He pulled over at a rest stop to relieve himself, bought a Coke, and the last bag of chips from a vending machine, and then popped open his onboard laptop. He pulled up a map of the US layered on a grid. A red dot pulsated, and he clicked it. The area around the pulsating dot magnified to show South Dakota. He clicked again, and a satellite image appeared zooming onto the town of Pierre.

"And there you are, darling," the colonel said to himself.

Back in Louisiana, when he had searched her medical kit, he felt that he might need to know her whereabouts at a later time. So he stuck a tiny GPS locater on the inside bottom corner of her medical kit underneath a box of nitrile gloves. He knew that it was completely unethical, but technically, ethics were not listed as a requirement in his job description.

At the time, he knew the truth was that he was attracted to her and hoped to see her again, and knowing where she was gave him a glimmer of hope. It was odd for him to do something so off the cuff, as he usually planned each expedition to a tee, but he was getting old. It was the only explanation for all the odd emotions and thoughts he had been having lately. Even getting blindsided by Lt. Finn was something that he would have anticipated more aggressively in the old days.

Col. Bragg sensed that this would be his final mission. He felt it instinctively, although he probably would not have admitted it out loud. The world would be different after this great pandemic, and it would take a long time for the world to return to normal.

Even then, it would be a new normal, fraught with reconstruction and rebuilding that would require a new energy, young energy. He knew that it would be beyond the number of years he could expect to live, for he could not see himself being part of a massive regrouping and rebuilding effort.

This was the colonel's last shot at redemption. He had heard Bible thumpers talk of Christ and His forgiveness, but he knew that the sins he had committed were appalling and beyond absolution. He felt his only hope was to accomplish something so good that it would even the score and erase the impact of all of his previous indiscretions. Even then, he doubted that he would make it to heaven, if heaven proved to be a real place. But at least he would settle for being even.

The whole notion of caring for such a thing as redemption was puzzling to him. It was a new idea, and new mind-set, and he felt driven to see it through—particularly, since the world appeared to be rapidly coming to an end. There was a reckoning coming. He could sense it.

Col. Bragg's plan was simple. He had acquired the source virus and was transporting it in a small vial locked in a dry icebox beneath the passenger seat. He knew that Dr. Van Lee would need it to further his research for a cure, and he vowed that he would get it to him at all costs.

He hoped that Van Lee was still with Dr. Harrison, but even if Van Lee wasn't with her, just seeing her face again would have made the whole trip worth the effort.

Col. Bragg flipped his laptop closed and pulled back on the interstate on a direct course to Pierre, South Dakota. He used his mobile GPS unit to identify low-traveled secondary roads that would lead him to Pierre with as little traffic as possible.

The Sons of the Apocalypse had built a convoy that stretched nearly a mile long. Jeremiah acquired nearly twenty-five thousand more converts by the time he left Lincoln, Nebraska, and the logistics of moving a crowd this size became increasingly more costly and more convoluted, especially as food in bulk became difficult to get hold of.

It would take time to identify the skills of his newest followers and train them to serve the organization. He assigned an accountant and a civil engineer to be Jessica's assistants, as well as another resource professional that dealt primarily with finding unique skill sets among individuals from the recently converted flock.

The work of organizing the rapidly-growing congregation went well beyond Jessica's mental abilities, so the help was necessary. However, Jessica was a symbol of obedience and its reward to the rest of the Sons because she was the first to choose His word. The fact that Jessica was meek but held such a high office inspired other members of the organization to have a goal, something to strive for, and it created a hierarchy that was important for controlling the large group. Jessica was also completely loyal and would throw herself in front of a bullet for Jeremiah; however for him, it was her commitment to God that was the main selling point.

Jeremiah rode near the head of the convoy in a large motor home. He ordered a few of his biker brethren to lag behind and keep on eye on the military woman. He had sensed her presence in Lincoln, and he knew that she was watching him. He believed it was a new gift that God had bestowed upon him. He sensed things, although he was not always able to communicate what it was he was sensing, but it was an early warning system, and it clued him in to the presence of the army woman.

His scouts told him that she had a heavily armed group of soldiers, approximately eighty men strong. The guns didn't bother him, his men were armed as well, and the number of men at her command certainly didn't bother him either; but he refused to kill them until he knew their identities and purpose. And besides, he felt they deserved a fair chance to accept the Word of God, no matter their intention.

However, Jeremiah wanted this group monitored closely, but he did not want them to know they were being watched. So he assigned a few stragglers who would act as decoys who would most likely get caught and killed, and two more trained soldiers behind them who had the proper skills to remain unseen.

Catching the first two would give the army woman's group a false sense of security and allow the second team to gather information on a regular basis unhindered. Jeremiah would deal with them all when the time was appropriate, but for now, he just watched.

During his campaign for God, Jeremiah had converted a great many people from a multitude of backgrounds. Computer hackers and government workers, farmers and ranchers, and even a few scientists that specialized in genetically modified organisms.

He used each one of these skill sets for the benefit of his flock and the God they served. Jeremiah knew that in this new world it wouldn't be money that was the bastion of power but food. So he mobilized bands of followers to take over ranches and farms in the midwest and in the south and later in the west.

In many cases, the farms and ranches were donated to the cause by willing converts and in other cases they were taken by force. Grain silos were guarded. Seed and grain facilities were taken over along with slaughterhouses, butcher shops, and grocery stores. Jeremiah knew that if he controlled the food supply, the populace would come to him and when they came he would offer them God's truth.

Jessica dropped a stack of reports on Jeremiah's desk. The reports showed the addresses of all the laboratories that were known to be currently working on cures for MADS, and she was the first to report to Jeremiah that the people called the new disease the Mad Hatter. The fact that the people nicknamed this plague infuriated Jeremiah. They didn't know this pestilence was God's will and that the only way to avoid the eternal fire of Sheol was to accept it.

Jeremiah dispatched fifty separate teams to destroy each of these labs. A cure to God's will was blasphemous and the work of evil, and anyone who attempted to find the cure would be stopped at all costs.

The convoy had a stopover in Omaha for a few hours, and Jeremiah could still hear the destruction going on. His methods seemed quite violent at first, but he knew the nature of people. God had showed him the most efficient way to get the attention of the people and make them vulnerable to His word. It was written throughout the Old Testament.

His advance party would drive through town making a ruckus, shouting the message of salvation. Those that resisted were killed immediately and without prejudice. It was unfortunate that so many had to die, but it saved many others in the end.

Courthouses and police stations were the first to be destroyed or burned. All established law needed to be eradicated for both practical and symbolic reasons. Allowing any resistance at all was not conducive to a smooth and willing conversion of hearts and minds.

Those that fled in the beginning were tracked down by units on motorcycles or in fast cars, and once captured, they were dragged back to face Jeremiah.

A knock at his door indicated that it was time to go. It was time for him to make his appeal, and he hoped and prayed that with God's help he would use words that would sway everyone to the correct path. The smell of smoke permeated the air as he walked to the center of town.

Omaha was no small place, and people ran and screamed down the streets all around him. His men and women did as they were instructed. Jeremiah viewed them as shepherds, and they herded the sheep to where they could hear him speak and then, and only then, could they make their decision to accept God's word.

A tractor-trailer had been parked before of a great mass of people in front of St. Philomena's Catholic Church. Jeremiah's men had Thirteenth Street blockaded and the people of Omaha's backs were up against the Missouri River. His troops brought in truckloads of people at a time to add to the crowd, and all of them were held at gunpoint.

Jeremiah saw the misery in their faces and the fear, but excitement welled up in him because he knew that soon, these heathens would be set free. He waited for more truckloads to arrive because the more people present when he started, the greater the glory to God. It also meant much less bloodshed.

Jeremiah guessed that nearly two hundred thousand people were gathered there, which he knew was approximately half of the city's population. If things went as well as they had been going after he spoke, he knew that he could expect about twenty thousand or so willing converts.

Another ten thousand would convert after some examples were made. He knew some of his followers had doubts, but they were kept in certain units and watched carefully until God's hand touched their minds. It didn't take long.

He whispered to one of the men standing near him. They would need buses, and there was a bus terminal in midtown. Each bus would need a driver, and they would need every single bus in the city. It was time.

Jeremiah climbed onto the top of the trailer and stood looking at the frightened and confused crowd. For a minute, all that could be heard was the wind and the subtle surf of the river behind them. He was an intimidating figure standing there, his more than six-feet-tall frame was over twenty feet in the air. His voiced climbed to a level that carried where everyone could easily hear him, yet he did not yell or even seem to speak loudly.

"I know you are afraid. Darkness has been set free in the world, and without help, we will likely all perish."

The crowd began to mumble collectively.

"I ask you, friends. If I could give you this help that would save you and your family and friends from this darkness, would you receive it? Listen to me. God made two great lights: the greater light to govern the day, and the lesser light to govern the night. He also made the stars. God set them in the expanse of the sky to give light on the earth, to govern the day and the night, and to separate light from darkness. All you need to save yourself is this light, my friends. God has given to me the gift to separate the darkness from the light, and I offer it to you for nothing, accept your promise to accept His mighty word," Jeremiah said eloquently.

Shouts erupted all around him, some asking for blessings and some yelling obscenities, but the crowd was too large for them to be distinct. Jeremiah raised his hands to calm them. An angry voice rang out loudly.

"Who the hell do you think you are?" it asked.

"I am the messenger, the deliverer, nothing more," answered Jeremiah.

"So what if we don't want any of your damn light?" another angry voice said.

Jeremiah looked sad but patient.

"Sons and daughters of Babylon, doomed to destruction. Happy is he who repays your disobedience for what you have done, and happy is he who seizes your infants and dashes them against the rocks."

The crowd began to buzz with agitation, and Jeremiah had to fight harder to calm them down.

"I ask you only to receive His gift of life. These are the days of His people, and I tell you this, that in the time of Moses, God sent a plague that killed all the Egyptian's livestock, but the animals belonging to the Israelites were spared. Tomorrow, the Lord will do this in this land. All your livestock will become sick and die, but not one animal belonging to those who accept His word will die. For all those that would like to know the gentle hand of God, find your way to my left and your way to peace and joy," he said, as flocks of people moved to be put in a line guarded by armed men.

"Terrorist!" rang out a voice from the crowd.

"False prophet!" rang out another.

The crowd caught on, chanting together, "false prophet, false prophet." Jeremiah waited stoically for the chant to die down and dropped his head in mock defeat.

"I see that some of you require more convincing."

The crowd broke into angry cheers, obscenities and threats of death valiantly coming from unknown sources.

"Then to prove the veracity of my faith, I offer you a contest. If you can best me in hand-to-hand combat, you may all go in peace, and I will trouble you no more. I will leave and take my men with me. For if I am righteous, then God will provide me with the strength to crush my enemies, but if I am a false prophet, I will be tore asunder."

Many men moved to the front of the large crowd. They loosened their shirts and cracked their necks, readying themselves to pulverize Jeremiah. He jumped to the ground into the center of them. He was big, bigger than most, but there were so many and the crowd took heart in the incredibly lopsided battle.

There was no hesitation as twenty men rushed Jeremiah at once, their weight collapsing him to the ground. Kicking and punching, the crowd watched the fight and grew more violent by the second, cheering for Jeremiah's death. Those who had chosen to convert began to loose their resolve as the battle wore on. It was at that moment, ten seconds into the fight, that eight men flew into the side of the semi trailer with intense force. Several others went tumbling to the ground, as Jeremiah stood erect, holding the limp forms of two large men by the neck in each hand.

The crowd murmured in disbelief as a fresh new group of men rushed in to the fight, seemingly by the hundreds. Jeremiah struck at a tremendous speed, each strike delivering a killing blow. The amount of violence and the efficiency in which he delivered death seemed impossible. He never once stopped preaching as he received and distributed blows.

Jeremiah's voice blanketed the sounds of battle.

"He poured out on them his burning anger and the violence of war. It enveloped them in flames, yet they did not understand. It consumed them, but they did not take it to heart," he smiled in revelry, looking to God as much as his assailants.

The bodies began to stack up, and Jeremiah climbed behind them, making his opponents advance more difficult. An older woman who seemed crazy came at him with a knitting needle, and he snapped her neck with barely a touch.

"As water pours from a well, so she pours out her wickedness. Violence and destruction resound in her. Take warning, I will turn away from you and your land will become desolate."

At that moment, a long metal pole slammed into the back of Jeremiah's head. The pure crack of bone and metal sickened those nearest to the battle, and everyone stopped as Jeremiah looked as if he would topple over. Barely keeping his feet, he reached to his head and wiped a steady stream of blood, which dripped onto his shoulders.

Jeremiah looked at his blood and caught the pole blindly with his bare hand as it came in for a second and deadly strike. He stared at the man holding the other end and bared his teeth. The expression on his face distorted into pure rage.

"Prepare the chains, because the land is full of bloodshed, and this city is full of violence! I will bring the most wicked of the nations to take possession of your houses! I will put an end to the pride of the mighty, and their sanctuaries will be desecrated," he said with intensity.

"When terror comes, they will seek peace, but there will be none!" he yelled.

Jeremiah pulled the pole from the man's grasp and began to swing it side to side. Death was abounding. The crowd shrunk from him and crushed one another to the ground, trampling and trying to save themselves from the madman who was a killing machine. As the crowd surged away from him, many fell into the river and were whisked away by the current. Jeremiah's armed guards watched in amazement as their leader manifested a superhuman ability that came directly from God, the extent of which none had ever seen before.

On a bluff across the Missouri River on the Iowa side, Col. Bragg watched the carnage through a pair of long-range binoculars.

"My God!" he said incredulously.

From this distance, it looked as if the people were just lying down before the large man, but it was clear that he was smashing them. The colonel didn't believe it was possible for one man to do so much damage, but he saw it with his own eyes. He had seen this scenario play out before. In a power vacuum, all sorts of leaders arise to exploit the weaknesses of others, and they typically leave the smell of death in their wake. But something was different about this man, beside the fact that he had strength that bordered on the supernatural.

Col. Bragg was only able to hear sporadic parts of the message, but what he did hear was enough to convince him that the man was some sort of cult preacher. He had performed some reconnaissance by walking over the pedestrian bridge to take a closer look, but things began to descend into a bad situation quickly, so he retreated to a bluff near Lake Manawa where he could observe.

He estimated the size of the cult to be at least thirty thousand, many of which were armed with guns and clubs. Too many guns to take a chance, he thought, so he decided that he would have to go farther north to find an alternate route over the river.

Col. Bragg stowed his binoculars and was locking down his gear in the back of the Humvee when he noticed a truck with large tires speeding his way. Instinctively, he felt for the presence of his hidden weapons as the truck skidded to a stop in front of him, spraying dirt and dust everywhere. Two thin middle-aged men jumped out, holding shotguns.

"What the hell you think you're doin', mister?" asked the passenger.

Col. Bragg could immediately tell that they were nervous. They were not comfortable with guns, at least not pointing them at humans, and that made them even more dangerous. Scared men were unpredictable.

"Minding my own business, and I'll just be on my way," he said and moved to get in the Humvee.

"Stop right there, you ain't goin' nowhere," said the other man, both men pointing their weapons at his head.

Col. Bragg stopped and elevated his hands slightly, trying not to show his annoyance.

"I think we goin' ta introduce you to Jeremiah, army man," said the driver.

Col. Bragg nodded toward the raging man across the river.

"Is that Jeremiah?"

Both men smiled and nodded, obviously in awe of the man.

"Well, I thank you for the offer, but I would rather not meet him. I have somewhere to be, so if you'll excuse me—"

The passenger hit Col. Bragg in the stomach with the butt of his shotgun and then across the face, which landed Col. Bragg hard on the ground. He lay in the fetal position for a moment, nursing his bloody nose.

"You do whatever Jeremiah wants you ta do. Whatever the Sons of the Apocalypse say. Here me, boy?" said the driver, who placed the barrel of his gun on Col. Bragg's cheek.

"I do," Col. Bragg said softly.

"Go get some rope, we gonna tie this boy on up and bring 'em ta Jeremiah," the driver said while making the mistake of taking his eyes off the colonel.

Col. Bragg slipped a Gerber from his boot and sunk the knife hilt deep into the inside of the man's thigh, grabbed the shotgun, and shot the other man at center mass. He died instantly. The driver wiggled around on the ground, moaning, but his movements soon became slower as he bled out.

Col. Bragg ignored him, gathered their shotguns, and searched their truck. He found a couple of cans of gas, a long-range portable two-way radio, and a few boxes of shells. The gunshot blast bothered him, as he suspected that it would attract attention and if this Jeremiah had patrols out this far, then others wouldn't be that far away. Col. Bragg didn't waste a moment getting back into his Humvee and heading north to find an alternate route across the Missouri River.

Jeremiah stopped swinging the pole as his blood began to cool. He stood on the bodies of a thousand men and woman, some dying, but most already dead. For the second time that day, nothing could be heard but the sound of the gentle breeze and the slosh of the river. All that broke the silence was the echo of a single gunshot blast from across the river.

Jeremiah dropped the pole, which was painted red with blood, and looked into the fearful eyes of the remaining men and women. He looked monstrous covered in blood, his clothes were saturated red and in tatters. He was a man who had just walked out of hell. When he spoke, he was slightly out of breath.

"There is only one way to salvation and I bring that to you. If you choose His word, then no longer will violence be heard in your land. Nor destruction, but you will call your walls salvation and your gates praise. The sun will no more be your light by day or the brightness of the moon shine on you, for the Lord will be your everlasting light and God your glory."

He stood in the sunlight, which reflected off his red-stained skin, colored that hue by a combination of blood and sweat. Almost forty thousand people converted that afternoon, and the rest were gunned down with their remains left behind to feed the birds.

Chapter 20

L T. FINN STOOD on the rooftop of a high-rise building surrounded by twenty armed soldiers. She had been watching the large man preach from the top of the trailer through a pair of long-range binoculars. She estimated that at least a hundred thousand people had been captured and brought there to listen to the man.

Most of the citizens had escaped the city, but she even saw some of those run down and shot by the man's security forces. She was familiar with these tactics because she had often employed them to intimidate and make people afraid to leave, discombobulate them, and slow their reflexes.

This man, whoever he was, had knowledge of military tactics, which was good to know. His force was at least twenty thousand strong and appeared to be growing, and she guessed this was his way of conscripting new troops. Social deconstruction was on its way and only the strongest would survive. She noted that he was gathering together a large force, while she preferred to be able to move fast and be agile, the lion in the brush so to speak.

One of her soldiers came through the door from below, followed by several others. The leader, Sgt. Thomas, was slightly out of breath, and she could tell that he was operating on adrenaline.

"Ma'am, we've been spotted. We lost Simms and Rodriguez. Acevedra caught a few rounds in the back. He made it to the building, but he'll be dead in an hour," the sergeant said, not pleased with losing some of his men.

Staff Sergeant Mathew Thomas was an army lifer. He was divorced twice and had one teenage son whom he never talked to. Not because he was an unkind father, but because his son had been programmed by his ex-wife to think he was. He got remarried to a beautiful girl within a year of his first divorce and drank a lifetime's worth of alcohol during the two years that they were together. He was demoted once during that time period and passed over for first sergeant more than a few times. He should have been a master sergeant.

Recently, Sgt. Thomas had gotten into the good graces of a certain colonel who recognized his particular skill set. Sgt. Thomas developed the reputation of being an efficient killer who had the ability to think for himself, particularly in tense situations. He was a natural leader who garnered respect from his fellow soldiers, and he was a brilliant ground tactician.

"Did they track you here?" Lt. Finn asked without taking down the binoculars.

"I didn't see them do so, but they're all over the place. I think it best to assume we've been made and move, ma'am."

She dropped the binoculars and looked at him as if she had never seen him before.

"What's your name, soldier?"

"Sgt. Thomas, ma'am."

"Staff Sergeant Thomas, when I require your feeble assumptions, I'll ask. Until that time presents itself, I would appreciate that you do what I order you to do. Although, it seems you can't even do that," she said and went back to looking at the large man.

Jeremiah was no longer on the trailer and from this vantage point, and she couldn't see on the other side. The crowd was moving, pushing forward. Something was going on, but she couldn't tell what it was. She stepped up onto the edge of the roof to gain a better view.

"Danger close," a soldier shouted, just as a shotgun blast made Lt. Finn spin around to see what was happening.

The soldier guarding the door collapsed when he was hit with the shotgun blast and a stream of hostile civilians poured in through the door headed for the rooftop, firing randomly. They were untrained but made up for it with zeal and numbers.

Two more of Lt. Finn's soldiers went down before the rest of her force returned fire. Lt. Finn's soldiers were well trained and immediately assumed assault positions by dropping down to their knees or stomachs, while some of the soldiers took cover behind vents and cooling units.

The civilians began to drop like flies, but they kept coming, a few of them heading straight for Lt. Finn. She watched with interest as they fired at her, but she did not flinch, only waited until they were close enough. The final shot was so close that several of the bee-bees from the shotgun shell hit her arm with enough force to spin her around, but she continued the movement using the inertia to catapult herself into the air, flipping over the two men that were charging her.

The maneuver was an extraordinary move that required incredible agility. She landed behind them and knocked the barrel of one gun sideways as it fired. The blast hit the second man in the head. Without pausing, she rolled over the dead man and drew out a long knife with a slightly curved blade that he carried in a sheath at his side.

The second gunman turned toward her but was met by a series of slices to his hands. Lt. Finn targeted ligaments in his wrist and elbows, severing them cleanly. The man dropped the weapon as he lost the use of his hands and stared at her in complete disbelief, the pain only beginning to set in.

As it turned out, the pain wouldn't have a chance to fully register. Using his shoulder to launch herself, Lt. Finn flipped completely over the man and sliced his throat deeply and cleanly, leaving a perfect red line just below his Adam's apple. He was dead before his body landed on the roof.

The lieutenant paused as she watched his dead form crumble before her. She was impressed with her own skill. She could feel her strength increasing and her senses becoming more acute. The virus had improved on the skills she desired most, those that she used to hunt, to kill, to cull. And she felt overjoyed to finally be completely free to do her work.

When the gunfight was over, twenty men lay dead, including three of her own men, and several others were injured. Her men knew something was different about her. The way she moved was inhuman, but no one said a word. Sgt. Thomas took stock of the situation and reported.

"Three dead, ma'am. Once the injured are checked out, we'll be able to move in five mikes. What do you want us to do with the bodies?"

"Leave them," she said, still watching the blood ooze from the neck wound of the civilian she had just carved up.

"Sorry, ma'am, I meant ours."

"So did I, and we move now! If the injured can't make it down the stairs, then they're not fit to be in my company."

She looked over to where the large man had been standing. Even without the binoculars, she could now see him standing closer to the river with a long red pole in his hands. Bodies were strewn all around him. Her lips curled into a smile; she liked him already.

Sgt. Thomas watched her leave, with anger building inside him. He never left a man. Quickly and quietly, he assigned two men to each injured soldier, and they worked their way to the stairs. The fire alarm had been triggered at some point in the original attack, and the elevators were not in working order. The sergeant waited until each man had left the roof and pulled a dog tag off each dead soldier and added them to a pocket that already had a few in it.

This mission didn't feel like a mission any longer to Sgt. Thomas. The world was changing, and Lt. Finn didn't allow access to the radio or any national media. He was not accustomed to being in the dark and would have to find a way to get more information. The large man, the one they called Jeremiah, was a worry, but Lt. Finn was running a close second to him.

Something had changed in her and not just her physical abilities. It was an empty look that appeared in her eyes. He knew that look, had seen it before in battle. It bothered him. He took one last look at his dead friends and heard a distant gunshot. It came from the river, but too far away to be of any danger to him, so he ran from the roof to rejoin his soldiers.

Chapter 21

Sara had been steadily getting worse. It was clear that the initial defense that her immune system mounted against the virus had been overpowered, which left her vulnerable. Her fever was high and spiked several times a day until, eventually, Carrisa decided it would be best to induce a coma. Keeping her asleep and controlling her body temperature were essential to buying them more time.

Don had become more and more reclusive, spending most of his time sitting in the room with her. He no longer wore a protective mask, which increased the potential of him getting and spreading the virus, but no one had the mustard to say anything to him.

Over the last couple of days, Tony had developed a tickle in the back of his nasal cavity, the beginnings of a cold that included just a touch of fuzziness in his head. He told no one, as he felt that they had enough to worry about.

Tony poured over everything that he knew about the pandemic, thinking and rethinking all the angles. He made a list of the things that he needed to understand in order to continue attacking the problem, and he racked his brain for a clever way to outfox a virus that had obviously evolved to exploit human beings at their own level of complexity.

Carrisa knew that getting Tony to agree to the induction of comastasis would be a bit tricky. His training as a virologist and subsequent experience in molecular virology was lacking in clinic experience, so Carrisa had to explain to him the merits of inducing such a state. But strangely, it was she herself who had the strongest misgivings about the procedure. Since the startling news of her pregnancy, she had been acting strangely maternal around Sara, and suddenly, she had become very protective of the little girl. The two had almost always been inseparable, but now Carrisa felt a strong kinship with Sara that she had not previously felt.

In her early years with Tony, Carrisa had always thought that she would become a mother and that Tony would be the father of her children. But somehow, she had imagined the whole thing happening with more joy and more happy deliberation. She had given up on this dream many different times over the years, with the final surrender coming when cancer had attacked her ovaries.

Doctors that she trusted had told her that the odds of her having children were next to nil. Only her mother had believed that it was still possible and her mother refused to let her give up completely. But secretly Carrisa had. So when she looked at the first home pregnancy test that she purchased on the trip to Pierre for supplies, she insisted that it was impossible. She repeated the test three times, and had Tony and Ramsey independently verify the results.

In the end, there was no question. She was pregnant, and Tony was the father. She remembered some of her more hopeful dreams about such a day and felt resentful that she and Tony could not put aside their differences long enough to celebrate this joyful news. She was resentful that it happened at such an uncertain time. She worried that the virus would take the child before it was born. Perhaps it was the uncertainty surrounding her unborn child's future that gave her pause regarding Sara.

Once Tony was brought up to speed on comastasis, his promise to Don and Sara propelled him to become a strong advocate for the procedure, even though it came with huge risks. He could sense that Carrisa's misgivings were fueled by her own fears, but he knew that he needed her support and expertise to accomplish it.

"This is her only chance," Tony began. "We have to assume the risks."

"And if it doesn't work, we will have killed her instead of the virus," Carrisa replied, playing devil's advocate.

"And if she lives, we save her. I promised her and Don that I would do whatever was necessary to save her life, and this falls under those parameters."

"Okay," she replied. "Lets do it. I'll get the room ready, you get Don's okay."

Getting Don to agree was not so difficult. He was an emotional wreck, and he was willing to do whatever was necessary to see his little girl back to health. He did not necessarily like Tony's bedside manner, but he trusted him. He believed that Tony would save her. He believed it with every fiber of his being, and so he surrendered to that impulse and turned his little girl's life over to the doctors.

When everyone was ready, Carrisa wheeled Sara into the makeshift intensive care room that had been set up in the clean room. She then administered the sedatives that would allow Sara's brain to reach a state of hibernation, retarding the onset of inflammation and stalling the long-term repercussions of brain swelling. Carrisa carefully monitored the sedative dose, and indicated to Tony that more was needed to induce her into the comatose state.

In addition to the coma, Carrisa set up a large water bath that had been chilled with ice. Once Sara reached the comatose state, her body was carefully lowered into the ice bath, and her body temperature was monitored. Ice bath therapy continued as a means of controlling her fever over the course of several days.

Meanwhile, Tony poured over the data that he had collected in the lab. He knew that the virus was infectious, and that even dilutions as low as one to ten million were enough to kill a monolayer of cells in twenty-four hours. Attempts to plaque purify the virus had failed because the virus replicated so efficiently that it managed to create enormous plaques that quickly overlapped with each other, even at the lowest dilutions.

They also tested a variety of cleaning solvents such as bleach and ammonia, heating, cooling, and UV irradiation in an attempt to kill the virus before plating, and in every case, it had no effect. Whatever this virus was, it was efficient at replicating in a variety of cells lines from two different kingdoms, it spread rapidly to other cells in the culture, and it was highly stable under a variety of temperatures and conditions.

The data further indicated that it was a non-enveloped virus with a spectacular protein capsid capable of withstanding a variety of harsh treatments, including boiling, freezing and thawing, UV irradiation, and high salt and sugar concentrations. In addition, they were still unable to isolate and detect viral DNA or RNA.

This was puzzling to Tony, but he reasoned that this could simply mean that the virus capsid protects the viral DNA or RNA extremely well, such that it is never separated from the capsid protein. In other words, nothing seemed to kill this thing.

Tony was impressed with this virus and its ability to adapt and evolve. He was quickly learning that it was far more complex than any virus that he had ever worked with or read about. It seemed to be engineered to perfection, and he wondered what environment would be required to evolve such a perfect viral machine.

Reports in the news indicated that people infected with the virus were becoming more aggressive. Many of those infected regained strength and agility, and some were becoming almost superhuman in strength.

Plants and animals, birds and insects, fish, and even some fungi were being destroyed by the virus at a record pace while some humans seemed to be improving. At least those that survived. The young and the old were succumbing to disease, but not all of the rest. Those that survived infection seemed to becoming stronger, and even more dangerous.

Tony wondered how nature could provide something so perfect for the exploitation of human physiology. Could it be some supernatural phenomenon? Was Don right? Did this thing come from outer space? If it did not use RNA or DNA, how was it replicating itself?

Tony had been working for over thirty hours straight when he decided to take a break and check in on Sara. He had been checking on her every couple of hours, and although she did not look good, her brain inflammation had been slowed by the coma, the swelling was under control, and the ice therapy reduced her overall body temperature. It was clear that the virus was no longer winning the fight by a mile, but it was still ahead by a lot.

Tony looked over at Don, who had been a fixture by his daughter's side. He had perpetual dark circles under his eyes, and Tony could see that he was losing weight.

"You do look tired, *mon ami*."

It took Tony a moment to register that Don had spoke.

"Yeah, you too."

"Is my sher' gonna die?" Don asked with no pretense.

"Not on my watch, Don," Tony said, trying to build confidence for the man.

"That do be good, 'cause you made me a deal. Where I come from, all a man has when he go from this world is his word and if he did keep it or no."

And then Don did something that he hadn't done in several days. He turned and left the room, not waiting for a response. Tony watched as he made his exit and realized that Don was on the verge of tears. Tony wondered what would happen to Don if Sara were to die, but he didn't wait for his mind to put together an image.

Instead, he made a list of every last thing that he would try in an attempt to save her life if the ongoing therapies failed to turn her around. After a few moments of thought, Tony walked quietly into Ramsey's quarters and shook him awake.

"What is it?" Ramsey asked, blinking the sleep away from his eyes.

"I need more supplies. I need you to make a call."

Ramsey shook his head, looked at Tony until he remembered who he was, and then went immediately to make the call. Tony handed him a list on his way out the door and then vowed to get some rest so that he would have a fresh mind for the next day. However, he was really wound up and had reached a state of complete exhaustion, so he decided that he needed a little help getting to sleep.

Tony lit a joint he had been carrying in his pocket and inhaled a monster toke. He could feel his body loosen and his mind relax as he exhaled the smoke. Tony took another deep inhale as his mind focused on the prospect of being a father. He was sure that he was the father of her baby, even though Carrie had said nothing about it. As he exhaled, he decided to stop by Sara's room to say good night. Don was still away, so Tony took the opportunity to speak to her, to explain to her what the situation looked like and to make peace with her.

Although the coma and ice therapy slowed the virus down, Tony felt that it was just a matter of time before she would succumb to the effects of the virus. They could control some of the symptoms, but ultimately, they could not control the cause, and unless something drastic happened within the next few days, he was afraid that she would die.

He looked at her sweet, young face and noticed how it looked lifeless and pale. He felt that it was unfair that someone so young would be robbed of the opportunity to experience life. It didn't make sense to him that someone with such a kind heart would meet such a cruel fate. It only added to his own agnosticism, as he could not believe that any God could blindly reside over such pain and sorrow.

"I'm sorry it's come to this, Sara, I really am," he started.

"I promise I'm doing my best, but I'm not sure if my best is going to be good enough."

There was a note of resignation in his voice.

"If there's a way, I'll find it, whatever it takes. There just might not be one, and I wanted you to know that."

When he finished talking to Sara, Tony noticed that the room was starting to fill with smoke from his joint. He had unintentionally taken it into the room with him, and he quickly left, feeling embarrassed. He had made it a habit to ridicule every idiot he had ever seen driving around in their car, smoking a cigarette with kids in the back seat. And now he felt like a bit of a hypocrite as he scurried out of the room before Don came back. But the joint had done for him what he wanted. He felt calm enough to go to sleep, and the tickle in the back of his throat was gone.

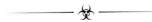

It took two excruciatingly long days for Ramsey to get confirmation on the requested supplies from Irish. But finally, the meeting was set, and Tony was eager to get there and make the pick up. Carrisa had asked to go, and he could think of no good reason to say no, although being alone in the truck with her made him a bit uncomfortable. They hadn't spoken about the baby at all, and as a matter of fact, they hadn't spoken at all unless it was about the virus.

Carrisa didn't say a word during the entire drive into Pierre, and Tony didn't have the courage to initiate a conversation either. Once they arrived in town, Carrisa said she had some things to pick up and left without further explanation. Tony waited for Irish. The town was eerily quiet, almost abandoned. Of the few neon signs in town, only one was lit up.

The sound of a truck soon echoed from around the corner, and Irish parked his truck in front of Tony in the alley. Something about Irish was slightly different. Tony had only met him the one time, but Irish was the kind of guy that left an impression on him.

The exuberance and energy he exhibited in the prior meeting was not present this time.

Tony nodded a hello but kept silent and alert.

"Well met, mate," Irish said and leaned on the back of his truck.

The silence was palpable, and Tony was a little impatient. Time was the one thing he didn't have.

"Well, do you have it?" Tony asked impatiently.

"Aye, I do, but there's been a bit of a change, I'm afraid."

"And what would that be?"

"I'll be needin' two hundred thousand dollars from ya for the load," Irish said with a sober expression, clearly not messing around.

"The deal was twenty-five thousand. A deal is a deal."

"Aye, that is true normally, I'm a man of my word."

"But…" Tony let it hang.

"But these are not normal times. And this load was especially difficult to come about, as I'm sure you are aware they're a bit valuable these days. I could get more than I'm askin' somewhere else."

Tony steamed; he never trusted Irish from the start. He was a little too charming, too put together. But Tony needed those supplies. Sara's life depended on them. He thought of the shotgun behind the seat in the truck, but he wasn't particularly experienced with guns, and he was sure Irish had some way of protecting himself.

"I have fifty."

"Not good enough, mate. Two hundred, I'm not negotiating."

Tony was desperate, and Irish knew it.

"I can give you one hundred, maybe a little a more. It's all I have, everything, but you need to understand how important that load is. It's not for me—"

Irish silenced him with his hand.

"You don't have two hundred thousand dollars then, do you?"

Tony knew he would have to lie. Everything relied on that supply of antivirals and antibiotics in that truck.

"How about a trade?" Irish said with his familiar charm returning.

Tony knew he was on thin ice. This wasn't where he was most effective, being a tough guy. He had always been able to outthink his opponents, but most often, they were in a glass vial.

"Trade?"

"Aye, trade. And I'll let you keep all your money."

"Nothing is free in life, Irish. Nothing."

"That's true, and neither will this be, but fair it is. You have my word on it."

"Your word, isn't that ironic?" Tony said.

"Aye, isn't this world a bit ironic?"

Irish lifted the roller door on the truck. It was full of boxes with medical nomenclature printed on them. Tony's eyes lit up. There were five times the number of medicines that he ordered. Tony noticed Irish flinch when he reached for the door and saw a blood spot soaked through his shirt, beneath his coat just under his rib cage.

"Seems a few boxes fell off a truck. I just happened along." Irish smiled, trying to keep the pain from registering on his face.

"So trade you say?" Tony reiterated.

"There has been quite a run on antibiotics and antivirals of late. Hospitals are hoarding, no longer prescribing them to patients they know are dying. People's lives are being decided in triage, just like in the wars of ancient days. There's irony for ya, mate. This is everything. I doubt there will be anymore, at least not that I can get." Irish flinched again and grabbed his side.

"What happened?"

"So are we agreed? You keep the money and the drugs." Irish clutched his side harder.

"I need to know the terms. What am I trading?" Tony said concerned about his injury.

"Safety. Food. Shelter."

Tony was confused.

"I don't understand. You need shelter and safety?"

Irish smiled with a touch of condescension and whistled. Out of the shadows of the truck, two young people walked out. The teenage girl was dirty and shy. She barely raised her eyes, but when she saw Tony there was an immediate connection. Her long dark hair covered most of her face, but from the portion that could be seen, she was still pretty. The only blemish on her youthful face was a large cold sore that sat prominently on the left side of her lip.

Also emerging from the shadows was an older boy, who looked as if he had been living in a ditch. He did not come across as being the shy type, but his posture suggested that he was guarded and very protective of the girl.

"This is Annie and Noah. They're brother and sister. They've been orphaned and need tending to. Tending to kids is not my business," Irish said as he leaned a little more heavily onto the side of his truck.

"You want me to take the kids, and if I do, you'll give me the load for free?" Tony asked.

"Aye, that's the deal, mate. Take it or leave it."

Tony watched him for a few moments, as the realization that he had misjudged this man overtook him. He shook his head, wanting very much to apologize but as per usual, his pride got in the way.

Tony laughed, causing a slowly fading Irish to smile as well.

"What's that, mate?"

"Annie. Little orphan Annie. There's some irony."

Both men laughed out loud, finding something funny in the middle of so much pain, and then suddenly Irish keeled over. He fell to the ground with his body bouncing off the bumper of his truck as he dropped.

A few blocks away, Carrisa dialed a payphone and waited for the person on the other end to pick up. Her eyes darted from side to side.

"Hello," said a scratchy voice.

"Sandy, it's Carrie."

"Hello?" the voice said again.

"Sandy, can you hear me?"

The phone clicked and a dial tone followed.

"Damn it," Carrisa said as she looked around again and withdrew her cell phone and redialed. She knew that Tony would not approve of the cell phone use, but she vowed to keep the call short.

"Who is this!" the scratchy voiced answered.

"Sandy?"

"Carrie, is that you? It's so good to hear your voice. I thought you might be… Where are you?"

"Out west. Listen, I need to know what's going on there in Atlanta."

"It's bad. Couple of labs got raided by looters or extremist…I don't know, but it's bad. Lot of sick people. The kids, Carrie, my God, they're all dead."

"Are you okay?"

"I'm fine. I have had a little chest congestion, but otherwise, I am fine. There is looting still going on downtown. We stay in at night. Quite honestly, I am worried about running out of food. All the grocery stores here are pretty much bare, and there are no trucks coming in to restock them. You think the White House screwed up Katrina? Well, nobody's even heard from this president yet."

"Look, are there any patterns or strange symptoms, anything? We haven't been able to track recent events very well."

"What are you doing, Carrie? And what do you mean we?"

Carrisa stalled for a moment and tried to sound upbeat.

"I'm with Tony. He's trying to find a cure," she said, her voice becoming more serious.

"He's the only one who can do it, Sandy, and there's this little girl. She's going die. Anything, any information might help," she said as a tear rolled down her cheek.

"I'll tell you what I know, Carrie."

Carrisa walked back to the alley where Tony parked the truck and saw him struggling to load an unconscious Irish into the back of Don's pickup. She ran the rest of the way toward them.

"What the hell happened?" she asked.

"I think he's been shot," Tony answered.

Carrisa helped him get Irish onto the bed and then pulled his shirt up, which revealed a bullet hole from which a steady stream of blood was pumping.

"We need to get him…" She stopped short when she saw the two teenagers standing on the back of Irish's truck, looking abashed.

"Who are they?"

"They're irony. You drive Don's truck. I'll get the other one and explain later."

They secured Irish in the back of the pickup, and Tony ordered the kids to get into the back with him to prevent him from moving around during the drive. The kids moved robotically, but obeyed.

Irish was a thickly built man, and it was difficult for Carrisa and Tony to get him to the lift inside the old Quonset hut and down to the lab. The kids followed quietly, staying close to one another. Once they were down, Ramsey ran over to help.

"What happened?" Ramsey asked.

"He was shot," Tony replied.

"You shot him?"

"No. I found him this way."

"Who are they?" Ramsey asked when he noticed the kids.

"Let's focus, we need to get him in bed, we can discuss it later," Carrisa ordered, feeling comfortable being the leader during a medical emergency.

"Once we get him on the table, I will need you both to scrub in and join me."

Fortunately for Irish, the old lab had been set up to perform surgical procedures on primates, and Ramsey had the foresight to update some of the basic surgical supplies before his guests arrived.

Carrisa took command of the operating room, almost reverting to her old form as an ER resident, even though it was a chapter of her life that had been long closed. Irish's operation was successful. Carrisa was able to remove the rather large caliber bullet out of his side, and unexpectedly had to remove his damaged spleen. During the process, he had lost a lot of blood.

Fortunately, Noah had a blood type of O negative and was able to donate some of his blood to be transfused into Irish to keep him alive. When the operation was finished, Carrisa removed the IV from Noah's arm and covered Irish with a blanket. They left the operating room, and as they walked down the corridor, Tony saw Don sitting in Sara's room, watching her vacantly.

"He hasn't moved," said Ramsey from behind. "Now, tell me what happened?"

"Not sure," Tony shrugged. "He was shot when I got there. Told me the price had changed and offered me a trade."

Tony pointed to the two teens. Noah was just taking a seat across the lab and scraggly Annie was eating ravenously while peering at them from behind her hair.

"We need to get the supplies down here and hide the vehicles," Tony said, trying to ignore her.

Lt. Finn rode in the passenger seat of her Humvee, followed by her company, which followed close behind in several Humvees and an armored truck. Staff Sergeant Thomas rode point just ahead. The point vehicle began to slow and pulled off the road just shy of the South Dakota border. Twenty miles ahead of them was Jeremiah's convoy, at least the rear guard, and she didn't want to lose them. Sgt. Thomas got out of his vehicle and approached her.

"Ma'am…"

"There better be a hell of a good reason to stop, Sergeant," she said, practically gritting her teeth.

Sgt. Thomas had noticed that on top of everything else, she could barely control her temper. Upon leaving Omaha, one of his privates contradicted her. It was a young person's mistake, but only a slight breach of protocol. Lt. Finn broke his arm in two places with blinding speed. She meant it as a lesson in subordination and humility. Many of the men were scared of her now, but not him; he was angry.

"Yes, ma'am. Two things, first I think we're still being followed."

"Ludicrous, Sergeant, I told you we dealt with them, don't bring it up again."

On her way out of Omaha, she had ambushed the second set of spies. Jeremiah, however, had placed a third set of military-trained brothers on her trail. He sensed her in Omaha, sensed her watching him and acted in accordance with his instincts. The plan had worked, and she was ignoring the experience of Sgt. Thomas.

"Go on," she ordered.

"We had a hit on that trace you asked about when we were back in Chicago. I've had the men checking on a regular basis. It was the same cell number."

Lt. Finn jumped up and seized Sgt. Thomas by the front of his vest.

"Where? Where is she?"

"They only had enough time to get a general fix, they couldn't triangulate, but within a couple hundred miles of Sioux Falls, best guess," Sgt. Thomas said, not liking the look in her eyes.

Lt. Finn looked to be on the verge of ecstasy.

"Oh so close, my little doctor. So close, and you too will find your place in this world," she said and came back to the present.

"Don't just stand there, Sergeant, let's get moving!"

Sgt. Thomas turned and jogged back to his Humvee and ordered the company to move forward.

Chapter 22

June 28, 2018

S ARA'S RECOVERY BEGAN as soon as she was taken out of the comatose state. Her fever stopped spiking, although she continued to run a low-grade fever. Her color was better, and she even regained a small appetite. Tony listened to her chest and nodded to Carrisa who had done the same thing a moment earlier.

"I'm glad you're feeling better, Sara," Tony said with a smile.

He and Carrisa walked out of the room to confer. Don watched them leave with suspicious thoughts, but he desperately wanted Sara to be on the mend.

"Did you hear it?" Carrisa asked.

"Fluid. She is really laboring to breathe."

"There's still an infection, I think, it just…stopped progressing."

"You mean it could be going from an acute infection to a chronic one?"

"I'm not sure…but she has improved in many areas."

"What else could be going on?" Tony asked.

"Maybe her immune system has started to overtake the virus…"

"Carrie, you know as well as I do that someone that sick does not just shift clinical courses that quickly. Whatever was killing that girl is still there, but something changed. Something altered the way it works. What could that be?"

"Perhaps the induced coma stopped the virus from replicating, put it into a sort of latency?"

Don interrupted, looking incredibly tired, but exhibiting the first smile they had seen on his face in a long time.

"I thank you both. What medicine did you use to make her better?" he asked.

Tony looked at his feet, trying to come up with an answer, but Carrisa stepped in.

"We haven't administered anything to her yet, Don," she answered.

"Well, is that a good thing?"

"I don't know," she said softly.

"Tony, what you think?" he asked in a pleading manner.

Tony sighed.

"I think this is temporary, Don. She might get better, she might get worse, there's no way we can know. We're going to give her some antivirals, interferon and ribavirin, and some others generic broad-spectrum protease and replicase inhibitors. If she gets worse, we will continue with the ice bath therapy and possibly put her back in a coma. Until we understand how the virus works, all we can do is try to stabilize her and do what we can to help her immune system kill the virus. Right now, it looks like we can slow the virus down, but we are not able to stop it."

"I see," Don said, trying to hold back tears. "Maybe she get better anyway."

"Maybe," Tony said reluctantly. "One thing I know for sure is that you can never count a young person out. They are strong and their immune systems are flexible. We just have to wait this out and keep supporting her as best as we can."

The fearful look entered Don's eyes once again, and he returned to the room with his daughter.

"I need an X-ray machine, Tony. I need to get a look at her lungs."

Tony continued to watch Sara laugh and her father pretended to not be worried. He nodded to Carrisa.

"I'll talk to Irish…"

"You'll talk to me about what?" Irish said from behind them.

Irish stood up straight but was in obvious discomfort. His shirt was off, but his lower abdomen was wrapped in bandages.

"You should be on your back," Carrisa said sternly.

"Are ya getting fresh with me, lass? Give me a day or two, and I'll take you up on your offer."

She smiled despite herself, and the flirting sent a tinge of jealousy through Tony's stomach.

"I need an X-ray machine. I heard you were a man who could get things," she said.

"There's a hospital in Sioux Falls that has an older machine in the basement. It's on wheels. It can be rolled out right into a truck."

"And film?"

"Aye, lass, that too, I'm sure."

"How would you know that?" Tony asked.

"You've got to know the right people."

"And do you?" Carrisa asked playfully.

"I do, but I'll need some help. Movin' a bit slow these days." He pointed at the wound.

Carrisa's expression changed to one of concern.

"Oh no, you can't travel. That wound will rupture. The chance of infection is too high. Sorry, doctor's orders."

Irish shrugged.

"I can do it," Tony said. "Just break it down and make it easy for me. I can get it done."

"Aye. Well, you know what they say, if you make something easy enough for a fool to do, only a fool will do it," he said with that charming smile.

"Murphy?" asked Tony.

"Aye and the Irish…"

"Are never wrong," finished Tony.

"No, absolutely not, I forbid it!" Carrisa said adamantly.

Irish stared over into the room where Don held his daughter's hand and made her laugh.

"She's beautiful, isn't she?" Irish said.

Carrisa followed his gaze and felt her resolve start to fade immediately.

"It'll be all right, lass. And I've got your strapping doctor here to get me through."

Tony touched her shoulder.

"It will be okay, Carrie. I promise."

Carrie never took her eyes off the little girl and placed her hand over her own stomach unconsciously.

Before they left the next day, Tony mixed up several different doses of the interferon, ribavirin, and other antiviral drugs and inhibitors that he thought might slow the virus. He knew that they didn't have enough time to test them all because Sara's condition could degenerate at any moment.

Ramsey's job was to test the different preparations by incubating them on the cell lines prior to or just after infecting them with the viral samples. Carrisa would administer any treatment preparation that she thought might work best based on Ramsey's results. The downside was that some of the treatments, in particular the interferon, were going to be hard on her young body, but it would be a necessary discomfort if the preliminary results indicated that it might work to kill the virus.

Ramsey escorted Irish and Tony topside to make sure everything was secure. He grabbed Tony by the arm and spun him around to face him.

"Listen to me, Genius, I don't have a lot of time left. So be quick about your business."

"What's that supposed to mean?" Tony asked with a laugh.

Ramsey squeezed his arm tighter for emphasis.

"I finished checking all the blood samples using the electron microscope. The large virus particles are present in everyone. We're all infected."

Tony looked incredulous.

"What? Everyone?"

"All but one."

"Don."

"Correct, Genius."

"Then we caught a break. Let's start running a series of…"

Ramsey interrupted.

"I don't have a lot of time. I find myself fading in and out. I'm not sure how much help I'm going to be. So be on your way and get back in a jiffy. Somebody's got to put a cork in this thing."

"Ramsey I'm sure…"

"Don't try to bullshit me, Genius. I'm ten years past sixty-five, and this virus shows no mercy for old farts. Just get the damn machine and get back here as quickly as possible," Ramsey said as he turned back toward the convex shelter.

They had to take Irish's big truck because it was the only vehicle large enough to carry the X-ray machine. Irish was tender, but he was tough, tougher than Tony thought.

"How did you start doing…what it is that you do?" Tony asked delicately.

"That's a bit rude, isn't it?"

Tony was embarrassed.

"Sorry, I jus…."

Irish laughed until he grabbed his side.

"Oh, that's magic. Just pullin' your leg, mate."

"Nice." Tony shook his head but smiled anyway.

"It's a three-hour drive, thought we could start with a smile," he said and became a bit more sober.

"I served in Her Majesty's Royal Army, then the IRA, and then I came to America."

"Why?"

"Why else? A woman." Irish smiled and remembered.

"I always knew how to find things or people, or people who knew things. We all have a talent ya know, even you."

"Really, well, what's mine then?"

"That's easy, mate. Yours is ignoring the fact that you're in love."

Tony smiled and shook his head. The intuitive remark took him by surprise but hit home.

"I don't know what you're talking about," Tony said with absolutely no confidence.

"No worries, mate, your secret's safe with me. So do you know where the Mad Hatter came from?" Irish changed the subject.

"I thought it was a genetically engineered virus at first, brought to us courtesy of the US Army or some other government faction. I thought that somebody probably designed it to do just what it's doing, to kill. But the more I think about it, the less I believe that. I had a friend at the CDC who showed us that even the army didn't know what it was or where it came from. And the fact that it kills everything, suggests to me that…"

"Sweet Mary, mother of God, mate, it's a simple question."

Tony smiled despite himself.

"Sorry, truth be told? I have no idea where this thing came from."

"Wasn't that easier?"

They rode in nearly complete silence for close to an hour. The day was clear and beautiful, save for the browning of the vegetation. At one point, Tony pulled the truck over and ran out into a corn field to retrieve a single corn plant with a single ear of corn on it. It was the only surviving plant in the whole field. He made sure the roots were thick with dirt and the plant was completely intact.

When he got back in the truck, Tony explained to Irish that it was always the mutants that taught scientists the most valuable lessons, and this plant appeared to be one of a very few that encoded some type of resistance to the virus. He assured Irish that if he could understand how the plant did it, then he could apply the same principle to finding a drug that would inhibit the virus.

Irish dozed on and off as they moved along the highway. Tony briefly remembered that he should be aware of rush-hour traffic, but the thought was quickly replaced by the fact that he neither knew the day nor the time. It made him realize how much of his previous life was spent worrying about things that really didn't matter all that much in the bigger picture.

In the passenger seat, Irish groaned and moved into an upright posture and looked straight ahead. The pain in his side had obviously been strong enough to roust him from his sleep.

"I owe you an apology," Tony said out of nowhere, although it hurt him to say so.

"Do ya now?"

"I misjudged you. I thought you were trying to squeeze me the other day."

"Well, honestly, mate, on a different day I wouldn't put it past myself, but I got a feelin' money isn't gonna be worth very much in the days to come. I think more people are going to die from being killed by other people than by the Mad Hatter. No, mark me words, things will change. They'll go back to the way they were in days of old. Survival of the fittest, kill or be killed, eye for an eye."

"Why do you say that?"

"I know people, mate, and I've seen it. They're okay one by one, but a mob has no brains…the food is close to being gone. They'll kill for it. You'll see a housewife slit her neighbor's throat for a loaf of bread. Things are about to become very bad."

"Why are you helping us?" Tony asked directly, which caught Irish a little of guard.

"Honestly, mate, I don't know," he said, looking out his window. "At times like these, you've got to choose your friends wisely."

Tony allowed Irish's insights to wash over him. He turned on the radio and went back and forth between National Public Radio and the British Broadcast Company. The outlook wasn't good.

The queen was dead, and so was Prince Charles. The coronation of the eldest Prince William was conducted without celebration, as MADS had killed so many, and they were in crisis, they needed leadership immediately. Tony saw that Irish was genuinely bothered by the loss of his queen. The prime minister was still alive, but the House of Lords and Parliament lost over half their members.

It was much worse in other countries. In the US, the president had signed an executive order establishing martial law. Curfews were set in all major cities. Looting had become epidemic, and soldiers were authorized to shoot looters on the spot.

A frightened Florida congressman had leaked information at a press conference indicating that the world's food supply was dwindling and would last approximately six months. The press conference set off a major run on supermarkets supplies and gasoline, and the excessive demand for supplies created widespread panic.

People were being shot in the street by their neighbors for food. Anyone with access to food was suddenly very powerful and very much at risk of being murdered.

Tony bristled at the report, which was prophesized only minutes earlier by Irish. Most summer harvests had failed, and the remaining cattle were dying at alarming rates. In some cities, the National Guard had been overrun by panicked crowds, and the military had been called in to surround the city, turning all of the citizens into prisoners who were trapped within.

Along with the looting, medical labs were being targeted and blown up all across the East Coast. Tony had friends at some of these places, and he wondered if any of them had made it out. He thought it odd that labs were being targeted, as it made no sense to him why someone would want to harm those who were trying to solve the problem. But then again, logic never did apply to an unhappy and frightened mob.

The strangest bit of news was the announcement of a pandemic of topical cancers in the South. Most of these were cancers that had been associated with HIV, hepatitis B and C viruses, human papilloma virus or herpes virus, and were rarely seen in the US. There had been a marked increase in Burkitt's lymphoma, Kaposi's sarcoma, hepatocellular carcinoma, and a variety of other cancers.

The commentators didn't have much additional information but did report that people suffering from these cancers were being directed to temporary tent hospitals that the military had set up. Many of these people had been showing up with large cancerous growths on their faces and or limbs.

"Jesus, mate!" Irish said angrily and slapped the dash.

The movement made him flinch painfully as he clutched he side.

"What's he got to do with it?"

"Who?"

"Jesus."

"What do you have against Jesus?" Irish asked.

"Not a damn thing. It would be the same as having something against Bugs Bunny or Mighty Mouse. They're fiction!" Tony said with an agitated tone.

Irish said not a word and forced an uncomfortable silence, which drove Tony to explain further.

"Fine! Give me one piece of evidence that there is a creature capable of designing all of this." Tony motioned to the outside.

"Just one bit, and not some supposedly esoteric book written two thousand years ago by fishermen. How many fishermen could read and write two thousand years ago? It's a ridiculous notion. Now science has several theories that do a very fine job of explaining the evolution of life and of man. Science offers us concrete evidence that supports its suppositions, not condemnation for not believing in an invisible, omnipotent giant who lives in the sky," Tony said, somewhat out of breathe.

"Hmm" was all that Irish said.

Tony was annoyed by his silence. He looked over several times trying to will him to speak. Irish knew what he was doing, but he kept silent until the tension was thick.

"Tell me, mate, can you see the virus in the air?" he motioned at the air around them.

"No," Tony laughed at Irish's ignorance.

"So how do you know it's there?"

Tony smiled pedantically.

"I know what you're trying to do, *mate*, but you can see a virus through an electron microscope quite well, I'm afraid. We call that empirical evidence."

"Aye, but before that microscope was invented—"

"In 1931," Tony broke in.

"Before 1931, it was impossible to do so?"

Tony soured a little.

"And?"

"And people knew about viruses before then by the way they affected the world."

"Sure," Tony said, "but they blamed those effects on all sorts of absurd superstitions and incorrect assumptions. The funny thing about people is that they tend to invent solutions to the problems that they can't solve. Before we knew there were germs, we bled people with leeches because we thought that sickness was caused by an imbalance of humors. Blood was considered one of the four humors, and it was often drained in an attempt to restore balance. We know that is complete nonsense now, because science has revealed the germ theory of disease."

"That was well done, now wasn't it? So life came from a germ or a bacteria, and then to animals, and poof, here we are millions of years later."

"You are oversimplifying it," Tony said, still impassioned.

"And God had nothing to do with any of that?

"No."

"So what does life mean then, mate? Are we just genetic accidents? What about good and bad, reward and punishment? An accident you say, where's the hope in that?"

Tony shook his head. *It always came to this with believers,* he thought. *When they ran out of lies to support their arguments, they always turned to the idea that morality and meaning could not exist without some anthropomorphic being dispensing it out from the heavens.*

Irish pulled a large silver cross from beneath his shirt.

"I'm not a very good man. I've done horrible things, but you asked me why I'm here. I'll tell you. The Good Lord told me I had to trust you, and that I would have to sacrifice myself to do so, but if I did, He would save me. So I did, and He kept His promise."

"Carrie saved you, not God."

"No, mate, God saved me through Carrie."

"There is no God!"

Irish stopped and smiled as Tony smoldered.

"Just maybe you haven't invented a big enough microscope yet. 'Cause, He's there, and you can tell by the way he affects the world."

Irish tucked his cross back under his shirt and watched the dying vegetation go streaming by through the truck window. Tony's jaw was tense, and he gritted his teeth with frustration as he searched his brain for a rational story that would help Irish see the truth.

"Then tell me why God would do this to his own creation?"

"Don't know," Irish stared hard into Tony's face. "The world as we knew it is gone. But we'll get through, He'll see to that."

"Hope comes from within," Tony offered. "You don't need a God to explain the resiliency of life. Like the one corn plant that I harvested today. It found a way to survive, and life will always find a way. That's the beauty of it. Look at every great natural disaster that has lead to complete devastation. A decade later, it is flourishing with life, with new beauty. That is the life cycle of the universe. Great disasters are always followed by periods of fantastic creativity."

"Aye, He did a good job with that one, didn't he?" Irish said with a laugh.

They reached Sioux Falls without seeing a single car along the way. Irish directed him to the rear of the Sioux Valley Medical Center and down a ramp where deliveries were made.

They could not see the front of the building, but from the rear, it looked abandoned.

Tony knew that Irish was in pain, but by the time they started to descend into the basement, the adrenaline must have kicked in, for he looked as if he had never been shot. Irish pulled a gun out from his waistband and checked to see if it was loaded. He pulled out another gun and handed the revolver to Tony.

"Are you familiar with these?"

"Not really," Tony said.

"It's easy. Point this end at the bad guys and pull this thingy here. Got it?"

Tony nodded as he stared at the shiny weapon.

"Are we expecting bad guys?"

Irish shrugged.

"Always mate, always."

They descended the ramp and went through a pair of double doors and then down a narrow corridor with several more double doors. They heard voices a few times, although Tony only became aware of them when Irish stopped him in his tracks, and then after a moment, he would hear them too. The corridors were only partially lit, with most sections completely dark, and all they had was a penlight to guide them on their way. Around every corner, Tony sucked in his breath and proceeded with extreme caution.

The sound of footsteps running echoed down the halls. Irish froze, and Tony ran into the back of him. The little penlight clicked off.

"Sorry."

"Shh."

The footsteps got louder and louder until they sounded like boots running, lots of boots. Voices began to mingle with the clumping of boots, and beams from flashlights shot from across the hall.

Tony and Irish crouched at an intersection of hallways. Irish put his gun barrel flush with the wall and waited. His hands were as steady as a rock. Tony loosely held his gun behind Irish, looking back and forth and feeling extremely nervous. The boots came very close to where Tony and Irish were hiding but began to fade with the voices and beams of light just as fast as they came. Tony and Irish were left in the dark. Irish clicked the penlight back on.

"That was close," Irish said and kept moving.

"I'm not sure what anyone would be doing down here. This hospital has been closed for nearly a month."

The rest of the way they heard nothing, but Tony saw a radiology sign on the wall and knew they were near the X-ray room. A pair of swinging doors thumped open, and Irish shined the light on a fairly obtrusive X-ray machine. Boxes of film cartridges lay on a shelf beside it. Irish wasted no time. He loaded the boxes of X-ray film cartridges onto a wheeled office chair, and then looked at Tony.

"Are ya ready?"

"Why rush? God tell you that we're gonna die?" Tony asked sarcastically.

"No, He's pretty sure *I'm* going to be fine. Let's go."

Irish didn't wait for a response and pushed the chair, leaving Tony to push the bulky X-ray machine. One wheel on the machine squeaked inconsistently, but each time it squealed, it seemed louder and louder as if it were a beacon announcing their whereabouts.

Irish stopped a few times but didn't rest for long. It seemed to take twice as long to get back as it did to get down there. Irish stood at the basement door looking through its small window back and forth.

"What are you waiting for? Let's go," Tony said impatiently, feeling a strong urge to get back to Sara.

"Something doesn't feel right, mate."

"Okay, I get it. I apologize about the God crack. Let's go."

Irish didn't move a muscle or respond to Tony; he only stared through the small window. He turned with a look in his eye that was new to Tony; it warned of danger.

"Stay here. Don't make a sound."

Irish wheeled out the chair with the box of film cartridges and slowly ascended the ramp to the back of his truck. They left the back of the truck open for easy access. He stood almost frozen staring at one end of the building and then the other. Finally, he unloaded the box into the truck and slid it to the side of a makeshift ramp and motioned for Tony to come.

Tony pushed hard to get the machine rolling and thumped open the doors. As he did so, he heard what sounded like gunshots. He looked up and saw Irish crouched at the back of his truck, firing his gun one shot after the next. After no less than ten shots, Irish ran down the ramp with dust flying up behind him as bullets ricocheted off the concrete walls surrounding him. Irish slammed into the door, pushing the X-ray machine back into the building and almost knocking Tony down.

"What the hell?" Tony asked, afraid.

"Don't know. It's the army."

"The army?" Tony grabbed his head. "Damn it, Carrie! I told her no cell phone."

"We've got to go, mate—now!" Irish said as he grabbed Tony.

Just before they began to run, Tony noticed that Irish's wound had opened and was bleeding through his shirt. They ran down the hallways taking turns at the lead and maintaining a solid pace. Tony lost track of the way back out after only a few turns, and the adrenaline coursed through his system.

After what felt like an eternity, they came upon an elevator. The small chamber was dimly lit, and it looked like a service elevator.

"Stand to the side," Irish said and pushed the call buttons.

Irish raised his gun and knelt as the doors opened almost immediately. No one was inside. They entered, and he selected the lobby button. Tony's eyes widened.

"You want to see the lobby?"

"We've got to see the front. See how many men, how many vehicles. Tell me why the army would be interested in your Carrie?"

Tony shook his head. "She was at ground zero when the virus hit. What interest they have in her specifically, I couldn't say, but a friend of ours was killed already for being involved. So I guess I'd rather not find out."

"Enough said."

The elevator door opened into an area that was poorly painted with old plaster coming off the walls. Mop buckets and other cleaning supplies on a rack provided evidence that this was a custodial area. The two men proceeded through the area with caution, Tony trying to imitate the posture of Irish.

Irish pushed open a door, which presented an orange-colored marble lobby with cherry wood furnishings and eclectic lighting. It was a nice lobby to say the least, and it was strange that it was so empty and quiet. At the doorway, Tony saw two men in army fatigues carrying weapons. Their postures were stalwart, weapons at the ready. Irish looked around at some other visible areas.

"Okay, there are four here, which puts their force at about fifty."

"How would you know that?"

"If they had less, they would have only left one or two guards. They have men to spare. That's what we heard in the hallways below. How would they have tracked you here, mate?"

"Carrie must have made a call when we went into town last. She's been acting…strange. It's not her fault, she's pregnant."

Irish raised his eyebrows, and Tony nodded.

"Well, congratulations are in order, but that'll have to wait until we make it out of here."

"If we make it out of here."

"You know you're a real negative guy sometimes. Stay here."

Irish left the lobby, walking at a fast pace. From behind the door, Tony heard four quick shots and a whistle. He tried to sneak out the door but saw that he was in the wide open. Four soldiers lay on the floor, red dots on each of their foreheads. Irish searched them, grabbing an automatic weapon from one as well as clips. He untangled a bone phone from around one soldier's ear and put it into his own.

Outside in the front parking area were ten Humvees and a large personnel carrier.

"Carrisa must have really pissed them off, mate."

"She has a gift for that sort of thing."

Irish froze and put his hand to his ear.

"Time to go."

He grabbed another automatic rifle and handed it to Tony. They went to the main elevator and saw that it was coming down. Irish indicated to Tony to stand aside, raised his newly acquired weapon, and waited. The bell dinged politely, and the doors began to open. Through the metal doors they could hear a voice.

"Kill dog actual, all clear," said the soldier who looked surprised to see Irish waiting for him.

Irish fired two shots and dropped the man.

"Let's go."

Tony followed his lead into the elevator car. He did not feel very comfortable with the soldier lying on the floor. Irish listened through his earpiece.

"Third floor."

Tony pushed the appropriate button and saw that his hands were shaking. He also saw that Irish's wound was bleeding freely now, dripping from his shirt, to his pants, to the floor.

"You need to do exactly what I say, when I say it."

"I think I saw this episode," Tony said with a smile.

Irish did not respond kindly.

"This is no movie. You lose focus, you die. You die, everyone dies. So shut the hell up and do as I say."

Tony saw for the first time that Irish was a very dangerous man, and ironically, exactly the type of man he needed to get him out of this mess.

The doors opened, and Irish led every step of the way with precise calculation. He listened to the bone phone and knew their positions. Based on this intel, Irish was able to make sure they were not sighted by any of the soldiers, but he knew it was only for a matter of time. Floor after floor, they went up and down. Tony had no idea what they were doing.

"Finally. They're out of the basement. Let's move, they've been rotating us, eliminating floor by floor, and we've been lucky. Once they find their dead mates, we're toast."

"Who's negative now?" Tony asked, his face pale.

They entered the elevator and started down. Irish's face dropped as he put his finger in his ear.

"Shite," Irish pulled the bone phone from his ear. "They found the dead guards, and they know we have been listening. We need to move fast. Don't lag behind."

Tony looked at the open wound in Irish's abdomen. The doors opened, and Irish hesitated only a moment, making sure it was safe. Two other cars were moving down toward the basement. They took off at a run, Irish running much faster than should have been possible in his condition. Tony had a difficult time keeping pace.

Irish navigated the maze of hallways as if he knew exactly where they were running. The sound of boots was close behind them, and for the first time, Tony was glad for the darkness of the basement.

Someone tackled Tony, and he fell hard to the floor and slid into a dimly lit area of the basement. Not knowing what to do, he balled up, expecting the worse, but looked up to see Irish scuffling with another man in an army uniform.

They disarmed each other quite efficiently, both moving with a grace and speed that Tony could not imagine. Where one would land a solid punch, the other would respond with a kick. Tony was frozen; it was like watching two men dance, a deadly dance. Irish managed to put the soldier's arm into a bar and pulled the handgun from behind his back.

The soldier somehow twisted his arm and reversed the move, which allowed him to take the gun from Irish. He pointed the gun at his head but noticed a blade pressed hard against his throat. The two men stood frozen, looking each other in the eyes.

"My name is Staff Sergeant Mathew Thomas, and I don't want to harm you."

"Then put the gun down, mate, and you won't."

"Not until you pull the knife away from my throat, slowly."

"Looks like we have a disagreement then," Irish pushed the knife harder, drawing a smidgen of blood.

The sergeant cocked the hammer back and held it there, while his finger pulled and held the trigger back.

"You cut, you die. Understand?"

"I cut, you die. Understand that?"

Tony was paralyzed and didn't know if ever in his life he had felt such a combination of fear and helplessness.

"Tell me, Sergeant, do you have kids? Or more to the point do you want to see them again?"

Sgt. Thomas's face fell only slightly.

"I believe they might already be dead. The East Coast is in complete chaos. Law is gone. I promise you, with God as my witness, I do not want to hurt you."

This time, it was Irish's face that fell. He pulled the knife back ever so slightly, taking some of the pressure off. In return Sgt. Thomas slowly allowed the trigger to return to its safe position. Then Irish pulled the knife so that it no longer touched his throat, and Sgt. Thomas removed the gun altogether. They remained close together just looking at each other, but breathing freer.

"Mind if I have my gun back, mate?"

"Not if I can have my knife back."

They switched weapons and stepped away. Sgt. Thomas looked at Tony for the first time.

"I'm Staff Sergeant Mathew Thomas."

"Tony, Dr. Tony Van Lee."

The soldier's eyes squinted curiously.

"Do you know a lady doctor named Harrison?"

Tony dropped his head and shook it. *Damn it, woman,* he thought.

Sgt. Thomas explained that he felt the chain of command had been broken and that his commanding officer had gone insane. He no longer felt that they were doing things honorably, and it was time for him to make a change.

They all looked through the original door to the ramp leading to Irish's truck. Sgt. Thomas eyed the X-ray machine.

"A little girl is sick. We need it," Tony answered the unasked question.

"I'm afraid that getting out of here will be hard enough without the machine, mate."

Tony stood his ground and elevated his chin. There was no way he would let Sara die because he was afraid to lose his own life.

"We don't leave without it. And I'm not negotiating."

Irish smiled in appreciation for Tony's resolve.

"All right, mate, the machine it is."

Irish and Sgt. Thomas both ducked for cover and peeked over the edge, getting positions on the other men. Sgt. Thomas shook his head.

"We can outgun them or outrun them. However, I don't feel comfortable trying to kill my own men, even though they've all changed…but I can distract them. I'll call in a fake report, which should buy us a minute or two to get the machine loaded and out of sight."

"I don't have anything better planned, but I promise, comfort or not, I'll kill any man who fires upon me."

"Agreed," Sgt. Thomas replied and spoke into his radio. "Lead dog actual, over."

"Lead dog bravo two, over."

"Bravo two, I've got four men, armed, floors fifteen and sixteen, stairwells, east corner, over."

"Roger, lead dog. That's four men, armed, in the stairwells east, floors fifteen and sixteen, over."

"Affirmative. Bring it all! Lead dog actual, out!"

"Roger that, lead dog. We're on the way. Bravo two, out."

The two men peeked back over the concrete walls and saw the army men who were there take off at a run.

Irish and Sgt. Thomas both helped get the machine up to the truck and pushed it onto the makeshift ramp, which snapped immediately.

"Can we lift it?" asked Sgt. Thomas, who checked his watch.

"It's got to be a thousand pounds. It's a dinosaur," Tony said, exasperated.

"Lead dog, actual. What is your position?" asked a cold female voice from the radio.

Sgt. Thomas looked disturbed.

"This is lead dog, actual. Say again."

Tony tried to pick one end of the machine up, but it did not budge. He would have had as much success if he tried to move a mountain.

"I said where are you, Sergeant!"

"Roger, sixteenth floor, west stairwell, over."

There was no immediate response. The three men froze and only a second passed before bullets began to rain down on them from above. They flattened themselves against the truck. A few bullets hit the machine.

"We can't let it get damaged," Tony yelled over the gunfire.

"Shame on you, Sgt. Thomas. I am so very disappointed to have to kill you," the radio squawked again.

Sgt. Mathew Thomas then stepped out into the open and fired several precision shots. It took Irish only a moment to join him, and the bodies of soldiers began to fall from the windows of the hospital. Once his clip ran out, Sgt. Thomas grabbed the machine and seemed to vault it into the back of the truck. Tony had to throw himself onto the ground to get out of its way. Irish took cover behind the truck again stunned with Sgt. Thomas's show of strength.

Suddenly, there was a sensational crash that brought Tony and Irish out of their collective dazes. Out of a fourth-story window, shiny pieces of glass and mortar came falling to the ground, followed by a woman wearing a hideous expression.

She landed gracefully and rolled onto her feet with no apparent injury. She leaped onto a car and over a six-foot-high chain-link fence, taking a straight line toward them.

"Holy mother of God," Irish exclaimed as he watched, his mouth opened with awe.

She leaped one last time and would have landed on Sgt. Thomas, but her route was pushed off course by several bullets coming from the opposite direction of the hospital. The crazed woman crumpled to the ground and lay motionless. She had been close enough that Sgt. Thomas had her blood spatter on his uniform.

Single shots were fired from that same position, forcing the soldiers in the hospital to take cover, but no one could not see the source of the gunfire.

"Now who the hell is that?" Irish asked, still mystified by what he had just seen.

"I don't know, but never look a gift horse in the mouth," replied Sgt. Thomas as he slammed the truck door closed.

All three men mounted up and drove as fast as the truck would carry them back to Ramsey's lab. Sgt. Thomas kept a careful lookout, but no one followed.

Col. Bragg had watched the two men park and go inside the hospital while lying on the hood of his Humvee, looking through the scope of his sniper's rifle. He was curious, and while he could not distinguish detailed features at that distance, he could tell that they didn't seem like soldiers. Probably just looters looking for anything of value; medicines were hard to come by, but they certainly picked the wrong hospital on the wrong day.

He had been tracking the group of Lt. Finn's soldiers for a day since arriving in Sioux Falls. Revenge would be sweet, he constantly reminded himself, and he remained patient. He followed Lt. Finn's army convoy to the hospital and then waited for the right time.

It didn't take long for the looter's situation to get sticky, but he just watched. When they came back, it seemed as if one of her soldiers had gone over to the other side. He took this as a good sign. Anyone who would serve under that woman was an idiot.

The trio came out with a bulky machine, and that's when the shootout began. The looters were sitting ducks. No cover and limited firepower left them completely vulnerable. That's when he saw her.

Lt. Finn smashed through a four-story window and landed on the ground. She then jumped a six-foot-high safety fence with almost no effort. Col. Bragg couldn't believe his eyes. He didn't have time to think about it, however, as she was about to attack the looters and the lone soldier.

Fortunately for him, she had made the mistake of getting out into the open. He fired twice, and she was blown straight from the air. After assessing the situation further, he decided it wouldn't hurt to provide the men a chance to escape by laying down some cover fire. He did so, and the truck made it to the main road and was free of her attack. With Lt. Finn dead, he didn't care anymore. His business was done.

He flipped the laptop open again, found the locator, and plotted his route on the map. The end of the rainbow was only three hours away. *Would it be a pot of gold or just a mirage?* he wondered.

Lt. Finn pushed herself up to a sitting position and sucked in a breath of air, as if she had just come up from under water in a deep pool. A large portion of her face was a mangled mess of blood and charred skin. The wound exposed bits of her teeth on one side of her face.

Lifting her shirt, she noticed that blood had stopped flowing at the entry wound of the other bullet. The virus acted quickly, repairing the wounds nearly as fast as her body could handle. Neural impulses were rerouted. Blood flow in certain arteries stopped. Muscles were primed to regrow, as well as her face where a new skin began to cover what damage it could, but it would have to be improved upon. She took her time standing, but her strength returned quickly, and she surveyed the damage. Twenty of her men lay dead on the ground, and several others were dead but hanging partially out of the hospital's windows.

Her remaining men came running in from different directions to check on her and asked about her wounds but stopped short, unnerved that she had lived with such an egregious wound. She barely acknowledged them because her mind was fixated on the mystery shooter.

She also silently acknowledged her mistake in letting Sgt. Thomas live. His change of heart had been obvious, and he needed to be dealt with, but she thought it prudent for him to lead one more mission before dispatching of him. She would make a mental note of this weakness, and not make that mistake twice.

When she spoke, her words were airy and slightly slurred, and each syllable was pronounced with a sucking sound. Her face was monstrous and came to resemble on the outside what Lt. Finn had always been on the inside.

"One team search that wooded area and track the shooter," she slurred. "We go north now."

"Ma'am, are you okay?" one soldier asked.

She looked at him with what was left of her smile, a smile that was an advertisement for pure malevolence.

"*Nur die stärksten überleben,*" she laughed, a horrible slushy sound emanating from her mouth, as the thought echoed in her mind, *Only the strongest survive.*

Chapter 23

A S SOON AS the lift touched down in the underground lab, Tony was off at a brisk pace. Carrisa came out of Sara's room, saw that Tony had returned, and walked toward him.

"Did you get—"

"I need to speak with you right now!" said Tony angrily, as he headed directly toward her.

Her attention, however, was on the bloody shirt of Irish, and Tony's voice disappeared completely.

"I knew it. Get in here," she said to Irish as she walked past, ignoring Tony.

Irish followed her instructions, albeit uncomfortably, not wanting to be in the middle of this argument. He pulled off his shirt and sat on the table.

"Are you listening to me?" Tony raised his voice.

"This needs to be dealt with first. Now's not the time, Tony."

The anger in their voices put everyone on alarm. Noah grabbed the hand of his sister Annie, and they pushed deeper into the corner as if they could blend into the wall.

Tony grabbed Carrisa's shoulders and spun her around.

"Who did you call? Why? Why the hell would you do that? They were waiting to attack us at the hospital!" he expressed angrily.

"This is not the time, Tony! Everything isn't always about you. Sometimes other people have to come first."

"That's a great point, I concur!" he said sarcastically. "So why in the hell would you make a call after I told you not too, Carrie?"

"You are not my superior, Tony, and stop calling me Carrie!"

"Stop changing the subject. We were almost killed because of you."

"I called Sandy, and I can call anyone I damn well please."

"Smart, *Carrisa*, very smart. Perhaps you should think of the welfare of the entire group the next time you get the urge to call one of your damn girlfriends."

"You're not the only smart one around here. You are a prideful and arrogant man who thinks he has the answers for everything. But the truth is, you know nothing about this virus and it's killing you. You finally met your match and you're cracking under the pressure. So go smoke something and stay out of my affairs!"

The shouting had drawn the attention of everyone. The room felt as if they were all standing on thin ice, and it was cracking beneath their feet. Tony was shocked, but he knew that there was truth in Carrisa's words. Her angry face lost its edges, and her eyes told him that she was sorry, but the damage was done.

"You're right. I don't know everything, I never have. I thought that's what you needed me to be, the man with all the answers, and I tried," Tony said quietly.

He turned and left the examination room. Carrisa wiped Irish's wound with a sponge full of iodine. His wounds were not open. On the contrary, they looked to have been knit for some days.

"Where's all this blood coming from?" Carrisa asked.

Irish stared at his wounds, just as mystified as she.

"It broke open, I'm sure of it."

Behind them, the sergeant cleared his throat. With all the excitement, no one even recognized that they had returned with another person who was standing in an army uniform carrying an automatic weapon. The sight of him caused quite a shock.

"Sorry," broke in Irish. "This is Sgt. Mathew Thomas. He tried to kill me, but we've come to an arrangement since."

Ramsey and Carissa stared blankly and shrugged in unison. Ramsey made it a point to make the sergeant feel at home by taking him on a tour of the facility. Tony entered Sara's room.

She and Don were playing cards. Her face was pale and covered in sweat, and her lips were blue. Sara tried to smile as her body trembled and her hands shook.

"Cards, I love playing cards. Rummy?"

"Hi, Dr. V. No, it's go fish."

"One of my favorites. How are you feeling?"

"My head feels really hot, but my body feels really, really cold."

"I'm sorry about that. We're going to take a picture of your chest and see if that tells us anything, okay?"

She coughed a wet cough that rattled in her chest.

"Okay, Dr. V. You wanna play fifty-two pickup?"

"Another time, okay?"

"Okay," she replied.

Tony nodded at Don who looked as if he hadn't slept in days. Carrisa was waiting for him outside her room. She seemed embarrassed.

"She's failing fast. Did you get the machine?"

"It's in the truck," he said as he tried to walk by her.

"I know you're angry, but there are some things we need to discuss. We're running out of time."

He didn't stop to wait for her.

Later that day, Tony, Carrisa, and Ramsey sat at a table, sipping coffee.

"That Irish's wound knit so fast should have been impossible," Carrisa said.

"Well, he's definitely infected with the virus, but it seems to have evolved in him. Although it maintains the same overall structure, the evolved version has a distinct phenotype. I'll test the soldier too," Ramsey added.

It took Tony a moment to wrap his head around the idea that the virus could do such a wide array of things to different people.

"There's something else, Genius. Carrie, you ought to tell him."

"When I used the cell phone the other day, I talked to a former colleague, Sandy. She worked at the CDC in Atlanta until it shut down due to the virus. She told me that there were some other pathogenic effects that the CDC thinks are related to the viral infections."

"Spit it out, Carrie," Tony said, still feeling hurt by the earlier conversation.

"For some reason, there has been a massive increase in virus-associated cancers, and this has been reported to have started right before things got out of hand. Sandy noted that many of the patients came in with lesions that had grown out of control and were painful. The demeanor of some patients became aggressive, and they displayed increases in body mass and strength."

Tony was nodding before she even finished.

"I heard about the cancers on the radio. Not to mention our newest guest practically threw the X-ray machine into the truck single-handedly."

Ramsey and Carrisa looked at each other, confused.

"I'm not exaggerating. When we were under attack…this is going to sound insane, but a woman crashed through a window four stories high and landed without injury." He put his hand up to prevent questions that they both had.

"Then she hurdled a six-foot chain-link fence. I was sure we were dead until someone shot her from behind."

The two other doctors sat in silence for a moment.

"Increased strength, almost superhuman strength, increased healing rates, increased aggression. I don't know what this means," Carrisa said.

"Well, we also tested the two kids," Ramsey added, "and they both have the virus, and the female—"

Tony interrupted him. "Her name is Annie."

"Fine, Annie has a herpes virus infection," Ramsey finished.

"Eighty percent of the population has some type of herpes virus infection," Tony stated. "What's different about hers?"

"The herpes lesion on her face is cancerous, and growing at approximately one hundred times the speed of a normal basal cell," Carrisa chimed in.

"And it is oozing herpes virus," Ramsey said.

"What? How can…no, it can't. It can't all be connected."

"Sandy had the data, Tony. She said it was widespread, an influx of apparent herpes virus infections and large-scale malignant cancer growths. It's all connected, but I haven't the faintest idea how."

Tony stood up abruptly, walked across the lab to a portable chalkboard, and began wheeling it back to where he was seated with Carrisa and Ramsey. In the process, he got a good view of Annie.

The sore on her face was nearly as big as a quarter now, but she smiled shyly at him and waved. He smiled back to her and continued with his chalkboard. He parked it at the table with the other two scientists and began to write at full speed.

"Okay, we have several different outcomes possible with this virus," Tony began. "The original virus outbreak, let's call it the alpha event, resulted in at least 128 human deaths in a matter of hours. We are not exactly sure how soon after this event plants and animals became infected, but we know that the alpha event killed marine animals. Next, the beta event resulted in a virus that appears to be attenuated in most humans, but lethal among the elderly and the young. It is unclear if this virus leads to increased strength in the other age groups. There is a clear phenotypic difference between several of us who appear to have the virus with little or no consequence, we'll call this the gamma group, and then there are those who develop rapid healing and acquisition of superhuman strength, which we will call the delta group. In addition, we can designate the epsilon group as those individuals who have an endemic, latent virus infection that accelerates to uncommon cancers. It's not clear if this is a different phenotype or if this is just a later phase of the gamma group." Tony wrote as fast as he could on the chalkboard, drawing the events and trajectory of the virus.

"And then finally, we have people like Don, who don't have the virus, and probably are resistant to it. That sound about right?" Tony asked.

Carrisa and Ramsey followed him and nodded silently. Tony expected an argument, but did not get one. This was the evidence they were faced with.

"Okay then. Carrie, I know you need to get film of Sara's lungs. Ramsey, you work on Sgt. Thomas. See if you can find out something in his physiology that has changed. I'd like to know more about the deltas, since they will be the most physically dominant among the infected. It would be good to understand more about it. I'll work on the herpes virus acceleration and cancer link," Tony said.

"Tony," Carrisa spoke softly, "we are shooting in the dark without more basic biology about this virus."

"I know, but we have to do what we can," he said.

"Oh, and, Carrie, wear a lead apron, okay?"

Carrisa looked him in the eye and was touched by his thoughtfulness. She unconsciously rubbed her stomach where the child was growing inside of her.

They all went on their way and to do their separate assignments.

Annie watched Tony come toward her with a shy look, but she was unabashed at the same time.

"Hi, Annie."

"Hello."

"I'd like to take a look at you if you don't mind. See if there's anything I can do to…help."

"Do you think I'm ugly?"

"What?" Tony was surprised by the question but smiled reassuringly to her.

"Of course not, Annie."

"I think you are beautiful," she said and immediately backed into her shy corner.

Tony fought hard not to blanch.

"I thank you for that. I think you're beautiful, too," Tony said as he noticed for the first time that her brother wasn't present.

"Where's Noah?"

She shrugged. Tony put his hand out, and she took it. He led her to a makeshift examination room. Tony examined the lesion on her face.

After Irish and Sgt. Thomas brought the X-ray machine down, Carrisa situated it to get images of Sara's lungs. The little girl was very weak, and it was painful for her to move.

"I'm sorry, Sara, I know this hurts."

"It's okay, Dr. Carrie, I can do it."

She rolled her over and put the film cartridge beneath her. They didn't have a target screen, so the cartridge had to go directly underneath, and it made her arch her back painfully. Carrisa pulled the controller box outside the room and peaked at the target light until in was exactly where she needed it.

"Try not to move, sweetie."

Carrisa took the requisite shots and then took the film to a computer that Ramsey and Tony had rigged to develop the film.

Ramsey had both Irish and Sgt. Thomas sitting on a table next to each other. Both men had well-developed physiques. Both men also seemed surprised that their bodies were in such good shape.

"So what you're telling me is that all of this is new?" Ramsey asked bluntly, pointing to the two men's well-defined muscles.

"I work out, but this is…" Sgt. Thomas looked down at his chest and abs, which were very defined.

"You too?"

Irish nodded as he felt the scar on his lower abdomen, which looked as if it had been healed for months.

"Not that I'm complaining, mate."

"Can you tell me about the strength? I heard you lifted something pretty hefty."

"I don't know. We were in a jam, and the doctor just said the machine couldn't get damaged. A little girl's life was on the line. I was thinking that I needed the strength of ten guys to lift it, but once I ran out of rounds, we were dead. So I just picked it up. I thought it was adrenaline…or something."

"If it was adrenaline, you probably would have shredded every muscle in your arms trying to lift that thing," Ramsey answered. "Anything else?"

"I'm a little antsy."

"Aye, me too, mate, hard to sit still."

Ramsey drew their blood and took measurements of their chests, arms, necks, and waists.

Tony rested in a room that was previously used for sleeping quarters. After sleeping for several minutes, a hand roughly shook him awake.

"There's a problem, mate. The lady doctor needs ya."

Tony flew down the hall into the main room where all the exam rooms and computers were located. He could hear Carrisa yelling orders well before he arrived. In Sara's room, Carrisa was in the process of pulling up the rails of the bed to prevent her from falling out. The seizure was violent and her little frame was hideous as it shook uncontrollably.

"Tony…"

"What happened?" he asked.

"She's burning up with fever."

A monitor at the side of her bed read 105 degrees. It continued to increase a tenth of a degree about every thirty seconds. Tony ran out of the room and to the freezer where he stored the drugs he had acquired from Irish. He knew that Ramsey was in the process of testing them, but it was still too early to know if any of them worked against the virus or the symptoms that Sara was experiencing. He searched through the different drugs and grabbed several glass vials and syringes of medications that he knew would work against many viruses.

"Okay," he said, "we have to give some of these a try. We no longer have the luxury of time."

Tony began filling syringes as Carrisa looked in Sara's eyes with a penlight.

"Her eyes are dilated, we have got to get control of her temperature or we will lose her brain," she said, trying to control her emotions.

"It's time to start the ice bath therapy again."

At that moment, the seizure stopped and everyone froze. For the first time, Tony noticed Don standing against the wall, his face as white as a ghost, as his features revealed that he was filled with terror. Tears rolled freely down his sunken cheeks as he looked at his baby girl as if no one else was even in the room.

Blood began to trickle from Sara's tear ducts. Her temperature reached 105.4.

"Where the hell is Ramsey?" Tony yelled.

"Don't know."

"Okay, ready?"

"Here." Carrie handed him the first syringe.

Tony injected her with a combination of four antiviral drugs, including ribavirin and interferon alpha. Irish came in with a wastebasket of ice and poured over the girl's small form. They made sure almost every part of her body was covered in ice and then stood by watching, knowing that there was nothing they could do except watch the monitor. Slowly her temperature came down, and everyone began to breathe the slightest bit easier. The emotion in the room was too much for Carrie, and tears escaped from behind her clinical façade.

At 103 degrees, Sara's eyes fluttered open, and she began to breathe deeper, although fluid could be heard in her chest with each raspy breath she drew.

"Sara, this is Dr. V. Can you hear me?"

"Daddy?" her voice was haggard and soft.

Don was there in an instant, holding her hand.

"I'm here, sher', I've been here the whole time. I'll never leave," he said with a shaky voice.

"Daddy, it wasn't your fault."

"What wasn't, sher'?"

"It was mommy's fault. She wasn't strong like you," she said, her eyes looked as if they were seeing something far away.

Don broke down crying, holding her as tight as he dared.

"*Ne laissez pas, mon amour.*"

"It's so beautiful," Sara said and squeezed Carrisa's hand as she took her final breath.

"No!" Carrisa exclaimed as she shook her head nearly out of control. Tears flowed freely now as she confirmed that the girl's pulse had stopped.

"She's gone," Carrisa quietly announced to no one in particular.

Don leaned over her tiny body, crying. Tony and Irish stood frozen, looking at the empty body of the small child. Annie was outside the room, tears in her eyes as well.

Tony looked into her small, lifeless face. It was pure and serene, as if she was only sleeping.

"I'm so sorry, Don…"

"No! You don't get to clear your soul. You hold onto the pain! You no did enough and now my sher' is gone. You keep that pain inside you, 'cause you no get to give it to me," Don said with fire, pain, and anger in his eyes.

Tony allowed the words to wash over him and left the room silently to let the man grieve. He was not accustomed to death. All his work had been onsite after events or in a lab. Death was a statistic to him, not a reality, but now he felt responsible for the death of this child.

In his grief, Tony began to question himself. He had dedicated his life to preparing his mind for events like this, and when it came time to deliver, all his academic posturing and intellectual prowess could not save one little girl. Not even a little girl that he had grown to love. He wished it were he who had died in her place, a thought that had never before entered his mind.

Knowledge wasn't enough. He had always relied on his knowledge and his intelligence. This time, it had failed. All his arrogance and pride, and he still could not save her. He walked down the corridor and found himself on the stairs leading to the garden. Once at the top, he saw Ramsey sitting on his bench in front of the flowers.

"We could've used you tonight," he said and sat down next to the old scientist.

"I don't get it. She was improving. How could she improve so rapidly and then just…there has to be a reason? I'm missing something, Ramsey. The whole world has gone to hell, just like that and I couldn't even save a little girl."

He could feel the pain and sadness well up inside of him. The tears threatened to escape his eyes, but he willed them away and stared at the purple flowers under the night sky. He nudged Ramsey.

"What do you…"

Ramsey fell over and slid from the bench to the ground. It happened so slow that Tony had a hard time believing it had happened at all. He stared into Ramsey's pale and frozen face, and he knew that the old scientist was dead before he even felt for a pulse.

The pain could not be ignored this time. It grew and grew in intensity inside his chest and neck until it burst forth. Tony wailed as the weight of humanity and death pressed down on his shoulders. He kicked dirt and clenched his hands into fists, as he glared toward the heavens.

"Fine, you win! Happy now? That child was innocent, what do you want her for? You son of a bitch, why didn't you take me? me!" Tony wept as his anger gave way to pure sorrow and he fell to his knees, feeling a little embarrassed that he had resorted to blaming a God that he did not even believe in.

And then he completely let it all go. The pain was so great that his intellect could not rationalize it away. He was faced with his own limitations and his own shortcomings.

He thought of all the people who he loved who had most likely already been lost to this pandemic or its side effects. First there was Ben, his friend who he loved. Did he ever tell him that he loved him? Probably never.

Then there were his neighbors, Darrin and Minnie. Why should they have had to die in this mess? They were just enjoying life, living on the beach. And then there was Dottie, Carrisa's mom. He had always liked her, and he loved flirting with her. Lost forever, and for what?

Even the entrepreneurial Dude, who dropped out of college to sell weed and was on his way to becoming a millionaire was most likely dead or sick or whatever. And now Sara and Ramsey were dead. Ramsey seemed to know his death was coming, but he could not get sweet Sara's smiling face out of his head.

The death toll was agonizing, and he wailed openly, no longer fearful of showing his weakness. He had been shown to be what he was, an arrogant charlatan. For too long, he had relied on his own intellect to survive and never before was it so obvious that he was failing miserably.

His thoughts turned toward those remaining in the underground lab. He thought of Carrisa and his unborn child. He could not let them die; his life would have no meaning without them. He knew that now. It had always been the case, but he realized it fully in this moment.

The time for feeling sorry for himself was at an end, and he realized the time for pride and arrogance was also at an end. He needed help and didn't know what type, but he needed it and had to swallow his pride and just ask.

"I'll do anything. Anything you want," he cried and pleaded to the invisible giant in the sky.

"Just help me help them. Please!" Tony begged as he looked up at the heavens.

A leaf tickled his face as a breeze blew through the greenhouse, but he ignored it and kept his eyes closed tight, concentrating on whoever it was or whatever it was that might be able to help him, supernatural or not. He knew nothing about how to pray. Only what he saw on the television or in movies. He knew that he was supposed to get on his knees and fold his hands together, but without fail, every person he ever saw pray closed their eyes tight. He reasoned that this must be the most important part.

It made no sense why any of these actions constituted proper protocol in the acquisition of a divine intervention request, but he could only do what he had seen.

Ignorance infuriated him. It was his most basic motivator, to know everything. Today his knowledge reached its limits for the first time he could remember, and he was reduced to groveling. Even in the midst of this, he was trying to deduce and configure the angles.

The leaf tickled his face a second time, and he brushed it away as his mind continued to spin overtime. The symptoms, he was treating the symptoms, he never touched the virus, never got down to the core issues.

How did it work? How did it exploit so many systems at one time? He squeezed his hands and eyes together as tight as he could. Unsure if it would make a difference or not, but he was ignorant and overwhelmed. He had no choice but to ask. This was not a task he could do without help.

For a third time, the leaf brushed his cheek, tickling it as a breeze blew through the room, bringing him out of his concentration.

"Damn it…" He froze as one of his marijuana plants licked his face while the wind blew.

A few weeks earlier, Tony had planted his genetically modified fruits and vegetables to be prepared in case they would be here for a while. He also planted some of his genetically altered marijuana plants, which grew rapidly and were doing quite well.

One of the leaves from a marijuana plant tickled his face now and a light began to glow in his mind. He thought of visiting Sara when she was in comastasis and smoke filling her room. He watched as the smoke entered her nostrils, as well as the breathing pump sucking up its vapors.

He remembered feeling the beginnings of cold symptoms and them leaving after he had smoked liberally. The fact that Sara had lasted so long, much longer than any of the other children, could easily have been explained by the fact that she was exposed to the smoke.

"My God…" He looked up to the heavens with an incredulous expression.

He had a hard time deciphering what had just happened. The scientific side of him said that this was a coincidence, however, another part of him said that he had experienced something much more significant. He didn't know and didn't have the time to inquire or meditate on the subject, so he got up and whispered, just in case.

"Thanks."

Tony spun around to go back inside to test his epiphany. However, when he turned, he noticed a large older man kneeling at Ramsey's side. The man wore an army officer's uniform and had his sidearm drawn and resting easily in his hand pointed at Tony.

"That was a helluva moment, sorry I interrupted. There's nothing quite as humbling as watching another man pray," Col. Bragg said.

He could tell that Tony was new to praying. He recognized the same discomfort in him that he had experienced himself.

"I've been pondering the idea of a God a little myself, lately. Not the Christian God, but more like Einstein's God."

Tony lifted his hands in a gesture that indicated he was planning no quick movements. He wondered how the army could have found them. And he surrendered to the idea that he would be arrested and taken to some military brig. But he accepted his fate without fear, as he felt calm and reassured.

"What's your name?" asked the colonel.

"Tony."

"Would you happen to be Dr. Tony Van Lee?"

"Yes."

"Is there a Carrisa Harrison with you?"

Tony hesitated and became protective.

"Why?"

Col. Bragg smiled and holstered his gun.

"I've brought you something, Doctor."

"I don't understand."

"I'm Col. Adrian Bragg, formerly head of the bioweapons division of USAMRIID."

Tony's heart almost stopped as he remembered the name from the file. His posture turned defensive, but the colonel remained non-confrontational.

"I know your name."

"How's that?"

"You killed my friend," Tony said coldly, letting the anger build.

Bragg unconsciously assumed a posture that bespoke of a man prepared to do harm, but his face said otherwise.

"Unfortunately, my friend, you are going to have to be a little more specific."

Tony gritted his teeth as he spoke.

"His name was Ben. Dr. Ben Epstein!"

As if the wind went out of Col. Bragg's sails, his shoulders sagged.

"I didn't kill your friend."

"I don't believe you. Why should I?"

"Because I shot the woman who did. And you saw her die."

"What are you talking about, Colonel? I have never seen you before in my life."

"You know, the other day at the hospital? I saved your life. I shot Lieutenant Finn before she killed the whole lot of you. She used to work for me."

Tony thought about the superhuman crazy woman that jumped from the fourth-story window.

"That thing used to work for you? How? I don't understand how she became that powerful and that frightening."

Col. Bragg widened his shoulders again.

"I don't either. She was insane, psychopathic, homicidal, I couldn't say. I'm very sorry for the loss of Dr. Epstein, but I can assure you that I had nothing to do with it. Finn tried to dispose of me and take over the whole operation."

Tony felt cynical, but he knew that Col. Bragg could have killed him at any time, including at the hospital. This wasn't the way a man acted when he wanted you dead. There was also something in the man's face that looked defeated.

"Here, take this. Call it an act of good faith to show you that you can trust me."

Col. Bragg handed him a glass container with a small rock inside. Tony took it and noticed nothing spectacular about it.

"What's this?" he asked.

"That, my friend, is what we believe to be the source of the virus you've most likely been studying."

Tony looked again at the vial and forgot to be cautious.

"The source?"

"Hope you're as smart as everyone says you are."

"I've been hearing that a lot lately. What exactly is this?"

"It's a piece of a meteor… We found it in the ocean near the gulf. It was frozen in a tiny ball of ice."

Tony laughed hysterically. Col. Bragg watched with interest, not sure what exactly to do.

"He was right."

"Who?" Col. Bragg asked.

"The father of the little girl that I just watched die. He said the virus came from a meteor, and I said he was wrong. Now, his daughter is dead, and he brought her to me believing that I could save her life."

"I'm sorry to hear that."

Tony lifted his head and picked up Ramsey's lifeless form. Col. Bragg helped him as they placed his body on the bench so that he was facing the flowers. Tony stared reflectively at the man for a moment and then turned back to face Col. Bragg.

"How did you find us?"

Col. Bragg only shrugged.

Chapter 24

July 4, 2018

JEREMIAH ARRIVED IN Bismarck, North Dakota, on the first of July with over one hundred thousand faithful followers. His reconnaissance teams had become quite expert at disorienting local populations and corralling the few nonbelievers that could not escape.

Since leaving Texas, the Sons had become quite efficient. They had fine-tuned the skill of targeting specific institutions, which they carefully burned without allowing the flames to spread to other buildings close by. After each town was conquered, Jeremiah thanked the rovers for their faithfulness and encouraged them to keep doing the will of God. Lavishing them with public praise was an important part of troop morale, and he knew how to generate good morale.

He felt that the loss of life was unfortunate, but he knew that any form of authority from the past must be destroyed or there would always be remnants of loyalty to it. People had difficulties accepting the truth when old lies walked around in front of them, constantly confronting them with temptation. Thankfully, there weren't many authority figures left at this point, and for this, Jeremiah thanked his Father.

Society had reached a breaking point. Groups of friends and their remaining family members had banded together to form small defensible units. These small groups of people were easily overcome by Jeremiah's Army, and the members of those groups often proved to be resourceful recruits once they saw that His word was the truth.

Moreover, they were often eager to believe in a power that was more dominant than the plague that threatened to annihilate the entire human race. Those who could not turn to God fled from the army and wandered the lands until they were eventually killed by other groups of violent and desperate vagabonds.

It was dictated in the master plan handed down from God through prayer that Bismarck would be the seat of Jeremiah's northern headquarters, and he decided long ago that his control of this region must be total. He would leave a large contingent of armed troops in the north, along with engineers and laborers to fortify the parts of the city he wanted to keep safe.

For most people in these parts, civilized society had become a fond memory as people known for their Northern friendliness now fought and killed each other for eggs and meat. Jeremiah vowed that he would restore order to this town, an impossible feat for a man, but not for God. And he knew God was on his side.

Jeremiah studied the reports prepared by his minions that sat in a neat pile on his desk in the large RV that had become his mobile office. He studied the maps of the city, and he marked roads that he determined would need to be blocked, established guard posts, identified which farms would be manned, and which livestock would be fed.

The Mad Hatter had not only been destroying the human race, but it had also killed many animals and nearly all the crops as it spread in all directions from the kill zone in Louisiana.

Jeremiah was acutely aware of the spread of death, and he was intrigued by anything that survived. Anytime he saw a small batch of soybeans, corn, tomatoes, or potatoes that survived, he stopped and had them carefully picked. If an animal appeared healthy in a flock or herd that was decimated by disease, he had them taken as well.

The animals he would breed with other survivors, and the offspring would be used to feed his people until such time as God called them all home. He had the seeds from the surviving plants saved and prepared for planting the following season.

Jeremiah made it clear to his followers that it was unlawful to slaughter the animals or eat vegetables until he gave the okay. The punishment for breaking this law was death because such violations put the whole group at risk of starvation.

He didn't know what God's plan was beyond the plague. He only knew his part, which was to share the truth and destroy anyone who did not accept it. He disliked the violence. Each time he put himself at risk, it was with pure faith that he would come out alive and unharmed on the other side.

The new extra sensory gifts that he believed God bestowed upon him had served him very well. First with the woman soldier, who he believed must have met her end. His scouts never came back, and neither did she.

Second, his extra sensory gifts were used to neutralize small insurrections that arose among his own people. Twice he had sensed plots against his leadership, and twice he had been correct. Each man, woman, and child involved were hung.

Twenty-seven people in all had been put to death by his hand and never had he felt such despair. The necessity of the act felt cruel and painful to him, because it was contrary to what he was trying to do. But in his mind, it solidified his position as God's most holy messenger and highest leader on the planet.

Men and woman treated him with respect, although he sensed that much of it was derived from fear. However, if this was the price he had to pay for complete obedience to God, then he vowed to pay it gladly.

Jeremiah realized there were positives that came with social collapse, and one of these was that people were more willing to accept His word. Fear was a great motivator for human change, and that made things less bloody for him and his army. That was a good thing.

Jeremiah looked at his watch. He was scheduled to address a large crowd in less than an hour. His troops had rounded up the crowd, which had already been standing there, waiting for him for over two hours. That was part of Jeremiah's strategy.

He knew that the crowd's weariness from standing and waiting for him worked in his favor because fatigue made them easier to convert. However, he learned the hard way that this strategy led to extreme agitation and unpredictability if it went on for too long. Three hours was usually the limit, and he wanted this to be a peaceful day.

In recent days, phone lines were nearly out of service, and cell phone towers were continually overburdened, making it impossible to send or receive calls. However, just before Jeremiah left for the stage, he received a call informing him that his teams on the East Coast had been successful in their mission to destroy all the known research labs working on a cure for the Mad Hatter.

It was good news. Jeremiah felt a surge of new power flow into him as he let this information sink in. There would be no cure for the plague, and science would not be directly interfering with or disregarding the word of God.

The mission leader who called him also informed him that social decline, and anarchy were much worse on both US coasts than they were in Bismarck. Jeremiah looked skyward and thanked his Maker. The apocalypse was coming, and his army was ushering it in. He felt tremendous pride, the good kind of divine pride, flow in and through his body.

A knock at his door pulled him from his thoughts. Jessica stood meekly outside, as was her usual stance.

She poked her head in.

"Jeremiah, may I enter?"

"Of course. Please."

"We're ready."

"Do you have the food tents prepared for the converted? I want them to feel blessed by their decision immediately."

"They are," she said, having a hard time not smiling in his presence.

He stared at her once handsome face, now damaged, but he saw more beauty in her scars because they stood for something so meaningful. Every single person who had chosen to accept His word had been converted by Jeremiah personally, and each one carried a scar of some sort on their face.

The healing of these wounds was at God's discretion as to what scars and marks would remain. Some healed well, some not so well, and some lost the sense of smell or sight in an eye, but they were the extreme cases.

Most converts bore a scar that was only visible when studying their faces. Oddly, a hierarchy formed, with those who had scars or disfigurements more apparent than others at the top. He decided to let it go until it became a hindrance to his message or a danger to his flock.

Jeremiah set aside his reports and left the RV. He greeted each person he met with a light tap on the shoulder, a handshake, or a smile. He liked to keep in touch with his people. A good general knew his men. That bit of knowledge came from his father. Actually, a good bit of knowledge came from his father, the war hero, who commanded a company of soldiers in Vietnam.

Jeremiah remembered his father's stories that he often told in a drunken stupor. His father had explained to him in no small detail the tactics and methods they used in battle, and he harped on the mistakes that were made by leadership. His father never left out the gory details even though Jeremiah was only a child.

Jeremiah missed his father, despite the fact that things had not been good while he was alive. He missed the idea of a father most of all. God had taken over that place now, but a part of him knew that he had missed out as a child and those things led him to a life of crime. His past life did not bother him. God used illiterate and sinful men throughout history to do His works. He was no different.

An old railroad boxcar had been converted into a makeshift stage where Jeremiah would address the crowd. A ladder was set up on the side of the boxcar to board it. Jeremiah scarcely remembered walking the mile to the center of Bismarck, but by the time he noticed, he was already there.

He knew that it was not smart to allow his mind to wander so, but he could not help but feel exhilarated by the news he had received. He smiled kindly to the men who stood guard below the ladder.

The crowd was relatively small. Jessica had arranged several days of smaller crowds thinking it would be safer than one enormous one. He guessed fifteen thousand citizens stood there before him. There were five times that many people being held by his army in camps until they had their chance to hear Jeremiah's words.

Jeremiah stood on the top of the boxcar until the crowd grew quiet. The demeanor of this group was nothing like the rowdy crowd in Omaha, where many people clung desperately to what once was. No, these people had begun to see the end. They wore a shroud of hopelessness, and Jeremiah knew that he could talk to them of hope, of the future, and of His great word.

"I am Jeremiah, and I have come to bring you the good news. Today, if you so choose, I can grant you the freedom and peace you have been seeking. Today is the historic day of independence for this country, and although God has condemned it for its sin, I bring to you salvation. Today, you will mark your independence from treachery and evil, and you will celebrate His glory and your gift of freedom."

The crowd remained quiet, and their eyes were all distrustful. He didn't blame them, they were afraid.

"Your throne, O God, will last forever and ever, and righteousness will be the scepter of Your kingdom. You have loved righteousness and hated wickedness. Therefore, God, your God, has set you above your companions by anointing you with the oil of joy. Accept the gift I bring you today, and peace will be upon you and your children will find peace."

A voice shouted from the crowd. The man tried to remain hidden, but to Jeremiah's senses, he was as apparent as the sun.

"I heard you kill people?" said the voice.

A rumble went through the crowd, and Jeremiah waited for it to pass before he began again.

"The Lord was very angry with your forefathers. Therefore, I tell you this is what He says, return to Me, and I will return to you. Do not be like your forefathers, turn from your evil ways and your evil practices. But they would not listen or pay attention. Where are your forefathers now? Do they live forever? Did not my words and decrees, which I commanded, overtake them? Then they repented and said, 'The Almighty has done to us what our ways and practices deserve, just as He determined to do.' I offer what He has asked me to offer, peace, love, and joy. I urge you to accept. Do not be tempted by the wicked ways your forefathers chose. Today, I offer amnesty, forgiveness, and the gift of His word. All I ask of you is that you sign your name in the book by blood."

It was the first such event where there was no bloodshed by Jeremiah. Each man, woman, and child accepted His gift. It pleased him immensely, but he knew that without an example, there might be those that did not truly believe. He would keep a watchful eye out.

After he descended the boxcar and began the act of conversion, some tried to flee. The violent act of converting by blood made some wary and some afraid of their decision. His men captured some, killed others, but all in all, the day went smoothly.

When he was finished converting the crowd, the skin on his knuckles was a bloody mix of dried blood and tortured flesh. When Jeremiah got back to the RV, Jessica dipped his hands in a bowl of warm soapy water and cleansed them. She swaddled them in a bandage, which was unnecessary. By the time she had them taped up, they were almost completely healed.

Normally, Jeremiah did not require much sleep, but today, he was tired and desired company. He pulled Jessica close to him as he lay down. She nestled herself within his huge frame and cooed silently, basking in the warm glow of his company.

She loved him profusely. He had set her free and given her life meaning. He, in turn, loved her only a little more so than most, but he could not have favorites, only moments.

The next couple of weeks went very much the same. He would address a crowd, and they would convert. He would spend five to six hours seeing to their salvation, and then he would retire to lay or eat with Jessica. She was a calming companion. Rarely did she ask questions and yet offered sound advice when he left a question on the table.

She was not the smartest person by far, but she was an exceptional learner and an extremely hard worker. He found her devotion to him to be extremely endearing. He realized this could only be a temporary situation, so he enjoyed every second he could.

In the coming weeks, the march would continue onward, and he would have to deal with more and more desperate people. His teams of scouts had captured several violent men from the scavenger groups. Some of them had tried to steal from his camp. All were dispatched with ease, but the problem was pandemic and would only get worse—desperate people, desperate measures. He could not afford to be too distracted by his female companion.

After dinner, Jeremiah asked Jessica if she would like to nap with him. He always asked, but she never declined. He wasn't tired, but he enjoyed the closeness, the quiet, the solitude. He longed for God's plan to be completely revealed to him. He longed for an ending to the pain and suffering of the people. His time with Jessica temporarily erased his worries and longings.

Jessica's hair was soft, and her breathing steady. She trembled when he touched her, but not from fear; no, this girl was in awe. He buried his worries in her thin frame and basked in the momentary respite. They shared nearly two weeks of relative peace and tranquility, but as Jeremiah had foreseen, it did not last.

A man wearing a sweater vest and sporting hollow eyes nearly fell flat while rushing into Jeremiah's RV without knocking. He was out of breath as he crawled to a standing position. Jeremiah did not budge, trying to savor the final moment of tranquility with Jessica. Tucked into him, she did not budge, trusting him completely. The man looked embarrassed as he entered the small room, containing Jeremiah's bunk in the back of the RV.

"Sir, sir," he huffed, "I, I'm sorry…"

"My door is always open, brother, but you might want to try knocking all the same."

The man nodded so hard it nearly dislodged his head.

"Well, go on, what is it?" Jeremiah sighed.

"Yes, sir, well, they found the girl, sir."

"Which girl?"

"I'm sorry, sir, the lady soldier. He said you would know who she was…"

Jeremiah was up and past the nervous man before he could get the last words out. She was alive, and that meant she had killed his men. This was a resourceful woman, and she was obviously dangerous.

Jeremiah charged out of the RV, climbed onto his motorcycle, and rode to where he had temporarily set up his headquarters, knowing this is where his inner circle would be gathered. Most of his inner circle was comprised of bikers and ex-military. Some were from Vietnam and knew of his father. Some were from Panama, Lebanon, and some were even from Iraq.

He liked bikers; they were honest in a brutal way, and nearly the only ones left that didn't look at him with fear in their eyes. True, they knew he was different, and dangerous, but that didn't mean they backed down. These were the men that would tell him "no" when he needed to hear it.

One scout had made it back, barely. He had wounds all over his body. How he managed to keep his guts from spilling out was a mystery. He was a younger biker, recently discharged from the army. He had been in the infantry, but his commanding officer noticed his natural abilities and had him sent to Georgia to be trained as a scout.

Jeremiah's temporary headquarters had been set up in an abandoned post office just outside the Bismarck city limits. The young scout lay on the counter next to several rows of mailboxes, bleeding.

Jeremiah held the man's hand and nodded to him once he opened his eyes. His organs were held in as much by the bloody shirt as anything. His time on earth was limited.

"Brother, you did well," Jeremiah told him quietly.

The man's lip trembled, and his eyesight faded in and out.

"She's not hu...human," he said with slurred speech.

The others in the room looked at each other, as if to verify that they all believed he was delirious, but Jeremiah knew this woman was a problem.

"Is the doctor coming?" he asked the others.

"The doctor...uh, passed on?" said one of his bikers standing beside the table.

Jeremiah looked at each of his men.

"You are saying that although we have a hundred thousand people here, we only had one skilled medical professional?"

Seemingly with a hive mind, they nodded in unison.

"Th...they have f-f-fifteen m-m-men. D-d-dangeroussss... stay away. Sh...she's the d-d-devil," sputtered the young scout.

Those words made Jeremiah's call to action an easy decision. The devil must always be met with the capable and the righteous. He was both, and she had killed too many of his men to escape His wrath. Jeremiah smiled and tried to put the young dying man at ease.

"The Father is ready to receive you, brother. He is pleased with you, and it's time to go home. Are you ready?" Jeremiah asked with loving gentleness.

The young man craned his neck around and looked out the window. The sky was blue, and a few fluffy white clouds drifted lazily by. Jeremiah didn't move and allowed him all the time he wanted. The quiet was eerie and made them all contemplate their own endings. Finally with very little strength left, his eyes met Jeremiah's.

"It hurts."

"It is commendable if a man bears up under the pain of unjust suffering, because he is conscious of the Lord. Bear it for a moment longer, brother, and you shall see the face of God." He kissed his forehead.

Jeremiah walked to the back of him and held his head in his hands. He closed his eyes and murmured a prayer that no one could hear but God and with a quick twitch of his wrist, he snapped the young man's neck instantly. He then carefully shut the man's eyes. It was a dignified way to die.

"See to the funeral arrangements. I'm gonna take some of the boys and be gone for a while. Jessica has the tasks I want completed, be sure to stay on schedule. I want to be ready to move south and west when I get back."

He did not wait for their replies. He walked urgently out of the post office to his motorcycle. He was angry and wrestling with revenge. This woman was clearly standing in the way of God's plan, and she needed to be dealt with. Somewhere deep down, Jeremiah knew he was talking himself into this, and anger won out this time.

She was a monster of some sort, a devil. He was the Word personified, and she had to be dealt with. God required that this evil be extinguished from the earth, and Jeremiah knew that it was his duty to do it.

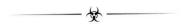

Lt. Finn had undergone amazing changes in the days since she had been shot. Her face was no longer a bloody monstrosity but was now covered by a thick, gray material more akin to an exoskeleton than skin. Her entire face was elongated, and her jaw appeared more reptilian than human. Her brow became thicker and eyes larger. She was hideous and bore a strange resemblance to a reptilian demon.

Normally, the virus didn't work so abruptly, but the damage to Lt. Finn was terribly severe. The needs of the host required upgrades. The virus responded to the host's strongest physical desires when they were at their highest levels. In fact, the virus could only alter the host if the host's desires were strong and consistent and came with complete willingness to become the manifestation of those desires. Under these circumstances, the improvements were easy and took little time.

Lt. Finn was obsessed with power, and her desire to dominate and destroy human life opened the door for the radical changes that reconstructed her form. To perform her work efficiently, Lt. Finn needed to be better protected, have superior senses, and have enhanced natural defenses. It was a miracle that the virus altered her physiology to keep her alive, but more incredibly, it appeared to surpass thousands of years of evolution in only a few painful days.

Along with the changes to her facial features came grotesque alterations to her body as well. Her arms were lengthened, and her fingers extended an extra three inches to end in sharp talons. Her legs grew in the same ratio as her arms, which gave her the look of a terrifying humanoid creature rather than a human being.

The changes also provided her with advanced agility and speed. The talons on her fingers were deadly weapons, and her eyesight and hearing improved exponentially, allowing her to see and hear accurately from long distances away. It had taken her nearly a week to heal into this new form, and the alterations to her body were painful at first, but now she was prepared to do her work well.

Lt. Finn believed that it was nature that had given her these gifts, because nature knew what she needed in order to fulfill her destiny. Her father had taught her that nature would one day cleanse itself completely, and she had slowly come into her own as the agent of this change.

It was her duty to purge the weak so that the strong could survive, and she knew that she would survive as the next step in evolution, for she was a greater being, born from nature's desire and need.

Lt. Finn's remaining force was comprised of twelve surviving men, and all but three of them had malignant cancers growing on their bodies and faces. As the Mad Hatter plague had wore on, these men had surrendered to the idea that they would all die, and therefore, had made an unspoken pact to do so as a band of brothers.

And while this gave them a sense of autonomy, an "us against the world" mentality, they remained loyal to Lt. Finn. Perhaps this loyalty was founded upon fear, or perhaps it was borne of familiarity, but whatever the reason, these men were committed to fighting to the death for the cause of Lt. Finn.

Lt. Finn was aware that she would need to move quickly in order to maximize the usefulness of her men. Her extrasensory perception had allowed her to hone in on Dr. Carrisa Harrison, and she knew that the woman was near, near enough that she could sense her presence. This excited Lt. Finn, and she methodically studied the scene at the hospital where she had been shot from behind. Her revenge for this shooting would be even more satisfying than extricating the coy doctor.

Lt. Finn matched the tread of the tires that Sergeant Thomas had left behind to skid marks left in the parking lot and followed them west. She had no idea where to look, but she knew that she would sense when she should stop.

The excitement welled up within her at the prospect of finding the woman doctor and crushing her head. She vowed that she would not kill her too quickly, not after all the trouble she had caused.

Lt. Finn sat in quiet contemplation from her throne on the passenger side of the lead Humvee, one of only three necessary to transport her unit. Her convoy had been vastly decreased by incompetence and disease, but she didn't care and actually looked forward to the day when all of her men would be dead and she could operate alone.

She felt the Earth calling to her. Soon, she would run free, culling the weak wherever she went. She would do what she was always meant to do with no one to stand in her way. But first, she needed these men to help her cut the head off the giant preacher and send his army into complete disarray.

Chapter 25

Col. Bragg's entrance to the underground lab was a surprise. First to Sgt. Thomas, who worked for the colonel on his last assignment as part of a tactical unit with a mission to secure and control the outbreak at Pecan Island.

Second, the colonel's appearance in the underground lab was a surprise to Carrisa, who remembered the tall man who had taken her samples, nearly by force, while flirting with her at the same time. Those events seemed like a lifetime ago to Carrisa, even though she quickly calculated that it had only been a couple of months.

"What the hell?" she exclaimed as she watched Col. Bragg walk into the room behind Tony.

Tony entered first and announced the visitor in an attempt to quell any alarm, but it had little effect on the group. Irish, who became startled when he heard Carrisa's reaction, slid into an adjacent room with his hand carefully wrapped around his pistol. Sgt. Thomas was incredulous, and his weapon was never far from his poised hand. Everyone else watched as Tony and the stranger entered. The only person missing was Don. He was still in Sara's room holding her hand, frozen in sorrow and lost in memory.

When the colonel first saw Carrisa, he froze and his stomach did a somersault; it was a sensation he had not experienced in years. It felt like he had been waiting a lifetime to see her face again, and now, here she was scowling at him with equal portions of hatred and shock painted upon her usually warm features. Even so, the sight of her set his heart at ease. He felt an inexplicable sense of fulfillment in her presence, and he was content to do whatever was necessary to be near her.

Col. Bragg slowly pulled his sidearm from his holster. Irish allowed his weapon to come forward, still out of sight from the colonel, and Sgt. Thomas reacted immediately, raising his weapon and pointing it defensively at him. Col. Bragg carefully and methodically lifted his free hand to show that he meant no harm, and then he laid his gun on a nearby table.

"I'm not here to hurt anyone," he said calmly.

Sgt. Thomas lowered his barrel to acknowledge Col. Bragg's gesture, but Irish did not dip his gun an inch as he slowly moved into the room. Col. Bragg saw the movement peripherally and recognized his situation was more precarious than he previously thought.

"Who'd ya say this was, mate?" he asked.

Before Tony could answer, Carrisa stormed across the room toward the colonel with a singular purpose.

"You son of a bitch. If you would have let things alone, we might have been able to control this!" Carrisa said vehemently as she slapped him hard across his face.

The colonel barely moved and smiled at her. He liked her even more. His memory of her tenacity was nothing compared to the real thing.

Tony stepped in, his face was hollow, but he knew he had to take charge.

"That's enough…"

"It's not enough. Tony, do you know who this is?" Carrisa nearly yelled.

Tony nodded, looking tired.

"I do, Carrie, and he brought us something we need."

He held up the vial, which contained the small meteor fragment. Everyone stared with no real comprehension of what they were looking at.

"It's the source," he continued. "Whatever we are dealing with was found in a meteor.

Carrisa put her face in her hands. The realization that Don was correct hit her hard.

Col. Bragg stepped forward slightly to explain but was met and stopped in his tracks by the freshly displayed gun barrels of Sgt. Thomas and Irish. The colonel froze but smirked as adrenaline and testosterone coursed through his veins.

"Sergeant," Col. Bragg said with clear meaning and a commanding tone.

Sgt. Thomas's military training made it difficult for him not to obey. He dropped the barrel again to a safe degree. Col. Bragg then stared fearlessly at Irish.

"I hate to be rude here, *mate*, but the idea of a bullet in my skull makes me a little jumpy, capisca?"

Irish studied him a minute longer and smiled an identical smile while lowering his weapon, the same testosterone running through his veins.

"We found this one frozen in a chunk of ice that hit the Gulf of Mexico. A fisherman retrieved it and kept it in his freezer. Others were retrieved from a glacier in Antarctica. Apparently, we were hit with ice meteors a couple of months ago. Most of them fell in the ocean, but a few hit land.

"This one was essentially a small ball of ice with small chunks of heavy metals. When we thawed the ice and put some of the supernatants on cells, it killed them almost instantly. It killed mice, hamsters, rats, ferrets, monkeys—hell, it killed everything it came into contact with," Col. Bragg stated.

The colonel recognized that these people were tired and defeated, but he knew that the human race was rapidly becoming extinct, and that they represented one of the very few opportunities to come up with a cure.

"The past is the past. There's nothing any of us can do about it now. For those of you who do not know, I am Colonel

Adrian Bragg. I used to head up the Bioweapons Division for USAMRIID, where it was my primary directive to procure threats against this country and provide biological weapons for our protection. I don't do that anymore. No one does anything anymore. Everything is gone or soon will be. No matter what the costs are, we have to find a way to stop this thing from going any further."

Col. Bragg paused for a moment to assess the reaction. His expression faded to one of deadly seriousness.

"So either come to terms with the fact that I'm here to help or put a bullet in my head right now. Got that you stupid, mick?"

Irish stood blank-faced for a moment, allowing the tension to grow thick, and then he smiled and laughed out loud.

"He's an arsehole, but I believe him," he said, and with that, he holstered his weapon, easing the tense moment.

Col. Bragg surveyed the lab. He immediately determined that most of the equipment was antiquated, but also recognized that clever modifications had been made. He knew the difficulties and limitations that they faced, and he found the challenge exciting.

He knew that for the first time in a very long time, he was going to be a doctor again. And he knew that the stakes would never be higher.

"All right, everyone, let's get to work. First thing's first, Colonel, let's compare notes," Tony said.

Tony, Carrisa, and the colonel spent a couple of hours reviewing each other's work and gathering specific details that each had learned about the virus. Tony shared the electron micrographs that Ramsey had taken of the virus, and the colonel was impressed.

"We attempted to get electron micrographs, too, but for some reason, we were unable to fix the samples correctly. They were still working on it when I had to run from my old lab."

"Why did you have to run?" asked Carrisa.

"The only reason to ever run," he answered.

"And what was that?"

"Woman problems."

Tony laughed while looking back at the micrographs and missed the moment Col. Bragg and Carrisa shared.

She couldn't figure this man out. Something about him seemed so intense and honest, although she knew he was completely capable of lying.

While looking at the micrographs, Col. Bragg just stared at the image for what seemed like an unbearable amount of time to Tony.

"Pretty cool, huh?" Tony said.

"So intricate, and beautiful. It's hard to imagine that something so small and beautiful could wreak such havoc," said Col. Bragg.

Tony kept a log of all their findings and discussions on the chalkboard. The colonel verified that the virus infected all eukaryotic cells that his lab had tested, too, and like Tony, they also discovered that plants and lower animals were hyper-susceptible to the virus.

The colonel had conducted preliminary studies in nonhuman primates, but everything except chimpanzees died within forty-eight hours. Chimpanzees survived for about two weeks before succumbing to the disease caused by the virus. Both Tony and the colonel's team had uncovered evidence that indicated that humans were initially hyper-susceptible to the virus, but discovered that the virus quickly adapted to its human environment. There seemed to be different phenotypes in humans, and they agreed on a temporary nomenclature to distinguish different events and stages.

The Alpha Event was characterized as an outbreak with the first virus released into the ocean. At that time, the virus was extremely virulent and caused rapid mortality in every eukaryotic cell that it infected. In humans, it caused rapid and complete mortality.

The Beta Event was characterized as infection by the virus that had the same deadly outcome in all other eukaryotic cells, but in humans, it appeared to be attenuated except among the old and young.

The Gamma Event caused infection with the attenuated virus where victims between eleven and sixty-four years of age were either asymptomatic or in a state of progression.

Tony hypothesized that the virus had to find a way to maintain a symbiotic relationship with at least one host or else it would be destined to die with everything that it killed. The virus had most likely adapted to be less virulent in most people but killed children under ten and adults over sixty-five.

They thought that this was due to some unknown intrinsic immune system factor that was not yet produced in the prepubescent population, and that experienced arrest or decline in geriatric populations.

The Delta Event was characterized as infection with the attenuated version of the virus that resulted in superhuman strength and an increase in aggression toward others. The colonel had been working on characterizing this event when he was arrested. He reported that his team found some interesting results.

They found that the virus encoded a factor that up-regulated androgenic and anabolic effects by turning up the activation rate of enzyme systems involved in protein synthesis. They tested six troops that had been infected at the kill zone and who exhibited the superhuman phenotype and discovered that in all six cases, the men demonstrated an increase in testosterone and an increase in the number of steroid receptors in muscle tissues.

This accounted for the rapid acceleration in muscle growth, bone, red blood cells, and enhanced neural conduction reported in these men. Further, they found in all six cases that there was a decrease in cortisol production, the enzyme associated with soreness of muscles after working out, which indicated that the virus allowed rapid muscle production with little pain.

The Delta Event was of great concern to the colonel, and he explained that if history were any indication, the deltas would take over as the country turned into a warring tribal culture, which would be inevitable if a cure was not found.

Carrisa excused herself to check on the others, but truthfully, she was worried about Don and began to grow unsure of her feelings concerning the intense looks she received from Col. Bragg. She needed a breather.

"I'll be back, I need some air," she said.

"Would you care for some company?" Col. Bragg stood as she excused herself.

Tony was absorbed in the evidence and didn't see Col. Bragg's open desire. Carrisa almost stuttered. She hadn't felt this desired in a long while.

"That's okay…maybe…rain check."

Col. Bragg watched her as she left. Tony went through the colonel's notes and was quite impressed with his findings.

"So you believe that the virus actually up-regulates strength?"

"In some cases, it appears to, very much along the same lines as taking steroids."

"What's the cost to the body?"

"I don't know. But I would bet that we are going to see the same type of burnout that has been described in habitual steroid users. Insanity, social instability, uncontrollable aggression, and extreme paranoia."

The colonel reported that his team also discovered that some viral factors appeared to up-regulate the mitochondria, resulting in increased energy production. In a nutshell, the virus was turning up protein expression and energy production so that it could make more copies of itself at an accelerated rate.

In the process, the virus provided a benefit to the host because it rapidly arrested age progression and reversed the aging processing, setting the stage for rapid muscle growth and increased strength. This resulted in an increase in weight and bulk, and increased the infected person's strength by 30 to 50 percent.

"Simply amazing," Tony began. "This has got to be a first. A virus that improves the host. Juventas," Tony said aloud to himself.

"Ju…what?"

"Juventas, the Roman goddess of youth. Perhaps, we should call this the Juventas virus."

"Good as any, I guess. Better than the Mad Hatter," Col. Bragg said.

"I don't know if we'll do as well with the merchandising."

Col. Bragg appreciated Tony's humor.

"So MADS is caused by the Juventas virus. The only problem is that if we find a way to destroy this virus, I am afraid that those that are cured are going to have severe long-term effects."

"You mean like those coming off steroids?"

"Maybe worse."

The colonel explained that once the virus was destroyed, the anabolic rate would return to normal, actually a new post-virus normal, which could have all of the classic features of the steroid junky, only magnified.

These effects might include rapid muscle loss with a decrease in strength, a decrease in testosterone production resulting in feminine features and shrinkage of the male genitalia and cortisol suppression of the immune system, resulting in increased numbers of sicknesses due to immune system failure.

Finally, there would be muscle damage, mitochondrial damage resulting in decreased strength and energy, and rapid onset of chronic depression that would seem insurmountable.

When Carrisa came back into the room, the colonel was dozing in a chair. Tony stared at the chalkboard, seemingly in a daze. They had made progress, but the problem was not solved. The virus was an amazing organism, more complicated than they could have ever imagined, but Tony had dissected it bit by bit, finding clues where no clues existed.

His display of mental energy was immeasurable. They were all children compared to him, but Carrisa knew it was important that he never know she felt this way. He would be incorrigible.

She tried to turn and walk out before he was noticed her, but Tony spoke.

She wasn't sure to whom he was speaking though because she noticed Col. Bragg's eyes were open by then.

"What about the cancers?" Tony asked.

Col. Bragg watched Carrisa turn back into the room. She was the most beautiful thing he had ever seen. He wanted to get her alone, but didn't want to push the issue. He was also unsure of her relationship with Dr. Van Lee. There was something there, a history, but it was not completely apparent.

"Have you learned anything about those that are infected with JV that develop cancer?"

"No," Col. Bragg said sleepily, "that is a relatively recent development. You got any ideas, Carrisa?"

She couldn't help but smile and feel a little bit self-conscious when he looked at her. She unconsciously fixed her hair as she spoke.

"From what I've learned, it appears that the cancers that have become rampant the past few weeks are those that are normally caused by latent human viruses like herpes and human papilloma viruses, etc.," she stated.

"A colleague at the CDC said that many of the patients she examined presented with human papilloma virus induced cancers, while almost everyone else had herpes virus induced cold sores or varicella zoster. Annie has a pretty extreme case that we can start culturing."

Tony thought it peculiar that Carrisa was acting a bit odd around Col. Bragg but went on to explained that JV suppressed the immune system, perhaps by hijacking the anabolic rate, which allowed latent viruses to become lytic infections that accelerated toward cancer. This was the Epsilon Event.

"Don't we all have some form of latent DNA virus infection? Are those that display the superhuman phenotype also susceptible to these lytically activated cancers?" asked Col. Bragg.

"I don't know," Tony replied. "I haven't seen anyone with the superhuman phenotype that had cancer."

"About 80 percent of us are infected with latent viruses," Carrisa added. "Is it possible that those who are latently infected with other viruses don't experience the Delta Event?"

"Possible," Tony said with a smile.

Carrisa smiled too, even though she felt embarrassed as she realized that she was delighting in Tony's approval.

"What other outcomes have you observed?" Col. Bragg asked.

"Irish mentioned that drug addicts were dying, and I've heard on the news that those infected with HIV or any type of disease that suppresses the immune system are dying, too."

"Okay," Col. Bragg said, "that seems to be related to the Epsilon Event. Everyone infected has a disabled immune system. Malnutrition in Africa has accounted for millions of deaths. Those with debilitating diseases like muscle dystrophy and cerebral palsy are dying. Those infected with malaria and exposed to JV are also dying. There seems to be no room for error in the Epsilon stage. This virus is a greedy bastard. It wants humans all to itself. But there has to be some portion of the human population that are genetically resistant."

"Yes," Tony began, "the mutants always find a way to survive. I have gathered a few plant mutants that have survived, and I have been doing some experiments to determine what they have or don't have that allows them to survive when everything else around it died."

"What about Don?" Carrisa asked. "He's the only one among us that has not been infected. And why are we not experiencing the viral infection as one of these events?"

"I think that Don carries a resistance allele to this virus. He has shown no signs of disease, and Ramsey couldn't find a virus in any sample from him," Tony said. "As for the rest of us that have been infected, I have a hunch."

"I spent a lifetime trying to create viruses that destroy humans," Col. Bragg said. "Now, we have to figure out how to stop this one," he said introspectively.

Tony went on to explain what he had learned by his observations and experiments. He described how every antiviral he tested was ineffective, and how every cell type he tried was susceptible to the virus. From these results, he hypothesized that the receptor would be highly conserved among all eukaryotes and would be commonly found on all eukaryotic cells.

He predicted that since the ubiquitous cellular receptor would be present on many cell types within the human body, this would allow the virus to infect respiratory cells through the aerosol route, cells in the gastrointestinal tract through the fecal-oral transmission route, and primary immune cells via the blood-borne route.

"I agree," Col. Bragg said. "It scares the hell out of me how this virus infects everything. It is clearly a generalist, and it obviously has not co-evolved with life systems on this planet!"

"This one plays by its own rules," Tony said.

Tony went on to describe how he characterized the difference between human and plant cells that he had infected in the lab. In humans, JV did not appear to target any specific cell, but rather seemed to infect them all.

"Was your team able to detect any viral DNA or RNA?" Tony asked the colonel.

"Nothing. It's got to be there, but it's an alien life form, so it might be different than what we're used to. Perhaps, it doesn't form the double helix that we are familiar with, or uses different bases or linkages to form the polymers, making it impossible to detect by methods we use."

"Or the virus is safeguarding its RNA or DNA by encasing it in a protective protein coat."

Col. Bragg shrugged.

"After seeing how complex the structure of the viral capsid is in the electron micrograph, it would not surprise me at all if it had evolved a unique mechanism for protecting the viral genetic template."

"Unfortunately, that leaves us shooting in the dark," Carrisa interjected.

"Well, not completely," Tony added. "We don't know what its genetics are, but we still might be able to stop it from entering the cell."

"The only way to do that would be to block the interaction between the virus and the cell," Col. Bragg said. "That would prevent infection, and perhaps limit the severity of infection in those who already have the virus, but that might not be a cure."

"You would need to know which receptor the virus uses, wouldn't you?" Carrisa asked.

"Not necessarily. We don't have time to work through all of those details. But we can use what little information we have against the virus."

"We're all ears, Doctor," Col. Bragg stated with an air of irritability.

Tony laid out his hypothesis. First, he described in detail the experiments he conducted using the mutant corn plant that survived virus infection in the field. He explained how he took lysates from the corn kernels, suspended them in solution and then used them to pretreat plant and animal cells. When this was applied to cells prior to infection with the virus, the cells were resistant to infection in all cases.

The next experiment was designed to determine if the corn kernel lysates were capable of stopping infection in previously infected cells. The results indicated that the virus could be slowed down, but not stopped.

"My theory is that the mutant corn plant makes a protein that inhibits the virus. It could be a receptor analog that's different enough to prevent infection, but similar enough to still interact with the virus. Or it could be some factor that down regulates a pathway the virus requires for replication," Tony explained.

"Actually, it could be any number of things, but the important thing is that you have evidence that an unknown factor in a mutated corn plant is capable of preventing infection. That's huge," Col. Bragg stated.

"So all we have to do is identify the factor," Carrisa added. "Sort of like finding a needle in a haystack."

Carrisa smiled and caught the colonel smiling back at her. Something about the man intrigued her, and she couldn't help a shy smile back, which she knew would further encourage him. He seemed too focused on her, and since she hadn't felt doted on for a long time, she honestly liked it.

"And my hunch," Tony began, "is that whatever gene gives rise to resistance in corn is going to be a highly conserved sequence that plays a role in basic cellular metabolism found in common among all eukaryotes. Actually, as crazy as this sounds, I think it will be found in my marijuana plants."

"Be serious, please," Carrisa chastised, "now is not the time to start that again."

"Wait a minute, just listen. Everyone in the lab has been exposed to my marijuana smoke. I don't hide it, and occasionally, neither do you. But remember when Sara looked like she was going to die and then recovered for a short time? The night before I stopped by her room to check on her, and I kind of accidentally filled her room with smoke. By the next morning, she had improved."

"So what are you saying?" she asked.

"My pot and the corn may be our answer."

Col. Bragg cleared his throat unconsciously. "You think a movie snack and a joint is the answer to save all of humanity?"

Tony didn't even hear the colonel's remark. His eyes sparkled with excitement, and his wheels were going a million miles an hour.

Annie's lesion had gotten larger since Tony last looked at it a day earlier, and the girl was growing more and more self-conscious. Tony was gentle as he examined her, and she did what he asked her to do.

"I want to try something," he told her. "It's kind of a long shot, but if it works, you will be the first human to know for sure."

"Will it hurt?"

"No, I think you might like this treatment."

Tony removed a few joints from his pouch and held them out for her to take.

"Do you know what to do with these?" he asked.

"I tried it once," she replied sheepishly. "Are you sure that I should do this?"

"Doctor's orders," he replied. "I want you to take a toke of this three times a day. You won't need much because it's strong, but three times a day until I tell you to stop, okay?"

Annie smiled. "You're the best doctor of all time."

Over the next several days, experiments and observations went on nearly around the clock. Tony fully investigated his genetically modified marijuana and determined that the modified THC from his GMO marijuana effectively reduced the number of steroid receptors on the cells' surface and slowed the virus infection in all of the cells he tested.

He observed Annie on a daily basis and was pleased to see that her lesion at first stopped growing and then by day three had started to decrease in size. She was ecstatic.

Tony concluded that the marijuana did not kill the virus but prevented it from replicating efficiently and, therefore, forced the virus into a state of latency. This allowed the immune system to fight back a little, and for those experiencing the Epsilon Event, it would be a very helpful medication. While this was encouraging, it was not the cure that he had hoped for, and so he continued to work.

Col. Bragg focused on trying to identify the factor that was present in the mutated corn. He tried to access his old Top Secret database records to determine if USAMRIID had discovered anything but learned that Lt. Finn had discontinued his security clearance.

He also quickly discovered that many of the scientific resources that scientists used for doing genetic analyses were no longer available online. Access to public databases had been discontinued and for hire services and companies no longer responded to e-mails.

The colonel was discouraged and felt defeated when he called Tony over to tell him there was no way to identify the unknown factor. In all honesty, Col. Bragg was even amazed that any of the satellites were still online whatsoever.

"We don't have the tools to do the complex trait analyses necessary to identify this unknown protein," Col. Bragg said, eyes looking toward the floor.

"It's our only hope," Tony said. "We may have to resort to some old-school techniques. What did they do fifty years ago when they had to identify unknown factors?"

"Molecular biology has really only been around for about twenty-five years. Before that, it was a lot of serendipity. Proteomics, on the other hand is even more modern, and identifying an unknown protein is…well, it sucks. We can't identify it without the proper tools."

Tony thought for a moment.

"What if we make the virus work for us?"

"How do you mean?" Col. Bragg asked.

"What if we incubate the virus with the corn kernel lysates for an hour, and then wash the virus through a series of Chamberland filters. Anything that attaches to the virus would be pulled through with it. I already know that the virus is too big to go through the smallest filter, so we could use it to trap the virus with the unknown protein attached. Then we purify the virus-protein complex, heat it up to force release of the protein, and then run it on a gel."

"That's actually a good idea," Col. Bragg said. "If it's not a receptor analog or a protein, then we'll be shit out of luck, but for now, it's our only hope."

Carrisa walked in, looking a bit haggard.

"I've got Annie's cultures incubating. It's going to be a while. I'm going for a walk," she said as she yawned.

"Is it daytime?" Tony answered without his eyes leaving the chalkboard, which had a multitude of ideas written on it.

"Good question. I haven't been outside in a week."

Carrisa flipped a couple of switches on the monitors that Tony had installed. It was day out and a nice one at that.

"Yeah, day."

"Take Sgt. Thomas or Irish with you," Tony said, again without taking his eyes off the board.

"Maybe I'll ask Don to go?"

"Sounds good," Tony answered, already slipping back into contemplation mode.

Col. Bragg stood off to his side, wanting desperately to go with her, but he knew this was not the time to indulge. There were more important things that needed tending to, but he couldn't resist a quick rendezvous.

"I'm gonna hit the latrine," the colonel said, leaving Tony focused on the board.

Col. Bragg caught up with Carrisa in the hallway. He could see clearly down either side of the hall, and he decided it was a good neutral place that would serve to staunch rumors if they were seen together.

"I drove halfway across the country just to see you," Col. Bragg said with a small crooked smirk.

Carissa stopped and turned toward him. It was dark in this hall, but she could see him just fine. He was handsome, and he seemed to be able to stare right through her. It made her feel nervous and excited at the same time.

"I bet you say that to all the girls during the apocalypse," she said.

"You got me. My best line," he continued to breathe her in with his eyes. "This is going to sound…well, rather odd, but I think I'm in love with you."

Carrisa could only stare at him. "That's not possible. You don't even know me."

"Oh, I know you. I knew you the moment I first laid eyes on you. Fearless, tenacious, beautiful," he said and drew closer to her.

Carissa didn't move. She was frozen by him; something inside wouldn't allow her to move. Only inches from her face, she could feel his body heat.

"Please don't look at me like that," she pleaded in a whisper.

Col. Bragg tilted his head slightly, giving her fair warning as to what was about to happen.

"I don't know how else to see you."

Softly he kissed her, and she did not resist. The kiss was deep and filled with passion. Their lips, moist with each other, separated and they stared into one another's eyes.

"I'm pregnant with his child," she said, nearly out of breath.

"I don't care."

Carissa blinked and pulled herself out of the daze and turned away, but not cruelly. She continued her walk to the surface.

"Did it work?" Col. Bragg asked.

"Did what work?" she stopped and looked at him.

"My line."

Carissa smiled and continued her ascent. Col. Bragg watched her go for a while and then turned to return to the lab. The colonel noticed Irish and Sgt. Thomas standing quietly on either side of the hall behind him. Both men had their heads down and were feeling awkward pretending they had heard nothing. Col. Bragg smiled to himself.

"Gentlemen," the colonel said to break the ice.

Both men nodded and waited for him to go by before following Carissa. They looked at one another silently as he passed and then laughed, finding it ironic that even at the end of the world, there was such drama.

The sunshine felt foreign when it first hit Carrisa's face, but she smiled and absorbed it. Irish and Sgt. Thomas sauntered out behind her, disinterested. They had been reduced to domestic servants because they were not doctors.

They cooked, fetched, and did a lot of waiting around. Neither was used to being idle, neither liked it. However, as two soldiers cut from distinct cloths, they had a lot in common and their relationship became quite friendly.

Carrisa set out on a course that only she seemed to know and she set a good pace.

"Guess she's getting cabin fever," Sgt. Thomas remarked offhandedly.

Irish nodded and kicked a rock.

"Aye. Gettin' a bit myself."

Carrisa set a blistering pace, which neither man seemed to notice until they were separated by a good clip. She was used to being independent and out of doors. The work they were doing was important, very important, but she stopped working in a lab for a reason. She hated being inside. It made her feel claustrophobic.

The sun and the breeze made her feel better already. North Dakota had steady weather in the summer, usually not rising above ninety degrees. Today was an exceptional day, a postcard moment.

She looked behind her and saw the two men dallying far off, engaged in a conversation that men loose themselves in. Why they did that she could not understand; men were a mystery. Tony was no different. Once he locked onto a subject, everything else in the world disappeared, and she was tired of being invisible.

She found a lone tree to sit under, and she leaned against the solid trunk as she turned her thoughts to her unborn child. This was a mixed blessing and circumstances had made the discovery less joyful than she would have liked, but it was a moment she had waited her whole life for. Years and years she had waited and prayed, and then one day, she realized it was too late. How quickly that had changed. But she knew that all good things came with a price.

It concerned her that she and Tony had not talked about the baby. She knew he had tried several times, but she didn't make it easy for him. She realized that he must be having nearly as many thoughts about being a father as she was about being a mother. She just couldn't let up and she did not know why.

She knew that they needed to speak and get it out into the open. She was also certain that they would need to figure out how the virus would affect the baby. It terrified her to think that she may give birth only to watch the newborn slowly die from infection with this virus.

And then there was Col. Bragg. She was attracted to him in a terrible way. He was the bad boy she had always made mistakes with as a young woman. He had all the attributes of one of her old flings that crashed and burned; but he was intelligent, a doctor, and so intense. It was that very intensity that she couldn't seem to resist, but she needed to figure something out or this would escalate into a problem.

While she was lost in her thoughts, she didn't register that a truck was driving in her direction at a fast rate of speed. It left a trail of dust behind it like a rooster tail. When she finally noticed it, she instinctually inched closer to the tree in an attempt to camouflage herself. The ruse didn't work, though, because the truck kept speeding her way. She wasn't sure why she didn't call out earlier, shock maybe. But the truck was impossibly close when she did.

"Irish! Sgt. Thomas! A truck!"

The two men were at least a thousand yards away, and there was no way they could get to her before the truck. Her only hope was that no one in the truck wished her harm. As the anxiety built within her, she saw a familiar face, Noah. He pointed at her and the driver skidded to a halt.

"Noah? What are you doing…"

A large and ominous man jumped out of the driver's seat at the same time as two others jumped out of the back. All three men had hideous scars on their faces, and they were all armed. The hope that they meant her no harm quickly vanished.

Noah had a strange look on his face, one she could only describe as a combination of fervor and insanity.

"I need you to get in the back of the truck, ma'am. You won't get hurt if you do what you're told," said one of the men with a deep Southern accent.

The other men said nothing.

Carrisa thought about ways to stall them, knowing her saviors were just over the hill. Her prevarication cost her a rough push into the side of the truck. At a nod from the driver, the two other armed men grabbed her and tied her arms behind her back and then threw her into the bed. No sooner had her face hit the cold metal, than she heard gunfire and men yelling. She could feel the vehicle spinning its tires and fishtailing in the grass, as bullets rang out at a near constant rate.

Soon the truck was speeding away at a high rate of speed, taking her to God only knew where. It was then that she realized she was crying.

Chapter 26

WHEN SGT. THOMAS and Irish arrived at the top of the hill, they saw two men slam Carrisa into the back of the truck. The truck had at least four men total, and Noah's face was immediately recognizable.

Men from the truck began firing almost instantly, but these were not trained men, at least not well-trained men. The fire was scattered and landed nowhere close to them. Irish and Sgt. Thomas knelt side by side and chose very carefully where to fire to avoid harming the doctor.

It was difficult to do any real damage from this distance with the truck moving away, but Noah stuck his head out, and Sgt. Thomas put a bullet in it. Another man attempted to lean out the window and fire at them, but Irish put a bullet in his chest just as the truck went out of range. The two men helplessly watched the vehicle disappear.

Irish gritted his teeth and shook his head.

"How fast you think they're going, mate?"

"Twenty, thirty miles an hour."

"We need to catch them before they hit the road. Last one's a rotten egg."

Irish took off at a run, with Sgt. Thomas right on his heels. They reached speeds that were not possible for most humans, drawing on the power that the Mad Hatter provided them.

Both men continued to accelerate and when they needed more, the virus had changed their physiology enough for them to have it. There would be a price to this, Irish thought, vaguely aware, but he needed to catch the truck and worry about consequences later.

Irish and Sgt. Thomas nearly caught the truck. Two small rooster tails of dust sprayed from behind them. The men in the truck saw two men pursuing them and one climbed out through the sliding glass window to the bed and began to fire at them haphazardly.

A bullet struck Sgt. Thomas in the shoulder, but he barely registered the hit. The road was only a couple of hundred feet ahead, and Irish wasn't sure if they would make it. Once they hit the road, the truck could speed away, and virus or not, they would be unable to catch them. So he pressed even harder. The man in the back fell many times as the terrain made it difficult to stand and fire his weapon with any accuracy.

Irish reached the truck first and grabbed the rail of the bed. He could see Carrisa's small, tied form in the fetal position, bouncing about in the back. For only a moment, their eyes met, and Irish saw the pure unadulterated fear in her eyes.

The man smashed Irish's finger with the butt of his gun, forcing Irish to let go, but Sgt. Thomas sprung into the bed from the other side. However, his momentum and an unfortunately timed bump ejected both men out of the back and onto the ground just as the truck hit the asphalt highway and accelerated away.

Irish watched it speed away, with the vision of Carrisa's scared face brandished in his mind. Behind him, Sgt. Thomas had knocked the man out cold and thrown him over his shoulder.

"Best we get back and interrogate this guy as fast as we can."

Irish nodded and looked back at the truck, which was now only a small black dot on the horizon.

"Aye mate, aye."

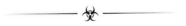

Lt. Finn watched the truck speed off from a distant tree. Although it was a long way off, she could see it quite clearly. She also saw the body lying in the back being pummeled by the bumps; she knew it was the woman doctor. It was the very thing that drove her, and the sight of the woman caused her to salivate. Her first instinct was to charge out, catch the truck, and kill the doctor immediately, but that was not prudent. She would be putting herself in unnecessary danger.

The woman doctor's captors, and other scavenger groups, had been tracking Lt. Finn for over a week. They had caught nearly all her men one by one and killed them. She didn't care at all for the men's lives, but the pomposity that the hunters displayed could not go unpunished. They mistook her for a victim and did not realize the truth of her purpose; she was the hunter! How dare they hunt the hunter.

There were only two men left from her original military contingent, and they were barely definable as men at this point. Cancerous tumors covered their entire faces and left only thin creases by which they could see. Dementia and insanity had settled into their brains, and she controlled them by providing food. They were animals with guns—fodder, and that's all she needed from them to get to the large preacher man.

Something about him was different; she could smell it when she was close, but getting close had become increasingly difficult. Somehow, he seemed to know when she was close by, and in turn, she felt the change in the behavior of his men.

At first, the preacher sent his men into the forested areas after her, but she easily dispatched them. The next attacks were coordinated and organized. The preacher learned quickly, and her men did not have the gift she received from nature, which allowed her to escape them. She was faster with a heightened sense of smell, and Mother Nature took care of her own.

Lt. Finn attempted to use fear to ward off the preacher's soldiers, so she captured several of his men in the dark and skinned them alive, leaving their flesh and bodies hanging upside down in separate trees. Their skin came off like warm butter with her claws, which were razor sharp.

Although she smelled the fear on the men who discovered their dead friends, their fear of the large man was greater than their fear of her. This infuriated her because this man was not called to the culling as she was, and therefore, he must be disposed of for his insolence.

Lt. Finn found it more and more difficult to stay focused because her thoughts were overcome by feral instincts and desires to feed on anything two-legged. In the back of her mind, she remembered that it was taboo to eat other humans, but like animals, they were far below her, and their flesh tasted so sweet it could not be resisted.

Eventually, some of the men that Jeremiah sent to kill her were captured, and she was no longer able to hold back her desires. She built a web of vines fifty feet high between two trees and tied the men firmly in her web. She did not gag them, and their screams and calls for help attracted more men who were trapped in the web. Lt. Finn kept the men alive as long as she could, eating only small portions of them at a time.

Lt. Finn held pace with the truck, keeping herself hidden in wooded areas. She was able to choose a path as if it was a road before her. She had no need to track the truck, she knew where their camp was located, and the smell of the woman doctor was hard to ignore.

The temptation to intercept the truck and kill the woman doctor was great, but Lt. Finn resisted and waited, albeit not so patiently. She would kill the woman doctor, but now she had to kill the preacher man first. She wanted nothing to distract her from the journey she would take with the woman doctor. The culling of the woman doctor needed to be perfect, Mother Nature demanded it, and Lt. Finn was her faithful servant.

Chapter 27

Tony and the colonel went to work, testing Tony's idea as soon as Carrisa went for her walk, not wanting to sacrifice any time. Tony really wanted to have a conversation with her because he knew they had a lot to talk about with the baby coming, but finding the cure had to take precedence, and he tried to keep the pregnancy from distracting his thoughts.

Both men were delighted to learn that incubating the virus with the corn kernel lysates was sufficient to prevent the virus from infecting cells. Something was obviously attaching to the virus and preventing it from attaching to cells or destroying the virus.

After, purifying the virus with the unknown factor attached to it using the Chamberland filters, Tony heated the sample in an attempt to unfold the unknown protein, knowing that if the protein unfolded, it would no longer be able to bind to the virus and then the virus and unknown protein could be separated on a gel.

There were two potential problems that worried him. First, if the virus itself broke apart at high temperature, it might also have proteins that would mix with the unknown protein, making it impossible to distinguish them on the gel. However, knowing what he knew about JV, he suspected that it would be able to withstand high temperatures.

Second, he worried that the unknown factor would not unfold, and therefore, would not be freed from the virus capsid. This could happen if the factor was something other than a protein or if it was a heat stable protein that could tolerate high temperatures.

The potential problems were immense, but Tony knew that he had to try, and he was extremely pleased when he looked at his results. After the high temperature incubation, he ran the solution on a protein gel and was pleased to find a single clean band, representing a protein of about 158 kilodaltons in size. There was a smear of other proteins that accumulated at the top of the gel, which he thought was probably the virus.

As he suspected, it looked like the virus remained intact, and the heat released the protein. Tony cut the protein out of the gel and purified it. To verify that the virus was still intact, he filtered part of the heated solution through the Chamberland filters and applied the purified virus to cells. All of the cells died as he had previously witnessed, indicating the virus was still intact.

Col. Bragg was impressed by Tony's isolation technique and had come to rely on his insight to guide his own experimentation.

"Too bad we don't have access to protein sequencing," Col. Bragg said. "We really need to know the sequence of that protein."

"Do you know how to run a mass spec machine?" Tony asked.

"I haven't done that sort of work since my graduate school days. I could probably figure it out."

"There's a mass spec down in the lower level here. It is probably thirty years old or more, but I think it is still functional."

"If it's that old, I may have used the exact same machine in grad school," the colonel stated with a smile.

"Take this protein band, resuspend it, and see if you can determine the amino acid sequence. If you can do that, we will be able to extrapolate a DNA sequence. Ramsey showed me a freezer full of expression vectors and plasmids that we can use to express the gene and the protein."

Col. Bragg found the old mass spec machine to be very similar to the one he used in graduate school and was able to identify enough amino acid fragments from the protein to determine its entire sequence.

The next step would have been to search the amino acid sequence against a variety of sequence databases to determine its identity. However, by this time, most Internet sites were no longer available.

"Have you searched the Internet for corn genomic databases?" Tony asked.

"There's nothing left of the Internet. It's damn near like an interstate on the East Coast."

Tony nodded, frustrated with their limitations.

"What about the human genome? I'm sure whatever protein you identified has an orthologous gene in humans."

"All the government-run sites are down. I'm pretty sure we don't have network access to anything."

Tony smiled. He knew that there were many problems that could potentially stump him, but getting information off a network was one of his specialties, and a skill that he took great pride in.

"Let me have a go," he said. "Do you have the sequence?"

The colonel handed Tony a piece of paper with a long series of amino acid letters on it. Tony took the sequence and promptly opened his solar-powered laptop. After a few moments, the machine beeped and flashed its way to life. He entered the amino acid letters into a website text box on the screen. Within minutes, Tony was gloating from behind his laptop screen.

"Here it is," he said. "It's a hypothetical protein, but I've got a gene sequence. There are actually two variants, a truncated version and a full-length version. The one you sequenced from the corn plant is the truncated protein. I'm checking for orthologous groups right now."

"What the hell did you do?" the colonel asked.

"Just took advantage of the past," Tony said. "I went to a mirror site and opened a cached copy of the NCBI nucleotide database. Sure, it's a few months old, but the information is there."

"Doctor, if I had you on my team, we could have destroyed civilization years ago," the colonel said with a loud chuckle that softened as he noticed Tony's obvious lack of humor on the subject.

"Looks like there are a lot of copies of the full-length gene that extend down to the kingdom protista. And there are only a couple of the truncated versions that lack an exon. I'd bet the truncated gene gives rise to the mutated protein," Tony said. "I'm betting this is a natural case of receptor mimicry."

They made quick work of cloning the gene and expressing it from a protein expression vector. As Tony predicted, the truncated protein they isolated from the corn plant stopped the virus just as effectively as the corn kernel lysates. This process gave them a system to make lots of this protein.

"I think the larger variant is the cellular receptor that this virus uses to attach to cells, and the shorter version is a rare anomaly that resembles the larger version, but functions in a different way," Tony said.

"Molecular mimicry," said Col. Bragg. "It makes its living copying the other protein, but it lacks its full cellular function."

"Let's grow up a gob and see what we get."

They produced large quantities of the unknown truncated protein, purified it, and determined that it was effective at preventing viral infection in cell culture if applied prior to infection.

If given after infection, it slowed the virus, but likely forced it into a state of latency. Tony named his new protein drug Saravirin after Don's daughter, and while he was delighted to have another weapon in his arsenal, he knew all too well that everything he had come up with so far was only a temporary solution.

He knew that he could slow down the virus a couple of different ways, but he could not kill it, and therefore, he could not cure it. He also knew that slowing down the virus was akin to throwing a life raft under the sinking *Titanic*.

Tony took inventory of what he had available for fighting the Juventas virus. First, he could use Saravirin as a prophylaxis to possibly prevent viral infection, as he knew that this protein would coat the viral capsid, preventing it from being able to attach to cells that it would normally infect.

Saravirin was capable of slowing down viral replication, but that it would return to normal if the drug regimen ceased. However, Saravirin was untested in animals or humans, and it could have toxic side effects.

Second, he demonstrated that the THC from his GMO marijuana reduced the number of steroid receptors expressed in the muscle, and therefore, was capable of arresting the effects of the virus in the short term. It also showed promise in reducing the effects of the Delta Event because it reduced the anabolic rate, which made him believe that it would slow the progression of the super-strength syndrome. It also slowed and potentially reversed progression of lesions associated with the Gamma Event, but it was not clear if it prevented the onset of cancer.

Unfortunately, neither of these treatments actually killed the virus. If anything, they just forced the virus to hide out inside of infected cells in a state of latency where it could wait for the next opportunity to spread the infection.

Tony stared at all the data he had collected and written on the chalkboard. With all his experiments and all his thinking, all he could really do was find a way to slow this virus down.

He knew that if he had more time and more tools, he could generate a vaccine, and probably some broadly neutralizing antibodies that could be used to control infection, but even those treatments would not help those who had already been infected. And that was probably almost everybody.

For the second time in his life, a problem presented itself that he could not solve. Last time, it was HIV, and he could always blame those around him for his failure at curing AIDS. *They threw me out before I could finish my work*, he had told himself.

But the truth was, he could not figure out how to kill HIV once it integrated its reverse transcribed DNA into the human genome. No one could. At least with HIV, you could teach prevention and protect most of the population, but JV was out of control.

Tony knew that if he failed at finding a way to kill this virus, humanity would fail on Earth. It was a hard thought that echoed in his mind as defeat overtook his body in a wave of grief.

Col. Bragg saw Tony's shoulders sag. He looked over the information on the chalkboard. They had done a tremendous amount of research and fact finding in a short amount of time. Dr. Van Lee was possibility the most intelligent and creative scientist he had ever seen work. If he was out of ideas, humankind was out of hope.

Col. Bragg tried to lighten the mood by chuckling.

"I barely remember what a bed feels like."

Tony didn't respond. He stared at the floor as if it might glean an answer.

"That Dr. Harrison is some woman. You two involved?" the colonel asked.

Tony lifted his head as the comment registered and tried to push through the cobwebs in his mind to clearly see what the colonel meant.

"It's complicated," he finally responded.

"Good," said the colonel.

"Excuse me?" Tony responded. This line of questioning was obviously something more than he thought.

"You like complicated," Bragg said. "It's probably why you can't figure this virus out. You're looking for something more complicated than it has to be."

Tony was pissed. "Then why don't you solve it?" Tony asked sarcastically.

"It's like that HIV thing. What was that ten, fifteen years ago?"

"My theory?" Tony asked.

"Yeah, that it was a synthetic bioweapon. You made it so complicated that it was unsolvable."

"I was very close before I was fired and blackballed by the agency," Tony said, anger growing in his voice.

"No, you weren't. You were never close. You were on the wrong track, and you never even considered the fact that you might be wrong. HIV was what it was, and so you hid behind a complexity of your own making. You are so sure of yourself that you become blind and didn't even consider options that weren't in line with your theories. It's your weakness." Col. Bragg didn't seem to be insulting Tony, just speaking his mind.

"Who the hell do you think you are?" Tony was furious now.

Col. Bragg laughed and raised his hands. "I'm on your side, Doc, but you're blind to simplicity. We don't have a lot of time here, and the human race needs you to be thinking of all options."

Tony was ready to scream, but his thinking was interrupted by the sound of the lift.

He decided to let it go for now, perhaps Col. Bragg was right. He would talk to Carrisa and see how her walk had gone. She had been gone a long while, and it was time to talk about their baby whether she wanted to or not.

Irish and Sgt. Thomas stepped off the lift with long faces, dragging the crumpled body of an unknown male behind them.

"Where's Carrie?" Tony asked, with panic rising in his voice.

"Listen, mate…you should sit."

"I asked you a question. Where is Carrie?"

Sgt. Thomas stepped in, measured and precise.

"We were ambushed. They took her."

"What! Who? You were supposed to protect her. Where, where did they take her?"

Col. Bragg's face was stone and fury, but professionalism kept him together.

"Not sure, but we brought him for that," Irish said as he lightly kicked the unconscious man with a terrible scar on his face.

"How did they find us?"

Sgt. Thomas grabbed the man's collar and dragged him off the lift.

"Noah."

"Noah?" Tony thought for a moment and then realized that he had been missing for some time.

"Why would he do that?"

"Don't know, mate, but he won't be talking to anyone anymore."

"Why won't he be talking?" Annie's voice squeaked out of the corner where no one noticed her.

She stepped out with unsure footing and looming tears in her eyes.

"Why won't he talk?"

Irish dropped his head.

"I'm sorry, lass. He's gone."

Annie began to cry quietly, tears flowing easily down her face. "How did he die?"

Sgt. Thomas looked uneasy and cleared his throat.

"I shot him. I'm sorry, very sorry, Annie. He betrayed us..."

She put a thin finger to her lips just under the lesion that was noticeably smaller on her face. The tears continued to flow, and the moment remained awkward and emotional. Tony stepped forward to console Annie, and she fell into his embrace, but for only a few seconds. She then approached Sgt. Thomas and stood directly in front of him.

"My brother was disturbed and angry, but he loved me and I loved him. I can never forgive you," she said and then slapped him across the face.

Sgt. Thomas did not raise his hands to protect himself or change his expression. He stared at her in the eyes, allowing her to get all the satisfaction she needed. He had seen a lot of death and knew how it affected people. He played his part.

Annie walked to the lift and mounted it, looking Tony in the eye. She smiled sadly.

"I love you, Dr. Van Lee. I love you, Tony. Thank you for being nice to me."

The lift grinded upward and delivered the girl out of sight. The men were left stunned and a little embarrassed, but no one went after her.

"What do we do?" asked Irish.

"Let her go," said Tony, seeing for the first time that human weaknesses were pressing in on their little group.

"Doctor, if she…"

Tony shook his head.

"She won't. Just let her go. Life is turning upside down, and I don't have the energy to nurse anyone through it." He tried to rub the sleep out of his eyes.

"How do we get Carrie back?"

Chapter 28

August 5, 2018

FOR TWO DAYS, Col. Bragg, Sgt. Thomas, and Irish used every technique they knew to get the prisoner to speak, but nothing they tried yielded any results. The prisoner was a hard man, whose yelling was as unending as his resolve. And it was apparent that his fear of the man he reverently referred to as Jeremiah was far worse than any immediate pain that Irish and Sgt. Thomas could inflict upon him without killing him. In fact, even the threat of death was unsuccessful as the man only muttered that he would finally get his due reward.

Col. Bragg described to everyone what he witnessed of Jeremiah and his army that called itself the Sons of the Apocalypse. The prisoner spoke about Jeremiah often and referred to the punishment he would face if he incurred Jeremiah's wrath.

The prisoner also spoke freely of God's word, and he spoke as if he had been given a glimpse of the *ultimate plan*. Sgt. Thomas and Irish worked well as a team, keeping him awake and disoriented. They worked in shifts, applying various techniques to keep him completely confused.

Tony disagreed with torture, as it went against his very nature, but with each scream, he felt his heart harden. It only took a quiet thought of Carrie and their baby for him to overcome the morals that would normally have prevented him from participating in such barbaric behavior.

Over the past few days, Tony had not seen Don, who now stayed in his bed most of the time. Irish and Sgt. Thomas had been checking up on him, making sure that he was not starving himself. Tony kept his distance. He couldn't afford the emotional energy it would take to console Don, and explain how Sara had succumbed to the virus.

Tony walked up through the narrow and dark staircase, and made his way into the greenhouse to Ramsey's bench. From there, he could barely hear the prisoner's screams. He sat in the solitude, looking at the violets that Ramsey had carefully cultivated over the years.

He also looked at his own garden, which was doing very well. They would all eat heartily, even though his appetite was gone for now. After a few moments of quiet meditation, Tony wrote in his journal, which had become the only outlet for the growing hopelessness that built inside him. He scribbled and erased and then wrote some more.

"Is this how life ends on Earth?" he read from the journal. "Damn it!"

Tony threw the book on the ground in frustration.

"What the hell am I missing? All the pieces of the puzzle are on the table, but I can't put it together. I can't even keep you and the baby safe," he said, his thoughts shifting to Carrisa and his unborn child. "I know that I am arrogant, and perhaps overbearing, but I love you with all my heart, and our child, too. And so, help me God, I will find you if it drives me mad…," he said out loud and to himself.

Tony's body operated on automatic pilot as he slowly picked up the book and pencil from the ground and placed them on Ramsey's old bench. He stared at them. Paper and pencil, simple tools. He froze.

"Simple…," he said in a soft voice.

Then, in a state of complete and uncompromising determination, Tony rushed through the trap door that lead from the garden to the staircase and ran toward the lab.

Irish and Sgt. Thomas stood outside the room where the prisoner was housed, exhausted and completely out of ideas.

Tony, however, had at least one, and Irish and Sgt. Thomas were glad to see the look of hope on his face. Tony went straight to the refrigerator where they kept the drugs and specimens, removing two vials and a culture tube from the shelf.

With these items in hand, Tony went into the prisoner's room. Irish, Sgt. Thomas, and Colonel Bragg watched Tony approach the room with his hands full, and with much curiosity, followed close behind him.

Col. Bragg spoke first as Tony stuck a syringe into one of the vials.

"Everything okay, Doc?"

"There's only one way to beat the Mad Hatter, Colonel."

The prisoner's face was beat and bloody, and he was tired but Tony's unexpected behavior kept him very focused.

"What are you doing?" the prisoner asked with a quivering voice.

"Are you going to tell us where they took Carrie?" Tony asked.

"Not a chance," he said resolutely.

"Then you are useless to us, and keeping you around is a waste of time and resources, right?"

Tony wasted no time in filling the syringe and injecting its contents into the arm of the prisoner. He then stood over him and smiled a smile that contained no amusement.

Sgt. Thomas was prepared to prevent Tony from giving the injection but stopped at a silent command from Col. Bragg.

"What's that gonna do?" the prisoner asked, fatigued and afraid.

The other men were alarmed, but something about Tony's demeanor made it clear that they should stay quiet.

"By itself it does nothing." Tony raised the culture tube. "And this, by itself, does very little. But, together..." Tony began to laugh and uncorked the culture, placing it right underneath the prisoner's nose, then placed it on the table by the man's chair.

"I don't get it."

"Correction, you already have it. You see, the combination of these two viruses is 100 percent deadly. But before you die, they will force you to reveal your true inner self, stripping away the mask you wear. No God to blame or serve, just you and your lust for murder. If I remember correctly, that means certain hell for you."

The prisoner's eyes got large as fear settled deep within his psyche. He shook as the adrenaline soared through his body.

"The Lord doesn't punish those that repent. Check your facts."

"Yeah." Tony laughed and continued. "You won't repent, you won't be sorry. You are a murderer and thief at heart, and this will reveal that to God."

The prisoner stared at Tony's uncompromising face, trying to decide if what he said was true. Trying to remember if God would still condemn him after he had already been saved.

The prisoner never really liked to kill in the beginning, but he was good at it, and he had begun to enjoy watching the weak take their last breath as a result of his hand. In fact, he had always felt guilty for feeling excited by another person's death.

"I'm also afraid that this won't be a very clean death, my friend. First, you will experience difficulty breathing as your lungs fill with fluid. Then, your organs will begin to hemorrhage and slowly shut down.

"Next, your brain will swell until you experience the kind of headache that will drive you…well, we've covered that. Finally, the excruciating pain will drive you to go on a rampage and kill everyone in your sight."

"Don't worry, we may not know where Carrisa is, but we do know where your Jeremiah is, and we intend to let you go there so that you can kill your own people. In fact, we'll use you to lead the charge."

Col. Bragg listened without changing his expression, he had been here before, but Sgt. Thomas and Irish recognized a new depth to Tony that they had not expected. Tony stared blankly at the man, waiting for a response.

Tony's years of scientific exile were enough to haunt any man, but failures resulting in loss of life were what haunted him the most. He was not emotionally prepared to take on the responsibility of saving the human race, no one was. But it was time to get on with it.

He was tired of sitting around waiting for an idea, he had been stuck in that rut his whole life. It was time to act. It was time to fight this disease on the front lines, and it was time to find Carrie and tell her that he loved her.

He was sick and tired of his own passivity, and he was tired of thinking about what would be the right thing to do. It was time for action. It was time to give it all that he had, and if he failed, then he could let go. But he would not end his life with a lack of action. He was determined to not go down without a fight. Instead, he would die trying. He would die on the battleground for a change.

Tony stared at the prisoner, his features hard.

"It's your call," he said. "Tell me where the lady doctor was taken, or burn in hell for all of eternity."

"Why are you doing this? I thought you were a doctor," the prisoner said to Tony.

"I have no further use for you. You are nothing more than a waste of my time. The only value you have for me is that you know where they took my Carrie. You are either going to tell us where she is, or…you know."

The man looked hard into Tony's eyes, which had become dark and haggard, with nothing but raw pain staring back.

"The good news is I have a cure to the Mad Man system that I injected you with," Tony said, lifting the third vial to show the man, "but the bad news is that you have to administer it within thirty minutes, or it's too late."

With that, Tony turned to the other men.

"Gentlemen, load the trucks. Regardless of the decision this man makes, we will be leaving in ten minutes. We don't have much time to get him to his people before the Mad Man virus takes over."

The prisoner squirmed oddly in his chair and tried to take a deep breath. He could already feel the effects of the Mad Man viruses taking over his body. His breath became labored, his skin became flushed, and his eyes turned red. He could feel a headache starting to build behind his forehead.

Even though he had been saved by Jeremiah, the man harbored secret thoughts that caused him much shame. Thoughts that he believed would land him in hell if Jeremiah found out. And even if Jeremiah never found out, God would know. And if this mad man thing caused him to kill others in front of Jeremiah, he knew that his punishment would be swift in this world and in the next.

"Okay, I'll tell you! Please! Give me the cure."

Irish, Sgt. Thomas, and Col. Bragg sat up at this admission. For two days, they had been unsuccessful at interrogating the prisoner, but now the answer was coming.

"Where is she?"

"North, northwest, twenty miles in the old National Guard Armory. Every two days we relocate three miles east. They'll be leaving soon. We only came for the woman."

"Why? Why would you want to hurt Carrie?"

"No, not her, the other one. The one that kills. The demon!" he said. "Please, Doctor, give me the cure, please. Hurry!"

"I think we know who he's talking about," Sgt. Thomas said.

"Why did you take Carrie?" Tony asked.

"Bait. The demon is obsessed with her, and we wanted to use her. Now come on, I've told you all I know."

Tony turned to Sgt. Thomas.

"Can you find them?"

Sgt. Thomas looked at the colonel for his approval before nodding in response, not sure of Tony's mind-set. The colonel gave his approval, and Sgt. Thomas nodded in the affirmative to Tony.

Tony breathed out a sigh and continued with the prisoner.

"Thank you. What is your name?"

The prisoner almost yelled.

"Frank! My name is Frank! Please, the cure?"

"Thank you, Frank, but I'm afraid there is no cure. I know that for you this is tragic, but it was necessary. I am sorry for that. But since you helped us, I will let you die alone instead as a murderer of your own people."

Frank glared at Tony and watched as he turned to leave the room.

"I will die a martyr, and I will reap a martyr's reward," the man said.

"Gentlemen, you may want to do whatever you feel necessary, if he starts convulsing, he'll be flinging those Mad Man viruses everywhere."

Irish and Sgt. Thomas looked at each other, not sure that they could believe the sudden coolness to Tony's demeanor. They quickly made sure that Frank was securely fastened to his chair and placed him inside the containment chamber and sealed the door.

Tony left the room immediately, with Col. Bragg hot on his heels. The colonel didn't want to question him in front of the others, but he felt it necessary to determine if Tony was operating from a sane mind.

"What the hell was that, Doc?"

Tony stopped dead in his tracks just as the other two men exited the room where Frank was contained.

"That may be the cure, and the price I had to pay to find it. I reengineered the Mad Man system based on our research, and I think we may have something. We don't have time to test it, but what the hell, we're all dead anyway. Frank is our guinea pig. If he survives and clears the virus, then we'll know it works. Now let's get moving. Time's one thing we know Carrie doesn't have."

Irish stuck his head in at the last moment, just in time to hear Tony mention a cure.

"What the hell do you mean by the cure?" Irish responded. "You mean a *cure*, cure?"

"I'll tell you on the way," Tony stated impatiently. "Somebody tell Don to look after the prisoner."

Sgt. Thomas and Irish armed themselves as Tony packed up multiple items from his research reagents. Col. Bragg stayed fairly quiet, but watched him like a hawk.

"What price, Doc?" Col. Bragg asked out of the blue.

"The Hippocratic oath?"

Tony laughed, his cynicism bleeding in.

"Do no harm. I wish I could say I was that idealistic, but I'm not. I'm not that kind of doctor. That's your oath. And besides, sometimes you have to break the rules for the right reasons, right?"

"That goes for bioweapons developers too?"

He never met Col. Bragg's eyes but nodded.

"I guess it does, and I guess I owe you an apology for a lifetime of being judgmental, considering our present circumstances. I gave that poor man hope when there may be none, just to manipulate him. That was wrong, disgusting, and evil. And no matter how righteous my reasons, I'll always be culpable for that."

"You did what you had to do to keep those you love safe."

"It's that type of interpretation that has doomed the human race to war, time after time. Now, I'm a part of it."

"You always were, Doc. You just didn't know it."

Tony finished packing and turned to leave.

"I'm in love with her, you know," Col. Bragg said.

Tony kept walking.

"Then you know how important it is to get her back," he said, leaving the colonel smiling at him with a renewed respect.

The Hummer sped over the rough terrain until it arrived at the spot where the truck that kidnapped Carrie exited onto the road. Sgt. Thomas double-checked the tracks.

"This is it," he said, looking at a compass.

Irish spied the landscape through a pair of binoculars, and Col. Bragg consulted a map. In the back of the Hummer, Tony ground some marijuana leaves into a fine powder using a mortar and pestle and then dissolved it in a small volume of liquid Saravirin.

"So, Doc, how about an explanation of this miracle cure?"

Irish and Sgt. Thomas, done with the scouting, came to listen. Tony kept grinding the leaves into the mortar using the large round pestle. The process looked archaic, considering the immense amount of research they had done.

"The short of it is this. From Don's immunity, we learned that the virus cannot infect everyone, and from his daughter Sara, we learned that we can slow it down…we combined these observations to find the virus's weaknesses. Saravirin can prevent it from binding to the cells it wants to infect, and the genetically altered pot slows down its effects. These are major findings, but there are still a few problems."

"It's too strong and adapts too quickly," said the colonel from the front seat, still looking at his map.

"That's right, and those drugs may force the virus to hide inside the cells it infects in a dormant state. So we need something to fight it where it lives."

"So what's the fighter then, mate?"

"Ramsey. He gave us the Mad Man system, a two-part viral infection system developed as a bioweapon that attacks the body's systems unilaterally. I reengineered it to have the Saravirin gene in the second virus instead of the lethal gene that Ramsey's team used for assassination. We have to get the first virus into their bloodstream somehow, and then we let the reengineered second virus fly." Tony held up another culture tube.

"That's what you used on that poor bastard back at the lab!" Sgt. Thomas exclaimed.

"Yup."

"Will this kill the humans too?"

"I believe that infecting them with the first virus will open the door for the second virus to express the Saravirin protein inside the cell where it should be able to inhibit virus assembly and possibly replication."

"Do you think this will kill it, mate?"

"I'm not sure. We don't have the time to test it properly. If this works, we will be able to stop the virus in its tracks. It may very well be the most important cure in all of human history."

"Are you saying you're guessing, mate?"

"Yup."

The colonel laughed, put down his map, and came to the back of the Humvee. He looked at the ridiculously old mortar Tony was using to crush and mix the ingredients.

"So the virologist of the century has developed a cure using a bowl and a rock. That's awful sixteenth century for you, Doc."

"You do what you have to do to keep those you love safe."

"I'm impressed, Doc."

"We'll see. First, we take out this Jeremiah and get Carrie back, then we focus on saving the world."

"Agreed," the colonel said. "So what's the plan?"

"The old drug cocktail," Tony said. "I am going to mix the THC, the Saravirin, and the two viruses from the reengineered Mad Man system together. Jeremiah and his people are about to be our proof of concept. If this works, they may return to a reasonable state of mind and refuse to fight us."

"So we go in and cure the group and then take Carrisa back?" the colonel asked. "Should we all sing kumbaya on the way out?"

"Let's try the cocktail first, and if that fails, we rescue Carrisa and take out Jeremiah. I have a syringe of the original Mad Man solution with his name on it just in case."

Thanks to Sgt. Thomas's superior tracking skills, they found the old armory within a few hours. Unfortunately, the sun had set, making it difficult to get a good assessment of Jeremiah's resources.

There were several small campers and many vehicles, but most importantly, the truck that had taken Carrisa was parked nearby. Armed guards were dispersed over the entire camp, and most appeared to be alert and vigilant.

Jeremiah's followers had parked all their vehicles in a semicircle, and many of the campers were mingling in the middle. From a distance, it appeared that everyone was talking in hushed tones. It was obvious that this was a disciplined camp.

Tony searched the crowd carefully but saw no signs of Carrisa. He also noted that there were no signs of the man, Jeremiah, who was described by Frank as "a hulk of a man with friendly features and an unnerving presence."

Tony's crew set up a camp a quarter mile away, which was plenty of distance in the dark. Tony had made enough of his concoction for about fifty men.

"I don't like how ready they seem. They're waiting for something," said Sgt. Thomas.

"The demon lady. The trap is set, they are waiting to spring it," remarked Irish.

Sgt. Thomas and the colonel shared a look.

"What do you think, sir?" asked Sgt. Thomas.

Colonel Bragg shrugged in response. He thought it irrelevant, as they had their mission to complete no matter what.

"I think it would be easiest to get this into their food," Tony said, holding up a Ziploc bag of his concoction.

"How do you propose we do that, Doc?"

"You're the Green Beret. You tell me."

"Look, mate, I've been in this type of fight before. Tell me what to do, and I'll get it done."

"There's got to be at least twenty vehicles, Irish, how the hell are you going to find where they keep their food? And more than that, how will you know what they'll eat tomorrow?"

"I can't tell you all my secrets, mate, plus I'm a man that can find things. Trust me."

"What about the guards?"

Irish looked for support from his more military-minded mates, and they all shared a quiet laugh.

Tony told him what to do with the concoction, which was simple: get it into something they would ingest in as high a concentration as possible. He knew that the original system was designed for injection into the person being targeted, but he also surmised from Ramsey's description of events that the viruses must be promiscuous, allowing infection from incidental contact. And besides that, injecting everyone was not an option without a gunfight that they would most certainly lose.

"How long is this going to take to kill the virus, Doc?" asked Sgt. Thomas.

"I don't know, hopefully the effects will be rapid."

"So we're basically guessing where their food is and what they're going to eat just to get this concoction into their bloodstreams, but we're not really sure its even going to work. And if it does work, we may not even know it for several days. Do I have this right?" Sgt. Thomas asked, hoping that he had missed something very basic.

"That just about covers it, Sergeant," Tony said, surprised at how much of this was really up to chance.

"Okay."

Zero three thirty had been established as the portion of the night when most people enjoyed the deepest sleep, and this was why Col. Bragg chose it as the time to infiltrate Jeremiah's camp. The colonel assumed command and ordered Tony to stay behind and to leave in a hurry if anything seemed out of the ordinary, which meant if they didn't come back by daybreak.

The trio wore the bone phones that Col. Bragg had taken from the depot, and each put them in their ears. The colonel assumed the lookout post and Sgt. Thomas took point. It was their job to keep Irish informed. Irish chose not to take a gun, only a knife. If he had to fire, he was dead anyway; at least that was his thought on the matter.

Col. Bragg had also brought a pair of night-vision goggles and was able to see the guards clearly, and he reported their locations to the others. He watched as Irish deftly snuck into the perimeter of the camp and brazenly went through the center of camp. Col. Bragg saw two guards on one side of Irish and two on the other.

"Okay, you're hot. You have two bogies at your eight o'clock moving north. They will reach you in one mike. Another two at two o'clock stationary," reported Col. Bragg.

"I'm on the eights, trailing northbound," Sgt. Thomas's voice came over the earpiece.

Col. Bragg saw Sgt. Thomas expertly shadow the two guards until he was within killing range. There was a small fire smoldering in the center of camp, and Irish sat down, hunched over on a rock as if he were keeping warm.

"They spotted you, Irish. Stay frosty."

Col. Bragg couldn't make out what the guard said, but Irish raised his arm in salutation. The wave seemed to quell the guard's curiosity, but he moved toward Irish anyway.

Sgt. Thomas sliced the throat of the other so fast that Col. Bragg almost missed it. The second came over close to Irish, but not close enough to make out his face in the dark. The guard kept his hand near his weapon. Irish moved slowly and without alarm.

"Five more seconds, and Sgt. Thomas is there," Col. Bragg reported and watched as Sgt. Thomas sliced the next guard's throat.

Irish immediately moved farther into the camp, not even waiting until the body hit the ground. Sgt. Thomas went straight to work pulling the bodies away.

"Both targets neutralized, sir. One mike to conceal them."

"Copy, Sergeant."

"Thanks, mate. I'm off," said the static voice of Irish over the bone phone.

Irish stayed close to the ground now, but he moved swiftly. He caught something on the air and sniffed. It was there and then it was gone, but then he picked up the scent of something else and followed his nose.

It was a bizarre thing, but not something he could ignore. His sudden heightened sense of smell was puzzling to him, but it allowed him to determine where the camp's food was stored.

An enclosed tow trailer attached to one of the trucks was locked, and Irish could smell the food inside. He knew that he would have to get in and close the door behind him, as the trailer was nearly in plain sight of all of the guards.

"I found it. I'll be blind while I'm inside, so watch me arse."

Col. Bragg watched as he entered the trailer.

"Copy that, all's clear. Sergeant, two o'clock, bogies moving south, west side of camp."

"Copy."

Sgt. Thomas moved around the area with ease, using movements gleaned from years of being on the battlefield. He marked where Irish was and then marked where he thought the other two guards were. Normally he would have just taken them out, but they lacked sufficient manpower for him to leave Irish alone.

Col. Bragg looked down toward a stopwatch he had started as the mission began. It just passed the five-minute mark, and everything was on schedule. The other two guards were now at the southernmost part of the camp where Irish and Sgt. Thomas had entered and were now a danger to their extraction.

"Sergeant, bogies northbound, six o'clock."

"Copy. I'm going to pull back a bit and take them down."

"Copy that. Irish stay put until I give the all clear."

"Right."

Col. Bragg watched Sgt. Thomas pull back into the shadows and ease his way toward them. They stopped where the fire distorted the night-vision gear Colonel Bragg used. He could vaguely make out their forms.

"I have limited visibility. Wait for them to move, over."

"Copy."

The guards orange silhouette in the goggles did not move, and Col. Bragg glanced at his stopwatch. It passed the ten-minute mark.

"What's the word, I'm done in here."

"Hold your position. Sergeant, report."

"They're not moving, sir. Should I engage? Over."

"Negative, hold your position," the colonel said and looked at his watch again.

Twelve minutes had passed, and with each minute over ten, they were in considerably more danger. If one of the guards shouted the alarm, the game was over. The light continued to wash out Irish's night vision, and he decided to disengage the gear, but a door opened on one of the campers, and two more armed men exited.

"Crap! Who changes shifts on the quarter hour?" he said to himself, annoyed with his luck and frustrated, knowing they should have been out two minutes ago.

"Okay, we're hot, two bogies exiting camper north, southbound. Looks like a shift change. That's a total of four bogies."

"Copy sir, four bogies."

"I'd really like to get the hell out of here. I'm a sitting duck."

"Copy that, hold your position."

Col. Bragg knew he had to make a decision now, and he also knew they didn't have enough manpower for this.

"Irish, I need you to exit in twenty seconds on my mark and follow the bogies. Southbound east side bogie is yours. Sergeant, I'm on my way in, I'll hit southbound west side bogie."

"Copy. I've got the other two."

"We have to hit at the exact same time."

"Copy."

"Got it."

"Mark."

Col. Bragg took off like a man who was half his age and as silent as a deer. He got to the edge of the campfire light just as the four guards saw each other. Col. Bragg didn't see Sgt. Thomas anywhere, but Irish was nearly in full sight against the side of the vehicles. He could only hope that they were taken completely unaware.

It was time, so the colonel disengaged his night vision and ran toward the guards. He had no time to see if Irish or Sgt. Thomas were there, but if they weren't, he was a dead man.

He flew past the first man, scaring him to death, and stabbed his Ka-Bar into the other's throat, viciously demolishing any vocal capability and slicing his gun hand wrist. The man went down, and Col. Bragg thrust his knife one last time into his heart. Col. Bragg had no time to wait as he pulled out his knife and rolled back to a defensive position. There was nothing to worry about, however, Irish and Sgt. Thomas had done their part and four men lay dead on the ground, and none of them made a sound.

They each grabbed a body and drug them far enough away from the camp that they wouldn't be found, at least by morning. Sgt. Thomas went back in for the final body and to hide any evidence of struggle, including blood spatter.

Col. Bragg and Irish met Tony at the camp and waited for Sgt. Thomas.

"Any sign of Carrie?" Tony asked a little anxious.

"Sorry, mate, not a peep."

"Don't worry, Doc, we're not leaving without her," Col. Bragg said, purposely not looking at him.

"Where's Sgt. Thomas?" Tony asked.

"Good question." Col. Bragg activated his bone phone. "Sergeant, what's your twenty, over."

No reply.

"Do you copy?"

Irish heard the empty silence and immediately had a bad feeling.

"Somethin's wrong, Colonel."

The colonel nodded and had the same feeling; something was very wrong.

"Let's go."

"What about me?"

"We need you to stay here. Remember, if anything happens, you'll be the only one with a chance to save the world."

And with that, Irish and Col. Bragg took off once again, leaving Tony feeling helpless and incompetent, but he knew his strengths were different than theirs. He certainly didn't like the idea of Col. Bragg being Carrie's savior, yet at the same time, he wanted the very best they had available to rescue her.

It occurred to him that it was a catch-22 situation, as were so many things in life. But it didn't matter because he refused to let Carrie go this time, and he was ready to assume the responsibilities of being a father to their unborn child. He made up his mind that he would apologize and accept responsibility.

It occurred to him that it was ironic that Ben, Carrisa, and he had set out to save the world when they were young and now he alone had the chance. They had never imagined that saving the world would unfold this way.

Hours went by and the sun began to glow on the horizon. Tony tried not to fall asleep, but he dozed now and again, and during one of these catnaps, Irish and Col. Bragg returned. He awoke to their sweaty faces and nearly jumped out of his skin.

"Find him?"

Irish looked at the ground. Col. Bragg only shook his head.

"What does that mean?"

"I think it means we have a third party, and I'm willing to bet it's the demon woman that fella Frank talked about."

Tony didn't know what to say or do. They had looked for hours, and there was no sign of Sgt. Thomas anywhere.

"We have a job to do, mate. We'll have to pick up the pieces later."

"Pick up the pieces? Sgt. Thomas is one of us…"

"If you want her back, we have to worry about him later," Irish said.

"He's right, Doc. Sun's comin' up. It's time to get ready."

They were right and he knew it, but he still didn't like it. As Irish and Col. Bragg secured their belongings, Tony studied Jeremiah's camp using long-range binoculars. Irish explained that he had mixed Tony's concoction into the coffee and spread it on the bacon. He explained that it was his best guess as to how to get it to everyone in camp. The three sat back and waited for a sign below.

Inside the largest Airstream camper, Carrisa lay dozing in and out of consciousness. She had been treated well once she arrived to the makeshift camp, but she still felt haunted by the memory of Noah's dead face. The gunshots continuously echoed in her mind, and she diagnosed herself with post-traumatic stress syndrome as a result.

Even though she knew that Noah had betrayed them, she could not forgive Sgt. Thomas for taking him out. As she lay there in her crude prison cell, reality settled in. She dared not hope of any rescue. How would they even find her? She was in the middle of nowhere with a bizarre group of religious zealots, all of whom seemed to worship the big man.

She had no idea what they wanted with her. The only question Jeremiah had asked her was about their progress on a cure. She didn't know quite why, but she downplayed what she knew and all the research activities that had been conducted.

Jeremiah was a frightening man, if in girth alone, but he seemed to have a gentle way about him. The other men treated him with as much respect as fear, so she knew there was a part of him she had not seen. Jeremiah slept across from her on the other side of the trailer.

And while she was uncomfortable sharing such a small space with a man she did not know or trust, he treated her with much respect and never came close to touching her, save to help her up and down the steps of the camper.

In fact, in the last few days, she was permitted to move around the camp, although the armed men kept a disinterested close eye. She watched Jeremiah as he slept, wondering how far she might get if she snuck out of the trailer and scurried off into the woods.

Unfortunately, the giant man seemed to have the uncanny ability to hear things that were nearly silent, to see things that were barely visible, and to sense things when they were barely discernible. When his eyes shot open, she nearly jumped out of bed.

"She's close."

Carrisa grabbed her chest, trying to catch a breath.

"Who?"

"The one we came for. Stay in the camper, I'll have someone bring you breakfast," Jeremiah told her as he rose and left the camper quickly.

Jeremiah looked up toward the early morning sky and gently sniffed the air. He felt her presence. In fact, he was aware that she had been patrolling the borders of their camp for nearly a week, but this time, he sensed something different. He sensed her heightened adrenaline. He sensed her desire to pounce. He knew that she was ready for a fight.

Jeremiah walked quickly to the center of the camp, alarming his men who immediately began scurrying around to get things ready. They knew the look that was on Jeremiah's face. They had seen it before; in fact, every time he had been confronted with news about the demon lady.

The battles against her and her men had been difficult for Jeremiah's army. Her persistent evil posed a significant threat to Jeremiah's stature as God's chosen Prophet and the abilities that he claimed were God-given. She was a dangerous foe, and he wished that he knew what she wanted, why she insisted on following him and challenging him. They had inflicted horrible losses on each other, and he had the feeling that she was running out of reserves.

A wiry man named Sticks brought him a cup of coffee. No one knew for sure why he went by that nickname, and he never told anyone. It was of little interest to Jeremiah; God knew everyone's name. He took the cup and drank from it.

"Thank you, brother. Tell the men to be ready. Something is going to happen very soon."

Sticks paused for a moment as the command sunk in and then went about his duties relaying the message. The activities in camp didn't change, but the tension elevated significantly. The sense of impending doom was palpable. There was about to be a showdown between good and evil, and everyone knew it.

As promised, Jeremiah had food taken to the camper for Carrisa, and she, too, could feel the tension mounting. Her nervousness left her with no appetite, and she left the breakfast untouched on the tray.

Col. Bragg watched all the action from his vantage point on the hill above the camp. "Something's wrong," he stated.

"Why?" asked Irish.

"Don't know, but they're getting ready for something."

Tony tried to peek over the hill. "Us? Do they know we're here?"

"Don't think so, mate. Probably would have picked us up already."

"Damn it. Well, did they eat?"

"Every single one, even that big bastard, and I think I know where Dr. Harrison is. Northernmost silver camper, connected to the blue Ford."

"When we go in, one of us will have to get in there and get out quickly. There's at least a quarter mile between their camp and our vehicle, so don't mess around."

"I don't understand," Tony said.

"We sorted it out last night. Without Sgt. Thomas, we're light," Irish said.

"Light? Speak English."

"Look, Doc, without Sgt. Thomas, we need one of us to cause a distraction, one to extract Dr. Harrison, and you to take out Jeremiah when it's time."

Tony felt for the syringe in his pants pocket to make sure it was there and then followed the other two as they slowly advanced on Jeremiah's camp. They had made it halfway there, moving quite slowly when they heard the sound of an engine running.

Col. Bragg dropped down and looked through his binoculars. He saw that the members of Jeremiah's camp were just as bewildered as he.

"Oh no," Col. Bragg said after a moment and dropped the binoculars down. Irish looked and had a nearly identical reaction and handed them to Tony.

Tony placed his eyes in front of the lenses and noticed off in the distance a Hummer driving slowly toward the camp. Tied spread eagle over the windshield and hood was Sgt. Thomas.

He had been stripped of most of his clothes and sliced open quite expertly in many places. What kept his organs in place was a mystery to Tony and the rest of the crew. At the last moment, he watched as Sgt. Thomas moved his head, and it became clear that his eyes had been plucked out.

"Oh God, he's alive."

Jeremiah's men armed themselves and took up defensive positions. Col. Bragg shook his head.

"This either helps or hurts. Which one, I'm not sure."

Jeremiah watched calmly as the Hummer crept toward his camp. He felt her, and he knew that she was very close. He also knew that it would end here the way God decided it would end.

He nodded to one of his men who ran and stopped the vehicle before it entered into the camp. After the vehicle was stopped, the man nudged Sgt. Thomas who moaned. This made the man flinch.

"He's alive...," the man announced with horror, letting his guard down.

In the instance that he turned to make sure his friends knew this detail, a razor-sharp claw emerged from the stopped vehicle and precisely sliced through his neck, removing his head from his shoulders.

In the next moment, the creature that originated as Lt. Finn jumped easily to the top of the hummer and faced the armed force before her.

"Give me the woman doctor and I won't kill you," she gurgled in a reptilian growl. She looked more like a carnivorous reptile now than a human.

Jeremiah stepped forward.

"You have done much harm to many of my friends, and now you demand things from me? I'm afraid you are in opposition to the word of God."

"God? Your puny little God? I am nature come to being, created by her to protect and preserve the strength and purity of her creations."

"Blasphemer!" Jeremiah shouted, openly angry.

"I am about to take away the delight of your eyes. In God's wrath through me, He will unleash a violent wind, and hailstones and torrents of rain will fall with destructive fury. I will tear down the wall you have covered with whitewash and will level it to the ground. When it falls, you will be destroyed in it, and you will know that I serve the Lord!"

Jeremiah ran toward the Hummer.

Lt. Finn's mouth creased, which was as close to a smile as she could manage in her present condition, and she braced and leapt high into the air, claws spread wide, ready to strike. Her momentum stopped dead when she hit Jeremiah, who caught her and smashed her body to the ground, but somehow, she manipulated his movement and flipped over him.

"Kill her!" Jeremiah shouted.

The shots came from all directions, and Lt. Finn ducked, bent, and ran for cover with her superhuman speed. She charged several gunmen, slicing them open with her claws as she ran.

In the panic that ensued, the armed men began to fire at her charging form, causing them to shoot many of their own men by mistake.

It quickly became apparent to Col. Bragg, who watched with Tony, that this was not by chance but strategy. As the colonel watched, he sensed something very familiar about the demon lady, something he could not shake. There was the sense that he had met her before. Then, suddenly his breath caught in his throat.

"My God, it's Finn."

Jeremiah saw that she had employed a devious strategy that caused his men to kill each other, and he could not stand by while they were dying; he had to act. He lifted a rock twice the size of a softball and carefully studied her trajectory as she ran.

After calculating carefully, he lofted the rock into the air leading her a great deal and watched as she ran smack into it and fell to the ground. She quickly got back up and circled Jeremiah, with her fangs dripping with saliva as her gnarled face sniffed at the air.

Quick as a viper, she leapt and spun in the air, striking Jeremiah twice in the face, but he managed to grab her and smash her torso into the ground. A claw ripped across his face, and a foot hit him in the stomach, sending him off the ground and ten feet into the air. As he tried to recover, Lt. Finn pounced on him immediately, claws out and ready for the kill.

Jeremiah grabbed her wrists and prepared to snap them in two. Putting all her weight on him, she twisted into a handstand, using his grip as a brace and forced him to let go. She fell backward awkwardly and landed them both flat on their backs and head-to-head.

She kicked from her prone position to his midsection, showing supernatural flexibility, but he caught her ankle and pulled her back as he rose. She flailed and fought, but he had gained position, and he used it to spin her like a lasso and throw her into the side of a camper, knocking it completely out of the bed of the truck it was in.

Col. Bragg watched the astonishing display.

"You think its ready, Doc?"

Tony was equally amazed and scared to death.

"No clue. It's been over an hour since they ate," he added a shrug to mark his uncertainty.

Each time Lt. Finn and Jeremiah were separated, his remaining men opened fire on her. Some hit their mark, some did not, but none seemed to slow her attack in the least. Standing toe to toe, they traded blows, both taking considerable damage, both refusing to fall.

Col. Bragg looked at Tony once more. He was anxious, they needed Jeremiah's army to be preoccupied to get Carrisa and get out of there alive.

"Okay, Doc, let's do it."

Col. Bragg took off to the side and began firing at both combatants. The unexpected attack caused Jeremiah to dive aside. Lt. Finn took cover behind a truck.

"She's mine by right, Christian, give her to me," Lt. Finn spat.

"You are not one of God's children, so I don't recognize that you have any rights," Jeremiah retorted.

Suddenly Lt. Finn began sniffing the air and caught a scent that she remembered well.

"Col. Bragg, I thought I smelled you about. How was your time in jail, hmmm?" She hissed.

Col. Bragg fired a couple of shots her way, one of which caught her in the arm.

"It was fine, how's your arm?"

She screamed a malevolent shout and flew at him, but she was caught by Jeremiah and slammed into the ground face-first.

Col. Bragg spun around to face Tony.

"Hit him now, Doc, do it now!"

Jeremiah froze at the sound, his face distorting with anger as he turned to size up his new foe.

Tony stood up in full view. Jeremiah walked slowly toward him but increased his speed as he realized that Tony was the doctor who was trying to find the cure. Col. Bragg had Jeremiah in his sites and pulled the trigger back into full auto mode.

Chink, chink.

The gun was empty. In haste, the colonel dropped the cartridge and prepared to reload, but Lt. Finn caught him full in the chest with both feet before he had a chance to insert it. He saw her gnarled face right above his, but for him staying conscious was equally as difficult as breathing.

"Well, if it's not my old boss. Hi, boss," she said as she raised her mutated claws high in the air to add to the drama of the killing blow.

Suddenly, something in the breeze distracted her attention, and she whipped her head around, sniffing the air.

Carrisa watched all the mayhem through the small window of the camper with a feeble sense of hope. It was obvious that her friends were entirely outmatched. Hopelessness came much easier since she had been kidnapped, and no small amount flooded her heart now.

A bang on her wall caused her to flatten herself against the opposite wall. But this banging came from the backside where there was no fighting. It came again and again until a pick came through the wall. After a few more strokes, the hole was large enough for a head to poke through. And one did.

"Hey there, lass. Want to have a go or are ya busy?" asked a chipper Irish.

Carrisa had never been so glad to see anyone.

Lt. Finn sniffed the air once again and jumped off Col. Bragg, leaving him injured on the ground and ran toward a camper being towed by another truck. She dove into the side of the wall, spinning like a missile and went right through.

Jeremiah confronted Tony's eyes with his own that were filled with a mix of anger and pity.

"You could have been saved and dined at the hand of God, if only you would have obeyed."

Tony did not know what to do, and he was convinced that he would not be able to get close to Jeremiah without getting killed in the process.

"You have no idea what you've done. God's will is in the balance, and you give hell the advantage. Why?"

"Because you took my girl."

At that moment, the entire sidewall of the camper exploded outward, and Lt. Finn stood looking as evil as her demon form could.

"Where is she?" Lt. Finn screamed.

Without waiting for a reply, she charged Jeremiah who had no time to worry about Tony and added his own yell to hers. With a rage never seen before, Jeremiah lofted her in the air as she drove her claws deep into his stomach and chest. He grabbed one arm and snapped it like a twig. Lt. Finn screamed in pain.

With one mighty hand, he palmed her head and repeatedly slammed it into the front of one of the trucks until the radiator burst. After several slams, Lt. Finn ceased to move, but Jeremiah continued until he was satisfied. He lifted her to eye level and stared at her ruined face and then dropped her body to the ground.

Col. Bragg tried to pick his head up and see what was coming, but his ribs were badly broken, and he could barely breathe. Tony stood in the exact same place, frozen, and watched as Jeremiah's attention turned his way.

"You see, brother, any door God opens cannot be closed by anyone or anything. He is the Alpha and the Omega, the beginning and the end."

"If I don't stop this, then it's the end of all of us," Tony said, pleading, trying to make peace, as his own life appeared to be coming to a close.

"The end is God's will."

"Why? Why does it have to end?"

"It's not my job to question His motives or reason, only to obey," Jeremiah said as he methodically closed the gap between them.

"You actually hear God speak?"

"I do."

"Are you sure it's God's voice you hear?"

Jeremiah stood less than a foot from Tony, towering over him. A true representation of David and Goliath was unfolding. Jeremiah looked down on him with pity and disappointment.

"Well then, it's time. God is benevolent, and I will give you a quick death, for God is not cruel."

"Then why would God set such a cruel disease upon his children," Tony responded with his chin held high. "It has been that question that has prevented me from believing in a God for most of my life. If God loves us, then why is there suffering?"

"Suffering is how God tests our faith," Jeremiah replied thoughtfully.

"Without suffering we would not know God's bliss. You can't have one without the other."

"Why not?" Tony continued, trying to buy time.

"If God is infinite love and goodness, then He could eliminate suffering. You haven't been touched by God, you've been infected."

"Brother, you will never know God for your mind's eye has been blinded by intelligence. There is no room for intelligence and faith outside of God. God is intelligence, and we must believe. If we seek intelligence on our own, then we worship a false god."

There was only one thing left to do. Tony had to inject the preacher with the syringe. Jeremiah put his hand almost completely around Tony's throat but did not squeeze. Tony removed the syringe from his pocket.

"Are you ready, brother?"

"I am," Tony said unsteadily, but looking directly into Jeremiah's eyes even though he was racked with fear.

Jeremiah nodded and gripped his throat tightly and lifted him off the ground. Tony grabbed Jeremiah's hands involuntarily and struggled with everything he had, Jeremiah's strength was incomprehensible. He dropped the syringe as he struggled for life.

"Do you got a round left for someone your own size, big fella?" Irish said from behind.

Jeremiah turned lazily, sized up Irish, and dropped Tony, who fell to the ground, gasping for breath. But it did not take long for the adrenaline in his veins to give him the strength he needed to fight back.

Tony picked up the syringe and charged Jeremiah from behind, injecting the two Mad Man viruses into the back of his leg with one injection. Jeremiah barely noticed and casually knocked Tony back to the ground with a random back swing.

"I'm afraid you are only delaying the inevitable, but there is no greater gift than a man willing to lay down his own life for another," Jeremiah said to Irish.

"Maybe, I won't be as easy as the little girl you were beating on earlier," Irish said with an arrogant smile.

The two men circled each other as Irish slipped out a hunting knife from seemingly nowhere and flipped it back and forth from one grip to another with practiced ease.

"I hope you brought one to share with the class," Jeremiah said playfully.

"Don't worry, mate, I'll be sharing this one with you soon enough."

Jeremiah stepped in and took a couple of swings, but Irish was faster, and sliced him across the chest and backhanded his face, causing his nose to bleed anew. With no time to spare, Jeremiah kicked directly at Irish, landing a full foot into his chest. Irish fell to the ground, as the arrogant smile gave way to a disgruntled groan. Jeremiah smiled at him and reevaluated his opponent.

"You have been blessed, brother."

"I've heard that before," Irish responded with a hint of humor, but he was much more aware of his precarious position this time.

Jeremiah stopped moving forward and blinked as if he were confused. His head began to throb with a powerful headache, the kind that he hadn't experienced since he had been called to be God's living prophet.

He reached forward and touched his eyes, trying to massage the pain away. As the intensity increased, he staggered forward a little, and then abruptly dropped to his knees. Sweat poured from his forehead as his eyesight faded in and out.

"You have defied the will of God, and for your disobedience, he will let loose seven plagues of death upon this world," he said through coughing fits.

"What could be worse than this, mate? I'm afraid your God and mine work out of a different zip code."

Tony watched as the scene became surreal. Death had its cold hand everywhere. Jeremiah defiantly refused to surrender. He lifted his hand and face to the heavens.

"Father, please do not forsake me!" he roared.

A moment of guilt passed through Tony as he saw the pain in Jeremiah's eyes, but it lasted only a moment as his heart had been changed forever. He had done what he had to do to keep his loved ones safe.

MICHAEL D. ACOSTA & ERIC F. DONALDSON, PH.D

"Many will rise up now," Jeremiah said to no one particular. "Without God at our head, there will be much death and much pain. Many will rise and scourge the earth as in the days of old. Many will rise, and they will steal, and murder, and rape, and die. You have doomed this planet and soon you will pay for the error of your ways."

With one last deep and clear look into Tony's eyes, Jeremiah folded and fell to the ground, seizing and writhing in pain. Panic raged through Jeremiah's remaining troops as their powerful leader succumbed to death. They scattered in their vehicles, many refusing to fight the dead preacher's battle now that he was dead.

Tony felt a hand touch his and looked back to see Carrisa staring at him. No words passed their lips, as they stared directly into each other's eyes. They had been through so much together, both before this pandemic and after. And now, here they were surrounded by so much death. They had won, but it was a pyrrhic victory.

Col. Bragg was on the ground, barely breathing. Irish held his midsection, obviously injured. Ten, twelve, maybe fifteen dead men were strewn about the campsite. Sgt. Thomas was still strapped to the hummer, a bullet through his forehead.

Jeremiah was dead and his followers were in disarray. And then there was the demon lady, Lt. Finn. Tony remembered where she lay, but when he went to find her body, she was no longer there. It was apparent from the marks in the dirt that she had attempted to drag herself off to safety.

She probably thought that she could escape, but Tony knew that she would most likely die of exposure. Nature was not kind to injured animals.

Chapter 29

IN THE WEEKS that followed, there was very little discussion about the bloodshed and death that occurred that day. There was no heroic homecoming and no celebrations. What truly lay ahead was an incalculable amount of work.

The reengineered Mad Man system seemed to work. Jeremiah's army lost its will to fight, and Frank the prisoner was alive and well at the lab when they returned. He told them that he felt like he did before this whole thing started.

But there were still a lot of questions to be answered about the cure and how to optimize it. It would have to be tested and refined. A vaccine would also have to be formulated, and a delivery system tested.

Tony knew that he could synthesize a vaccine with his genetically altered plant genes, but he also knew that a vaccine would only help those who had not encountered the virus, and he wasn't sure if anyone was so lucky. However, future generations would need a vaccine. His child would need a vaccine.

In order to have a real impact, he knew that he had to figure out how to get his drugs and a vaccine out into the world if they were to be used to eradicate the virus. That required organizations and infrastructures in a world that was fresh out of both.

He had no idea how many people were left alive, or how many more Jeremiahs and Lt. Finns were out there as a result of Delta Events. No one knew if there were any working elements to the government left. There were so many questions and no information. It was apparent that they had much work to do.

Carrisa was in her second trimester, and she had begun to sport a slight potbelly. Tony was both excited and afraid at the prospect of being a father. He was even more afraid of the change that had occurred in his heart.

The memory of injecting Frank without knowing what harm could come of him haunted Tony, and he was afraid that he would never stop obsessing about it. This made him think of Ramsey who was haunted his entire life by something very similar.

The baby notwithstanding, he still had Carrisa to work out. They had talked only a little since coming back to the underground lab, and she had changed too. While he loved his relationship with her, it was an enigma. They had acted like man and wife since the defeat of Jeremiah, but neither had spoken a word about their problems in the past.

Carrisa spent her time looking after Col. Bragg, who was on the mend, but his injuries were quite severe. Her attention toward him made Tony jealous, but he held his thoughts in check. It wasn't the time, and he had no right.

Irish seemed to be much the same as he had always been, but he had borne his burdens for years. Don, on the other hand, remained aloof. He congratulated everyone on a great victory and earnestly mourned Sgt. Thomas's loss, but he remained distant and continued to avoid Tony.

Tony retreated to Ramsey's bench and looked at the blue flowers still in bloom. Fall was coming, and they would have to ration well to make it through the winter alive. He wasn't even sure that spring would have any fresh food to offer to the world.

He marveled over the changes society had endured in such a short period. A brave new world was on the horizon, but the definition of that world was ambiguous and frightening. He still wasn't sure if the future held a place for humans. The Mad Hatter was the least of their troubles. For now, they had turned on themselves. Jeremiah was right. The fighting would begin. The fight for dominance and food, for life itself.

Life was resilient, and while it appeared that JV would wipe out everything, the mutants found a way to survive. Mutants always did. It was the basis of evolution, a random bubbling up from simple pieces, to create complexities capable of surviving under all circumstances.

In some ways, science and evolution were far more meaningful, far more simple and elegant than a God could be. And yet, Tony could not help but feel the presence of some form, some entity, some type of benevolent energy as he looked forward upon the new world.

Life would find a way, as God had found a way in him. The Almighty had a sense of humor, always using the most unlikely characters to cast forth his message and to do His work. He definitely had a sense of humor.

Tony realized that he had a role to play. Despite all his intellectual gifts, he recognized for the first time that he was one of the smallest parts of life, but an important part. Despite the death, and loss, and pain, he felt a touch of peace come over him.

A plague fell from the heavens, and he found a way to slow it down, and possibly a way to defeat it. He had won the battle, and for now, that had to be enough. The war would be waiting.

Tony strolled over and looked at the flowers as he took a seat on Ramsey's bench. He should have felt vindicated and proud, but he felt alone and humbled. He opened up his diary and smiled at the pages as he allowed the stubby pencil to find it's way into his fingers.

"We did it, Ramsey. We did it."

With a sad smile, he recounted all of the loved ones that he and his fellows had lost along the way, listing their names one by one on the pages of his diary. It would be more than just a diary now. It would be history, a chronicle.

Sgt. Thomas
Noah
Ramsey
Sara
Charlie
Dottie
Sara's friend Thomasina
Ben

There were hundreds of millions of other nameless and faceless souls gone forever. They were not his responsibility, but now that he had access to a potential cure, he had to act fast. He would set out to save the world, and JV had a big head start. It was time to begin and he had faith.